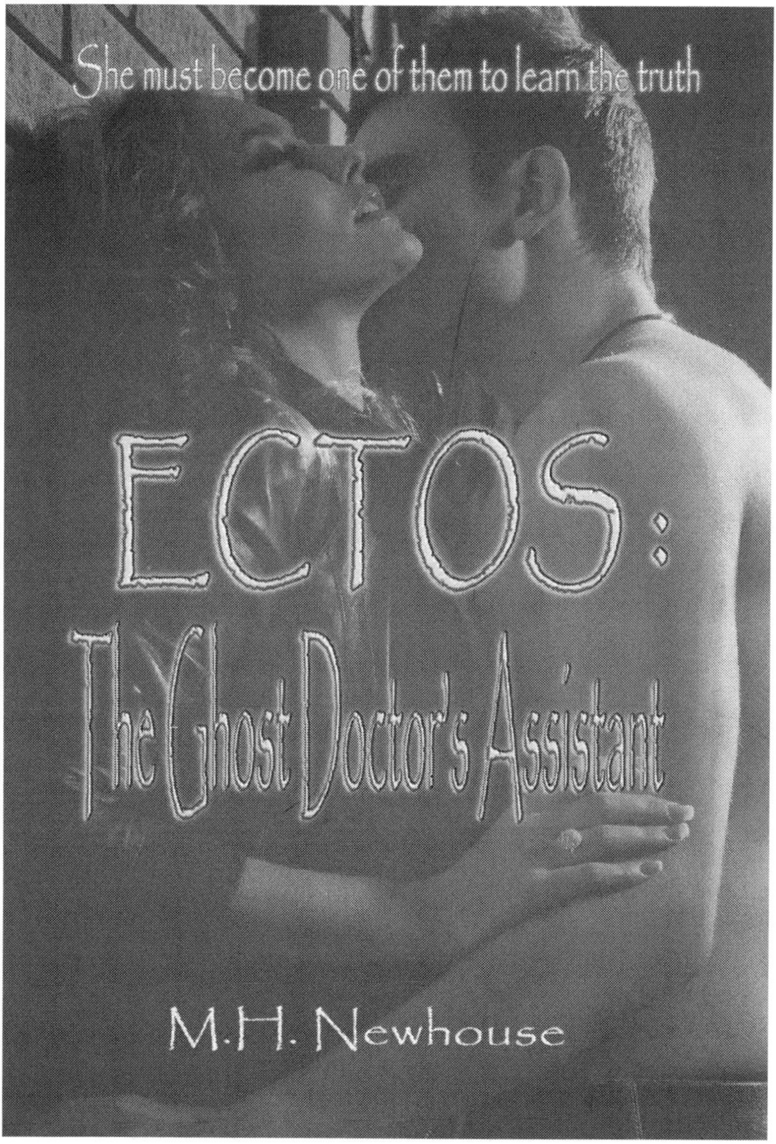
She must become one of them to learn the truth
ECTOS:
The Ghost Doctor's Assistant
M.H. Newhouse

ECTOS:
The Ghost Doctor's Assistant

By:
M.H. Newhouse

ALL RIGHTS RESERVED

No part of this book may be reproduced or transmitted in any form or by any means, electronic or mechanical, including photocopying, recording, or by any information storage and retrieval system, without permission in writing from the author, except in the case of brief quotations embodied in reviews.

Cover Art:
Deborah Melanie

Publisher's Note:

This is a work of fiction. All names, characters, places, and events are the work of the author's imagination.

Any resemblance to real persons, places, or events is coincidental.

Solstice Publishing - www.solsticepublishing.com

Copyright 2014

Mark Newhouse

ECTOS: The Ghost Doctor's Assistant

Ectoplasm: ghostly substance: the substance believed by spiritualists to issue from a medium who is communicating with spirits. *Encarta Dictionary: English (North America)*

Ectos: term used by parapsychologists for those believed by some to be sensitive to ghostly manifestations. *Dr. Joel Lasker, PhD, Stone Wall University, Department of Parapsychology.*

GRATEFUL THANKS

Thank you to my editor, Leslie Fish, and the great team from Solstice Publishing for 'exorcising' my ghostly novel and freeing my soul. Special thanks to my good friend, Louis Emond, who went ghost-hunting with me through the maze of my original text. And of course unending love to my wife and family for keeping me happy by 'haunting' my thoughts every day.

PROLOGUE

He could see her clearly. She was young and tempting, the way he liked them: no makeup or lipstick, just naturally cute. He liked them cute, petite, not large, busty and brassy. He preferred soft honey-blonde hair, long enough to dance over slender shoulders. She was all that, and equipped with large blue eyes that could search a soul. Was she searching his? What would she find there? Would she be afraid? What would he find if he could probe her soul?

He saw her moving toward him, her mouth parting and her hands reaching for his face. He wanted to pull away, but couldn't. There was something about her that was holding him in place, waiting for her, anticipating her next move, even though he knew exactly what she was going to do. He always did. That was the curse.

He dropped his hands to his sides, pretending to let her take charge. Her hands felt warm against his cheeks and her lips were soft as they pressed against him, at first gently, very gently, and then with more passion. When he didn't move, she pulled slightly back, gazing at him with questioning eyes, then she moved her hand to the top button of his shirt. He winced as the button opened. He felt her finger touch his neck, then trace the line of his jugular. He didn't like being exposed to her nails like that; it made him feel too vulnerable. One well-placed puncture by her nails and it would be over – but she was gentle, tenderly drawing a light line over his flesh with one nail, barely touching him, but just enough to send a quivering electric pulse to his brain.

Then he saw her hand lower to the next button, and the next. Slowly she undid each of his buttons, her hand now sliding under his open shirt, caressing his chest with gentle rolling touches of the tips of her nails. *She knows what to do*, he thought, *Just as I figured. She's got to be that type of girl.*

She pulled the shirt off his right shoulder and placed her lips on his skin, running her lips slowly down his chest. He still hadn't moved, but he shivered when she removed his shirt completely and he watched it fall to the carpet -- which, he noted, was an oval rug over a white-tiled floor. *What color is it?* he thought, trying to see the rug in the dimly-lit room. *Is it pink? That figures too.*

His attempt to focus on the rug was interrupted when he felt her hand lower to the front of his jeans. He didn't stop her. Maybe this time it would be different? Knowing what was coming next made it difficult to become excited. It was amazing how his apparent indifference excited them, forced them to take the initiative. They thought it was a ploy, an act. It would have terrified them if he told them the truth.

She looked up into his face with those haunting blue eyes, her hand reaching for his belt. She wasn't wearing a ring. A clue? Her fingers were thin, dainty, and he could see no nail polish. *Do most students wear nail polish today?* he wondered, as he let her open his belt buckle. She reached for his zipper and he still didn't stop her, but noted she appeared to be left-handed.

He saw it just the way he knew it would happen – in a few days. He didn't know exactly when; his powers weren't strong enough for that. She backed away from him, that questioning look still on her face. He still wasn't reacting. He saw her smile coyly as she slowly removed her top, her hair resting lightly on her shoulders, lush strands barely touching the top of her breasts – which were firm, but not large. They were tempting, but he still wasn't giving in. He saw her eyes again, and then felt her hand move into his open jeans.

I can see her eyes. So why can't I see her face? How can I find her if I can't see her face?

He concentrated harder, trying to conjure up the vivid images again. He saw her drop to her knees, and he found himself gazing down at the girl's naked back. If only there was a tattoo, a birthmark. He felt her touching him with her fingers, felt it as if it was really happening now. She was gentle, more caring than he expected. He felt strange; she was having an effect on him he hadn't anticipated. He fell back against the wall.

The girl was still below him. He was looking at the room, searching for clues to where she would be, where he could find her. All the dorm rooms looked alike, so how could he find her? He felt her move her head backwards, her eyes aimed up at him. "Enough," he heard escape from his lips.

He saw himself gently drop his hands onto her bare shoulders, enjoying his first touch of her skin, but unable to decide – once again – if he would make love to her, or tighten his hands on her throat and kill her.

CHAPTER 1

Shelly stretched her well-formed limbs. Running helped clear her head of the headaches that had plagued her since she was a little girl, blinding headaches for which doctors hadn't found a physical cause. They hadn't found a reason for her horrifying nightmares, either.

Shelly's sneakers softened the impact of her feet hitting the asphalt. Her pace was unhurried and her breathing easy. This was going to be a pleasant run. Her eyes were concentrating on the gently twisting track while randomly taking in the canopy of trees and thinking how serene everything looked, very different than the city where she had commuted to Queens College while living at home with her mother. Being new to the Island, she didn't realize that the jogging track at the rear of the campus gymnasium had two major advantages over this pathway within the deserted park. The quarter-mile oval near the gym was shielded from outsiders by a wall of sixteen-foot-high chainlink fence, and there had never been a murder there.

She studied the oak trees, planted a hundred years earlier, now untended and growing wild. They protected Shelly from the sweltering late August sun, but also concealed Ralph Estes. His face was almost invisible against the bark as he observed the few joggers running, in pairs or small groups, sporadically all day…no loners anywhere. What shitty luck!

Estes had little sense of time, no real need to keep time, except when the darkness told him to return to the shelter in the basement of a nearby church. "I'll kill the bastard who got my watch," he had said the day that it disappeared, but now it was all but forgotten, like everything else he had once cared about. It was all lost in a haze of drugs and mostly petty crimes to support his habit. Only his present needs drove him, and he had waited all afternoon for just the right opportunity to satisfy them. The preferred target would be a young woman alone. He fingered his knife hoping he might still use it, hoping she was pretty. She wouldn't be after he finished with her. They never were.

Shelly felt the sun setting. She had been warned by her mother who still lived in their Flushing Queens sixth floor apartment, many times, not to run alone.

"You worry too much. It's beautiful out here, really nice neighborhoods," Shelly comforted her mother during their nightly phone calls. She remembered how each relationship she had in college had made her mother warn her to be careful – a natural enough warning from someone whose husband had caused her so much pain, finally leaving her for a younger woman, a familiar story. Shelly would have liked to kill her 'sperm donor' for that, and for the nights when she heard her mother weeping in the small apartment they had moved to after the separation. There were times she prayed her 'wishes' for him could become real, and the cops would find his body but never be able to explain how it was done. Some of her nightmares involved murder. Sometimes she saw his face as the victim, sometimes her own. Other times she just saw a featureless blank mask of a face, ghost-like, covered with blood.

It was a relief when Shelly was accepted into the graduate education program, to become a reading specialist at Stone Wall University, a chance to finally be on her own. She had thought the nightmares and headaches would stop in a new environment, but only the daily runs seemed to keep them at bay. Up to now, except for a few gawking undergrad males trying to match her stride, her runs had been uneventful – especially since she didn't want to complicate things with a new boyfriend and wasn't interested in a hook-up. She wasn't into casual sex and relationships were just too tough, she thought, as the runs liberated her from all other concerns for a brief span each afternoon. The park a mile from the university had seemed a good change of pace.

* * * * *

Ralph saw the park as his hunting ground. He folded his knife back into its red plastic handle, and shoved it in his jeans pocket. "You're lucky I can't reach you, you little bastard," he shot at the squirrel above him. *What the hell does squirrel meat taste like?* he wondered, as he felt for the few coins he had in his gray sweat-pants pocket. "Shit! Not enough for even a damn cube."

About to leave, he heard a faint sound. It was a rhythmic slapping sound…not a heavy tread. A lustful grin appearing on his lips, and he focused his eyes a short distance away. He had guessed right; it was a woman. He peered around her, behind her. Yes, she was alone. Unfolding the knife, he hid tighter behind the tree. His heart thundered in anticipation.

The girl was running at a steady pace, long honey-colored hair tied in a ponytail whipping behind her. *It's a beautiful day for a run,* Shelly thought, as she concentrated on her breathing.

To the predator, it didn't matter what she looked like – although he preferred pretty. It didn't matter if she helped charities or was the mother of a new baby. All he prayed for was that she was alone. He waited hungrily, his eyes following her yellow jogging suit. She was not a human being, but a faceless creature: his prey.

Shelly had heard of ESP, even studied it in a psychology class at Queens College, but considered it largely science-fiction, a pseudo-science at best, akin to ghost hunters and alien abductions. She found the case studies interesting, but not very convincing. She had never heard of the data from experiments by the Rhine Institute. She had never had indications that she might possess ESP or any other special talent related to the occult or supernatural – only the terrible dreams.

As she ran along the tree-lined park she could not see into the future, so she had no idea that death was only a few yards away.

CHAPTER 2

Ralph was aware that the knife barely protruding from his hand was the wrong kind of knife for this kind of work. The blade, only three inches long, was too short and too dull to make a clean cut – but it was easy to conceal, small enough to perhaps get away with an excuse for having it if someone caught him with it. "It's only for cutting meat," he could say. The red plastic-handled knife was also cheap, found in any hardware store or Wal-Mart, and far too common to easily trace. But there was another plus, which to him was more important than all the rest.

Ralph loved the power-surge he felt, the rush of having to use all his strength to tear through female flesh, pounding his knife into a soft female body over and over until his ambushed victim was no longer able to fight back. And they did fight back, screaming and kicking and clawing with their nails. Sometimes it took many hard thrusts of the blade before they stopped resisting. He liked that. He liked watching sweet little rich girls – in his depraved mind, they were all rich -- writhe in pain and terror, finally forced to realize they were helpless to stop his brutal attacks. He couldn't wait to throw them to the ground, rip off their blouse or jacket, pull down their pants, rip through their panties and bras, and do whatever he damn-well wanted to their bodies before stripping them of their jewelry and money. Most would give in, praying he would spare them if they just kept their mouths shut and stopped fighting him, pretended to like him, made sounds like they were enjoying it. Some would scream, as if that would save them. He had a simple solution for that. If they screamed, and refused to stop after he slapped them in the mouth, he'd just slit their throats. Nobody else could hear the gurgling sounds, but he could -- oh yeah, like the sound of a stream bubbling, but far more pleasure-giving. He got off on their shock and agony. Why shouldn't he?

He had been suffering far longer than they would. Their pain would be intense, concentrated, too soon over, while his was endless, endless, endless. Brain-dulled, he felt nothing for them or anyone else. This girl would be just like the others – he wished he could remember how many: two…three…four…more? They were all the same once he finished with them – almost unrecognizable.

Something caught his attention. He heard a noise ahead. *Sneakers?* "What the…?" *How did she get past me?* He couldn't understand how the girl was now jogging ahead of him. *I must have been daydreaming.* He let out an angry curse. Afraid it was too late, now fully alert, Ralph's eyes zeroed in on the girl. She was not too far away to catch. *But how did she get past me? Could I have gone off that long? I thought she was wearing yellow… My damn eyes are playing tricks.*

Ralph trotted clumsily after her, the knife clutched tightly in his hand. He hoped she would be tired, or too busy concentrating on running to notice him, pursuing. He'd fix her extra special for forcing him to chase her. *I don't like running,* he raged, as he searched the path ahead. All he had to do was find a good spot, tree covered, away from the road and the few cars meandering toward home in the darkening sky. *Oh man, I'm going to mess this one up good!*

The thought of what he was going to do to her excited him, consumed him. He could almost feel her under him, her clothes in shreds, her naked body thrashing, unable to fight him off as he held her pinned to the ground, maybe breaking her back so he could enjoy the panic in her eyes longer. He wondered how big and juicy her breasts were. *…Almost there…almost.* He felt the throbbing inside him. The anticipation was overwhelming. He wondered if he might be able to actually have sex with her. He hadn't felt this lustful in a long time. It was her fault for making him chase her. *Almost…almost.*

The shadows of the trees reached across the sky and made it hard for Ralph to see where his shoes were landing. He turned on a burst of speed and finally was catching up…or was she slowing down? They were near a particularly dark area, thick leafy branches blocking the sun – the area in which another jogger had been killed three years earlier, but Ralph didn't know that. Neither did Shelly.

Ralph could almost reach her with his knife. "You're mine now, bitch," he rasped, his breathing fast and hard, as he braced to thrust the knife deep into her back. "Hey, bitch," he shouted, hoping to terrify her, hoping she would turn around and he'd see the terror in her face. That would really do it, he thought, the spark he needed to explode into violence.

Why didn't she stop? She must have heard me? Why isn't she turning to see who called? I want to see her damn eyes! Bitch!

Now totally morphed into a predatory beast, Ralph pounced, the blade fully extended in his fist. "Damn you," he screeched as he threw all his weight behind the deadly thrust into her spine. "Die, you bitch!"

Fully launched, Ralph let out a blood-curdling scream as his body followed the knife – and seemed to be falling through a cloud, a translucent mist, shaped like a human being.

"What the hell?" Ralph's shocked brain cried, as he crashed to the ground – head bursting open against a jagged rock, his knife plunging inches below his heart. He couldn't understand how he had fallen like that. *Am I that clumsy?* he asked himself, as he almost burst into laughter at the ridiculousness of missing the girl, an easy target, and falling on his own knife. He thought he could get up and finish his job…

And then he tasted his own blood.

But I'm still here. I can still get her. "Damn you, bitch," he moaned. "You're dead now..."

He tried to pull the blade out of the small wound, but something was forcing it to stay where it was. He pulled up again, but the knife seemed to be digging deeper, as if something invisible was pressing down on his hands and forcing the knife inwards.

"What the hell is this?" Ralph's brain screamed, as he gradually realized he was powerless against what felt like strong invisible hands pressing down on the knife, pressing down, and inch by inch yanking it up toward his heart, with Ralph screaming in agony at each thrust. "Who's doing this?" he screamed, writhing in the last throes of pain and terror.

And still the knife was pushing in and out, now sawing through his sternum and up to the neck with greater speed.

In the end, Ralph's hands finally slipped off the knife. He gave up fighting. The knife no longer moved. Gradually his breathing stopped...his heartbeat went on a little longer...his eyes remained open, searching for his invisible assailant, even in death.

Shelly had kept a safe distance, frozen by the incredible scene. She snapped out of her shock, her first thoughts racing to the girl who had been so brutally attacked. "Where's the girl," she muttered, looking for the second corpse, the body of a young female runner. *Where is she?*

Where she expected to see the blood-soaked body of a young jogger, there was only the unbent carpet of grass. Shelly didn't understand.

Where is the other girl?

CHAPTER 3

Shelly couldn't move. Her conscious brain unable to process what she had seen, she tried to retrace the strange events. When she had first noticed the other jogger, she didn't think there was anything unusual about a man trying to catch up with an attractive female runner. It happened to her all the time when she ran, in her neighborhood or in school. It was how she had met Jeff. She wished he'd been running with her today, but he was at UCLA – *Probably hooking up with another runner,* she thought, the image of Jeff and his new running partner in the back of a car momentarily flashing before her eyes. Then she remembered what had just happened. *I've got to stay focused on the here and now. But what the hell* did *happen? Where's that girl?*

Shelly recalled how she had seen something, a reflection, the gleam of something in his hand. At first, she wasn't sure what she was seeing. She didn't believe it when she finally realized what it had to be, but she kept running, running and shouting a warning to the jogger, panic replacing common sense and her need to protect herself from the knife in his hand. "He has a knife! Run! Help!"

Strangely, her screams didn't seem to stop the jogger, nor make her speed up. The girl was doomed unless Shelly could get to her. The two of them could maybe frighten or fight off this stumbling attacker. There was no time to get help. She would have to depend on the few self-defense classes she had taken in college. Almost there…

Shelly screamed when the attacker finally lunged, his knife plunging full-blade into the jogger's back. "Oh God!" She froze, then screamed loudly again – to frighten off the mugger, to prevent another strike. She kept screaming, as she grabbed her phone from her fanny pack, fumbling with it, dropping it to the ground. She searched the grass for the phone, found it, and just as she was about to press down on the 9 of 9-1-1, something incredible stopped her cold.

The jogger whom she had witnessed being brutally stabbed seemed to be fading into a smoky mist, and the attacker was falling, face-first, to the ground. Shelly saw his head burst into a bloody fountain. "Oh God," she repeated, unable to believe what she was witnessing. "The girl! That poor girl! Got to help her!"

The girl was gone.

Shelly peered at the spot where the other girl's body should have been, but there was nothing. "I don't believe this," Shelly murmured, unable to move, not wanting to get closer.

The mugger lay still. Shelly thought he was dead.

Then he twitched.

"Oh, damn, he's still alive," Shelly gasped, watching in horror as the man moaned and then began to roll slowly, obviously in agonizing pain, rolling onto his back.

Shelly searched around her for a large rock, but then she saw the knife. She could have sworn he had thrust that knife into the girl's back, so how was it now inexplicably sticking up from the bloody mess that was his shirt? *How could that happen?*

Shelly remained a few yards away, as she watched the man raise his reddened hands to the knife handle. She wondered if she should try and help him—he was human after all, and needed help. Could she just stand near and watch him die?

But Shelly was paralyzed as she saw the man's hands, covered with blood, clenched around the knife handle as if ready to pull it out of the wound, but instead his hands appeared to be pulling the blade up – and then down hard, not out of his body, but tearing more flesh and bone as it slowly sawed its way up his chest in jerky motions that made the man let out tortured screams with each thrust...terrible screams like those she heard in her nightmares.

"That's impossible," Shelly muttered, her fingers hovering over the phone, hypnotized by the sight of the man apparently impaling himself repeatedly with the knife. "The girl," she reminded herself, scanning the area, searching for the wounded jogger again, but she didn't see anyone else around. "I don't get it," she murmured, "What happened to that poor girl?"

The mugger let out a final awful wail, and thankfully became silent.

Shelly didn't know what to do. She had to look closer, so she cautiously approached the mugger's body – now completely still. She saw the blood flooding around the body and felt faint, her hand steadying herself on the back of a park bench. "Oh God! What the hell happened?" Unable to explain what she had witnessed, Shelly searched the area again. "She can't have gone far after that attack," Shelly said. "I need help." She moved her finger to push the emergency buttons on her phone. "How the hell do I explain this?" she asked aloud. "This is impossible. Just damn impossible!"

"Nothing is impossible," a male voice calmly replied.

Shelly whirled to where she thought the voice came from. Nothing. She whirled around again, her eyes searching desperately. Was there an accomplice? Panic surged through her body and again she searched, and then searched again. She braced herself for an attack, her nails ready to be lunged at the accomplice's throat, her knee ready to be pounded into his testicles, thinking, *Please, don't let him get that close!*

Sudden darkness.

CHAPTER 4

Shelly felt a hard surface against her side. Opening her eyes, she was dismayed to discover she was lying on a park bench. *It's dark. How did I get here?*

Her hands automatically checked her clothes. Her jogging jacket was still zipped and her pants were in place. Had she been attacked? *I could have been raped! Why was I so stupid?* She could hear her mother scolding her for not listening to her warnings. She sat up. *I'm okay,* she thought, breathing a sigh of relief. *Everything is fine.* She gazed up at the trees, recognizing that she was in the park. *What am I doing here?*

Everything came back to her with a jolt. The last thing she remembered seeing was a body...a man... lying dead! At least she thought he was dead. He was on the ground. There was blood...

Her eyes searched the dark area behind the bench. "I've got to call 9-1-1," she muttered, recalling what she was about to do before blacking out. She reached into her fanny pack. "Where the hell is my phone?"

"You dropped it on the ground before you passed out," a voice replied. "Are you okay now? I was concerned about you. One minute you were all fists and nails, and the next you were down. Out like a light."

Shelly recoiled as her eyes darted toward the voice. *A man's voice!* She prepared to fight him off, terrified of the voice of someone in the dark. She remembered now. She had heard a man's voice before... But where was he? "Who's talking?" she asked, rearing up on the bench. He had to be near, but where? She shook her head. *I must be in shock. That would be logical.* "Is someone here?" She looked more intently. "I don't see anyone. Where are you?"

She began to laugh at how ridiculous she felt, hearing voices, seeing bodies melt into nothingness. "I must be nuts," she said, dropping back onto the bench, relieved nobody was near. "I'm probably just dehydrated. Where's my water?"

"Please don't be afraid—"

"What the hell?" Shelly reared up again and searched quickly in the dim light. Was this a trick? Was someone playing with her? "Stop messing with me. I called the cops!" Her eyes tried to pierce the dark and search the surrounding trees. "The cops will be here any second," she threatened whoever was hiding behind the bushes.

"While you were sleeping? With your phone missing?"

"Who the hell is this? I'm warning you!" She held her fists in front of her, wishing she had the man's knife... *Was that knife even real? Is this him?* The thought that the mugger was back, was hiding to terrorize her – waiting until he could attack, and God knows what – forced her to search the darkness again for her tormentor. "Just stay away from me! The cops are coming."

"Don't you think that if I wanted to hurt you, I would have done it by now?" the voice asked. "You're not going to try swinging at me again, are you? You almost knocked yourself out with that last kick. Pretty high though. Good legs."

"You're not a mugger?" *Or a rapist,* she thought. "I'm hearing things," she said. "There's nobody here." She sat back against the bench, relieved.

"I'm here," the voice replied. "Right in front of you."

"What the hell are you?" Shelly reared back further, searching desperately. "I've got a knife," she lied, wishing she had taken the one from the body. *...the body. Holy crap! This could be the killer?* "I can defend myself! Stay back whoever you are! This isn't funny." *Where the* *hell is that damn phone?* She aimed her fists, her body circling to ward off any possible attack.

"Calm down for heaven's sake. I just saved your life. Why would I hurt you? By the way, you look angelic when you're sleeping." He would have said sexy, but thought that would spook her even more than she already was.

What the hell is going on? Shelly moaned, wishing she could see who was tormenting her, her eyes searching every inch around the bench. "What do you mean you saved my life? You're not even here." *I don't see a damn thing,* she assured herself, still on guard.

"Don't you remember seeing that creep lying on the ground over there? Oh, I forgot, you can't see me. That's why you're so afraid. That's how you missed me with those chops of yours. Not bad…for a girl."

Shelly tried to stop shaking. It wasn't a good idea to show she was afraid of whoever this character was. "I'm not afraid of you. You don't exist. I'm in shock or something like that. You're not real. You're not real. You're not--"

"Boo!" the man suddenly shouted.

Shelly jumped a mile off the bench. "Hey, don't do that!"

"Sorry. But now do you believe I'm real?" the voice asked.

Shelly turned her body to where she thought the voice was coming from, eyes still searching. She told herself to act calm. Maybe whoever was doing this would think she had everything under control if she sounded calm. She tried to speak firmly. "I don't understand. Who the hell are you? How come I can hear you but not see you?"

"I don't know."

"You don't know?" Shelly was still searching for a face, a body, a bit of clothing, dandruff, anything that would make this thing seem real.

"No. I seem to have no memory at all…before I saved you. That's strange, isn't it?"

His voice was soft. He didn't sound as if he was going to attack her. He hadn't up to now. She had seen on T.V. that if you personalize things, make friends with a kidnapper or hostage-taker, there's less chance they will hurt you. It was worth a try. "What's your name," she asked, still wondering who exactly she was talking to, wondering if her legs would hold her if she tried to make a run for the middle of the street where a car might see her. It was worth a shot. "What about your name?"

"My name? That's a good question. I don't know."

This has to be a trick. I'm being punked. "What about an address, a phone number, email?" Shelly thought she could probably make it to the street from the bench, but was it worth the risk? Her legs felt rubbery. What if he had a knife…or a gun? "Come on, you must remember something?"

"I'm telling you the truth. I can't seem to remember anything from before I saw you." That wasn't quite true, but why scare her more than she was already, he thought.

Why was she still here, Shelly wondered. The mugger was dead and so, probably, was the girl. This guy, whoever he was, was somehow involved. *Staying here is not smart.* She lowered her feet close to the ground, hoping he didn't notice.

He did.

CHAPTER 5

Shelly inched closer to the edge of the bench, her hands ready to launch her forward. "Are you saying you have no memory of anything before me?" *Keep him talking. Wait for the right moment.*

He sensed her tension and knew what she was thinking. If only he could stop her. But how could he do that? He hesitated before answering, "That's right. I have no past before you." It wasn't time to tell her the whole truth yet. She was still huddled at the far end of the bench, but her feet were now on the ground. "I wish you weren't so afraid of me," he said, deliberately softening his voice for her. "I told you I'm not going to hurt you. I mean it. I protected you while you slept. I'd never hurt you."

Shelly thought his voice was soothing, not like her father's raspy voice when he shouted at her mother before hitting her. This voice sounded sincere... if he was real. She still couldn't see him, so how could he be real? Now was the time to run, but something was holding her here. Perhaps there was something about the disembodied voice that made her believe he really meant her no harm. "Are you still here?" Shelly peered into the darkness, hoping he had left.

"I'm trying to remember things. I haven't talked to anyone before. I've tried, but nobody could hear me... until you."

"Just my luck!" Shelly let out a nervous laugh, thinking again it must be from shock at seeing the other jogger attacked so brutally. "Mom says I find every stray—"

"I'm not a stray. I saved you from that creep." He wished he hadn't sounded so irritated, desperate, but he was. She had to stay. It was his only hope.

Shelly's eyes automatically found the dead mugger again. She'd almost forgotten about him. What did the voice mean, he had saved her? "You said that before." *Somehow he...this thing... must have killed that mugger. Not safe. Distract him and escape. No more fooling around.* "Okay, how did you save me? I remember seeing that guy stabbing the other jogger, and then suddenly he's falling flat on his face. I've never seen anything like that before." The picture of the mugger slicing up his own chest sent a shiver through her. She had to shut it down. "Where's the girl?"

"That bastard thought he was attacking you," the voice interrupted. *What the hell was she doing out here by herself at this particular date and time? There had to be a reason why she was here when he was. Was it an accident?* He didn't think so. She was meant to be here. He had to tell her, or she would leave. It might take forever to find someone else who could help him. "I don't want you to be afraid, but... You were his target."

"Me? That makes no sense. I saw him. He was way ahead of me. He was after someone else. I saw him stick his knife into this poor girl... and then...there was nobody there. It looked like that girl vanished into a puff of smoke or something. I saw the knife. That girl must be lying somewhere. Can you help me find her?"

"That 'poor girl' was me," the voice said. "I was the other jogger."

How could that be? That would have been funny if she hadn't seen the knife thrust hard into the girl's back. "Stop joking. This is serious."

"I'm being serious. That girl was me."

Shelly thought he must be an idiot. "That girl was you? I don't understand?" Shelly wished she could see his eyes to see if he was telling her the truth, but she couldn't see any of him. She could only trust the voice, and that she wasn't willing to do. "How could that guy see you? I can't. You sound like a guy, not a girl. This is insane!"

He could hear the agitation in her voice. He had to keep her calm. "I don't know. I was wandering around, minding my own business, when I saw this creep stalking you with a knife. For some reason, I couldn't let anything happen to you. Suddenly I was running in front of him, and you. I have no idea why. When he tried to thrust his knife into my body, he fell right through me. That was a hell of a surprise! I was just desperately trying to help you." *I had to,* he thought, wondering what it was about this girl that had forced him to protect her. He'd never thought of anyone in the park before, so why her?

Shelly thought he sounded as if he really believed he had saved her. Suddenly she had a flashback of the knife plunging into the female jogger's back. *I could have sworn it was a girl!* God, that knife must have hurt. "Did it hurt? I mean the knife, when he got you with it. I'm confused. He did stab you? Or didn't he?"

He was surprised by her questions. Did she care? Could she care for someone she didn't believe existed? "I didn't feel a thing," he replied. "I am tired, though. I guess saving your life took a lot of my energy. I'm like a ghost of my former self." He let out a bitter laugh. "That's a joke."

Shelly didn't laugh. She was stuck on the word, "Ghost". It hadn't occurred to her before that this invisible creature might be a ghost. *I've been watching too many movies,* she thought. *There's no such thing as ghosts.*

"Yup. Saving you took a lot out of me," the voice continued. "I barely had enough strength left to drag you up onto the bench. Thank goodness you're a light-weight." He guessed she weighed about a hundred and ten pounds…five foot one or two…taut muscles, but not body-builder type…smaller breasts, but hard to tell in that awful yellow suit. "I would have had to leave you on the ground if you were fa— less light."

"Thank you, I guess," Shelly murmured, still thinking she must have hit her head.

"You're welcome," the voice said. "It's funny. I've been stuck here a long time, and you're the first person who can hear me…except for the creep, and I have no idea how that happened. Damn, I've tried to talk to others, really hard." He studied the girl's face. *I like her eyes, blue, kind of innocent looking…no make-up…dirt on her forehead makes her look like a bad little kid. But why her? She has a nice enough face, but why, of everyone else I've tried, can she hear me?*

Shelly had the oddest feeling he was studying her. But how could she know that? "So I'm really not cracking up? I'm not in shock? I'm really having a conversation with a…with a…with a ghost?" Shelly felt frightened again as the realization she was talking to a ghost seemed the only possible explanation. *But aren't all ghosts evil and scary?* "I never believed in ghosts. Are you sure you're a ghost?"

"I'm pretty sure. There's nobody around here to tell me." He was still examining her face, her soft lips, no lipstick or gloss, and light blue, barely blue, eyes. He felt a strange stirring inside him, the same feeling he had experienced before he jumped in front of her attacker. He classified the feeling as some instinctive, unexplained, need to protect her. It was a feeling he had not felt before as he had watched countless humans in various places in this and other locations around the park, some not behaving all that nicely either. He had often tried to scare those naughty teens in their cars away, but had never succeeded in materializing enough to do that until now. *Hell, I couldn't even flick a pair of panties away*, he thought, amused at the memory of a pair of lacy panties hanging on the front seat of a car while a boy and girl were going at it hot and heavy in the back. *Get back to work,* he scolded himself. *She has to be the key,* he thought. Somehow he had to keep the connection going. "What is your name?" he asked, trying to keep his voice soft, afraid he might scare her off, but wanting to keep her talking.

"My name?" *I'm not going to tell him that! Nobody will believe this,* Shelly thought, trying not to burst into irrational laughter. *Like I'm going to tell anyone? They'll think I'm crazy. I think I'm crazy!*

"I told you I won't hurt you," he repeated, his voice gentle. "I'd just like to know who I'm talking to. You don't have to be afraid of me. I'm not a bad kind of ghost..." *At least not to you,* he thought, hoping she didn't pick up on the anger inside him, anger which erupted unpredictably when he thought about how he had gotten here, why he was still here.

"I'm not afraid of you," Shelly lied. "I know if you wanted to hurt me you could have done that, just like you said." It sounded right, but you never knew with ghosts. *If he is a ghost and not some vicious demon. What a mess this is!*

"Thank you. I'm glad you believe me." He sensed that she did not, but there did seem to be a slight, very slight, lessening of her fear.

Shelly was not the type to be afraid. She enjoyed trying new things, taking risks. That had worried her mother before she let her go away to grad school -- as if she could stop Shelly once she made up her mind. "Just stay away from strange men," she had warned. *Who could be stranger than this character?* Shelly mused, but still there was something about him... "My name is Sheila...but I like Shelly," she said, knowing her mother would not approve of her talking to a stranger, especially a ghost.

"Shelly? I like that. Hi, Shelly." *It's a nice name,* he thought. *Suits her...unlike that awful yellow thing she's wearing.*

"Hi." Shelly relaxed a little at the soothing tone of his voice. "You really don't know your name?"

"No. I've tried hard to remember, but nothing pops. Hey, why don't you give me a name for now? You're the only one who can hear me anyway."

Shelly had a feeling that this was getting in too deep even for her.

"It will make it easier for us to talk to each other," he continued.

Shelly gasped. *Talk to each other? Does he see a future to this?* "I've got to go now." Shelly wondered how he would react.

"But we just met! Surely you can stay a little longer," he said, his voice smooth, friendly, not at all threatening.

He really does have a nice voice. Just my luck to meet someone with a nice voice -- who just happens to be dead and with amnesia! "I have to go," she repeated, hoping the ghost would take this calmly. So far he had been pretty good -- for a ghost, that is. "It's been a real plea…very interesting." She couldn't bring herself to say it had been a pleasure. "I wish you luck." She lifted herself off the bench, still unsure if her legs would hold her, praying that whatever this thing was it would not be on top of her the instant her feet hit the ground.

She can't leave. "Shelly, please, I need your help. I think I'm still here because I was murdered." It was his one chance to keep her talking. What woman would not be curious about a statement like that?

Shelly stopped moving. *Damn! And I was just about to leave.*

CHAPTER 6

Oh crap! He was murdered? The way he'd said that, "I was murdered" there wasn't any emotion. And yet, she could feel tangible sadness in his voice…and danger. So why wasn't she leaving? Maybe because she thought she wouldn't be able to get away? Or maybe, it was something else that was keeping her here?

Can you feel sorry for a ghost? That's what she was feeling for this thing that sounded so human, so vulnerable, but which also frightened her. *Who knows what a murdered ghost might do?* She felt a chill race through her body. "You're not making that up?" she asked, feeling foolish afterwards. *Who asks someone if they made up a story about being murdered? That's just stupid. Provoking a ghost? That's just idiotic and dangerous.* "I'm sorry," she hurried to say. "I didn't mean that the way it sounded."

She apologized to me? "Oh, I know I was murdered," he said, forcing himself to sound calm, still sensing her fear. "It's the only reason I can think of that I'm still here. I have to find out what happened before I can have my… rest." *And my revenge,* he thought -- and quickly suppressed that emotion. The last thing he wanted was for her to somehow sense the violence seething inside him. That would be enough to terrify her.

"Like in the movies?" Shelly asked.

"Yeah. Like in the movies," he replied, not telling her the whole truth -- not revealing the rage he knew was waiting to be unleashed if he ever learned who had killed him. He felt as if someone, or something, had programmed him to explode if he ever found out who was responsible for his death. It was beyond his control, and had been his sole purpose for being… at least until she came along. *But why her?*

Shelly couldn't understand why she was picking up impressions of anger, rage, from this entity whose voice seemed so calm. It was as if she was sensing -- correction, sharing -- what this creature was feeling. She didn't like that at all. She felt threatened by the violence coursing through her body, her lack of control over emotions that weren't hers. Just what could this ghost-thing do? What did it want of her?

She decided to try and distract him, look for an escape before she got any deeper. If she pretended to be his friend... What had he wanted? *A name.* Giving him a name would be a token of friendship, a way to throw him off her real desire to get away and not come back. But what name?

It seemed to pop up out of nowhere. "I think I'll call you Allen, if that's okay," she said. "How does that sound? Allen."

"Allen?" He repeated it several times, the rage temporarily side-tracked. "Yes, I like it." He let out a little laugh. "I was afraid you were going to pick out some medieval name like Sigfried, or Olaf, or something that sounds more ghostly. Allen's cool."

Shelly suddenly thought he sounded unexpectedly manly, even sexy. *Again? Sexy? A sexy ghost?* "No. You don't sound medieval. Your voice sounds like an Allen," Shelly said, puzzled by her reactions, becoming more convinced she was going crazy. *How do you even think for a second that a ghost can be sexy?*

"Okay. Allen it is. Thank you. I feel better already. I've been very confused," the ghost, now called Allen, said. "Yes, I like that name a lot."

"I'm confused too," Shelly admitted. *At least we have one thing in common.* "What are you confused about?"

How much could he tell her? "It's like I have unfinished business...something I still have to do," Allen said.

Of course he has something to do. He was murdered! I'm getting out of here." Well, I'll leave you to it then," Shelly replied, leaning forward to get up from the bench.

"Please don't be afraid of me," Allen said again, picking up on her thoughts. "I'm not going to hurt you." *Maybe if I repeat it, she'll believe me,* he thought.

Why am I not running? Shelly wondered. There was something about his voice that seemed to assure her that he didn't want to hurt her, but to trust a ghost? "I just don't understand any of this. I've never met a ghost before." Shelly was not at all sure she wanted to know one now. She glanced at her watch. Her mother usually called at eight. "I've really got to go. It's been nice talking to you."

"Aren't you going to help me?"

"How can I help you?" Shelly asked, checking her watch again out of nervousness.

"I have no idea. But one minute I'm walking in this park minding my own business, and the next I'm saving your life. That should count for something."

"Thank you," Shelly said, realizing she sounded cold. Not a great idea.

"No, I didn't mean it that way. I just meant, how did I do it? I have no idea what I can do."

"So nobody ever told you?"

"You'd think that someone would do that, wouldn't you? After all, how does a ghost know what he can really do if nobody shows him? It's not like the movies, I guess."

"I suppose you have to find out for yourself, pretty much the way we do all our lives," Shelly said. "Trial and error, my father says." *Like trying one wife and deciding that was an error, and then trying another wife -- damn slut!* She tasted the bitterness she always felt when thinking of her father and the divorce.

"That doesn't seem fair," Allen remarked, suddenly picking up anger signals from her. "I think, after a hard life of learning from one mistake after another, we'd have someone teach us the ropes of this ghosting thing."

Shelly sighed. "Life isn't always fair." *Holy crap, I sound like Mom!*

"Hey, I'm not ALIVE anymore! So shouldn't I get a break after dying?"

He sounds like a pouting little brat. A thought occurred to Shelly. "How old are you?"

"How old do I sound?"

Great! I'm playing guessing games with a ghost! ...Why not? If I'm going crazy I may as well go all the way. "Ancient. You sound really ancient!"

"Do I really sound that old?"

"No, I was only kidding. I can't believe a ghost can be vain! Next you'll ask me if you sound good-looking."

He hesitated. "Well, do I?"

"Oh, brother!" Shelly had enough. "I've got to get back to the dorm. It isn't safe after dark around here. Too many ghosts!" She started to walk away. "By the way, thank you again for saving me today. I hope you have a great life... I mean after-life."

"Wait a minute! Are you just going to leave me like this?"

Shelly heard her mother saying, "Oh, oh."

"You can't just walk away, and that's it. I saved your life. That means you owe me."

The "Oh, oh" sounded louder, but was it safe to upset a ghost? "Okay. Let's say I believe you saved me, but what can I do? You're a ghost and I'm a new grad student. I can't help you. I want to help, but seriously?"

He noticed soft brown freckles on her cheeks and nose and a slight dimple in her chin. She really was cute, even if she looked worried right now. "I don't know what you can do, either. This whole thing is confusing. It's kind of lonely…or it was until I found you."

Her mother's warning was even louder. "I guess it could be lonely, not being able to talk to anyone. How about this? Were you married? Did you have kids? Maybe they could help you?"

"I told you, I don't know. I think I have amnesia or something?"

"A ghost with amnesia? This is getting better and better."

"I guess some things we're meant to forget after we leave," Allen said, knowing there was one thing he desperately wanted to remember. He would do anything to remember the murderer. He would make him, or her, suffer the most excruciating death any ghost had ever inflicted on anyone. Until this encounter with this stranger called Shelly, finding his murderer had been his only reason for being. Even now his thoughts were on how he could use this girl to help him get justice. He just wouldn't tell her. If she knew it might terrify her, and he'd lose the only person who might be able to help him.

Shelly shivered. A strange cold draft was coming from somewhere near the bench. She sensed it was coming from this ghostly creature she called Allen. Were there secrets this thing wasn't telling her? Dad was like that, pretending to love her while he was out having sex with someone only a few years older than she was. Secretive, soothing voice and gentle words aside, this creature was not to be trusted. *Hell, you can't trust a man, even alive, so how can you trust a dead one?*

She remembered the icy coldness in Allen's voice when he had said he had 'unfinished business'. She had a feeling she knew what unfinished business the ghost of a murdered man might have. Whatever it was, Shelly didn't want any part of it.

CHAPTER 7

"It's getting late. I really have to go," Shelly muttered, afraid of the hostility she sensed around her. It was as if a moist chill was passing through her body.

"No," Allen said, "You can't leave me."

He isn't going to let me go. Shelly wondered how far a ghost would go to get his own way. "I have to go or my friends will come looking for me." Would Jeff have come looking for if he was still around? Would any of the so-called men she had dated care if she was late? *...Unless I was preggies,* she laughed. *I'm on my own.* She had to sound logical, not frightened. *Keep my voice calm.*

"I see," Allen said. "Just when we were getting to know each other."

"What if I come back tomorrow? We can talk some more. Maybe I can think of some way to help you by then." She knew she didn't mean it. She had no intention of coming back. *Just like Jeff had no intention of coming back.* She felt the bitterness, but held it in check. *First things first. I could have been mugged, or killed, and now I've got a ghost after me. I'm never coming back here again,* she vowed.

"Why don't I go with you?" Allen asked.

Oh, oh. "To the girls' dorm? I don't think so!" Shelly imagined what kind of trouble a ghost in the girls' dormitory could cause. She didn't like the idea of any male being able to see her any time he wanted, without her being able to see him. "That is a definite no."

"It could be fun! Just imagine what we could do together. We could spy--"

"NO! I don't think so! Even a ghost can see that a male living in a girls' dorm is not a great idea." *What is he? Some kind of a pervert?* she thought. He didn't sound like one, but you never knew.

"Why couldn't you have been a guy?" Allen groaned. "We wouldn't have this little problem if you were a guy." *But then I wouldn't be feeling this way about you either,* he thought, wondering exactly what it was he was feeling for her. She certainly seemed to arouse something in him. He felt oddly protective toward her. Wasn't that why he had risked whatever existence he had to save her from that knife-wielding killer?

"That would have been better." Shelly said, thinking that anyone else but *her* would have been much better. *How do I get away?* "I promise I'll be back tomorrow afternoon, and we'll talk some more. Maybe you can go jogging with me. Would you like that? You looked like you can really run well."

"I don't know how I materialized like that. I've never done it before."

"You must have the power. What did you do before you 'saved' me?"

"No idea. It just happened."

"I saw you," Shelly said, thinking aloud. "Before the mugger jumped you. I thought you were another jogger…a female?"

"You did see me. That's a first."

"That mugger must have seen you too… to attack you like that."

"You're right. I hadn't thought about that. But how did I do it?"

Shelly's eyes wandered to the corpse in the shadows and she shivered, having almost forgotten about him. *What if someone finds him and I'm sitting here chatting with this ghost? They'll think I did it, and lock me away in a crazy house somewhere. It's one thing to stab someone in self-defense, but this guy looks as if someone sliced him up. That's not self-defense. How would I explain this?*

Allen was still talking. "I know that bum saw me, but I have no idea how I did that. All I remember was seeing you in trouble. That's all I could think of. I suddenly wanted desperately to help you."

"Well, maybe that's it. Maybe when you focus like that, without any other distractions, you're able to materialize."

"That could be it. Like when someone is in trouble and suddenly has almost super-strength…like adrenalin can give you in dangerous situations. That might explain it."

"It makes sense," Shelly said, and suddenly realized that Allen might have been so focused on saving her that nothing else had mattered to him. She closed her eyes, trying to remember what he had looked like when he had materialized, but no picture appeared. She gave him a small smile, the first he'd ever gotten from her. "I think I know what happened. Allen, you were so worried about me that you took physical form. Maybe you can do it again?"

"Let me try! I'd love for you to see how really handsome I was… am."

Oh brother, Shelly thought, but was surprised that she was curious about what he looked like, her desire to escape momentarily put aside. She settled back on the bench. "I'll be quiet so you can focus all your energies…."

"Shhh. I can't concentrate if you keep talking."

"I'm trying to help."

"Then please be quiet. I'm trying to focus."

"Okay, I'll be quiet. Now you try to concentrate."

"Shhh."

Shelly gave him a dirty look, but kept quiet.

Several seconds went by. Shelly kept searching for any sign that Allen had materialized, even one part of his body, but there was nothing. Suddenly she heard what sounded like a burst of air escaping from a balloon. "Are you okay?" *I'm asking if a ghost is okay? I really must be nuts!*

"It's no good. I tried my best, but I can't do it. It must have been a fluke."

Shelly thought he sounded tired. "You probably just need practice. If you did it once, you'll do it again."

"I don't know. They really should have an instruction book for all this stuff."

"Why don't you write one?" Shelly said, thinking how crazy that sounded -- but maybe it would give him something to do so he wouldn't bug her anymore. Anything was worth a try.

Allen laughed. "We could do it together. Shelly and Allen's Ghost Instruction Manual. You'll be my 'ghost-writer'." He laughed. "That's a joke. But seriously, we make a good team."

Shelly sagged on the bench. *This guy is planning on a long-term relationship.* That was enough to frighten anyone. *Relationships with humans are scary enough,* she thought, bitter again that Jeff had gone to L.A. even though she'd thought they had something that might last.

"I think you and I were fated to meet," Allen continued. "I only wish I knew why."

Shelly had a feeling she knew why he needed her, but why on Earth would she need him? If he thought he was going to involve her in some insane scheme to get revenge for his murder, he was sorely mistaken. It was time to tell him good-bye. "I think—"

"I think we have a special connection, and that's why I was able to save your life from that guy over there."

Shelly glanced back at the dead mugger. If Allen had really saved her life, as he kept on insisting, didn't she owe him at least a little help? Shelly sighed. There were plenty of boyfriends she had had trouble getting rid of in the past, so how on Earth was she ever going to get rid of a persistent ghost?

CHAPTER 8

"I really do have to go now," Shelly said lifting up from the bench again, wondering if this ghost she called Allen would materialize and push her back down. "People are going to start worrying about me—"

"You promise you'll come back?"

His voice seemed to be coming from right in front of her now. He had moved. She braced herself in case he grabbed her. Maybe he was lying about not knowing how to do that. "Yes. I give you my word I'll come back tomorrow afternoon and we'll talk."

"Okay. I believe you. Please don't let me down!"

Had he moved away? Was it safe for her to leave?

"I'd hate to have to come to your dorm to look for you."

Shelly shivered. *Was that a threat?* "I said I'll be back." She felt like telling him she didn't like being threatened, but why provoke him? "I always keep my word." *Am I really going to?*

"Okay. I'm sorry. I need to be sure. You're the only one who can help me. I have no idea how long I'll have to wait for someone else." His voice trailed off, as if he was sad.

She sensed the loneliness again. "I'll do what I can. But you have to let me go now."

"It's fine. Go on." He wished he could hold her here, but knew that even if he could physically restrain her, it would do no good. She had to want to help him, but who would want to help a ghost? "I... Good-bye, Shelly. I'm sorry I kept you so long. I'll understand if you don't..."

She waited for him to say something else, ready to give him an argument. When he didn't, she slowly took a few steps forward. *Is he gone?* Was it relief she felt, as she walked cautiously to the street and then broke into a gentle jog – which, when she thought she was safe from him, became a run. As she raced toward the dorms she wondered if at any second he would reappear and attack her. *You just can't trust a male…a ghost.*

* * *

Allen had mixed feelings as he watched Shelly sprint out of the park. At first a sudden fury rose within him, his insides bubbling up with anger -- anger that he had let her go, anger that he had let her lie to him, knowing she didn't have any intention of coming back. "How could I have been so damn stupid?" he asked aloud. And then he remembered her face. It was an easy face to like…to trust. Perhaps it was her eyes, or maybe her natural looking brownish-blonde hair? She had worn no make-up, not even a hint of gloss on her lips…and she had small dimples on her cheek when she smiled. "Cute," he said aloud, surprised he could still have such thoughts. *Maybe I'm not a ghost,* he thought. *Ghosts can't have feelings for…* "I'm just confused."

Allen sat on the back of the bench, unsure of what to do next. "What if she doesn't come back?" He realized that was pretty likely. He let out a deep sigh. "I have no choice. I have to trust her."

He prepared to wait for her there, for as long as it might take before she either came back or he was finally allowed to go where ghosts with unfinished business were eventually sent.

* * *

Shelly didn't stop running until she reached the three-story brick dormitory, known by the girl residents as the Hot Box because of its aged AC system which had the nasty habit of cutting out in the hottest weather. The boys called the girl dorm that for an entirely different reason.

Shelly raced past the unguarded glass doors of the brick building and up to the third floor. She shoved the fire door open and made certain it was completely closed again before she started down the long corridor with its regularly spaced wooden doors, each decorated by its tenants with various items, some of which belonged anywhere but on a door visible to the public.

Shelly fished out her key and pushed it into the door marked Room 306. She was relieved to see that her roomie, Lisa Denning, wasn't there. "Probably partying, as usual," Shelly thought, as she closed the door behind her and clicked the twin locks. "I should have gone with Lisa, wherever she is; then I wouldn't be in this mess."

With the door secured, and the window checked and locked, Shelly stood in the center of the room and listened intently for any sound that might indicate the ghost had followed her. She wouldn't put it past any male, and definitely not past a ghost. She even wondered if he was telling her the truth when he said nobody had ever heard or seen him before she did. Could that be a sneaky way to hook up? *With a ghost?* Shelly scolded herself for even thinking such a crazy idea. *Where the hell do these crazy ideas come from?* she asked the empty room.

Shelly waited several minutes, and finally threw off her sneakers and let herself fall backwards onto the thin mattress of her cot. She closed her eyes, realizing she was exhausted. She wanted to sleep, but was afraid of what she might dream. *If he is a ghost, if such a thing could really be, then what is he after?* If he was really murdered -- something she found hard to believe, something much too terrifying to accept -- why was he still here? She had felt his seething anger when he had mentioned murder... *This ghost is out for revenge.*

Shelly's eyes closed. Her breathing slowed. She saw herself leaning against a wall. It was painted a sickly yellow. *...My room...I see my bulletin board...Jeff's picture...I have to take it off.* Shelly felt strange. *I'm not alone.* She saw herself staring as a young man came toward her. He was tall and thin, with long wild-looking dark hair and brown eyes that were aimed at her face. He suddenly stopped in the middle of the room and dropped his hands to his sides. She felt a strange sense of excitement, and after a brief pause she saw herself walk toward him, her hands rising to reach his face. She lifted herself on her toes and gave him a tentative kiss, which became more passionate as she held on. The strange thing was that he didn't seem to be responding. She dropped back, her eyes questioning, but when he didn't move, she began to open his shirt buttons, touching his neck, teasing him with her fingernails. And still he didn't move, so she slowly ran her fingers over his flesh and suddenly felt him shudder. That was enough for her to keep trying, especially when she gazed into his eyes and saw he was following her every movement. Carefully, she ran her lips down the front of his chest. There was hardly any hair; the skin was smooth and flawless. She heard him sigh. She removed his shirt from his shoulder. His skin was pale but perfect, no marks, a smooth canvas for her lips.

      By now Jeff would have been wild. He would have thrown her on her bed, or the floor, and started pumping her crazy, even if they were both still dressed. This man wasn't moving, wasn't showing any desire for her other than remaining still as a statue, waiting for her fingers and lips to explore each stone-like feature. She pulled off the rest of his shirt and found herself gazing at a back that looked like that of a teenager, and not a grown man. She felt more aroused than she had ever felt, even with Jeff, by this mysterious man with the dark hair and impenetrable eyes who was standing so still, making her do all the work. It was the aloofness, the mystery, that was now driving her, making her want him. It was time. She moved to his front and her hand slid down to his jeans. She wondered what she would find. Would he be aroused? He had shown almost no sign of interest in what she was doing to him. He was a mystery…a mystery she had to solve.

Standing in front of his eyes, she slowly removed her blouse. Surely the sight of her breasts -- firm, rounded, always arousing to Jeff -- would make him move. He left her standing there, naked on top, excited, wanting him, but not touching her breasts which were longing to feel his hands. Would they be gentle, as the slenderness of his body, the paleness of his skin, seemed to suggest? Or would his hands be rough and callused as he finally grabbed her in his palms? She had to know. Even if this was a one-time hook-up, she wanted to feel his hands and see what he would do.

This is new. This is strange. She had never met a man who could not be aroused by her, but this one was still resisting. Even if his body was clearly showing signs of his interest, he just wasn't moving.

Shelly saw herself drop to her knees and slide her hand into his opened jeans. She was pleased to see he had been aroused by her, and looked up and met his eyes gazing down at her with what she thought was passion. She lowered her eyes and touched him, with her fingers, drawing him out and caressing him, teasing him, running her lips around him the way Jeff had liked so much.

When she felt him shudder and gasp, "Enough", she looked up and saw his hands were lowering toward her. *At last,* she thought, now eager with lust, making her want him to touch her shoulders, to raise her up so they could make love. His standing still, making her wait, had been so damn arousing, and now she was eager for him to show his passion, to show that he too had been overcome by wanting her. But the strange thing was, when she gazed up this time, she didn't like the look on his face. It looked as if his finely etched features were twisted in some horrible torment as his hands moved with open fingers slowly toward her neck. Her eyes met his eyes, and she saw that they were hollow.

She heard someone scream.

CHAPTER 9

Shelly's eyes blinked open. "What the hell kind of dream was that?" she asked aloud, realizing that she was sweating. She was surprised she remembered so much of it, but could not remember the man's face. It was as if he had been invisible…invisible…like a ghost? Was that a dream too? *No wonder I had a nightmare like that.* "What the heck happened to me today?" Her mind wouldn't let her stop thinking about the crazy things she had experienced. Was it a real ghost, or was it a hallucination from the shock of almost being attacked? Had she been attacked? Was the attacker so close to killing her that only a freak accident had saved her? Was Allen her way of explaining what happened? Her mind kept working the puzzles over and over, not letting her sleep again. Not that she wanted to, after that erotic yet horrifying nightmare. *Imagine being so turned on by a dream, and then having it end like that? What a night!*

Another thought-track to drive her nuts: at the back of her mind was the gnawing realization she never called the police. "I was going to. But how could I call the cops? They never would have believed me." Shelly wondered what kind of trouble could she get into if they found the corpse and connected her to it. Wasn't it a crime not to call the cops if you found a body? "Holy crap! What a mess! And a ghost too?" She closed her eyes again, overwhelmed by all the problems that had dropped on her, like giant boulders, just because she went for a jog in the park. "It almost makes you want to burn your jogging shoes," she said, knowing she could never do that, but also swearing she would never go to that park again. "I don't need no damn males, ghosts or real, to complicate my life," she said, staring up at the ceiling and wishing she could fall asleep and wake up with all of this gone.

I wonder what Allen looks like, she abruptly mused, and then scolded herself for even thinking about that ghost or whatever he was. "He isn't even Allen. I gave him that name." She found herself wondering if the reason the man in her dream, a dream still vivid in her mind, could not be seen by her was because it was a ghost -- Allen. She couldn't believe that dreaming about him could make her almost climax, but then morph into a nightmare that made her scream with fear. "I'm going crazy," Shelly whispered, suddenly feeling very alone in the cluttered dorm room. "Where the hell is Lisa?"

Shelly thought of telling Lisa, but guessed her boy-crazy roomie would think she was either insane or pulling her leg. Anyway, she rarely saw Lisa without some boy in bed with her. It was as if the girl, unlike Shelly, was eager to try every hook-up she could find. Shelly had woken up many nights to hear the sound of Lisa and some guy or another making the bed-springs rock. No, Lisa would be no help at all.

So who could help?

She could hear her mother saying, "I told you so. I told you to stay home where you're safe." And her father would laugh it off as some dumb-ass kid stunt, trying to get attention away from his bimbo and her new baby boy. "I hate him," she said, feeling the familiar anger well up inside her. She closed her eyes again. *Who would ever believe I talked to a ghost?* "I don't even believe it."

She felt one of her headaches rising from behind her right eye. "I need a doctor," she groaned. "A head doctor."

She jumped up. "That's it! Why didn't I think of that before?"

Shelly leapt out of bed and ran to her laptop on her cluttered desk, waiting impatiently as the internet slowly came to life. She typed quickly, opening the home page for the university -- named after the short stone walls that were built to protect the American rebels during the

Revolutionary war, a few sections still standing around the perimeter of the sprawling campus. Few students knew that a tiny, but bloody, battle had been fought here hundreds of years earlier. The university did not publicize this battle for some very good reasons; the bodies of the fifteen rebels that had died here had never been recovered.

Shelly hesitated at the computer, muttering, "What am I doing?" She answered her own question: "If there is a ghost, and I'm not saying there is one, then I've got to get help to get rid of it." She continued typing. It was a long-shot, but worth a try. She searched the left margin of the university's home page, and clicked on the long list of departments.

Scrolling down the list, she finally landed on what she was seeking, the Department of Psychology. "I'll just find a professor to talk to." She pressed the button on the mouse to stop the scroll, but it kept going.

I passed it, she thought, and tried to scroll backwards with the mouse.

The scroll moved up, stopped, and then back down again as if on its own.

"Damn," she cursed, about to clear the screen, when it began to scroll out of her control again. Course after course scrolled down quickly until a heading read, "Graduate Courses" and the scrolling slowed. "What the heck is going on?" Shelly muttered, watching as the grad courses slid slowly by.

Near the bottom of the list the scrolling stopped, leaving Shelly staring in disbelief at the last course on the list: Parapsychology 666, Clinical Research Seminar. *I've never heard of that one before,* she thought as she clicked on the course description.

It was blank. Only the professor's name was listed, and the building in which the course was supposed to be presented. A notation read, "By appointment only."

"That does me a lot of good," Shelly grumbled. She flicked the previous page icon, and the screen returned to the university home page. Suddenly it began to scroll quickly downward again by itself, stopping at the same course number, Parapsychology 666.

Shelly read the notation again. *What kind of department offers only one course and by appointment only?* she wondered. "That's not very hopeful," she mused, but jotted down the name of Dr. Joel Lasker, Ph.D., Psych Building B, Room B101. "I have no idea why I need this, but what the heck."

She started to scroll back to find someone in the Psychology Department who might be able to help her, but was startled when the screen suddenly went blank. The battery icon revealed the laptop was still half charged, so why had it gone off?

Shelly stared at the blank screen and then at the scrap of paper on her desk. Why had she even bothered? It probably was a waste of effort, but then why had she written it down?

Shelly heard a noise at the door. She closed the cover of the laptop and jumped into bed. For some unknown reason, she had no desire to explain to Lisa where she'd been tonight or what she had decided to do. Not yet.

Closing her eyes, she waited anxiously for the door to open, hoping it really was her roommate. Even if Lisa was drunk and dragging in one of her playmates, even if she had to listen to the bed moving with thrashing bodies, the moaning and giggling, she hoped it really was her. *Please, let it be her!*

CHAPTER 10

Finding Dr. Lasker's listing in the on-line college catalog worked better than a sleeping pill. Shelly slept through Lisa stumbling into the room, cursing at Shelly's sneakers in the narrow path between their beds, and falling onto her bed on the other side of the cramped room after a bit too much to drink -- but at least, for once, alone. She also slept through Lisa's snoring and sleep-talking.

Shelly didn't know it was the sleep-talking and recurring nightmares that were the reason Lisa always tried to go to bed late, and as often as possible with a bed-mate. It was also why she'd been an undergraduate, and now grad, psych major.

Lisa had been a sleep-talker since childhood, and alarmed her parents when they learned she not only talked in her sleep but sometimes walked in her sleep. Several times her parents had found her in the large pantry of their kitchen, staring at the rear wall of the closet lined with wooden shelves. On one occasion they heard scratching noises in the kitchen closet, and were shocked to see Lisa's nails had almost broken off from scratching the back wall. It was then they discovered the hidden panel that, when pulled open, revealed a staircase leading to a small concealed room at the top of the house. The hand-drawn plans for the house, constructed in the early eighteen hundreds, and the leather-bound records they had found in the basement, offered no evidence that the room existed.

When Lisa was five, she revealed to her parents that she had heard low moaning sounds emanating from somewhere above her room, almost every night in that house. Nobody believed her, so she stopped telling them after a while. She never told anyone else either. She had hoped that getting away to college would end the moaning and the nightmares, but it hadn't. That small room and the eerie noises seemed to be imprinted in her brain, emerging in her dreams unless she drank herself to sleep or exhausted herself with sex. She had read in one of her courses that dreams have sexual roots, and was doing everything she could to sexually uproot her dreams.

    In her application for a roommate, Lisa asked for someone who didn't smoke and who wasn't noisy after ten p.m. The last requirement was forced on her by her parents, who hoped sending her away to college would "straighten her out" and turn her into a 'studier'. Lisa, afraid of her nightmares and her sleep-walking, refused to go to sleep until, all partied-out, she was convinced she wouldn't be able to dream. It seemed a good plan and had worked fairly well, until tonight. Something was causing her to talk in her sleep again. Something was making her cry into her pillow. She hadn't done that in a long time. She had never dreamt about Shelly before, either. The truth was, she didn't like her room-mate much, maybe because she didn't go partying with her. So why was Shelly in her dream tonight?

    Why did she see Shelly slowly undressing some unidentifiable man who seemed frozen as she touched and kissed him for what seemed like hours, and then dropped down on her knees before his open jeans. She'd never seen Shelly with a man in the three weeks they had been on campus together and couldn't imagine Shelly servicing any man with her lips as she was doing in the dream. Lisa felt her own excitement building as she watched Shelly's head, her hair bouncing off her shoulders, as the man stood gazing down at her hidden by some kind of mist. And then everything changed. The man, who had been a stone-like statue, lowered his hands and placed them around Shelly's neck. *I didn't know she was into that,* Lisa thought as the man began to slowly grip tighter with his fingers. The harder he squeezed, the more Lisa felt as if her own breath was being stopped.

Shelly would have been alarmed if she'd been awake to hear Lisa moaning her name. As it was, she slept through it all and woke up at six-thirty as usual. The sun was peeking through the venetian blinds. Nobody ever dusted them, and the cheap plastic was like a dust magnet. She was about to bend down for her sneakers, eager to head for the park and take a morning jog, when suddenly she remembered what had happened at the park yesterday. She sat on the edge of the bed, paralyzed. Had he been real? Was any of it real?

"No," Lisa cried out in her sleep, feeling the fingers clamping down too tight.

What now? Shelly thought, wondering if she should wake her air-head roomie.

"No... Shelly, please no! Don't go there!"

Shelly jumped. *Was Lisa calling my name? What's going on?* she thought, as she looked at Lisa wrapped in her blanket, still wearing the clothes from last night. *Should I wake her?* she wondered. She leaned closer and smelled alcohol on Lisa's breath. *Idiot,* Shelly thought, and she decided to leave Lisa exactly where she was, since now the drunken roomie was just snoring. *If she misses her classes again it will be her own fault. I'm not going to fight with her again. That's for sure.*

Shelly picked up her robe and flip-flops and her little plastic bucket of soap, shampoo and conditioner. She listened at Lisa's breathing again. No more moaning. *I must have not heard right,* she thought, and headed for the shower room. Before she left the dorm room she locked the door. She almost never did that until she left for classes, but something about this morning was different, and locking the room had been instinctive, automatic.

The shower room was still deserted. Most of the girls who shared the showers were still asleep. Shelly flicked the wall switch, turning on the overhead fluorescent lights, and searched for a stall that looked cleaner than the others, less slimy. She hated to think of what went on in these disgusting stalls when nobody was looking.

She found a hook to hang her bucket. The pipes and faucet had corrosion bumps on their chrome surfaces, but at least this early the water would still be hot. Later in the morning, with so many girls and guys taking showers throughout the building, the water cooled quickly. That was understandable, the heating system being almost as old as the dorms -- some of which had been built nearly fifty years earlier when the school had been a girl's reformatory and experimental penal farm, complete with cornfields and a pig slaughterhouse. It was a past well buried by the founding trustees of the college, now a state university.

Shelly slipped off her robe and yesterday's panties, and dropped them to the bench outside the stall. She lifted her tee shirt over her head, tossed it after the robe, and turned on the water. At first it was cold, but then it became too hot. *Typical,* she thought as she leaned in to adjust the two faucet handles that always seemed to be working against each other. *A person could get badly scalded with this crappy system,* she thought, as finally the water seemed to be beating down steadily, if not powerfully, at a decent temperature.

Careful not to slip on the soap residue on the tiled floor of the stall, she stepped into the spray. It felt good, the stinging droplets hitting her soft skin. She let the water wet her hair and then drip down her body. To save time, she applied shampoo first. She watched the shampoo foam through her shoulder-length honey-toned tresses and trail down her front. The pressure of the water was good this early in the morning, relaxing her as it cascaded down her back. She felt as if her worries were fading. *I'm naked in a waterfall,* she mused, hoping nobody else would come and take another stall, so the pressure would drop or the temperature slide to freezing cold. *Maybe I won't bother going to see that professor after all,* she thought as she let the shower spray down her ever more relaxed body. "I must be crazy," she laughed. "Ghosts? Impossible."

The gentle spray of the water reminded her of her last night with Jeff, when he had joined her in the shower after they'd made love in her bedroom. Her mother had been out working, so she and Jeff had played hooky from classes to be able to use a real bed -- not the back seat of a car or a rental for an hour in a motel. That was when she thought he was going to marry her, before he told her he was going to film school in California. She remembered how he had looked at her, his eyes seeming to pick out her flesh from the soapy water streaming down over her hair, shoulders and breasts. Just before he kissed her and they made love in the shower, he had whispered, "You are so beautiful," and she had believed him.

Shelly reached for the faucet and gave it a hard twist. Conditioner stinging her eyes, she used the towel gently on her face and then her body. "No more men for a while," she told herself.

When Shelly finished patting down, she wrapped the towel around her torso and prepared to step out of the stall. Instantly she felt a chill race through her. On the tiled wall of the shower, written in streaks of white soap, were six shaky letters,

LASKER

When Shelly looked down, she saw an almost used up bar of white soap in her hand, one end crushed.

Shelly dropped the soap. *Did I write that? How did it get there?* Her legs felt rubbery. She was unable to move, staring at the name, unable to grasp what it was doing there.

When she finally felt steadier, she took her washcloth and wiped the words from the tiles, then aimed the shower head at the wall and watched the soap scum drip down to the tiled floor and the tarnished drain.

When she looked at the wall again, the word was still there, its outline barely showing against the dull tiles, but still clearly there -- the name of the chairman of the Parapsychology Department.

LASKER

CHAPTER 11

Shelly was still staring at the wall when she heard the bathroom door open. She tightened the towel around her body.

"That Jack is a real dud," Shelly heard a voice she recognized, a girl from somewhere in the South. "He takes me to a movie and then expects me to pay half! What a jerk!"

"Actually, Ronnie, I think that's not bad," another voice replied.

"Are you serious? What kind of boy takes a girl to the movies and doesn't pay?"

"A guy who's telling you he doesn't want you to feel obligated," the second voice said.

"You don't know the rules, Sue," Ronnie said, and burst into laughter. "We play different in Atlanta. The boy pays, period."

"That's not what's important," Sue said, sounding irritated. "Did you have a good time with him?" she asked.

"Yeah. kind of," Ronnie replied.

"Did he hit on you?"

"No. Not even once."

"Well, that proves it. I think you found a good guy there."

Shelly had never gotten to know Susan Robinson, a black girl from Harlem, but was suddenly impressed by the intelligence she was expressing to Ronnie -- whom Shelly grouped with Lisa as an airhead of the first order. She stared at the stubborn letters on the shower wall and decided Sue might be just the person to help her. It was worth a try. Anything was worth a try. She stepped out of the shower stall.

"You startled us," Ronnie said, not bothering to cover up with a towel. "We didn't know anyone else was here this early."

Sue was silent, her black body covered in a thick white robe. She seemed to be studying Shelly with her dark intelligent eyes.

"I'm sorry," Shelly said. "I'm an early riser."

"Not like your roomie," Ronnie said with a wicked look, finally covering her lower body with a towel, but leaving her ample breasts exposed. "She sure can party. I saw her at Crotch's Pub last night. You should go with us sometime. Your roomie loves it there. I've never seen anyone so hot for it."

Shelly felt like saying *it takes one to know one,* but was looking at Sue who was still staring at her. "Is everything okay?" she asked, feeling threatened.

Sue frowned. "How about you? You look like you've seen a ghost…or Ronnie's tits. Hey, Veronica, why don't you cover up for a change?"

"Why should I? If you got them, flaunt them, I say."

"Fine. You just keep letting those things hang out, and one day when you're old -- if I know you then, which I doubt -- those melons of yours will reach your knees."

Shelly laughed at the shocked expression on Ronnie's face. She knew she was making the right choice. Susan was smart enough and honest enough to help her.

"I apologize for Boobsie over here, but did you want something from me?"

Shelly trembled. *Did she know? How could she?* Sue was definitely worth a try, but what about Ronnie who was now covering up with her towel, at last? "Can you two come with me a minute, Sue? I want to show you something."

Ronnie shook her head. "You'll excuse me, but I have to rush. I'm late for breakfast as it is. I'm meeting that jock, Bill. I'll bet he's willing to pay for a damn movie. Y'all have fun." She turned to Sue. "I'll think about what you said, but if you like that boy that much, maybe you should go out with him. He just doesn't do it for me...if you know what I mean?"

Sue shook her head and followed Shelly toward the shower stall. "Some girls don't know when they've got something good. Now what's going on?"

Shelly wondered if that had been her problem with Jeff. Had she not realized how good he was? Was the breakup really her fault? *No! Damn it! No!* She hesitated, and then pulled back the shower curtain. She pointed to the wall. "Do you see that?" The letters on the wall were still visible to her.

Sue peered into the stall. "What exactly am I looking for?"

"You don't see the letters...right there on the back wall of the shower?" Shelly touched the letter L with her finger.

"Sorry," Sue said. "All I see is a wet wall. You just took a shower."

Shelly stared at the name again. "I'm sorry I bothered you," she muttered, pulling the curtain shut. *I was really hoping she could see it*

Sue gave her a smile. "Just because others can't see something doesn't mean it isn't there."

"I don't understand," Shelly mumbled as the taller girl pulled the curtain back again and searched the wall. "You still don't see it?" she asked, surprised this girl was apparently believing her.

Sue turned back to Shelly. "My Grandma used to see things all the time. Everybody thought she was nuts, but she wouldn't give it up. One day she told me she had a dream that I would be the first in our family to go to college. My mother laughed and said I'd be a cleaning girl just like all the rest of us, but Grandma said I'd be a doctor. When anyone asked how she could come up with such a crazy idea, she told them the ghost of her husband told her that."

Shelly froze at the word ghost. "Do you believe in ghosts?" she asked.

Sue looked over Shelly's shoulder toward the shower stall. "Is that what's going on with you? Do you think you've seen a ghost?"

Would this girl she hardly knew think she was totally insane? "I don't know," Shelly answered honestly. "I don't know what's happening to me." She sighed. "You hardly know me, and I put you on the spot like this. Sorry."

Sue studied Shelly's face. There was something she was sensing, something not quite right. "I don't know what's happening to you either," Sue said, giving Shelly an anxious smile. "Just be careful."

Shelly nodded. "Thank you. I plan to be."

"And don't tell anyone else about this. They'll think you're whacked."

"Do you think I'm crazy?" Shelly asked.

Sue tightened her robe. "No. At least I hope not. I really hope there are ghosts somewhere out there. Maybe someday I'll see my Grandma, and be able to thank her in person."

Shelly nodded. "I hope you can."

"Thanks," Sue said. "I'd give anything to have that chance. Later."

Shelly watched as Sue walked to another shower stall. She wished she could tell Sue the whole truth, but wondered if someone who was a stranger would believe her. Sue's warning, "Just be careful," echoed in her brain.

Shelly pulled the curtain open again and saw Dr. Lasker's name scrawled in the residue on the wall. What was it doing there? Was it a message from some unknown source, hopefully friendly, affirming her decision to go see the chairperson of the Parapsychology Department? Was it her imagination again? The name was still there. *It must be someone who wants me to see him,* she decided.

It never occurred to Shelly it might be a warning from someone who did *not* want her to see Dr. Lasker, someone who would do anything to stop her.

CHAPTER 12

It was difficult enough for Shelly to concentrate on classes, at eight in the morning, without having so many other things to think about. First and foremost was the possibility of being acquainted with a real, live -- okay, dead -- ghost. The second was her involvement with a violent death -- the mugger -- although she wasn't exactly sure what her involvement was. Had the police found the body? Was there a body? *I'll have to check the news to see if the crime -- accident? -- was reported.* This was all too confusing. And then of course there was the erotic dream of a man she could not see, a man without a face... *A man without a face?* Was she dreaming of Allen?

Shelly was usually a good student, earning substantial scholarships for academics which allowed her to go to college, but she'd never had a ghost to contend with before. It was almost impossible to concentrate, and her notes on the lecture were, at best, chaotic. She still didn't believe she had really seen and talked with a ghost, but then what else could the young man -- he sounded young -- what else could he be?

"I'm getting nowhere," she groaned, realizing until this was somehow settled, she would never be able to concentrate on her classes. She had been ready to forget all about the ghost whom she never intended to see again, until Lasker's name had shown up in her shower stall. Why would it be there? Why was she the only one who could see it? The whole thing was driving her crazy.

As soon as the first period ended, Shelly headed for the bus stop at the corner of the sprawling, brick-faced education building. She had no idea how long it would take for the bus to travel the circuitous route from this portion of the expansive State campus all the way to the other side, where the map showed the Parapsychology office was situated. It was as if they'd deliberately separated the building from the rest of the campus, as if trying to protect the "normal" students from the psychos in the department, Shelly mused. *Everyone knows it takes a psycho to become a psychologist,* she thought, as the bus seemed to take longer to arrive than usual, *So what does it take to become a parapsychologist?*

That question amused her, but it also made her a little afraid of what she might be getting into. All she knew about parapsychology was what she had seen in the movies and on TV, and that was always weird and bogus to her. "Check your brains in at the door when you see one of those," she told her friends, but now she wasn't sure of anything.

"It must be traffic," a young man unexpectedly commented as Shelly was peering in the distance for the Blue Bird bus. "They really have to do something with the roads here. It's getting worse all the time."

Shelly nodded, taking in the long, dark brown hair and wire-framed sunglasses that hid the boy's eyes. *Quite cute,* she thought, and then scolded herself for being so easily distracted. *I sound like Lisa or that damn Ronnie,* she *laughed,* wondering if she'd ever have the balls to run around with her boobs hanging out like that.

"Where are you headed?" the young man asked, putting down his backpack, a perennial feature of student attire.

Shelly wondered why he wanted to know, but quickly decided he was just making conversation, harmless talk. "Over to the other side of the campus...the Psychology buildings."

He looked surprised. "Hey, that's where I'm headed too. You a major?"

Shelly shook her head. "Graduate Education. I want to be a reading specialist, like my mom."

"My mom's a teacher too. Coincidence, huh?"

Shelly was hardly listening. Where was that darn bus? *I'll be late for my afternoon class...*

The young man brushed back his hair, which was over-long and wild with brown curls that danced inches from his shoulders. "So, are you new here?"

Shelly sighed. She was in no mood for hooking up with anyone, even if they were good-looking. "I don't understand why the bus is taking so long."

"It was fine first period, when I came over here." He looked down the road and she saw the sharpness of his facial features. There seemed to be a slight twitch of his cheek. He removed his sunglasses, and she saw that his eyes were dark blue, very intense. She'd seen eyes like his somewhere before, but where? "Don't worry, you'll make your afternoon sessions," he said. "It'll be fine."

"Well, it's not fine now," Shelly said with a sigh. "I'll have to try this later." She began to walk away -- and suddenly realized he had said something about her missing her afternoon classes. *How did he know?* She turned back, about to speak, but he beat her to it.

"You didn't tell me your name," the young man said.

Shelly hesitated. Her eyes focused on his face...dimpled chin... thin lips. His eyes were dark blue, which was interesting considering his hair was dark brown, making his eyes stand out more. *What am I doing? No more Jeffrey,* she sighed. "Shelly," she said, and started to cross the road, giving up on the bus. "See ya," she called back, only half-hoping she would see this interesting-looking man again.

The man looked surprised, his eyes darting toward the road and then back to her. "Shelly? Did you say Shelly? Shelly what?" He walked up to her, his backpack forgotten at the bus stop enclosure. "Shelly what?" He slipped his sunglasses back on, as if he knew the intensity of his eyes was disturbing her.

Shelly suddenly felt uneasy. "What do you want?" She backed away from him.

His mouth was tight, his sunglasses a mirror hiding his eyes. "Please, what's your last name? I really have to know."

"Why? Why is that so important? I'm not interested ...." Shelly was backing toward the curb. He looked harmless enough, but his eyes were like a mirror.

He must have sensed her discomfort because he pulled off his glasses again. "Please don't be afraid," the young man said. "My name is Dodd. I came here to find someone named Shelly."

"Oh, bull!" Shelly laughed, strangely relieved. "That is the worst pick-up routine I've ever heard. Just give it up already. I'm not biting." She backed away faster, intending to cross the road.

"Wait a minute! Just look at this!" Dodd reached into his pocket and extracted a folded sheet of yellow lined paper. "Explain this to me!" He unfolded the paper and held it in front of Shelly's face, his dark blue eyes probing hers.

On the paper, in what looked like red ink, Shelly saw her name, first and last, scrawled in shaky letters.

Shelly Adams

Why was she shivering? "How did you do that?" she asked, reaching for the paper and taking it from his hand. "It's some kind of trick, isn't it?" She thought of the word in the shower. Was the handwriting the same?

Dodd looked all around and then aimed his eyes directly into her face. "Is this you? Are you Shelly Adams?"

"I asked you how you got this." Shelly kept feeling chilled, as if she had a fever, but worse. "You knew who I am. Why?"

Dodd was staring down the road. "I had no idea who you were until you told me. It was in my textbook when I opened it this morning."

"You didn't write it? Someone didn't give you my name, and you didn't write it for some kind of sick joke?"

He shook his head, his eyes probing her as if asking, *How much does she know? What is she capable of?*

Shelly was trying to maintain contact with his eyes. *Where have I seen those eyes before?* she asked herself again, unable to tear away from his intense gaze.

Dodd shook his head. "Someone wants me to find you. I don't know who, how or why."

"Maybe to warn me about something," Shelly mumbled, remembering the lettering in the shower again. *What the hell is happening?*

Dodd nodded slowly, his eyes still studying her carefully. She didn't look as he had expected, much softer, innocent looking. He felt confused, finally stammering, "You shouldn't go anywhere today. You should stay here until we can figure this out." *What am I doing?*

We? Shelly studied his face again. He looked as if he was telling the truth, but what if he wasn't? What if this was all some kind of weird trick? "So you came here to find me? From where?"

Dodd looked around the corner and then back into her eyes. It was time to drop the bombshell. "I'm an assistant to Dr. Lasker of the Parapsychology Department."

"What did you say?" Shelly looked as if she'd seen a ghost again. "Say that again?"

Dodd heard the sound of a large vehicle approaching. *It might be the bus.* "Hey, calm down." He could see her face had gone white. He almost felt sorry for her. "Do you need something to drink, a place to sit down?" He was sure now this was the right girl, but she was nothing like what he had expected, what he had feared. And yet, his visions had never been wrong before... Well, that wasn't quite true, but what should he do? Should he trust a girl he hardly knew, or the visions that had been with him all his life?

Shelly gasped, still wondering if this was some kind of weird trick. "I was on my way to see Dr. Lasker. You work for him?"

"Now you're kidding me, right?" He looked at the road. It was not too late, but he'd never gotten it wrong before. This time he couldn't make a mistake. Too much was at stake.

Shelly was confused. This was too much of a coincidence. It had to be a setup, but who could do something like this? Why were his eyes studying her so intently? Why did he look so dark and distracted? She had found him handsome, his hair wild and his mouth sensuous, but now she thought she saw something else, a darkness that frightened her. She backed further from the curb into the road. "I don't know what's going on, but it isn't funny. I'm leaving."

Dodd saw the bus out of the corner of his eye. It was finally almost here. He heard the voices inside him arguing, screaming that he had to make his decision. He only had a few seconds. He reached for Shelly with both hands.

Shelly heard screams, but it was too late. The bus was heading right for her.

CHAPTER 13

Shelly was like a deer frozen in the path of the bus as it turned the corner. She couldn't move. Even the loud screams all around her did not seem enough to get her to jump out of the way. Her eyes found Dodd, who was close but not moving. *Is he in shock? Is he too far away to save me? He's nice looking,* she found herself thinking, scolding herself for wasting her last thoughts on some boy who was not only a stranger but also strange. Those damn eyes!

The bus roared toward her. Trying to move, she stumbled, her ankle giving way. The ground was rushing toward her. The bus was about to crush her and throw her broken body a mile. Good-bye, Shelly, she thought, closing her eyes before the impact and laughing irrationally inside.

She heard the brakes screaming on the bus. *It isn't real,* she thought as she waited for the collision and night. *It isn't real. It isn't real.*

None of it seemed real. The bus was almost here, the shining metal front about to hit her. *It isn't real. It isn't real.* Shelly was unable to move or scream as the bus seemed to be coming for her in deadly slow motion.

She believed she was going to die, and there was nothing she could do about it. Her eyes hit on Dodd's face. Was it real or a vision? Was his face a smile or a grimace of paralyzing fear. He was wearing his sunglasses and she saw her body falling in the reflection of his silver lenses. Crazy last thought: *I want to see his eyes before I die.*

Suddenly a strong pair of arms grabbed her from the path of the bus and flung her hard onto the grass.

"My back!" she screamed. "You could have been more gentle." She knew she wasn't making sense.

"That was too damn close," she heard a voice gasp, as the bus screeched to a stop a few dozen feet away. "Do you make these things a habit?"

The voice, male, struggling to breathe, seemed weak -- as if exhausted from saving her, she thought. There were tears in her eyes, and she felt her body stinging from the impact against the grassy earth. "What things?" she murmured, still in a daze.

"Needing me to rescue you." It sounded like a whisper now, tender, gentle.

Shelly struggled to sit up, but fell back again, looking for her savior, and saw a face through blurry eyes. "You're real? I didn't imagine you?"

"Of course I'm real," Dodd said, gazing down at her with a puzzled look on his face. "You're alright? How did you do that? How did you get away from the bus?" He looked all around to see if he could find any explanation for her amazing escape from what looked like certain death. "I was too far to help," he mumbled, wondering why he hadn't noticed the rescuer before the bus arrived. He'd seen everything else.

"You saved me," Shelly said, her lips forming into a weak smile as the tears flowed down her cheeks.

Dodd didn't reply. He was studying the faces in the crowd.

Shelly was slowly coming around. She recalled how surprised she had felt when she hadn't seen Dodd rush to her aid as the bus careened toward her. *He must have been too far...or maybe he didn't see? But then he miraculously did it.* "I thought you were too far," she said. "Thank you."

Dodd nodded, his eyes still searching the crowd, his mind trying to understand how she managed to escape what he'd been sure would be certain death under the wheels of that bus. "You have to be more careful," he said. "You should rest."

A stocky man in a bus driver's brown uniform was bending over her. He smelled of perspiration, and his breath in her face was sour. "I'm so sorry!" he was wailing. "I don't know what happened. I don't know!"

Dodd hadn't anticipated him. *What do I do now?* he thought, trying to figure out how he should react. "Are you the driver?" Dodd roared. "What the hell is wrong with you? You could have killed her!" He glared furiously, his eyes blazing.

Shelly wondered why he was so angry. She was still dazed, but wished he would stop shouting, wished his eyes would be less sharp and look down at her again. She wanted to see a caring look, not this angry, frightening... Yes, frightening.

The driver, a Black man with dark eyes that shouted his guilt, could have pulverized Dodd with one hand tied behind his back under normal circumstances, but he was allowing Dodd to shout at him, bully him, as he tried to see if the girl was okay. "I don't understand it," he said. "It was like the bus was aiming for you. I couldn't control it! I had no control at all. I'm so sorry."

"Bull," Dodd spat, wanting to cut off this driver before he convinced Shelly the bus had not been under his control. "You're the damn driver! What the hell were you doing? Are you drunk?"

The driver shivered under Dodd's glaring eyes and brutal scolding. "I'm telling you something was steering my bus! I don't drink! Not for years! I'm telling you the truth. It was like the bus was driving itself, straight toward her. It wasn't me. It wasn't me!"

"Get the hell out of here," Dodd said in a menacing voice. "It was your fault. How else can you explain it?" He was pulling the driver away. "They should arrest you for what you did."

The driver shook his head, walking a few steps away as if in a trance. "I'm sorry. I'm so sorry." He turned to Shelly, tears streaming down his face. "I can't believe it. Are you okay, Miss? Please, tell me you're okay."

Shelly felt strange. She felt sorry for him even though he had almost killed her. "I'm...okay. Please, don't worry about me. I'm okay." She tried to lift herself off the grass.

"Stay down," a voice she recognized said softly. She quickly searched for its source. Why couldn't she see who said that?

And then she remembered Allen.

* * * * *

She searched for anyone else who could have spoken, but there was nobody near except Dodd and he was busy with the driver. It had to be Allen's voice. Had he pushed her in front of the bus? She had felt someone's hands shoving her in the path of the bus. *Allen?* "I want to get up," she said, but sank back onto the grass, her legs still rubbery.

"Can you walk? Maybe you should wait for an ambulance?" The driver was staring at Dodd with sweat pouring down his face. "Best play it safe. You don't want to be hurting more. I'm so sorry."

Dodd stared hard at the driver. "Just get in your damn bus and wait there for the cops. They'll know what to do with you." His voice was stone cold.

"Don't go on the bus," Shelly heard that same soft voice warn. "Don't trust him."

Shelly shook her head to clear it. A voice was warning her not to trust the driver. Was it him? What was he doing here? "So I should trust you?" Shelly asked, searching for any sign of the ghost.

The driver looked as if he'd been slapped. "I'm sorry, Miss. I didn't mean it. You can trust me. I ain't goin' anywhere. I'll tell the cops it was my fault. The damn bus wouldn't stop. It was like a missile aiming for you. I'm so sorry."

Dodd needed time to think. "Shelly, you look weak," he said. "I'll take you back to your dorm so you can rest."

"What about the police?" Shelly asked.

Dodd aimed cold eyes at the driver. "They'll talk to you in your room. You need to get some rest. You, driver, tell the cops her name is Shelly Adams, and she's on the third floor of this building." Dodd's eyes were drilling into the driver's brain.

"I'll tell them it was my fault," the driver repeated, as if in a trance. He had already forgotten the young girl's name and what she looked like.

Shelly felt Dodd take her arm and help her to her feet. It felt good to have someone to lean on. She suddenly realized how tall and strong he was, and found herself gazing into his eyes. *He's taking care of me,* she thought, letting herself be guided by him, supported by him.

"Don't trust him," she heard Allen's voice warn again. Or was it her brain still recovering from the shock?

"Oh shut up," Shelly said, tired of the voices without faces, suddenly feeling completely drained from her close call with the bus.

Dodd dropped her arm. "I was only trying to help!"

Shelly pursed her lip. "I didn't mean you," she said, wishing she could see her ghost who kept getting her into trouble so she could tell him to get lost. "Dodd, I didn't mean you." *Believe me, I didn't mean you, not after you saved me.*

Dodd looked confused, but grasped her arm again. *She's weird,* he thought, but that was exactly what he had expected when he came to find her. After all, every Ecto in the Parapsychology Department was unusual in their own way. You might say it was a departmental prerequisite.

CHAPTER 14

"Which room is yours?" Dodd asked as he helped Shelly climb the stairs to her room on the third floor of the dorm.

"Oh, him you let into your dorm room," Allen rumbled, following along. "I don't trust him."

"Shhh," Shelly hissed, now aware that Allen had really appeared again -- this time not in the park but here, on campus, in her dorm. *This is bad,* she thought. "I told you, you're not supposed to be here."

Dodd was confused. "I thought you wanted my help. Are you okay? Are you in shock?" She was having trouble getting up the stairs. She was leaning on him, depending on him. It was a long fall. If someone tripped on these stairs, they'd most likely break their neck. He held her tighter, helping her move up one step at a time. "Do you feel dizzy," he asked.

"No. I just have a headache," Shelly said, realizing she had to be more careful when she spoke to the ghost with others around. "I have a really big headache!" She wondered if the ghost understood she meant him. She decided to focus on Dodd. He was holding her, helping her. *Dodd is stronger than he looks,* she mused, feeling his arms around her back. *Good thing.* Her legs still felt shaky and her head was swimming.

"Don't worry. I'll leave as soon as I get you to your room," Dodd said, realizing they were almost at the third floor. She would be safe in a few short steps.

"A likely story," Allen hissed. "He's not going to leave. He's got the hots for you."

"Not everyone is like you," Shelly replied.

"Thank you...I think," Dodd said. "You sure you don't want me to call an ambulance? You're acting a bit strange." Even for an Ecto, he thought, aware that in two steps he'd be on the third floor. He suddenly wondered just how powerful her sensitivity was. *Is she more powerful than I am?* One shove down the stairs and he wouldn't need to know.

"No ambulance," Shelly said. "I'm fine. Just a bit tired and a HUGE headache!" *Why doesn't he leave me alone?* she thought, wishing Allen would leave.

"So which room is yours?" Dodd was still holding Shelly up as she limped down the corridor. "Wait a minute. I bet I can guess."

"How can you guess?" He was teasing her. He hadn't shown any sense of humor up to now, but had appeared dark and kind of mysterious. A sense of humor would be a nice touch, she thought.

Dodd smiled. "Don't you remember? We were talking about parapsychology before that idiot bus driver almost ran you down." He had decided to try and learn the truth before he did anything else. He had been so certain she was the right one, but something had stopped him. He couldn't help feeling she was nice -- not at all what he thought she would be like. He almost wished she had been the self-serving, arrogant, greedy witch he had expected. How could he hurt someone like her, someone who was making him care about her? *I'm confused,* he thought, voices arguing inside him. *I've got to be sure.*

Shelly vaguely remembered something about wanting to go visit the psychology building that morning… "Dr. Lasker," she suddenly exclaimed, happy she remembered his name. "That's who I was supposed to see." She eyed him curiously. "You said he's your boss? I remember." *His eyes are so blue,* she thought as he gazed down at her.

Dodd nodded. "He's chairman of the department."

"Isn't that weird," Shelly said. "You work for the guy I was going to see."

"That's very weird," Allen echoed. "I told you I don't trust him."

They were almost at her door. "What's he like?" Shelly asked, fishing for her keys in her fanny pack.

"Lasker's a unique character." Dodd hesitated before he continued. "He specializes in unexplained phenomena like ESP, mental telepathy and of course ghosts." He suddenly looked hard at Shelly. "Is that really the kind of person you want to see?" He hoped she would change her mind; it was her only chance.

Shelly wondered just how much she should tell him. "I'm considering taking a course with him. Ghosts have always fascinated me. You know, all the movies and all." Why was she lying to him? Had she come to the point where she didn't trust anyone, even someone as cute as this tall stranger who somehow rescued her from the bus and was now helping her through the hall? Were other girls looking him over? There was nobody around... *All in classes,* Shelly thought, embarrassed that she had hoped at least some would see her handsome escort. *Not like me at all,* Shelly scolded herself. *Must be shock.*

Dodd didn't reply. He was studying the doorways along the hall. There were at least a dozen doors that could pop open at any time, far too many. "That's your room," he pointed to room 306. "Am I right?"

Shelly turned toward him, a look of amused surprise on her face. "How did you do that? Do you have ESP?" He looked perfectly normal, nothing out of the ordinary, except for his eyes which seemed too blue for his face, framed by all that wild brown hair that hung almost to his shoulders. She had always been a sucker for blue eyes and dark hair. *What the hell am I thinking,* she scolded herself for not staying on track. *Must be the accident...but he is cute, in a mysterious way.* She thought of Jeff's face, so square, framed by boy-next-door blond hair...no real depth...definitely, not mysterious...a one-dimensional jock whose tanned skin was so different than this boy's pale flesh...she saw Jeff naked in her bed, but wondered what Dodd would be like…Jeff was rough and tumble…Dodd looked like he would be gentle… *What the hell am I thinking about?* Shelly scolded herself again.

Dodd laughed, but he found nothing funny in this quest to find out just how much she knew. " ESP? No, I'm just as normal as you."

Shelly was beginning to wonder how normal she was, seeing a ghost and all. "So how did you pick out my room?"

Dodd pointed to the notepad on her door.

Shelly looked at the scrawled note, a shiver running through her body.

Shely I WARN U

She grabbed the note and crushed it in her fist. "We always get some joker writing on this thing. I should get rid of it."

Dodd noticed the note was written in red ink…red as blood. *I wonder who wrote that one? Could it have been Chan? Does he finally believe me?* he thought, as he crushed the other note in his pocket.

CHAPTER 15

"I'm very tired," Shelly said, sitting on the edge of her unmade bed. "Forgive the mess."

Dodd couldn't help being suddenly amused by his surroundings. The room was a shambles. Her roommate's side of the small chamber was more of a disaster than her side: used panties, a bra and a pair of white socks all on the floor by the bed. The panties were black and lacy, which Shelly wished were not so visible, but Dodd seemed unaffected by them, his eyes focused on her. She liked that.

"Now that you're safe..." Dodd wanted to get back to the Department and find out if Chan had finally decided to help him. Who else could have written that damn note?

"Dodd... Is that really your name?" Shelly thought that was an odd name. ...*odd Dodd,* she thought and realized he might not find that humorous, even if she was struggling not to giggle.

Dodd was standing in the center of the room. The rug was an ugly pink shag. He should have guessed. His eyes moved to the messy bed where Shelly was sitting. He was surprised at how much he thought she looked like a little girl, the brown blanket covering her knees, her sneakered feet poking out from the bottom. He shook his head. She wasn't anything like what he had expected. "Yeah, I'm stuck with it."

"It's unusual," Shelly said. "Is it short for something? Like Dodsworth or something like that?"

"Get rid of him," Allen rasped. "We need to talk."

"Oh no! Are you here?" Shelly looked around the room. "I made it clear you can't be here. This is a girls' floor. Someone could barge in any minute."

Dodd looked confused again. "Shelly, are you okay? You're talking to me but looking at the door." He looked, but saw nothing there.

Shelly was still scouring the room for Allen. "Am I what?"

Dodd's eyes were studying Shelly, wondering if she was right and someone could barge in on them. He felt the tension in his fingers and let his hands drop to his side. "Are you okay?" he repeated. His eyes were on the door. If he was going to make a move it had to be now. Any second, the police might come to get her statement about the bus driver. He had almost forgotten about the driver. He almost felt sorry for him. But then again, the man would remember nothing about the incident. Dodd had made sure of that. "I asked if you're okay."

"That's a dumb question, you dick," Allen rasped. "She was almost killed, so how do you think she is?"

Shelly wished Allen would leave the room. She had this urge to risk everything and reach over to Dodd, her rescuer with wild dark hair and gorgeous blue eyes, and push her lips onto his in one damn grateful kiss. *...Oh, who the hell am I kidding? Grateful, my ass. I just want to feel his lips against mine and see what he's feeling.* "Are you gone yet," she asked Allen.

Dodd sighed, still very unsure of himself. The girl had aroused a protective instinct in him, something he hadn't expected, something he didn't want. And yet she was crazy -- one minute warm and inviting, and the other asking him to leave. He had wondered if she really was an Ecto, after all she hadn't seen the bus before it almost killed her...and now he wasn't sure. The only other female Ecto he had known -- Swan, a Native American -- had been independent and almost masculine in her mannerisms. This one was totally different, which he was finding disarming, confusing. Maybe she wasn't the one? In his visions, he had never seen her face. How could he be sure?

Shelly realized how crazy she must appear to Dodd and tried to focus all of her attention on him, not scare him off. He looked very distracted, as if he was deep in thought. She wanted him to think only of her. "Sorry. I guess I am a little in shock after all." She gave Allen a glare, hoping wherever he might be he got the message to get out.

Dodd frowned. "That would be natural after what you went through," he said. He glanced at the door and thought of locking it. *I'm just not sure,* he told himself. *Make a move on her or not? Damned if I know.* He heard a siren in the distance. It was late. Soon the other girls in the dorm would be back. He found himself hooked on her lips and pale blue eyes. Swan's eyes had been almost black, piercing. Shelly's eyes were see-through, not threatening at all. "If you're okay, I'll leave now."

"It's about time," Allen rumbled. "I thought he was never going."

Shelly's eyes instantly moved to where she thought the ghost might be. "Not on that bed," she said to Allen who seemed close to Lisa's bed.

"Nice undies," Allen said.

"You leave those undies alone," Shelly warned.

Dodd looked shocked. "I wasn't going anywhere near them." He was used to the strange people in the Parapsychology department, but this girl seemed even stranger than any of the others. He had always believed the more sensitive an Ecto the weirder they had to be, but this girl took the cake.

"Please leave," Shelly begged Allen. "I'll keep my promise."

Dodd got up. "What promise? I'm going. You need your rest." *Why is she acting like this? If she is as sensitive as she is weird, then her powers have to be pretty awesome. She's looking for something.*

"I'm sorry," Shelly said to Dodd, seeing he was about to leave. "Maybe I'll see you at the Parapsych Department," she added hopefully.

Dodd sighed. She still wants to pursue that. Maybe his first instincts were correct after all. He walked toward her. Now or never. "Good-bye, Shelly," he said softly.

"I didn't mean you have to leave," Shelly said quickly, glaring at Allen and hoping he could see her. She realized Dodd was staring at her as if she was insane, and didn't blame him one bit. "I'm really sorry," she said, thinking he was about to leave because she had been acting so crazy. "I'm just not myself."

Dodd stared at her and his eyes saw a young woman, nicely built, with a smile that seemed to be asking him to kiss her. *Maybe it's her freckles,* he thought, as he realized she looked very young and innocent. He gave her a thin smile, still deep in conflict with what he felt and what he knew, a battle between his heart and his brain. "Well, I think I'd better go now and let you rest," he finally muttered, steering deliberately clear of the bed with the panties. "You're going to be alright now."

Shelly's voice was husky. "Do you really have to go?"

Dodd gazed into her eyes. She was hard to turn down, but he knew what would happen if he stayed. "I'll see you again. I promise."

Shelly nodded reluctantly. "Thank you." She wanted to ask him if she could make it up to him somehow…later or another day? He really did have an interesting face, eyes intensely studying her, warming her, but mysterious. They seemed to lure her toward him, making her want to get to know him better, make her want to feel his arms around her again, feel his lips exploring her lips, and much more. She moved toward him.

"I'll see you when you feel better," Dodd said. "Give it a few days before you leave the dorm again." That would buy him time to sort things out, to figure out how he really felt. "A few days of peace and quiet and you'll be fine."

"Once you're out of here, she'll be fine," Allen said.

Shelly held her reply to the meddling ghost. "Thank you for saving me," she said, inches from his lips, hoping he would take the bait. She could feel her body begging him to take the bait, even if that damn ghost was watching. Maybe that would chase him away once and for all.

Dodd was so tempted by her, but weighed his options quickly. How much of the truth could he tell her? What if someone had seen what really happened at the bus stop? The cops were below, taking statements. She was approaching… It was her! Oh God, it was her. He knew what was coming next. He had seen it before, and knew she was going to reach her hands to his face and place a tentative kiss on his lips. He swallowed hard, anticipating how her lips would press harder and harder, trying to get him to react, while all he could do would be to let her proceed with the ritual -- while he decided if he should make love to her or kill her.

CHAPTER 16

Shelly raised her hands to his face. "Thank you for saving me." She wondered why he wasn't reacting. A kiss. It would only be a small kiss, a tiny token to thank him. She leaned toward him and placed her lips tentatively, gently, on his. *Why isn't he moving?* she wondered.

"Please. No more," Dodd said, wondering if he could change things. Was it too late? If he stopped her before she began, could he at least delay the decision? *She isn't what I expected,* he thought, arguing with someone inside him who had warned him of the threat she posed -- the voice that had convinced him she had to be stopped, no matter what he had to do. "I'm sorry, I have to go," he said.

She backed away, crushed by his obvious rejection. "I only wanted to thank you for saving me." Why did he look so strange? Was he afraid of her? Of women? *He's got beautiful, fine-etched features, tall, thin…is he gay?*

Dodd saw an out, but did he want to take it? *Nobody is around. Why not let the vision happen? If she's gone there's no doubt, no reason for my brain to ache like this trying to make a decision.* He felt as if his head was exploding, and all because of her. The voices arguing her fate were never going to stop until he did it. He knew he could do it. The bus proved that, but did he really want to? *I need more time.* "I didn't save you," he finally said, knowing it would stop her cold.

Shelly was confused, more than ever. She really believed that Dodd had saved her. But now he had made it clear that it wasn't him. Why would he lie about that? "You didn't? I don't understand."

Dodd shook his head. "No. I didn't save you."

"Dodd, you were there. What did you see? Who saved me if it wasn't you?"

She really doesn't know? "I thought you could tell me," Dodd replied, again intently staring at her, hoping she would have an explanation different from what he suspected, an explanation that could change everything. "I didn't see who it was. He vanished before I could get to you…or to him, to thank him properly." Dodd held his breath, his eyes more intense than ever. *Please tell me I'm wrong,* he begged silently. *Tell me you're not an Ecto and it will be over.* He could almost taste her lips.

Shelly heard someone whistling.

"It wasn't you?" she asked Dodd again. "Are you sure? Are you positive?"

Dodd shook his head. "That bus driver had you in his sights, and then suddenly you were lying on the grass. I have no idea how that happened. I wish I did." *Oh God, I really wish I did.*

"You know," Allen said.

Dodd waited, but Shelly remained silent. *Okay,* he thought, as he saw she wasn't going to answer. He forced a smile. "I wanted to tell you the truth." *Jackass,* he heard the voice scold, *Why did you tell her that?*

Shelly nodded. "I appreciate that." *If he didn't save me, who did?*

Dodd was thinking, trying to regain his advantage, his control of the situation. "Maybe you'll let me take you for coffee after dinner tonight? If you're feeling better, after a rest?"

"I told you so!" Allen said in triumph. "Do I know my horny boys or don't I?"

Shelly almost barked, "Shut up!" but was learning to focus on the real faces in her life and ignore what she still hoped was a figment of her imagination, a troublesome creature she created for some unknown reason, to whom she had given the name Allen. Besides, she now suspected Dodd liked her, maybe a lot. That was the best news she'd had in days, the best since Jeff had dropped his little bomb.

Your loss, Jeffrey, she said silently. "I'd like that," she said, smiling at Dodd and then giving Allen a defiant look.

Dodd didn't smile back. "I'll pick you up at seven, okay? I'll bring my car this time."

"Hey, you have a date with me tonight. Remember? We're jogging in the park together," Allen said, wishing he could make something move so that Dodd -- what a name for a boy -- would run out of here screaming. "I'd like to scare the crap out of him," Allen said, eyeing Lisa's lacy panties and wondering what Dodd would do if they suddenly flew right into his face.

"Seven is fine," Shelly replied. "Maybe you can take me over to the parapsychology quad tomorrow too? I really would like to sit in on one of Dr. Lasker's classes, but I don't feel like taking the bus."

A strange look came over Dodd's face. *She isn't going to let that go.* He sighed. "Sure. But I have to warn you, Dr. Lasker is not…well, he's not for everyone." *One last chance.*

"I hear he's really interesting," Shelly said, wishing Dodd would be more open. He really didn't talk much, but maybe it was better that way. Allen talked too damn much! And Jeff was full of bullshit, even in the shower. A flashback of his muscular body holding her while he whispered, "You are so beautiful," sent a warm shiver through her body. *What would Dodd be like in the shower?*

Dodd sighed. "Oh yeah, he's interesting alright." *You have no idea. Every damn Ecto is interesting.*

Shelly wondered how Dodd meant that, but decided not to question him too much just yet. "See you later, then. And thank you again for helping me." She held back from giving him a kiss, even though she wanted to.

Dodd looked around the room. She still wanted to see Lasker. He had hoped she would change her mind. *There's still nobody else here,* he thought. His eyes landed on the unmade bed, the black lace undies. *Damn, she's so young and dumb and naïve!* He had a flashback to his vision, her eyes gazing up at him as she toyed with his belt, his hands slowly lowering. Dodd felt his head pounding, exhausted from wrestling with his thoughts and all the conflicting voices in his brain. *One more day won't hurt,* he decided. "You're welcome," he said. "I'll see you tonight." He walked quickly through the door before he changed his mind.

Once outside the room, Dodd paused and stared at the notepad taped to the door. He could see the impression on the blank page over which the warning message had been written. He looked up and down the hallway and tore several sheets from the spiral binding. *I really wonder who wrote that one,* he said to himself as he headed for his car in the parking lot behind the dorm.

Shelly watched the door close, wishing she had asked him again to stay. For once she thought Lisa might be right, a bedmate like Dodd might be just the thing tonight. She wondered why Dodd had almost sounded angry when he had said, "You're welcome" and had left. Maybe he was disappointed that she hadn't invited him to stay? She had been tempted, had tried to send signals to him, but he had seemed distracted. She stared at the door, wishing she would hear him knock. As tired and confused as she was, she had decided she wouldn't turn him away if he returned. She found herself wondering what Dodd would be like in bed. He seemed to have a nice body, a bit thin, but still promising and sexy. "What the hell am I thinking about?"

A yawn shook her body, and she dropped back onto the bed. It didn't matter that she was fully dressed; the mattress, a barebones college cot, felt like a cloud tonight. *I'm exhausted, but I should have invited him to stay... Oh, who the hell knows?* She raised her fingers and began to unbutton her blouse. In her mind, she imagined Dodd's fingers gently unfastening each button with tantalizing slowness. She sat up, reached behind and undid her bra. It would have been nice to have help with that, she suddenly thought, wondering what his hands would feel like cupping her breasts. She let her jeans fall to the floor. They were dirty anyway from the roll in the grass. She didn't bother picking anything up, but fell back against the pillow.

Dodd's face was easy to conjure up, his intense blue eyes and that amazing black hair...his features, fine but strong...those eyes half-closed and his lips slightly parted.

She saw him falling gently down over her, his body arched inches from her own. She felt his lips pressing onto her lips, his eyes gazing into her eyes, measuring her responses as he moved lower, and then up again, letting his hair and flesh brush lightly on her skin. But it was his eyes that were holding her eyes, her soul, in their magnetizing grasp...eyes that were robbing her of all control, all restraint. Even as he sank lower and then inside her, even as she saw his eyes were haunted, unfeeling eyes, she could not break away.

Shelly's eyes began to close as her hand wandered below the sheet. It was Dodd's hand and it felt so gentle, so delicate...*he's tall and thin and those eyes....*

"Don't tell me you're going to sleep?" Allen startled her. "We've got to talk right now."

Shelly sat up as if she'd landed on a trampoline. She'd forgotten about her invisible intruder. "You're still here?" She pulled the blanket up to her chin, wondering how much Allen had seen. "Damn it, Allen! How long have you been here?"

CHAPTER 17

"You're really cute when you sleep," Allen said, glad Dodd was no longer around. "I don't know what you want with that guy when I'm here," he added, surprised at how that sounded.

"I don't really believe in you," Shelly said, closing her eyes to make whatever it was bothering her vanish forever.

"That's fine," Allen said. "I don't believe in you, either." *Then why do I feel so damn protective over her?* "Although you are fun to watch."

"I'm real," Shelly replied, becoming angry. "I have no idea what you are, other than an invisible Peeping Tom!" *--And a pain in the ass,* she thought.

Allen laughed. "Whatever I am, I seem to be linked to you."

"Not to me you're not," Shelly said, bolting from the bed in just her panties and shirt which she had buttoned while covered by the blanket. "You've got to leave. You've got to leave me alone. Please?"

"I wish I could," Allen said slowly, "But you're the only one who can hear me. Before you came along I was stuck in that damn park, but here I am! It has to have something to do with you! I have no idea why, but doesn't that tell you something? Like I said, we're linked."

Shelly opened the closet, looking for a robe. A mirror was hanging on the inside of the door. Her hair was wild. She brushed it back with her hand. *I'm a mess,* she thought, and instantly grew angry. "I don't care! I don't want a ghost in my life! I'm sorry if that offends you, but look what's happened to me since you came into my life. Look what I look like!"

"You look fine. That Dodd character was eating you up like you were a Girl Scout cookie."

"Oh crap! Mind your own business," Shelly barked, wondering if what he said was true and then realizing she had more important problems to think about...especially one major problem. "Why can't you just leave me alone? Please! All I'm asking is that you get out of my life! What have I done to you--"

"If I had been minding my own business, you'd be dead right now...twice." Allen paused. "Interesting..."

"What do you mean 'Interesting?'" Shelly asked, not finding anything interesting in this whole insane situation. Dodd was interesting, but this ghost? *More like frustrating, annoying, stubborn...a plague!*

"Well, think of it. If I hadn't saved you twice, you might be a ghost with me. Do you think that's what this is all about?"

"Wait a minute. *You* saved me? From the bus?" She had still hoped Dodd had been modest, or that someone, anyone, human had saved her.

"Yes. I saved you twice. Do you think Dodo-boy could have saved you? That's a joke!"

"His name is Dodd." Shelly plunked down on the bed. "Oh crap, I've got some headache!"

"Unfortunately, ghosts don't carry aspirin," Allen said, "Or I'd be saving you again...from your 'headache.'"

Shelly scowled. "For once I didn't mean you. I have a real headache."

"What do you mean 'for once'?" He wondered how she could sound so ungrateful.

Shelly wished he'd stop saying how he had saved her, but had to admit she was curious. "Okay, I'm sorry. I should be grateful, but I really thought some human... But how? How could you have saved me from that bus? You can't move anything! So how did you pick me up and pull me out of the path of that bus?" Was he lying to make Dodd look bad? *Anything is possible. Isn't that what Allen said when I first met him?* "Oh, damn! This is so confusing. I'm sorry. I should be helping you. How do you think you did it?"

Allen was silent and then muttered, "I don't know. It's like every time you're in danger, I seem to be able to energize somehow and, poof, you're saved." He laughed. "I'm just meant to protect you I guess."

Shelly was having a hard time grasping this. If it were true, then Allen -- or whoever he had been in real life -- was definitely not a figment of her imagination or a delusion. "Okay, I guess you're real," Shelly said. "I don't like it, and don't want to admit it, but you're actually real." She shook her head hard. "I don't see any other answer."

"That's what I keep trying to tell you."

"And if you're real, then you must be a ghost."

"As opposed to what? A result of a bout of you drinking?" Allen asked.

"I thought you might be some kind of creature I'd made up." Shelly wished she could see him so she could be sure he was a ghost.

"Oh, thank you. I love being called a creature."

"I'm sorry. I'm just having real trouble taking this all in."

"How do you think I feel? They really should have an instruction manual or something. Did I say that before?"

"Yes, but you're right. So you're a ghost and you saved my life twice, but you don't know how you did it?"

"That sums it up," Allen said.

"And you have no idea who you were in real life, and what happened to you?"

There was a long silence.

Shelly could almost feel the sadness emanating from the ghost. It made her feel kind of sorry for him again, even if he was a pain in the ass. "Sometimes we're better off not knowing ..."

"No! I have to know! I want to know why I'm here like this. If someone killed me...well, I just have to know. Wouldn't you?" He realized his anger was showing, and knew he had to stop it before she became frightened, too frightened to help. "I think if I find out, I might be able to go..." He knew that if he put it that way, maybe she would want to help him.

Shelly sighed. She'd had dreams of being murdered, horrible nightmares. What must it feel like to be a ghost, and know someone in your previous life murdered you? "It must be awful," she murmured, "Knowing someone...someone you might have known...killed you."

"It is."

"I didn't know ghosts could feel things like being sad."

"I didn't until I met you," Allen said. "I don't understand this at all. I just know that you're the only one who might be able to help me."

"How can I help?" Shelly asked, feeling an overwhelming sense of sadness and confusion.

"I don't know." He sighed. "May I stay with you? I don't like being alone."

"You can't stay here," Shelly said. "I promise I'll come back to the park today. Wait for me there."

"You told that Dodo you were meeting him," Allen said. "You can't be in two places at once. I can't even do that, and I'm a ghost."

Shelly sighed. "I almost forgot about him."

"He's not very memorable," Allen said. "Kind of spooky looking."

"You should talk? You're the ghost! Dodd's a nice guy," Shelly said, feeling irritated with her ghost again. "How about this? I'll meet you at the park at four. That will give me plenty of time to get back--"

"For your date with that Dodd?" He said the name with obvious distaste. Why should he feel so angry about some boy being interested in her? *This is ridiculous,* he scolded himself. *I'm a ghost!*

"It's not a date," Shelly said, wondering why she felt she had to defend herself.

"That Dodo thinks it is. I could see it in his beady little blue eyes. Have you ever seen such weird looking eyes in your life?"

Shelly had found Dodd's eyes interesting, kind of intense, sexy in the way he had been looking at her, obviously appraising her. But she wasn't about to share those thoughts with a ghost. "He can think what he wants, and so can you, but it is not a date. I just think he's nice, and he asked me out for coffee, to talk." *I'm lying to a ghost,* Shelly thought, feeling warm at the thought of Dodd being with her tonight. She felt excited about the possibilities. It had been months since Jeff left. "It's not a date."

"That, Shelly, is called a date."

Shelly sighed. "You sound like my father when I first dated." She sighed again. Her father hadn't sounded that interested in her for a long time. He had a new family of his own.

Allen replied, "I am anything but your father." *What the hell am I saying?*

I know, Shelly groaned. *I know.* "Are you still here?"

There was no answer. Shelly wondered if he was deliberately hiding somewhere in her room. How could she know for sure? She couldn't see him, and he left no footprints, butt imprints, or any sign of his being there. "I can't get undressed if I don't know if you're here," she said, clearly exasperated by his being invisible and being able to see her naked if he wanted to. "Come on, be fair. Tell me if you are here?"

When after several seconds there was no response, Shelly cautiously undid the top button of her shirt. She was emptying her jean pockets onto her countertop when she noticed a crumpled sheet of paper. She recognized it as the paper torn from her notepad on the door. She picked it up, and was about to toss it into the plastic trashcan under her fake-maple veneer desk when it fell to the floor.

As it fell, it slowly unfolded until she could read it as it lay on her rug. It said, "Lasker", but there was a large X drawn through it in red ink. "What is that?" Shelly said, reaching for the note for a closer look.

Just as her fingers were about to grab the yellow square of paper, it burst into flame.

She pulled her hand back. "What the hell do you want from me?" Shelly shouted, as the burning ashes danced in the air around her.

CHAPTER 18

The ashes fell to the floor and fizzled out on the tiled surface.

"Did you do this," Shelly asked, but realized Allen couldn't have, not unless he was lying about his abilities to materialize and make things move.

"Allen, are you still here? Please tell me?" Shelly wondered if Allen was still lurking somewhere in the room. One thing was sure; she wasn't going to get undressed in front of this annoying intruder. Who knew how male ghosts got their jollies at seeing young women naked? "Oh, this is bad." She sat on her bed and leaned against the wall, going over all the strange things that had happened to her. "It all started with that mugger," she said, recalling the blood-soaked corpse, the knife protruding from his chest… *Allen sawing through his chest.* She shivered at the memory of the knife moving up and down, up and then down into flesh and bone. "Damn him anyway," she cursed.

Unable to relax, Shelly walked over to her laptop and sat down on the college-issued plastic chair. *Thank goodness I brought a cushion with me,* she thought as she settled onto the chair and lifted the cover of her laptop. Her fingers dangled briefly over the keyboard. She began to type. The search engine listed several sites that looked promising. She highlighted one, and the local crime reports appeared on the screen.

She began to scroll down the reports, eager to make sure she hadn't dreamed up the entire episode in the park. "Damn!" There in bold print was the headline: "Brutal Rapist Found Stabbed in Park by Cute Coeds." *Typical sloppy journalism,* she thought. *Was he found by coeds or stabbed by them?* And of course there was a picture of the two 'cute' coeds, dressed in tight jeans and shirts tied just below the breasts, revealing flat midriffs, staring with wide-eyed horror at the corpse still on the ground. Did these two really find him, or were they planted by the sensation-seeking reporter? Shelly felt lucky that her picture wasn't included.

The article was short on details, and what details were provided were definitely more graphic than factual. The reporter was clearly playing it for sensationalism. She tried to pull the facts from the descriptions written to titillate and give the readers a vicarious thrill. "The man's head had smashed like a pumpkin against a rock, blood coloring the asphalt...the girls had screamed in terror at their first sighting of the bloodied corpse." *Well, what else would they do?* She glanced at the alleged coeds again and sighed. "Fifteen seconds of fame...tight blouses and all."

What was more interesting to Shelly was the statement that the police were stymied by the ability of the man to stab himself in his heart -- in what appeared to be a self-directed rampage, since no fingerprints were found other than the deceased's. The pathologists theorized that the victim fell or was pushed down, somehow impaled himself on his own knife, and then turned over onto his back and proceeded to finish the job. How he could repeatedly stab himself was anybody's guess.

Shelly read the article again, especially noting, "There were no other fingerprints on the knife, and too many footprints from joggers to determine if anyone else was there when it happened." *No fingerprints...Allen.*

Shelly sighed. At least they wouldn't be able to use footprints to find her. That was the first good news since this whole mess started. She continued the article. "Without any apparent witnesses, the police are at a loss for an explanation." *So am I,* she thought bitterly. *So, damn it, am I.*

Shelly leaned back, trying to think. She wasn't a suspect, not even a known witness. *I'm home free,* she thought, but almost instantly realized she really wasn't free.

The article, as lurid and sensational as it was, had proven that the events in the park were real. The mugger was real. The dead body was real. "Damn! That means my "ghost" is also real." *--And the only one who could have sliced and diced that bastard up like that. He's capable of such brutality... He could be anywhere in the room. I've got a cold-blooded butcher of a ghost somewhere in this room! Or was he just trying to protect me? I saw that mugger creep...he wasn't dead.* Something told Shelly that Allen could not be that brutal butcher she had imagined. If he had stabbed the mugger, it was because he had felt forced to do so to protect her. She owed him her life.

"You're too stubborn to show yourself," she said. "Okay, you win. Enjoy while you can!"

She pulled a clean button-down shirt and a gray skirt and matching jacket out of the closet. Next she dug out a plain white bra and pair of white lacy panties. She thought of stockings and low heels, but decided to go with grayish flats.

There was still no sign of Allen. *Have it your own way,* she thought, angry that she had no real way of knowing if he was playing Peeping Tom with her. She sighed and pulled on her robe again. With the robe covering her, she removed the panties she had slept in and slid the fresh pair on. She then held the bra under the robe and slid the robe off with her free hand. The bra was dangling against her breasts. She needed both hands to clasp it in the back. "I hate you," she said as she threw the robe on the bed. She was standing now by the bed in her bra and panties. Was he watching? *What difference does it make?* she thought, as she gave up all effort to conceal herself and pulled on her shirt, skirt and jacket. "So now you've seen me," she said, slipping into her flats. "Did you like what you saw?"

No answer. "Okay, fine. But I guess this proves that a visit to Professor Lasker is my best option." She waited for a response in vain. "I've decided," she said in a threatening tone, "I'm going to the parapsychology department. I'm going to see if I can get rid of you once and for all." She stormed out of the room, locking the door behind her.

The hallway was deserted, oddly unfriendly looking, the lights on the ceiling dimmer than she remembered. She quickly checked her notepad on the door. No new warnings. "I'm going now," she said and started toward the stairway.

She was at the top of the stairs when suddenly she grabbed the banister. She was looking down, frozen at the top of the landing. Sweat was beading on her face and her eyes were locked on the stairs. She had had a vision of falling down the marble steps. She could see her body crumpled up and broken at the bottom of the steps. Who was reflected in her eyes?

CHAPTER 19

The sensations rushing through her were chilling. She had felt this before, when Dodd was helping her up the three flights of stairs after her near miss with the bus. At that time, she had the eerie feeling Dodd was going to throw her down the stairs. *But he was helping me...I am going crazy, being paranoid. Dodd would never hurt me. But Allen? Would he?*

Shelly turned back to the staircase, unable to move. *Someone is behind me,* she thought, sensing invisible hands about to shove her down the steps.

But there was nobody there. And yet she still felt certain that someone was there, someone was going to push her.

Her hand held the brass banister, fingers clutching tightly as she gingerly moved down, one step at a time. She wished Dodd was here to help her again...just as he had helped her climb the stairs before. *Why didn't I call him?*

Shelly breathed a huge sigh of relief when she finally reached the ground floor, her legs still trembling, and her hands still clutching the banister.

Was it my imagination?

She looked up.

For a second she thought someone was looking down at her, but when she looked again, she realized there was no way she could see around the corner to the landing. "I've got to get control of myself", she said, as she headed for the large plate-glass doors that fronted the building.

The bus was sitting on the corner, the door open wide as if it was waiting for her. A white driver leaned toward her. "Need a bus, Miss?" he asked.

"I'm not taking a bus," Shelly said, as she tried to calm herself on the sidewalk outside the dorm. She gazed up at her window half expecting to see flames from the note licking at the cheap cream-colored shades, but everything looked as it always did, her window totally uniform with all the rest along the brick façade of the building. "What the heck is wrong with me?" she asked, starting to walk away from the bus stop.

"Need a lift?" Shelly heard a voice ask.

When she turned toward the street, she saw Susan peering out from her PT Cruiser. There were brownish patches where rust had eaten through the body, either that, or the girl was the worst driver in the world, with more accidents than anyone she had ever known. "I don't know," Shelly replied, walking parallel to the car, but away from the curb.

"You don't know?" Sue asked, the car rolling next to Shelly. "Where are you headed?"

Shelly suddenly wondered why everyone lately seemed to be questioning her about where she was going. She remembered the warnings she had received about going to see Dr. Lasker, and wondered if Sue was someone she should trust. Could she have been the one writing the warnings? That would explain her saying she couldn't see the writing in the shower. Shelly turned back to the car. Somehow the patches on the body seemed to reassure her, after all, who would use such a car if they were plotting a kidnapping or something awful like that? And yet, she had only just met Sue this morning, in the shower-room of all places...just before the bus incident. Shelly frowned. Why would a black girl she hardly knew suddenly want to help her? *This is stupid,* she scolded silently. "I'm headed for the Student Union," she lied, not knowing why she didn't want to tell the truth.

"Hop in. I'll give you a ride." Sue leaned across the bucket seat and pushed open the car door.

Shelly hesitated, but how do you turn down a ride without offending the driver? The car was moving slowly next to her, its door wide open, hard to ignore.

"Come on. I'm not really as bad a driver as the car looks." Sue gave a good-natured laugh.

I hope not, Shelly thought, wishing there was some way to avoid getting into Susan's car. "It's a nice day. I was looking forward to walking," she said.

"Hey, I'm heading to the S.U. myself, so get in."

Shelly hopped reluctantly into the car and pulled the door shut. She heard the click of the locks as she pulled the shoulder-belt around her. "Thank you. I wasn't expecting a ride."

"No biggie," Sue replied. "I was heading there anyway."

"Everything okay?" Shelly asked, sensing Sue wasn't telling her everything.

"Can we talk a little?" Sue's eyes were hidden behind sunglasses.

Shelly felt Sue was studying her. Her curiosity was piqued. "Sure. What's up?"

Sue was driving slowly, her eyes still on Shelly. "I was looking out my window this morning."

Shelly froze. This was a strange way to begin a conversation.

"Well the thing is…I saw something…something weird."

Shelly's eyes were glued to the mirror reflection of Sue's shielded eyes bouncing back and forth from the road to her face and back. She was glad the car was moving so slowly. Sue seemed unable to keep her eyes on the road, another accident waiting to happen. "What did you see?" She held her breath, afraid to hear what this girl was about to say.

CHAPTER 20

Sue stopped at a crosswalk, a group of students lugging backpacks strolling by as if they had all the time in the world. A few looked questioningly at the Cruiser with its dents and rust patches, as if asking, "How is that broken-down wreck still moving?" She felt uncomfortable with what she was about to say. Would Shelly believe her?

Shelly was waiting. She sensed Sue was holding back. "Please tell me what you saw. You don't have to worry. After what I've been through, I'll believe anything."

Sue nodded. "The thing is...well, I saw you. I screamed from the window the bus was going to hit you, but there was no way you coulda heard me. But I saw it. There was no way it could miss...but it did. Thank God it missed." She pulled up her shades, her eyes now pinpointed on Shelly's eyes. "But I know it's impossible. Girl, there was no way in hell that you could have gotten away from being creamed by that bus! No way. How... I know there's some explanation!"

"What did you see, exactly?" Shelly asked. "Please tell me! I need to know."

Sue pulled the car into the Student Union parking lot. "You don't know?"

"I guess the accident made me block it out."

Susan leaned closer. "I saw you fall in front of the bus, and suddenly...."

"Did you see who saved me?" Shelly hoped Sue had seen someone real, a real human being, pull her away from the bus just in the nick of time -- and then, for whatever reason, ran off before she could thank him. That would make Allen a liar, and she would be able to free herself from him and all this trouble once and for all. "I didn't see him, and he was gone when I came to. Please, tell me what you saw! It will really help me."

Sue stared into Shelly's face. "You really don't know?" She gazed out the car window. "Okay, I know it sounds crazy, but I swear it's what I saw. I mean, it was from a distance. I was up in my room, and you were...you know where you were." She felt confused. Was Shelly playing some kind of joke on her? But how could she have? "Shelly, I know you won't believe me, but it was like you were pulled up from in front of the bus and tossed in the air...but I swear, it looked like nobody was holding you. I swear it. I was screaming, so maybe I saw wrong. I don't know!" She stared into Shelly's eyes. "Did you do it yourself somehow? Did you get up by yourself?"

Shelly felt frustrated. *This can't be happening,* she thought. "Nobody was there? Are you sure?" Shelly didn't want to believe Allen had saved her a second time in two days. She didn't want to believe in ghosts, and definitely not one to whom she owed her life -- not once, but twice. But now Sue had seen it...or not seen it...nobody was there who could have saved her.

Sue shook her head. "Uh-uh. I looked and looked, but only a guy with long brown hair was anywhere close, and he was just standing and watching. There was nobody else close enough. I mean, I looked really hard."

Shelly fell back into the bucket seat. "I was really hoping you saw something different."

"I swear to God, Shelly, I didn't see anybody near you, yet you were being carried away. It lasted only a split second, and I thought you were really still under the tires, but when I ran downstairs...thinking you were dead...some boy was helping you up -- the guy with the brown hair."

"That must have been Dodd," Shelly said, thinking aloud.

"I was sure you were dead," Sue repeated, as if she thought Shelly was a ghost herself. "I don't understand."

"I don't either," Shelly said softly. "Sue, would you do me a small favor?"

"You really don't know who saved you?" Sue asked.

Shelly shook her head. "Like you said, nobody was there."

Sue bit her lip. "Does this have something to do with what you were trying to show me this morning, in the shower stall?"

Shelly had forgotten about showing Sue, a perfect stranger, the writing only she could see on the shower wall. "Yes. At least I think so."

"What do you want me to do?" Sue asked, her hand resting lightly on Shelly's hand. "I know you don't know me, but I want to help."

Shelly wanted to trust her. She had to trust someone. But was Sue the right one? *I have to chance it*, she thought. "Can you drive me to the other side of the campus? I know it's out of your way..."

"Your wish is my command," Sue said, and immediately the Cruiser pulled out of the lot.

Shelly felt the seat belts tighten around her. As Sue drove, now at a thirty mile-per-hour pace, Shelly found herself looking expectantly around every corner and into every side street for anything suspicious.

"You're quite a backseat driver," Sue joked, uneasy after their conversation. She couldn't get over that Shelly didn't seem to know how she had escaped the bus -- didn't know, or didn't want anyone else to know. *Maybe she doesn't trust me yet*, Susan thought. *I can't say I blame her after that narrow escape.*

Shelly let Sue think what she wanted. Only she knew the truth -- she now firmly believed that someone or something was deliberately trying to stop her from meeting Dr. Lasker. And whoever or whatever it was, was willing to kill her to accomplish its goal. But who had the motive, the opportunity and the ability to stop her?

Shelly stifled a gasp when she realized there was only one person she knew who could have caused that bus to careen toward her, one person who would do anything to stop her from seeing Dr. Lasker and freeing herself from this situation. She closed her eyes and heard his voice. It was a soft voice, gentle, yet somehow attractive, masculine. It was soothing her, reassuring her. "I would never hurt you," he said.

Hadn't Jeff said that too? *"I would never hurt you, but we need our space. We both do."* It wouldn't have hurt that much if they had not made love just a few minutes before. *And what about my father? Hadn't he promised not to hurt Mom…and me…* She couldn't finish. She heard someone echo, "I would never hurt you."

It was coming from the face of a demon, a demon she had named Allen.

CHAPTER 21

It was only a twenty minute ride by car to the psychology quadrangle, but it was one of the longest rides in Shelly's life. She kept searching for a hurtling car or a falling lamppost, anything that could cause an accident and prevent her from reaching her destination. *It could be Allen,* she thought as her eyes searched the road ahead. *He might have guessed that my real reason to see Dr. Lasker is to get him out of my life. Who else would want to stop me?*

"You must still be nervous from the bus accident," Sue commented, observing Shelly's anxious reactions at each intersection. "Don't worry. I'm a safe driver. This is a used car. It's all I can afford right now."

"Sorry," Shelly replied. "That bus was very close. I guess I am being a bit of a back seat driver. Sorry."

"No problem," Sue said. "Maybe if we talk it will calm your nerves. Where are you from?"

"Long Island…Queens, like almost everyone else on this campus."

"I'm from Harlem," Sue said. "Your folks visit often?"

"Not really. My dad wanted me to live at home and commute. It's a lot cheaper." She almost added, *and he's spending his money on his new bimbo wife and her baby.*

"What about your Mom?"

Shelly sighed. "Mom goes along with most of what he says, even if they're divorced." *What else can she do, with him controlling the purse strings?* Shelly thought bitterly. "Where are your parents," Shelly asked, only half interested, still scanning every possible site for an ambush.

"My grandmother raised me. Mom ran off when I was little."

"Sorry." Shelly was beginning to like this girl. She remembered the common sense Sue had shown in the shower room with Ronnie. "My dad waited until I got older."

"My grandmother passed away about two years ago. She left me enough money for college." Sue smiled sadly. "I told you about her already though."

"You said she had a dream and saw you graduating as a doctor. Am I right?"

Sue nodded. "Tell you the truth, I wish I could see her just once more so I could thank her." She stared at Shelly. *And so I could ask her a few questions,* Sue thought to herself.

Shelly wondered why Sue was looking at her like that. *What does she think? Does she think that I can talk to her dead Grandmother, or something? Is that why she's helping me?*

Sue sighed. "My Grandma, she saved all her pennies from cleaning houses so I could go to school. That's why I take my studies so seriously." She laughed. "I guess I'm a bit of a wet blanket compared to your roommate and a lot of the girls in the dorm, but I can't let Grandma down."

Shelly was feeling antsy. Was this the right way to the Psychology Buildings? Why was this trip taking so long? She glanced at her watch and back at the road. It was almost fifteen minutes already. *Why did I trust her?*

"There they are," Sue said, spotting the twin buildings that housed the Psychology Department. "Which one do you need?"

"I didn't know there were two buildings."

"They're pretty far from everywhere else," Sue said. "Any idea which one you want?"

"Which one has the Parapsychology office?" Shelly replied, and realized she was saying more than she wanted.

"Is that where you're going?" Sue asked, making a left turn toward the building known only as Psych B. "I've never been there."

"Yeah, I'm thinking of changing my major," Shelly lied, wondering why Sue seemed so interested in where she was heading.

"A lot of kids do that, but usually not in their first year," Sue said. "I don't know too many that are in this department, though. Are you sure this is what you want?"

Shelly wondered if this was yet another person trying to keep her from seeing Dr. Lasker. "Well, I'm just exploring my options," she said. "You can let me off here. It's got to be in one of these two buildings."

"It's in B building. The other one is named after some billionaire, Dr. Howard Hudson; nobody wants to sponsor this one, though. Are you sure this is where you want to go?"

There she goes again, Shelly thought, wondering again if even Sue could be trusted. "I've always been fascinated by parapsychological...uh...studies," she lied, knowing that she really knew almost nothing about the strange world of ghosts and other such make-believe creations of the imagination except from T.V. and movies. She still didn't believe in ghosts. Allen might be a ghost, or he might be something even worse. "Thanks for bringing me," she said, not wanting to discuss this any further. "I'm sorry I took you out of your way."

"How will you get back? Want me to stay with you?" Sue was reaching toward the passenger side of the car, leaning toward the window. "I don't have anything urgent."

Shelly gazed at the tall windowless building. Without windows, it was hard to tell how many floors the building had. She turned to examine Psych A and noted windows along all the walls. *Why no windows here?* she wondered, strangely disturbed by the building's solid concrete façade. "I'll catch the bus later. Thanks for the ride," Shelly said, knowing she was lying again. Dodd's phone number was in her purse. It would be the perfect excuse to give him a call.

"Call my cell," Sue said, handing Shelly a printed card. "I carry these in case I meet some handsome African prince who wants my number," she laughed. "Seriously, call me when you're done, and I'll zip back to get you. The Student Union isn't that far from here."

Shelly couldn't help being suspicious. *Why does she want to help me?* ran through her brain again. She took the card and slipped it into her pants pocket. "Thank you, Susan," she said, deliberately formal. "I'll be fine, but if I get stuck here late, I'll give you a call."

"Whatever time you finish, call and I'll get you. And by the way, call me Sue. All my friends do." She gave Shelly a warm smile.

Shelly was surprised by the friendliness of the girl. In high school, most of the Black kids tended to stay to themselves, and she had expected pretty much the same here. Maybe that was why she was suspicious of this girl. *What does she want from me?* It was natural to be suspicious, and yet she found herself liking Sue. She seemed genuinely friendly and eager to help. But that was what made her more suspect. Just when Shelly thought about asking Sue to stay with her to meet the infamous Dr. Lasker, her show of friendliness and eagerness aroused Shelly's suspicions again. She hated feeling this way, but everything that had happened in the last day had made caution seem the best route, and something told her that whatever she was about to face she had to confront alone.

The sound of the P.T. Cruiser pulling away made it very clear she was now getting her wish; she was completely alone. The sight of the windowless, nameless tower drawing closer with each step made her wonder if she was making a fatal mistake.

CHAPTER 22

A small sign with an arrow, painted on the wall in orange, indicated the front door of the building. Shelly realized this tall building was at the very furthest corner of the sprawling campus when she saw the sixteen-foot high concrete walls marking the campus' outer perimeter. She noticed that the wall was topped with coils of barbed wire. Exactly what was being walled out -- or walled in, she wondered. She didn't remember walls like this anywhere else on the campus, but then again, she was new to the place and probably hadn't seen even half of it yet.

She peered past the wall. Thickly wooded forests, rising on a hill behind the wall, added to the sense that this isolated building was in some kind of pit, with no sign of housing or commercial property anywhere nearby. Even the parking lot, smaller than those on the main campus, was located a good distance from the building -- which looked like a monolithic rectangle made up of large concrete blocks stacked on top of each other, gray planes rising unbroken like a giant tombstone. It looked unfriendly and cold compared to the older, more traditional, buildings on the other side of the campus.

"Who designed this thing, Frankenstein?" Shelly asked as she approached the building. Even a scrawled message, a valentine embedded when the concrete was fresh, would have been some relief from the stark uniformity of the slabs that made up the sidewalk, she thought.

Shelly approached the single glass door with a large red B on its pane. It looked nothing like the grand double doors that marked the entrances of the other buildings. She pulled at the plain-looking door handle, half expecting it to be locked. She almost hoped it was. Entering this concrete building felt like walking into a gigantic mausoleum at a cemetery. *This place is creepy,* she found herself thinking.

"May I help you?" a uniformed guard sitting behind a desk in the lobby asked as he pulled what looked like a smart-phone from the counter top of his desk. "ID please?"

"I'm looking for Dr. Lasker," Shelly said, digging out her university ID and handing it to the guard, who popped it into his handheld scanner.

"Okay, thank you," the young guard said, returning Shelly's ID. "You said, Dr. Lasker?"

"Yes, sir," Shelly said, replacing the ID in her purse.

"I don't know him." The guard poked the letter L into his machine and looked into Shelly's eyes with some surprise. "I'm a temp here. Is that the Parapsychology Office?" he asked, peering into the scanner.

"I guess so," Shelly replied. The guard had a serious expression on his face as he fumbled with the device in his hands.

"Basement," the guard said, his eyes still on the screen. "You did say Parapsychology, and not just regular Psych?"

"Yes," Shelly said.

"Okay," the guard replied. "You're the first one that's asked for that." He gave her a slight smile. "I'm sorry, but it says I'll have to call ahead to confirm your appointment. Please wait over there." He pointed to two chairs along a wall about twenty feet away. "What time is your appointment for?" he asked, still punching away at the hand held device.

"I'm sorry," Shelly said. "I don't have an appointment. I was just hoping to sit in on a class. I'm thinking of changing my major."

The guard looked up from his phone. "My instructions are to announce all visitors to that department only if they have an appointment" He saw the disappointed look on her face. "I'm sorry. I'm new here. You know what, let me see if I can help. Please wait over there, and I'll be back to you in a minute."

Shelly walked over to the wall and leaned against it. She felt weak, wondering if it was from her close call just a few hours earlier. The few minutes it took for the guard to call down to the lab seemed like an hour. She dropped into the chair. It was cheap plastic, hard on the butt. *Obviously they don't want anyone sitting here for long,* she thought.

"Miss," the guard called. "They're sending someone up to see you. It'll take a few more minutes." He gave her a smile. "At first they didn't want to see you without an appointment, but then I told them your name and the man said he'd make an exception."

"Thank you," Shelly said, returning his smile. He had a nice smile, she thought, for a security guard.

Shelly returned to the wall and waited again. Her legs felt as if they were going to buckle, and her head was pounding with one of her violent headaches. She wondered why the guard seemed to be staring at her. Maybe he was sizing her up to ask her for a date. He was kind of cute, although she didn't like the uniform. Some girls like men in uniforms, but Shelly found them too conservative. Her mind wandered to Dodd's wild look, that unkempt hair and his eyes...wild eyes. *I should have called him,* she thought, wondering why she hadn't.

"It shouldn't be much longer," the guard said, still giving her a curious look. "I guess they're pretty busy."

Shelly gave him another smile.

He looked as if he wanted to say something, but was just studying her. *Maybe he's undressing me with his eyes,* Shelly thought, wondering why he seemed so reticent. She aimed her eyes at him, challenging him to speak.

To her surprise he turned quickly to a notebook lying on his desk.

What is wrong with everyone lately? Shelly wondered. Why was he deliberately looking away from her? She fished out her cellphone and quickly checked her reflection. Everything looked fine. Her eyes caught her attention. Even in the dim reflective surface, they seemed to stand out from the rest of her features. She smiled, and her teeth -- straight and white, after years of invisible braces, the best invention ever, she thought -- were now competing with her eyes, as if eyes and teeth were floating on the dark surface of the screen. She pushed a button and the phone lit up. No messages. *I guess Dodd isn't all that interested,* she thought, hoping he would have called on any pretext he could come up with. *Maybe he's into boys?* She let out a little giggle, remembering a line from a Seinfeld episode: "Not that there's anything wrong with that." But somehow she couldn't picture Dodd being interested in boys, not the way he had looked at her with those smoldering eyes.

The guard looked up. "I'm sorry this is taking so long."

Shelly smiled. "I guess I should have made an appointment."

The guard nodded, but was clearly studying her. She noticed he had sideburns that came more than halfway down his cheeks, and his nose looked as if it had been broken. *Maybe a bar fight,* she mused, *Probably over a girl.* He looked muscular under his white shirt, gray jacket and light blue tie -- not like Dodd, who was lean and scholarly looking. She felt herself flushing at envisioning Dodd's body. The chair was making her uncomfortable… or was it something else?

"Do you want to keep waiting?" the guard asked. "It doesn't look like they're coming for you after all."

Shelly thought he looked sincerely apologetic. "I'll wait a little longer, if that's all right with you," she replied. He seemed nice. *Why can't I like the nice ones?* What was it about Dodd that attracted her? The guard looked clean-cut, with light hair and gentle brown eyes. Suddenly it hit her. *He's the All-American boy! Damn it, he's Jeff!* "That's it," she mumbled, causing him to look at her with surprise. "What's your name?" she asked, hoping it was anything but Jeff.

"Jimmy," the boy replied, smiling again.

She studied him further and smiled back, but couldn't get worked up over another Jeff look-alike. *There's no mystery to him, no real depth...Dodd was mysterious and wild looking...dangerous.* Was that what she found so difficult about him, why she found him so sexy? She turned back to the guard and wished he would suddenly smile and ask her out, anything to break the spell. With Jeff she always knew where she stood, until the very end, and even then he had been honest -- too damned honest. With someone like Dodd, someone who looked like he had the genetics of a weasel, it was hard to tell just what they were thinking, what secrets were concealed by those sexy eyes and strangely cold smiles.

The guard looked up again from his book. "I'll call them again if you want," he said.

"No. That's okay, Jimmy. I'll wait a few more minutes and then go. I really should have gotten an appointment."

"Sorry," he replied. "I wish I could be of more help."

Why doesn't he try and ask me out? Shelly wondered. *I'd say yes.* She thought of approaching him in some way, but something was holding her back. She knew what it was. She closed her eyes and saw his face again. *This is crazy,* she scolded. She took a deep breath and began counting backwards from one thousand, a trick she had learned to help her relax her brain. Counting back like this required total concentration, blocking out all the twisting thoughts that had been plaguing her while she waited.

The guard saw her eyes close. She was a nice-looking girl, he thought, neatly dressed in a buttoned shirt, gray skirt, matching thin jacket, with light hair dropping down to her shoulders. *Good figure...athletic...possibly a runner...nice smile and dazzling eyes.* How could anyone keep her waiting like this? He picked up his phone and dialed the department number again. He cupped his hand over the mouthpiece and said, "She isn't leaving." He listened to someone calling some strange name. "Is someone coming for her or not," he demanded, wondering why these guys couldn't be more gracious. "She's been waiting patiently for over an hour." He knew he was risking his job, but it didn't seem fair to leave her waiting endlessly like this. "Do you want me to tell her to leave and make an appointment?" he asked.

"I'll be right up," the voice on the phone said.

He hung up, almost disappointed. He had almost gotten up the guts to ask her out, but what would someone like her see in a guard, a temp at that? He glanced quickly at her legs and then let his eyes rise toward her face.

Shelly was falling asleep. Nobody else had entered or left the building while she waited. She shook herself awake, sat up, gazed at her watch and sighed. "Five more minutes", she said softly, "And then I'm out of here."

Not counting, not thinking, she became more aware of the silence of the large lobby. It was an eerie silence. It was like nobody ever came here. She noted that the walls were completely smooth: no fingerprints anywhere, not on the smooth metallic railings, the glass panels on the doorway near the bench,, and no scuff marks on the highly polished floor. She got up and walked over to the elevator, to look at the directory encased in a sheet of highly reflective glass. There were only a few names listed. When she looked for the Parapsychology Department, the office was listed simply as Basement and Sub-Basement. The individual classrooms and professor's individual offices weren't listed at all. *That's it,* she thought. *I'm out of here, but first I'm going to thank the guard. No more waiting around for me!*

"I didn't expect to see you here today," a voice from behind startled her. "You said you were coming tomorrow."

When she turned, Shelly was surprised to see Dodd standing behind her in a white lab coat. She couldn't help notice he wasn't smiling.

CHAPTER 23

Almost instantly a smile appeared on Shelly's face. He looked as handsome as she remembered, sharp eyes and wild hair, but what was with the lab coat? "I didn't expect you," she said, surprised at how glad she felt to see him.

"You must be feeling better."

Shelly saw Dodd gazing at the guard who was watching everything from his desk. "I am. Thank you again for before."

Dodd saw the guard watching. He wished he could tell him to mind his own business, but that would arouse suspicion, make him easy to remember. "It wasn't anything." He gave her a hint of a smile.

Shelly felt better seeing Dodd smile. "I was a real shit," she said, recalling how confused he looked when she had been talking to Allen, that pest. "I'm sorry. I was in shock."

"I've forgotten about that already," Dodd said, his eyes again darting over to the guard who he now was sure was watching them from his desk. "I'm really surprised to see you here though," Dodd said. "Didn't you say tomorrow? You should be resting."

Shelly tensed. Was he going to tell her she couldn't meet with Dr. Lasker today? Was that why he'd been sent up to meet her? "I didn't want to wait," she said. *I can't wait.*

Dodd turned to the guard. "I'll take care of her," he said. "Thank you."

The guard nodded, but his eyes were still on Shelly. For some reason he couldn't explain, he wanted a photograph in his brain of her face. "Sure," he said, wishing he had sent her back before this weird-looking character in a lab coat had shown up.

Shelly wondered what it was that was making the guard look at her so intently. *Maybe he's jealous,* she reasoned, feeling Dodd very close to her. "I'd really love it if you could help me see Dr. Lasker today," Shelly said to Dodd, giving him a warm smile. "Is that possible? I don't have an appointment."

Dodd glanced over to the guard again, as if checking to see if he was eavesdropping. He leaned closer to Shelly, so close he could smell the strawberry scent of her shampoo. "He rarely sees anyone outside of classes, and definitely not without an appointment. Dr. Lasker is extremely busy."

Shelly nodded. "I understand. I'll just have to keep trying. I'm not going to give up until I see him."

Dodd wished she hadn't said that. It would have made life so much easier. He heard a voice saying, *"I told you so."* "You don't have to worry. I've already told him about you, and that you would be coming to see him. Everything's been arranged. You're just a day early…but it will be okay. You'll just have to wait awhile." He called to the guard, giving him a smile. "We'll be a bit late, so you won't be here probably when we leave."

The guard nodded. Apparently the girl knew this guy in the lab coat, so it would be fine. "Thank you, sir," he said. "Thomas will be back tomorrow."

Dodd nodded, pleased the guard was apparently just a temp. It was about time he caught a break, he thought.

Shelly sensed that Dodd was trying to take credit for helping her obtain an audience with the great parapsychology genius. *All males are alike,* she thought, wondering if this was his way of gaining an advantage over any other possible suitors she might have. Was Allen right after all about Dodd's true intentions toward her? Was he really just another horny boy, using his position with Dr. Lasker to coax her into bed? She wondered if that would be such a bad thing. She realized she wanted that too…at some point, sometime soon. "I really appreciate your help, Dodd," she said, trying to cut him off before he delayed much longer. "You're a good friend." *That should raise some questions in his macho brain,* she mused. She suddenly had an image of Dodd standing by her bed wearing only an unbuttoned white lab coat. *Whoa! Not a good thing to think about right now.*

Dodd's face showed no disappointment at her remark about 'friendship'. "Sure. I'm happy to help. But you are feeling better? No more close calls?" He hadn't counted on her getting here a day early. *Damn,* he thought, as he weighed his options given this change of circumstances. "How did you get here?" He had to find out if someone was waiting for her. Who else knew she was here? The guard would be leaving soon. His shift was almost over. He'd think she left after he was gone....but who had brought her? "Did you take the bus?" he asked.

"Not after yesterday. No way! I got a ride with a friend," Shelly replied, wondering why she felt the need to hide Susan's name.

"That was nice." *A friend?* He found himself wondering if the friend was male or female, but knew there was no time to be jealous now. He touched her arm with his hand. "I'll be happy to give you a ride back, unless someone's waiting for you."

Shelly smiled. *He's jealous. That's why he sounds so strange.* "That will be very nice," she said. "I'll have to call my friend after we're done, and tell her I've got a ride."

Dodd nodded, his mind racing. "We were expecting you tomorrow, though, so Dr. Lasker is in a class, finishing up. Want to sit in? I'm sure he won't mind. He's quite the lecturer, very animated and definitely opinionated. Students either love him to pieces or want to kill him. I'm not sure myself, sometimes," Dodd remarked, a cloudy look coming onto his face. "I'm kidding of course." He quickly replaced the dark look with a warm smile. "So, do you want to see the Doctor in action?" he asked. He would find out who the friend was later. It wouldn't be difficult, not for him. After all, he had found Shelly. "I think you'll find this an interesting experience."

"That would be great," Shelly said. "Are you sure he'll be okay with that? I don't want to disturb him."

Dodd put his hand on her shoulder. "I told you, I told him all about you. He's excited to meet you."

Shelly felt Dodd's hand on her arm, but wondered why it felt cold. She glanced at him out of a corner of her eye. He was a foot taller than she was, and his hand seemed muscular, stronger than she expected. She realized his eyes were probing her again and suddenly felt uncomfortable... It was as if his eyes, so blue, so intense, could see through her clothes. *Wishful thinking,* she groaned inside. "Are all the classes in the basement?" she asked, forcing herself to focus on her mission again...hard to do with those eyes on her.

"Not all. What do you think, we're moles or something?" He laughed, and his eyes lost their intensity for a second. "We have to fight for every inch of space we've got. Most people don't consider parapsychology a real academic subject. The university trustees and the state gave us a terrible time getting recognized as a science. Dr. Lasker always complains that the bean-counters, that's what he calls the powers-that-be, would still like to give us the boot."

"So that's why you're here? I mean, in this building at the end of the world?" Shelly saw the guard look up when she said that. "It looks like a headstone," she said, and realized maybe she shouldn't have been quite so honest.

"That's funny," Dodd said, but he wasn't smiling. "In a way, you're right. It is the end of the world, but as you're going to see, it's also the beginning of another world." *My world,* he thought, *Not yours.* He dropped his arm and pointed to the stairwell. "I like to walk. Is that okay?"

Shelly still felt a little weak, but the elevators seemed oddly ominous. There were three in this building, three doors to choose from. Right now she didn't want to make any choices... all she wanted was to be led, by him. "Walking is great," she said, even though she still felt dizzy and her head was throbbing.

"I never trust elevators," Dodd said as he pulled open a doorway marked "RESTRICTED."

Shelly couldn't believe the weight of the door, like it was constructed of solid steel, no window.

"It has to be fireproof," Dodd said, as if reading her thoughts.

Shelly was surprised when he reached back and she heard the unmistakable sound of lock cylinders moving into place. "Are we locked in or are they locked out?" she asked.

"They're locked in," Dodd replied. He reached for her hand to guide her down the six flights of metal stairs. He didn't say who "they" were, and Shelly hoped it was a joke. He seemed to have a peculiar sense of humor.

Shelly was surprised that she felt winded by the short descent to the next landing but realized it was a result of her traumatic day.

"You still look beat," Dodd said. "That accident took more of a toll on you than you want to admit. You could still be in shock. We should go to my lab. You can sit there, rest up a bit, and wait for the Professor."

"No," Shelly replied. "Please take me to his lecture hall. I want to hear him."

"You really don't look well. How about some water, at least?"

Shelly felt out of breath. The headache was getting worse. The windowless basement prompted a wave of claustrophobia. Even Dodd, so kind and considerate, seemed too close, his breath smelling like burnt charcoal…too close…stifling. "Yes. Okay. Water would be great."

Dodd smiled. "That's better. We've got to take good care of you."

Shelly followed as he led her to the last door on the left side of the hall. The sign on the glassless door read Lab C. She watched as he punched some numbers into the keypad and pushed open the door.

"This is my lab," Dodd said. "Come inside and I'll get you some water." He held the door for her. "I'll be right back." He walked a short distance away, returning with a glass of water. She drank hastily.

"What's that smell?" Shelly asked, a pungent odor assaulting her nose.

"There are always odors in the labs," Dodd said. "Nothing to worry about."

Shelly nodded, but the smell was strong, making her feel dizzy. "I'm not well," she groaned seeing a look of concern on Dodd's face.

"Just relax," Dodd said, placing the paper cup in the trash. "It will be over soon."

"I've got to go," Shelly said, moving toward the door.

As Shelly reached for the doorknob, her legs buckled.

Dodd grabbed her before she hit the ground.

Shelly felt his arms holding her and saw his eyes looking down at her. She felt weak, as if she was melting under his gaze. He was close now, his lips inches away.

Why doesn't he kiss me? Shelly thought just before her eyes closed.

CHAPTER 24

"What are you doing in my lab?" Shelly heard a voice ask, as she tried to focus her eyes. "How did you get in here?"

Shelly saw a man with a grayish beard staring down at her through wire-framed eyeglasses. She wanted to pull away from him, but seemed to have turned to rubber.

"I asked you, what are you doing in here?" the man repeated.

Shelly thought he sounded rude and loud. She wanted to go back to sleep.

The man was shaking her. "Damn it," he said, as he shook her again. "Stay awake! I can't afford you dying in here."

Dying? Who's dying? Shelly thought. "Stop shaking me," she suddenly shouted. "Who the hell are you?" She felt her eyes closing again, and wanted to stand and get away from this lunatic who was shaking her as if he was a dog with a rag doll.

"Wake up, damn you!" the man shouted. "If you don't stay awake, I'll slap your face." He raised his hand.

"I'm awake," Shelly said. "What happened? Who are you?"

"That's what I want to know," he demanded, his eyes angry and large behind the thick lenses.

Shelly wanted to close her eyes, but heard herself say, as if in a distance, "There was a smell...a funny smell." She was searching her memory which seemed fuzzy. "I think I passed out." She pulled her legs backwards, as far away from this bearded stranger as she could get. *Where the hell is Dodd?* she wondered, remembering his had been the last face she'd seen, remembering she thought he was going to kiss her...that he did kiss her...and then she fell asleep. Was he that bad a kisser? *What the hell is going on?*

The man frowned. "It was gas. Someone left a gas canister open." He eyed her sternly. "Did you? Did you? You could have been killed, young lady. Young lady?" He shook her again. "Damn you, wake up!"

Shelly felt woozy still. "Gas? Gas!" *That was the smell. Is Dodd okay? Where the hell is he? Maybe he's going for help. Why can't I see anyone but this guy with his big owl-eyes?* "I feel sick."

The man was in her face, staring at her, his hand still ready to slap her if needed. "I guess I should ask if you're okay, but you're trespassing. This is my office, and it was locked. How did you get in here? Are you going to be sick on me?" He ran for a plastic bag. "Here. In here."

Shelly held the bag under her mouth. Nothing happened.

The man shook his head. "Are you on something? I won't tell, but you must tell me what the hell you are doing in my office."

"Your office?" Shelly said, still in a daze. *How did I get in here?* She was trying to remember. "He said this is his lab." Shelly felt for the buttons on her blouse. They were open. "Did you do this?" she shouted as her fingers rushed to close the buttons.

"Are you insane? You break into my laboratory and then accuse me of --"

"I'm sorry. I'm a bit fuzzy still. I'd better just go." She tried to lift herself off the chair, but slumped back down, her legs still too rubbery, her brain still fuzzy. "I'm sorry. I can't seem to stand yet. Another minute..." Where the hell was that damn Dodd? Was he unconscious too? She felt a spike of fear race through her brain.

"Hold on Miss. What's your name anyway? Are you a university student? I know you're not in my department." The man pulled an old-fashioned cellphone from his pocket. He saw that the girl was struggling, and despite his anger at having his office invaded he felt a little concerned for her. He was also thinking that if she had died here, it would have been a real mess. That would have nailed the coffin shut on this place, for good. He looked at the girl and realized that if she talked, complained to anyone, that would also be the end. He could imagine her telling the campus cops that she had been almost killed here, her blouse opened... raped. *Oh my god!* He had to be nicer to her. No choice. "Okay, Miss, you're getting some color back. You're feeling better, right?"

Shelly was trying to focus, definitely in defensive mode. She was angry -- angry at Dodd, angry at being here with this lunatic, angry at finding her breasts exposed. "I'm not telling you anything! I have no idea who you are. I just know that he brought me in here and said it was his office, and was getting me some water when--"

"For the last time, this is *my* office!" the man exploded, despite his resolve to keep calm. *I've got to get to the bottom of this. I'll put her on the defensive.* The man pulled out his phone. "I'm calling security. You have a bad attitude, young lady, considering you are the trespasser here. What is your name? Now! I have no time to waste." He knew he could be very intimidating if he wanted to be, and this was one time when he definitely wanted to be as frightening as he could. He had to convince her she had more to lose than anyone if this 'incident' got reported. "Now tell me, who let you in my office? It's more his fault than yours."

Shelly shook her head, still trying to clear it. "Dodd," she said, still not convinced this was not Dodd's office.

At first he thought she had said, "God", but then the full impact of what she had said hit him. The man looked around the room quickly. "I don't know anyone by that name." He felt his stomach sinking.

"What do you mean, you don't know Dodd? He said he works in this department. He brought me here! Where is he?" She was coming to and wanted answers.

The man stared silently at her. *What am I supposed to do now?* he wondered. She seemed genuine. What was she doing here? Why had Dodd brought her here? Had he turned on the gas? Not even that insane kid could do something like that. "I would know this Dodd of yours if he existed. I'm chairman of this department." He sighed, weighing his options. The most important thing was to silence her. Fear would do it. He aimed his eyes at her and said, with masterful cold authority, "I've heard enough. You don't belong here. Now be silent while I get security to take you wherever trespassers are taken on this crazy campus." He picked up the desk phone.

Shelly groaned. "Wait a minute. You said you're the chairman of this department. Is this the Parapsychology Department? Are you Dr. Lasker?" She studied him quickly and noted he looked younger than she expected, his beard neatly groomed and his hair just showing signs of gray. She also noted he was shorter than Dodd, perhaps five and a half feet, and stocky, with a paunchy belly made larger by his plaid jacket.

Dr. Lasker gave her a surprised look. "Exactly who are you? How do you know my name?"

Shelly tried to shake herself awake. Her head was still so fuzzy. What a way to meet the chairperson of the department. *Oh my God, he saw my breasts!* She felt a red flush fill her face. "Sir, I'm so sorry. I was supposed to meet with you. I heard you might be able to help me." She involuntarily pulled her blouse tighter. Had Dodd done this? *Where the hell is he? Why do men always disappear when you need them?*

"Help you?" Lasker looked at her. *She was coming to see me? Dodd tried to stop her? Why?* The girl looked young, barely conscious still. She had almost been poisoned, gassed. *...in my office,* he thought, wondering how such a thing could happen, again all too aware of how a complaint from this student, her blouse found undone, almost gassed to death, in his lab, could seal the fate of his department once and for all. *What was Dodd thinking?* Looking at her body, even now, he had a feeling he could guess. *Damn Dodd! Imagine if she got it to the papers that she had been molested in my office. Dodd would get his revenge, all right.* He sighed. He had to try and help her, even if it was a damn nuisance. *"You can kill more flies with honey..."*

Shelly was slowly regaining all of her senses, and realized she was in big trouble. If this guy reported her as a burglar, even a trespasser, especially in this weird lab with all the exotic equipment, she'd get booted out of school at least, maybe even end up in jail. *Where the hell is that damn Dodd?* "I'm feeling better," she muttered. "I think I can go now."

He blocked her rising from the chair with his body. He tried to smile, but it wasn't easy with all he was contemplating. "What kind of help were you seeking?" he asked, hoping he could help her quickly and then be rid of her forever.

Shelly wasn't fully awake yet, but awake enough that she wasn't sure how much she should tell him. He would really think she was crazy, after finding her half naked in his office with the gas jet turned on. "I've had a terrible time," she began, almost laughing at the realization of how many awful things had been happening to her lately. "I was almost mugged, witnessed a murder -- it doesn't matter who -- almost got run over by a bus, and now I was almost poisoned by some kind of gas in your laboratory." *And you saw my boobs,* she thought, wishing she knew if that was all he had seen. *What the hell does it matter?* She sighed. "Dr. Lasker, I was warned not to come here. Maybe I should have listened?"

Dr. Lasker sat down on a rolling stool and moved it closer to Shelly, who was still seated on a chair fighting for balance. "I'm listening," he said, his voice showing concern -- partly for her, and partly for himself if she decided to file a report. *Damn Dodd! Why didn't he play with his new 'friend' at her place, or in the back of his car? I never should have let him stay on.*

Shelly felt tears in her eyes. "I can't believe what I've been through. A damn bus almost ran me down on my way here. I thought Dodd saved me, at first--"

Dr. Lasker interrupted, "Okay, let's start with your name. What is it, and are you a student at the University? I can't help you without knowing who you are and what you're doing here." He was trying to sound helpful, friendly, two qualities he wasn't known for.

"You're really Dr. Lasker?" Shelly asked again, wondering if she should ask for some ID. He looked like a professor -- sport jacket, brown plaid, tie half mast, corduroy trousers slightly sagging at the beltline, a blue belt totally out of place against brown trousers and jacket. She looked up at his face, and the beard was what she noted most: brown, some gray, kept reasonably short, probably hid cheeks marred by acne scars, slightly graying eyebrows -- forty to fifty years old -- reddish complexion, furrowed forehead, brown mud-ball eyes made larger by wire-frames…but not bad looking…for an old man, she thought.

"Would you like to see my identification?" Dr. Lasker asked. "That's not going to happen. Now stop wasting my valuable time. Tell me your name now and what happened, or you can spend the rest of the semester in jail or back home." Maybe if he played tough he could scare her enough that she would just want to get back to wherever the hell she belonged. He had little patience for playing Mr. Nice-Guy, and so far that hadn't worked at all.

Shelly detected the change in his tone. *He sure sounds like the Dr. Lasker I've imagined,* Shelly thought, finally able to see his face clearly. "My name is Shelly Adams, and I'm a grad student... in the Education department."

"Education Department?" He let out a disdainful growl. "So Miss Teacher, what are you doing all the way over here?"

Condescending sonofabitch, Shelly thought. If she didn't need his help, have hope he could help her, she would have stormed out of there, but not before telling him exactly what she thought of his snottiness and his poison-spewing lab. One last attempt and then... "Dr. Lasker, I came to see you because...." Shelly hesitated. "You've never heard of an assistant named Dodd? Really?"

Dr. Lasker was becoming annoyed that she kept bringing Dodd into the picture. "No, Shelly, I have never had a student or an assistant named Dodd. I would know. We have a very small department here, for reasons which do not concern you at this moment. Now Shelly, one more question before I boot you the hell out of here. No more beating around the bush, no more wasting my time with your insignificant questions, exactly why were you coming to see me?"

Shelly felt her anger rising. She had anticipated he would be tough and impatient, but now he just seemed rude. Was he someone she could trust? She had trusted Dodd, and now where was he? *And he looked so cute,* Shelly thought, remembering how she had thought of making love with him. *Where the hell is Dodd?* She found nothing cute or loveable about this pompous and inconsiderate ass of a professor. And she didn't like being threatened. She wanted to leave. Would she be able to make it to the door? Would he stop her?

"Miss, I really have no more time to waste. Security will be here to check on the poison gas that you claim was used on you, and hopefully then they will take you with them, and you and I shall enjoy wonderful lives…apart from each other. So speak now or forever hold your peace." He rose from his chair and was about to push it back toward the wall when he heard the young girl sitting in front of him say, "Dr. Lasker, I think I have a ghost."

CHAPTER 25

Dr. Lasker took off his glasses and burst into laughter.

"Why are you laughing?" Shelly shouted, thinking this was the rudest man she'd ever met.

"Who put you up to this?" he asked. "I should be used to these pranks by now, but ...and I guess the smell wasn't gas after all? A ghost? Good prank. I was really fooled." He pushed his stool away.

"I'm not kidding," Shelly said. "I've got a ghost!"

The doctor saw Shelly wasn't laughing. In fact her face looked deadly serious. She was either a great actress or a complete nutcase. "Now listen, Miss, I've had others try this before on me, and I have no patience ..."

Shelly tried to get up, but she still felt woozy from the gas. "I'm not kidding," she repeated. "I can't explain it any other way. I really think I've got a ghost who can talk only to me…and I don't like it." *I don't like you either,* she thought.

Dr. Lasker had heard almost every kind of crazy story before, but there was something about this girl that made him wonder if maybe there was some truth to her story. Maybe she didn't really have a ghost, but sincerely believed she did. "What makes you think you're being haunted," he asked, standing over her and peering into her eyes, as if he could tell if she was lying by just studying her pupils. "Make it snappy. I'm a very busy man."

Shelly felt nervous, wondering how she could ever convince him, if she wanted to convince him -- he was horribly rude and inconsiderate after all she'd been through. "I didn't believe it either," she said, "But I have no other explanation for all that's happened to me, since he saved my life at South Island Park yesterday, from a mugger, while I was jogging..."

"Whoa! Slow down! Take a breath! You said he saved you from a bus accident before? Which is it? Bus accident or mugger?"

"Both," Shelly said. "He says he saved me from both."

"How is that possible? Ghosts, if they exist at all -- and we'll discuss this soon, if I don't have you arrested -- there's never been any conclusive proof that ghosts can manipulate real objects, let alone perform the kinds of rescues you describe. I respectfully submit you've been under some kind of stress lately, and this ghost of yours is conjured up by your own fertile imagination -- something like a childhood make-believe friend. No real harm, unless you do something stupid -- like breaking into my office."

She glared at him, but realized she had to restrain her response if she wanted any chance of getting help from him. "I thought I was imagining him, too," she began slowly, "I really did think he was a result of shock at first -- but someone else saw me being miraculously pulled from in front of the bus. She said there was nobody there... nobody who could have saved me."

Dr. Lasker sighed. "This so-called witness might want the notoriety, or have some other ulterior motive. I've seen a lot of crazies—"

"I can't think of any motive she would have. She has no reason to lie."

"Well, I only have your second-hand reporting of what she allegedly said."

Shelly jumped up from the chair. Her temper erupting. "I'm not lying to you! I have no reason to make any of this up! I hate the whole damn thing! I don't want a ghost, and I don't want to talk to someone as rude and pig-headed as you!" She staggered toward the door. "You can send the cops to room 306 D Dorm to find me, if you still want me arrested. You've given me one damn big headache. I'm sorry I ever found your name! The cops will want it, though."

Dr. Lasker looked stunned, and then he shouted at Shelly in an even louder voice, "Stop right now young lady! Nobody ever yells at me! I'm head of the department here! I'm God here!"

Shelly whirled around. "God at least listens when you ask for help. All you do is make me damn mad!"

Dr. Lasker was surprised by the fury in her voice and face. Would she look like this if it was a prank? He stood and blocked the door. "Okay. Fair enough. You can yell loud, and I can yell louder. Just stop. Let's both calm down." He forced a look of concern. "I'm not saying I believe you, but let me show you something." He reached into a drawer in his desk and pulled out a manila envelope. "I found this on my desk a few minutes before I found you down here in my lab. Did you leave it there?"

Shelly was still fuming and just wanted to leave. "I've never been here before, and I don't plan to come back."

"Please look at it." Dr. Lasker held it up. "Is this your note?"

Shelly felt like tearing it out of his hand, but instead stared in disbelief at the red ink. It was dripping off the page from the printed letters that said,

Hep Lab!

Dodd must have scrawled it, she thought, but why did he disappear? And why did this guy who said he was Dr. Lasker claim never to have heard of him? *I'm totally confused,* Shelly thought, shaking her head, as she couldn't take her eyes from the clumsily written note.

"That note may have saved your life," Dr. Lasker said, holding his hand out to retrieve it. "You are certain you didn't write this?"

"I already told you--"

"Then who wrote it?" Dr. Lasker asked, examining the note for any clue. "Why is the L missing? Surely they can spell Help?"

"I wish I knew," Shelly said, wondering if maybe Allen had written it, leaving out the L to conserve his energy. Holy crap! Had he somehow managed to save her yet again? Impossible, she thought, but what other explanation could there be?

Dr. Lasker sat down on the stool again. He replaced the note in the envelope and put it back in the top drawer of his desk. He locked the drawer with a key. "Please sit down. No more shouting or threats." He gave the girl a weak smile and felt grateful when she sat down on the chair again. He took a deep breath and spoke softly to her, "There are things in your story that make no sense to me," Dr. Lasker said, his voice more reassuring. "But I see you need some help. I think you are a fairly honest young lady …"

"Fairly honest?!" Shelly was turning stormy again. *Who the hell does this guy think he is?*

"Okay, I mean completely honest. Yes, you do strike me as being honest. Maybe deluded a little? Maybe suffering some sort of severe trauma? You mentioned a bus accident and a mugging… also a murder?" He found it hard to accept that all those things could have happened to her in such a short period of time, but she seemed to believe it, and was acting as if they had all happened. "Each of these alone could cause such problems, but all? Yes, they very likely are the possible causes of your problem with what we shall call an 'unspecified manifestation'."

He saw her tense and quickly added, "But then again you may actually have seen a ghost. Do you really believe you have? Such sightings, while frequently reported, are rarely if ever substantiated. You do understand that, don't you?" He had interviewed countless students who had claimed to have the special sensitivity that was required to become Ectoplasmic Researchers -- Ectos, as the students called themselves for short -- and only a rare few had met even the minimal standards of the testing procedures. *A true Ecto,* he mused, *is very rare*, and looking at this blonde with her cute nose, darling freckles and slightly disheveled hair, he doubted if she could possess even one iota of that magic quality.

"We are a department of Ectoplasmic Researchers, Ectos," he explained, "But to be frank, I have never yet been able to substantiate the existence of ghosts, despite numerous attempts. We may want to believe such spirits exist, to bolster our religious beliefs and to offer the end of eternal condemnation for failure to uphold our moral, political and religious precepts." He saw that she looked confused. "In other words, if we believe in ghosts, we believe in the after-life -- and therefore it behooves us to live as righteously as we can. It's a very convenient antidote to our innate criminal instincts if we believe we are facing grim punishment, as we are doomed to roam the Earth as ghosts."

Shelly shook her head in frustration. "Dr. Lasker, I am telling you the truth as I know it. Will you help me? Yes or no? I don't feel well, and dammit, I'm sick of all this. Please tell me you're going to help me, or let me just go and—" Shelly began to tremble.

Dr. Lasker sighed. The young woman in front of him seemed sincere enough, but he had been fooled before. He studied her eyes. She looked like she was going to cry. "Yes," he said slowly. "Yes, I will help you as much as I can -- if you are genuine. If not, it will be a short relationship."

"You'll help me get rid of this crazy thing?"

Dr. Lasker nodded his head, not sure if Shelly herself wasn't the 'crazy thing'. *But aren't all Ectos technically crazy?* He had a clear image of a young man's eyes, wide-open, staring without emotion as he was forced into a straitjacket by a team from the university hospital.

"Got him," one of the heavier associates shouted. "Man, I never thought someone so thin could put up such a fight."

You have no idea, Lasker thought, as he watched them guide the now docile assistant onto the ambulance. "His name is Dodd, Thomas Dodd. Please take good care of him. It is not entirely his fault."

Lasker shut off the images. He didn't want to see Dodd's tortured expression. He didn't want to see the eyes that made him feel so guilty. "Your breakdown wasn't my fault," he murmured as the van left. But he knew that wasn't quite true. He also knew Dodd wasn't crazy, not in the commonly understood definition of the word.

Hadn't others called Lasker himself crazy? Wasn't that particular craziness what he looked for in his assistants? It seemed to come hand-in-hand with the sensitivity. Dodd was prone to insanity because of the very gifts that made him such a powerful Ecto. And all true Ectos wanted, demanded, that he help them hone and develop their ability. Dodd had wanted that more than any of the others. He had pushed and pushed…

But enough of the past. In the back of Lasker's brain the wheels were turning. *Here, in front of me, dressed in a lab coat that makes her look damn sexy, is a young woman who seems to sincerely believe she is being haunted. Maybe this girl is crazy? I wouldn't doubt it… but just imagine the possibilities if her ghost is for real!*

CHAPTER 26

"Is your so-called ghost with you right now?" Dr. Lasker asked, feeling he was being played.

"Are you?" Shelly peered around the lab for any sign of Allen.

"Am I what?" Dr. Lasker asked, following the girl's eyes as she scanned the room, not realizing she was addressing her ghostly presence.

"I was talking to him," Shelly said. "It can be confusing to others."

"I guess it might be." *This girl is batty as hell.* "Did he answer you?"

"No. I don't think he's here now. I told him I wasn't coming here until tomorrow."

"You lied to a ghost? Isn't that kind of dangerous?"

"I don't think he wants to hurt me. He claims he saved me twice." Why did she trust him?

"That is the part I find incredible. Ghosts are mostly malevolent spirits, mischievous at best. A kind-hearted ghost is stretching things a bit."

"I still don't believe it all, but he says that when he sees me in danger it somehow makes him focus his energies, and he can materialize… do things he normally can't do." Shelly gazed at the professor. "Do you think that's possible?"

Dr. Lasker sucked in his lip. "There is much we don't know about all these phenomena, enough to fill the pyramids of Egypt -- another mystery I shall someday explore, if we don't run out of money." He let out a laugh.

Shelly looked anxious. "Have you ever heard of anyone being haunted like this before?"

Dr. Lasker looked at the rows of books behind his desk. "There are some cases similar… but as I stated earlier, there is very little substantive evidence to back up the existence of these creatures." He wasn't ready to tell her the truth…not yet.

"Please don't call them that. He doesn't like it?"

"What?"

"Creatures. He isn't a creature, I don't think." She remembered the gentleness of his voice, almost sexy…okay sexy…and tried to picture what Allen might look like. One thing for sure, he probably didn't look anything like this professor with his arrogant ways and old-fashioned jacket. *Who wears plaid these days?*

"You said he's not here?"

Shelly looked around the room. "I never know for sure. Only when he talks do I know he's around."

"So you've never seen him? You have no idea what he might look like?"

"He says he's good-looking, but he can't see himself. He doesn't even know if he's naked or not…" She paused at that thought. "That's not the way they show it in the movies, is it?"

Dr. Lasker laughed. "I apologize. I shouldn't be laughing at another human being's predicaments, but I keep picturing the sight of a middle-aged male ghost completely naked and--"

Shelly began to laugh too. "I told him he couldn't stay in the girls' dorms with me."

"What are you two laughing at?" Allen asked, suddenly making himself heard.

"You're here?" Shelly asked, not sure if she felt relieved or annoyed that she couldn't get rid of him.

"Yes, I'm here. But you're not supposed to be here until tomorrow." Allen sounded irritated. "I told you I didn't think this was a good idea, but you're stubborn. You could have waited for me."

"I had no idea where you were. Were you in my room?" She wanted to ask if he had seen her lying on her bed, her blouse open, but realized again that they weren't alone. "I'll talk to you later. We've got some things to settle," she said and turned her attention to the professor.

Dr. Lasker had become silent, observing the girl as she seemed to be talking to someone in the right corner of the room, near the file cabinet. He flipped on a recorder hidden on a shelf nearby.

"He flipped on his recorder," Allen said. "I wouldn't trust him. He looks like a Parapsychology Professor, a real 'egghead', only interested in what he can get from you."

"You think that about everyone," Shelly said.

"And so far I've been totally right," Allen replied.

"I take it he's here?" Professor Lasker asked, scanning her face to see if he could detect any sign that she was having a joke at his expense.

"He's here alright," Shelly said. "He says you look like a parapsychology professor, a real 'egghead'. Shelly had to agree with Allen for once. *That awful jacket!*

"Where is he?" Lasker asked, trying to follow Shelly's eyes. "Can you see him now?"

"I never see him," said Shelly. "He sees me and hears me all the time, whenever he wants to." She said that loud enough so even Allen would get the idea that she didn't like him invading her privacy. "Do you understand? I can't get away from him. He can see me at any time or any place. I have no privacy." She wondered again just how much Allen had seen the night before. *Can you imagine, three strange men might have seen my boobs in one day? Must be a new record*, she thought, slightly embarrassed, definitely annoyed.

"Privacy is overrated," Allen said. "Besides, you have a lovely body."

"You *have* seen me," Shelly said, horrified that a complete stranger might have seen her naked.

"That's for me to know," Allen replied, ending it with a teasing chuckle. "Even a ghost needs some entertainment," he added, clearly enjoying her discomfort.

"What's going on now?" Dr. Lasker asked, searching the area where apparently the ghost was—where Shelly was looking as she spoke.

"Nothing," Shelly said, blushing, "Please, you've got to help me. And maybe you can help him find out what he needs to know, too."

"You mean, if he was murdered?" Dr. Lasker asked, wishing he had sufficient brain-power to be an Ecto, so he could see the ghost -- if there really was a ghost. "The truth is, Shelly, we're in uncharted waters here. I definitely think we need to check out a few things before we give you the necessary approval. I can't risk the accreditation of my entire department without being certain. I'm sure you understand. I'm also sure you understand the need for discretion."

He wants me to shut up about what happened here today. She weighed her options, and decided nothing was more important than obtaining his help to rid herself of this ghost. "How long will all this take, Professor?" Shelly braced herself for the answer. "I really don't know how much longer I can do this."

Lasker sat back. "To check your claims properly, to document it for future use, I'd estimate at least three to six months."

Shelly fell back in the chair. "Do you mean I have to have a ghost chasing me around for another six months? No way!"

"Sounds like fun," Allen said.

"I'd guesstimate that's about right…give or take a few months."

"That settles it! You are not staying in my room," Shelly shouted.

"I never had that in mind," the professor replied, indignant she could think that he wanted to stay in her room, but wondering how he could best take advantage of this very interesting situation. *She's either a kook or the best thing that's happened to the parapsychology department since Dodd first appeared. Poor, insane, Dodd, thank you for bringing her to me.*

CHAPTER 27

Dr. Lasker wished he could learn more. He was hurriedly thinking of how he could check if this was a set-up or for real. She looked as if she was seriously talking to someone, but maybe she was just a good actress. *These young girls, especially the pretty ones, can be pretty deceptive,* he thought.

"I don't want you following me around anymore," Shelly said.

"I guess you don't want me saving your life, either? That's three times! Three times in two days that I've saved your life, and you won't let me even stay in your room?"

"I have a headache. Ever since you've shoved your way into my life, I've had the worst headache ever!"

"At least you're alive to have a headache! Stop feeling sorry for yourself and think of somebody else, for a change."

Shelly nodded. "Okay, you're right, but that doesn't change anything. You can't stay in my room. That is final!"

There wasn't any reply. Shelly realized the professor was staring at her. "He gets stubborn sometimes and refuses to talk," she explained. "He's like a child sometimes."

"I am not," Allen shouted. "You take that back!

"Now he's threatening me," Shelly said. "He doesn't like to hear the truth."

"You are the only one who can hear him?" Dr. Lasker asked.

"Yes. Can you? Listen carefully. Say something to the professor, Allen."

"I will not."

"Did you hear that?"

"What?" Dr. Lasker was concentrating very hard but heard nothing.

"He can't hear me. Only you can," Allen said. "Consider it a special gift. We have a special link, like I keep telling you."

"Did you hear him that time?" Shelly was praying Lasker had heard Allen. It would prove she wasn't having delusions or hallucinations or whatever else this haunting could be called.

"He spoke?" Dr. Lasker was still scanning the room.

"Yes. He said I should consider this a special gift." She looked angrily at where she thought Allen might be. "It's more like a curse! Ever since I've met you, all I've done is face one insane thing after another, and now I'm here in this basement lab after almost being gassed by…" She gasped, "Allen, could Dodd be another ghost?"

"I don't know," Allen said. "I suppose it's possible. If he is a ghost, he may be far more expert at ghosting than I am. He seemed quite real to me."

"To me too." Shelly turned to the professor. "Are you sure you haven't got an assistant, or know a student, named Dodd?"

Dr. Lasker looked annoyed. "I've told you before, I've never heard of Dodd, and I still haven't seen or heard your apparition either."

"So I guess I'm stuck with IT," Shelly said.

"We're both stuck," Allen remarked. "We're stuck with each other, since nobody apparently believes in ghosts around here."

Dr. Lasker was studying the girl with almost twenty years of experience behind him. Her whole body seemed to be aimed at wherever her ghost might be while he was supposedly talking to her. Her body language seemed the best proof that she really believed in this ghost. "You don't seem like someone who would lie about this ghost of yours, would you?"

"Why would I do that? He's caused me nothing but trouble! You've got to believe me. I'll do anything to get rid of him if I could."

"Oh thank you. This after I've saved your life three times in just two days!"

"I'm sorry. I didn't mean it that way. I just mean that my life was so simple and straightforward until you showed up." Shelly involuntarily pulled the top of the lab coat she was wearing tighter. "It's not personal about you. It's just I want my life back. And my privacy!"

"I only showed up because you were about to be mugged by that hideous character in the park. I don't know what would have happened if he had gotten to you. It was destiny that we were both in the same place. How else do you explain that you're the only one who can hear me?"

Shelly realized Allen was telling the truth. She could have been raped or killed if he hadn't been there. Her voice was softer when she said, "You're right. This really isn't your fault."

"What isn't?" Dr. Lasker asked.

Shelly realized she had been more focused on Allen than on Dr. Lasker, again. "I'm sorry. He just said that his showing up at the park wasn't his fault, that he had to do something to save me from that mugger. I guess he's right."

Dr. Lasker shook his head. Kook or saint? So convincing, so damned convincing. How could she be a fake? He had to take the risk. "I am going to take a chance on you. As crazy as this whole thing sounds -- and I've been in this parapsychology business a long time -- I've never quite experienced something like this association you may have, I did say "may", with something or someone from another dimension. It is possible--"

"You believe me?" Shelly sagged with relief back into her chair. Maybe he wasn't such an ass after all.

"He doesn't believe you," Allen grumbled. "He just wants to use you. You'll see."

"Not you again!" She aimed furious eyes at Allen. "What if he can help you? Isn't that worth taking a chance?"

Allen didn't reply.

"What did he say?" Dr. Lasker asked, searching for anything to prove she wasn't faking.

"He says you don't really believe me, and you just want to use me and him. He's paranoid."

Dr. Lasker frowned. "Well, he's partly right. Before I admit that this thing you seem to be conversing with is real, I would have to run some tests on you. Shall we say tomorrow morning?"

"I have classes until one," Shelly said.

"Forget your classes. If this thing is real, you will be changing majors. I am not investing my time and expertise in a part-time project. If your 'friend' is real, he is right; I do have a special use for you -- as a member of my department. I assure you, there is nothing more exciting than becoming an Ectoplasmic Research Assistant. But if you are not the genuine article, then you may go back to your former life and become a teacher or whatever pedestrian occupation you wish. I will not press charges. I give you my word. Do we have a deal?"

"I don't like him and I don't trust him," Allen said.

"Shhh," Shelly barked. "I'm thinking. Maybe he can help you find out who you are. Wouldn't that be worth a few tests?"

"Your friend doesn't know who he is?" Dr. Lasker asked.

"He says he has amnesia. He doesn't even know his name." She realized how insane that sounded.

"A ghost with amnesia?" Dr. Lasker mused. "Now I've heard of everything. Well, what do you and your amnesiac ghost say? Do you want my help or not?"

"Can you start the tests right now?" Shelly gave Dr. Lasker a hopeful smile. "You have no idea what I've been through!"

"You really want to get rid of me that bad?" Allen said. "Fine, I'll give this joker a chance, but only for you. I don't trust him one bit. How do we know he isn't lying about Dodd?"

"He says he never heard of Dodd, and I believe him." Shelly looked questioningly at the professor. If Dodd really wasn't his assistant as he had claimed to be, then who was he? Shelly tried to picture him in her mind, but all she saw were those blazing blue eyes. Were they eyes of love, or the eyes of a murderer?

Dr. Lasker shivered at Dodd's name.

CHAPTER 28

"I don't trust him," Allen said, "But I'm not the human around here, so I'll leave it to you since you'll do exactly what you want anyway. Stubborn!"

Shelly felt she had little choice but to believe Dr. Lasker if she wanted his help. If anyone could help her, it had to be this strange, irascible professor. "Please, can we start now? Whatever you want I'm willing to do?"

"Hey, do you know how that sounds?" Allen barked. "You never know what he might want. He's probably a letch, like Dodo-bird."

"Will you please shut up?" Shelly was really getting annoyed. "He's a professor, for goodness' sake. They don't think like that!"

"He's a man, you naive idiot! We all think like that. Hey, even I'm thinking like that! Do ghosts do that?"

"I refuse to discuss this with you any further," Shelly said. "You piss me off!"

Dr. Lasker was staring at her as if she was crazy, so Shelly decided to relate what Allen had said. "He says I have to be more careful around you about what I say."

Dr. Lasker looked uncomfortable. "I'm not sure we should start this tonight. Perhaps tomorrow morning would be more suitable, since I'll have my assistants with me to verify the results." *And to make sure this looney doesn't charge me with molestation or worse,* he thought, regretting his offer.

"Not another delay! Please, I have to know I'm not crazy," Shelly said. "I trust you, even if he doesn't."

Dr. Lasker frowned. The girl was somehow burrowing into a side of him he didn't often show his students or assistants. What was it about her? He suddenly felt protective, as if she was his own daughter. *I don't have a daughter anymore,* he reminded himself, angry at his confused feelings, disturbed at how she had brought up a tragic memory from his past, something he didn't want to think about "You should trust no one. Have you told anyone else about this?"

"No. There's one girl in the dorm that I almost told. She's very trustworthy."

"You must tell no one else! This must be our secret... at least for now." Dr. Lasker wondered who the other girl was and how much Shelly had already told her. He tried to master a smile, but felt uneasy. "I'm sorry. I know you understand the need for secrecy, at least until we know more." He made a mental note to get the other girl's name and decide later what had to be done. "Truly, we must preserve the special nature of this research at this time. You understand?"

"Okay, I guess," Shelly said. "I really don't want anyone else to think I'm crazy."

Dr. Lasker was lost in thought. "I admit I still have misgivings, but I would like to help you."

"Right out of your panties," Allen grumbled.

"Stop it," Shelly barked.

"You wish me to stop?" Dr. Lasker had gotten off his stool and was walking toward a locked cabinet.

"No, Doctor, not you. I'm sorry. He keeps warning me about trusting you." She looked sheepish. "It's hard to ignore him. He has a big mouth!"

"Forgive me for living," Allen said, then added, "That's funny."

Shelly gave him an annoyed scowl. "I wish you'd stop it already. I am trying to help you."

Dr. Lasker unlocked the cabinet and extracted a rectangular metal box. "Do you know anything about ESP?"

Shelly nodded. "Extra Sensory Perception. I've seen it on enough television shows—"

"Well, most of what you see is fiction, but I've seen examples enough to know it exists in a rare chosen few.

What you may be experiencing is a variant of ESP we call Personalized ESP; the random perceptions are somehow perceived as embodied human-like voices and shapes. Often people think they are ghosts, also called spirits, but really these are just a series of random images that cannot be explained -- at least not yet."

"I think he has 'Extra Stupid Perception' if he believes that," Allen grumbled. "I am not just a collection of random glimpses into the future."

"Stop it. I need to concentrate," Shelly said. "Don't you want his help?"

Allen sighed. "Okay, I'll be a good boy… for now."

Dr. Lasker pulled a metal rolling table between him and the girl. He unlocked the box. "Inside this box is a simple test we do for ESP. It's very rudimentary, but indicative."

"Will it hurt?" Shelly asked, noting all the exotic equipment situated in various parts of the laboratory. It looked like a torture chamber, she thought, wondering if that was what Dodd had in mind when he brought her here. She had a flashback of her open blouse. Had Dodd done that too? She remembered how immobile he had been as she had tried to kiss him in her dorm room. What was his secret? Why did this strange creature known to her only as Dodd seem to turn her on?

The Doctor had been watching her. She looked distracted. Suddenly he laughed.

To Shelly it was the sinister laugh of the mad scientist from a horror movie.

CHAPTER 29

Shelly felt hesitant. There really was a lot of exotic-looking equipment scattered around the room, and she recalled that the entire department was isolated in the locked basement of this remote building. There was nobody around to help her if things got out of hand. Would anyone hear her scream in this heavily insulated windowless basement room? "Are you still here?" she asked Allen, for once hoping he was.

"Yes. Are you okay?" He sounded gentler, concerned.

Dr. Lasker smiled. "I guess you didn't like my evil laugh. I always do that the first time with newbies. It makes them squirm a bit."

"I'm squirming enough, thank you," Shelly said.

"He has a bit of the sadist in him, if you ask me," Allen said.

"Like you didn't scare me when you yelled, 'Boo!'" Shelly glared at him.

Allen sighed. "That's different. I was practicing."

"You can do better than that," Shelly said, and turned back to the professor.

Dr. Lasker shook his head. This girl was nice looking, but very possibly insane. He had second thoughts as he opened the metal box. "At any rate, this is the first test I usually give when an ESP candidate is being screened." He pulled a deck of cards out of the box.

For some reason Shelly's brain flipped to Strip Poker. *I'm really nervous,* she thought as she tried to refocus.

Dr. Lasker flipped through the deck and pulled out four cards, placing them face up on the counter. "We have four different cards in the deck, all outlines of basic geometric shapes: a square, triangle, circle, rectangle. We use shapes rather than numbers, as they're easier to visualize and harder to pronounce if someone is cheating." He gave her an inquisitive look.

"Only four shapes means you have a one in four chance of getting it right," Shelly observed. "Isn't that less challenging than a regular deck of cards?"

"Purposely so. Early ESP trials utilized this type of deck, and so we have some basis for determining the standard at which we may assume some kind of ESP phenomenon is occurring. As I said, this is a very crude preliminary examination, and will only tell us if it is even remotely possible that you are a candidate for further study."

"Like an insect specimen," Allen grumbled. "The man's a butterfly collector, and he plans to pop needles in your beautiful body and put you on display, a prized trophy in his hidden torture chamber somewhere in this windowless hole."

"Will you please just shut up already and let me do this test?" Shelly snarled.

"I'm sorry," Dr. Lasker said. "I was only trying to set you at ease by explaining to you--"

"No, not you! It's him again! Please, let's do this so I can get back to normal."

"You understand this is not definitive?" Dr. Lasker covered the cards and returned them to the deck. He turned around to be sure there were no reflective surfaces which she could use to cheat, and began to shuffle the cards. "Are you ready? Concentrate." He pulled out a card and placed it face down on the table. "All right, what is the shape you see?"

Shelly forced herself to concentrate on the card. "Nothing."

"Try harder," Dr. Lasker urged. "Try to make your mind blank."

"Like his," Allen laughed. "This is a waste of time. You haven't got ESP. You have a ghost."

Shelly tried to shut him out, but still couldn't see any shape. "A circle," she guessed.

Dr. Lasker pulled up the card. He tried not to show any emotion or reaction, but noted that it was a circle on his pad.

"Did I get it right?" Shelly asked.

"I'll give you the results afterwards." He pulled up a second card and immediately flipped it face down on the table.

Shelly tried to see the shape in her mind. "A triangle? I think it's a triangle."

Dr. Lasker noted the card was a triangle. He was beginning to feel the tingling that came whenever he suspected someone might have the elusive ability called ESP. He remembered how excited he had been with Dodd's incredible scores. "One more, please?"

Shelly tried again. "A rectangle?"

Dr. Lasker noted the card was a square. Close, but not correct.

Three more cards in a row Shelly got wrong. "Are you concentrating? Do you see shapes, or are you randomly guessing?" He sighed. *Another failure.* There were so few successes.

"I'm not doing well?" Shelly asked, noting impatience in his voice.

"That's irrelevant," Dr. Lasker said, trying to suppress his disappointment. "Let's try a few more, and then I'll have a score for you."

They tried a total of ten cards, and Shelly got all of them wrong except the first two.

"This is totally stupid," Allen barked. "You don't have ESP. Tell him to hold the cards up and I'll tell you the shapes."

"That's a good idea," Shelly said.

"What is?" Dr. Lasker asked, about to report that Shelly did not have ESP…at least not at this time or on this test. Further tests at another time, perhaps when she was not as tired, might indicate otherwise, but he doubted it. She seemed a nice enough girl, but not Ecto material.

"Allen says, if you hold up the card so only he can see it, he'll tell me what it is."

"He said that, did he?" Dr. Lasker turned around again to make sure there were no hidden reflective surfaces on the ceiling or floor. He searched for a hidden video camera she might have planted. "I suppose there's no harm in trying that," he said, selecting a card. "What card am I holding?" He held a card inches from his chest.

"It's a circle," Allen said.

"No tricks," Shelly hissed.

"Me, you don't trust? I said it's a circle," Allen repeated. "I can't believe you trust this character but not me!"

"A circle," Shelly said, giving Allen a dirty look.

Dr. Lasker noted it was a circle on his score sheet. He held up a square against his chest.

"A square," Allen said promptly.

"A square." Shelly wondered if Allen was giving her the right shapes, since the doctor gave no sign she was getting them right. She had to trust him. What other choice was there?

The doctor tried three more times, and each time Shelly listened to Allen and reported the right shape. Lasker's hands were shaking as he pulled a card from one above the bottom card on the deck. "What is this shape?" he asked.

"He's cheating," Allen said. "I told you not to trust him."

"Never mind. What's the card?" Shelly demanded.

"A question mark," Allen said. "Real ingenious."

"A question mark," Shelly said, hoping Allen was not the one playing tricks.

The look on Dr. Lasker's face told her Allen had not lied.

"I'll be damned," Dr. Lasker stammered. "Maybe you do have a ghost!"

"That's what I've been trying to tell you," Shelly said, sagging back into the chair, totally exhausted.

CHAPTER 30

Dr. Lasker was studying the results of Shelly's test. His mind was racing. If this simple test was even a slight indication, then something strange was at work here. The girl called it a ghost, but that part remained to be seen. She had gotten every one of the last cards right. Even Dodd had not gotten more than sixty percent on any of the tests. No Ecto had ever scored this high.

"Are you convinced yet?" Shelly asked, seeing him studying her again with his eyeglasses raised above his nose.

He had to hide his excitement. "It is rather remarkable," Dr. Lasker said, his mind still working on the possibilities this discovery might offer for his department. "We will of course have to do more tests."

"Oh, for heaven's sake!" Allen roared. "No more tests! Either he accepts I exist or let's try something else. I'm losing patience with this clown."

"Like what?" Shelly asked.

"I have a whole battery of tests," Dr. Lasker replied, thinking she was talking to him. "We'll have to run brain scans, body electrical evaluations, neuron tests and quite a few more."

"I told you, Shelly, to this quack you're just a specimen, a butterfly to add to his collection."

"I'm not a butterfly!" Shelly roared.

"A what?" Dr. Lasker looked confused.

Shelly sat up taller. "I said I'm not a butterfly, a specimen for your probing needles."

"No. Of course not," Dr. Lasker said, surprised at her strong response. "I never thought you were. It's just that before taking you into the department, I must ascertain exactly what we are dealing with here. We don't train just anyone for this kind of intensive research."

"Probe, probe and more probing!" Allen roared. "Let's just get the hell out of here and solve this thing on our own."

"How? How do we do that?" Shelly asked. "You don't even know who or what you are! And frankly, I'm beginning to wonder what I am too."

"You're my partner," Allen said. "We're meant to be together. Can't you see that? Why else was I sent to save you? Three times! Count them!"

"I've heard all this before," Shelly said.

"You have?" Dr. Lasker asked, thoroughly confused. He thought of putting on his usual stern voice and authority face, but was afraid he'd lose her. She was showing surprising strength for a newbie. Most new students were terrified of him, but this one was refusing to show any sign that she was cowed by his reputation or presence. Still it was worth a shot. "My dear Shelly," he began, deliberately making his tone sound condescending and authoritative, "I have been a professor of parapsychology for twenty years, chairperson of this department for nine. My work is published all over the world. I am one of the leading authorities on supernatural phenomena. I do not expect to be questioned by an untrained student in my own laboratory. What I say goes. Is that clear?" He glowered at her with all of the authority he could muster.

"He needs you," Allen said. "He's scared stiff you're going to walk out of here and take your ghost with you."

"Are you sure?" Shelly asked.

Dr. Lasker couldn't believe this petite girl was actually questioning him. "I am positive. Absolutely positive," he barked.

"He's terrified," Allen said. "Just walk out. Right now! Get up and walk out. Trust me."

Shelly nodded and rose from her chair. "Thank you, Dr. Lasker," she said and headed for the door.

"You're leaving?" Dr. Lasker asked, fighting the urge to block the door with his body. "If you leave, don't bother coming back. We're done here."

Shelly's hand was on the door handle. *I hope Allen is right,* she thought as she turned the knob.

"Wait," Dr. Lasker said. "Wait!" He exhaled a gust of air. "Perhaps we can run these tests a bit later? I see no harm in, shall we say, on-the-job-verification. We'll call it probation. No harm done if it doesn't work out. I'll get you back to your former program. I give you my word."

"See? I told you so," Allen said. "I've got this guy's number!"

Shelly nodded, her hand still on the door handle. "I don't know. You haven't been very nice to me, or to Allen."

Dr. Lasker waved toward the chair. "Please come back. Let's talk. This is a rare opportunity for you." *And for me,* he thought, praying she was what she appeared to be.

"Tell him you're not a specimen. Tell him you'll only stay if he promises to show you proper respect," Allen said. "You deserve that, at least." He was surprised she had shown such strength after all she'd been through since meeting him. He wondered if he'd underestimated her. *Just because she's cute doesn't mean she has to be a bimbo,* he realized. But then why did she seem to always get into so much trouble?

Shelly nodded again and repeated, "Dr. Lasker, I would very much like your help, but I will only stay if you agree to show me proper respect."

Dr. Lasker felt his whole body tighten at this ultimatum, from a newbie yet. He forced himself not to explode, quietly nodding his head. *There is something about this one,* he thought, aware that she had him over a barrel...at least for now. "Agreed," he said, finding the word hard to dislodge from his throat.

"I need you to understand that I, and my ghostly friend, Allen, are not specimens for your collection." Shelly smiled at Allen.

"Your ghostly friend? I like that. Thank you," Allen said, wondering if he had finally made a small breakthrough with this stubborn human female whom he seemed destined to protect.

"You're welcome," Shelly replied.

"I haven't said anything," Dr. Lasker said, fighting to hold back his notorious temper.

"I was talking to Allen," Shelly said. "He thanked me for calling him a friend, which I now know he is."

Dr. Lasker sighed. He had never seen anything like this before, this young girl having a very complex and congenial conversation with a ghostly, at least invisible, companion. He examined her test score again and determined that to have, for lack of a better understanding, a ghost on his team was worth the humiliation he was now suffering in silence. It was worth almost everything. "Please tell...Allen? Is that his name?"

"I told you he doesn't know who he was in real life. I gave him that name to use until we can help him."

"Forgetful old coot," Allen said.

"You should talk," Shelly shot back. "You forgot your own name."

"I know my name," Dr. Lasker said, again feeling his temper simmering.

"No, I was talking to Allen again. You have to get used to that. I'm trying to get used to it," Shelly said. "He's a bit of a chatterbox. He says he hasn't talked to anyone in ages." She leaned toward the doctor. "I think he's making up for lost time with all this talking."

Dr. Lasker nodded. "Hello Allen," he said, not sure in which direction he should be speaking. "I am Professor Joel Lasker, PhD, Chairman of this department, and I am very pleased to meet you." He turned to Shelly. "Can he hear me? Should I speak louder?"

"Oh, for Pete's sake! Tell him I hear him loud and clear. Too loud and clear."

Shelly shrugged. "Allen says he hears you fine. And says he's glad to meet you too."

"I never said that, you little liar."

"You actually can hear him right now?" Dr. Lasker asked. "Well, perhaps someday I will be able to hear him too. At any rate, Shelly and Allen, welcome to the Parapsychology Department. I have a feeling we are going to get along just fine."

"I wouldn't bet my life on that," Allen murmured.

CHAPTER 31

"I think perhaps the best thing at this point is for you to return to your dorm, gather up a few things, and we'll house you in our rooms right here," Dr. Lasker said. "Yes, I think that would be best."

"Hold on, Professor, I never discussed moving out of my dorm into this…" Shelly paused, she almost said prison. The tall building with its windowless façade did remind her of a prison. "What I meant to say was, is this really necessary?" She thought the good doctor had a kind of lecherous expression on his face. Perhaps he wasn't quite as 'uninterested' as he pretended to be. He certainly seemed so sure of himself, he might be thinking of other means of persuading her to bend to his desires, perhaps more than just being part of his department? *Maybe Allen is right about him,* she mused, *But I can take care of myself.*

"For the work we do here, I'm afraid it is essential that you remain close." Dr. Lasker was wondering how much he could tell her. He didn't want to frighten her off, not until she was well on the hook.

"What about me?" Allen said. "You don't want me in your room at the girl's dorm…even if that would be quite delightful for me… Sorry about that, but I haven't seen a girl in a very long time, except of course for you. Very nice too."

"Behave yourself," Shelly said, a warning look on her face.

The professor nodded. "You're talking to Allen, I hope?"

Shelly nodded. "Sorry. He has this thing about moving into the girl's dormitory with me. It's his dream -- and my nightmare!"

Dr. Lasker smiled, his first genuine smile of the evening. "I can see why you wouldn't want that," he remarked.

"Tell the old goat to mind his own business," Allen said. "I don't go around spoiling his fun."

"You're a letch!" Shelly barked. "Not you," she said to Dr. Lasker, who looked shocked at the accusation even if he had harbored some such thoughts about this cute intruder. "You keep getting me into trouble," she barked at Allen who was having a good chuckle at her expense.

Dr. Lasker was almost disappointed that she found him so non –threatening. "Thank you," he said, wishing he was ten years younger, but of course even then he probably would not have been her type. *She probably likes the athletic, clean-shaven beach boys, or the dark and forboding gangster types, not a college professor with a beard -- brown with gray, as befits my station...* No, he was not her type, more like a father figure, he mused. But what about this Allen character? From her side of the conversation, it sounded as if she had her hands full.

Shelly was still arguing with Allen. "I told you, you can't, cannot, will not, stay in my room! Period! End of discussion!"

"He's giving you quite a fight, I see," Dr. Lasker said, wishing he could hear both sides of the argument.

Shelly sighed. "He's very lonely. It's tough being the only one he can talk to."

"Perhaps we may be able to do something about that later on," Dr. Lasker said, wondering if any of the other researchers might be sensitive enough to hear this Allen. *Dodd might have been sensitive enough,* he thought with regret.

"Later on doesn't cut it!" Allen roared. "And I wish you wouldn't give him all my personal information."

"You don't have any personal information, remember? You have amnesia -- supposedly," Shelly argued back.

"What do you mean 'supposedly'? Do you think I like not knowing who I am?"

"No, I guess not."

"Do you realize I don't even know whether I was married? I mean what if I have kids somewhere? What if you're my kid or something?"

"God forbid," Shelly said unable to stop herself.

"Thank you very much. I think you'd be lucky to have a father like me. I saved you..."

"I know, three times! And that's only in the two days since I met you!" She felt exhausted again. "I have an idea. Dr. Lasker, could Allen stay here?"

Dr. Lasker barely heard her. He had been busily thinking about all he could accomplish if this ghost was for real. "I have an idea," he suddenly said with a smile. "Perhaps I can help resolve your little housing problem. Why doesn't Allen stay here too? We have wonderful rooms downstairs."

"Oh no!" Allen shouted. "I'm going with you or right back to the park, where I can wait and rescue some other cute damsel in distress. This guy reminds me of Dr. Frankenstein. Just look at this place! It looks like a torture chamber with all these gurneys and equipment. I can guess what that Dodo guy was going to do with you, once he knocked you out with his sleeping gas. Just look at these hooks and chains! Hey, is that a straitjacket? What a place! You need me with you. That's final."

"You're not going with me," Shelly said firmly. "Why don't you be a good boy...er, ghost... stay here tonight and give it a try? I'll come back first thing tomorrow morning and we'll decide where we go from here."

"I don't like it here," Allen said.

"I don't like any of this," Shelly said, "but we have to make do for now."

"My place is with you," Allen persisted. "What if that Dodd character shows up again?"

Shelly wondered why she shivered at Dodd's name. "You had to remind me? You're a real pain!"

"I'm just worried about you," Allen said, wondering how a ghost could have caring feelings about someone still alive. What was he feeling for her?

It was strange how whatever it was he was feeling seemed to be getting stronger each time he saw her. "I'm not kidding now. I really am worried about you. Please let me take care of you. I think that's why I'm here." He knew that even if that was true, it was only a part of why he was still here.

Dr. Lasker yawned. He looked at his watch. "I didn't realize it is so late," he muttered. "So what is it to be?"

"Allen?" Shelly aimed her eyes at where she thought he might be. "Please? I need a good night's sleep. Please stay here. I promise I'll be back early tomorrow morning, and we'll sort this whole thing out."

"I tell you what. If you stay here, I'll stay," Allen said. "It's too late for you to be out on your own anyway. That crazy Dodd could be out there waiting for you."

"I don't even have a change of clothes," Shelly said.

Dr. Lasker smiled. "I will be happy to lend you a fresh lab coat, if that helps."

"I think you look very sexy in a lab coat," Allen said.

Shelly shot him a dirty look. "Okay, I know when I'm beat. Just one night. I'll stay here one night, and only if you give my 'friend' his own room."

"Only if it's next door," Allen said.

"You're pushing your luck," Shelly replied. "He wants a room next door to me," she informed the professor.

"Very well," Dr. Lasker said, "But may I ask, how will you know he isn't in your room if you can't see him?"

"Because if I even think he's violating the rules, I will cut him off faster than you can say parapsychology," Shelly said, aiming her fiery eyes at Allen.

"Everyone wants to spoil my fun," Allen moaned.

"He says, everyone wants to spoil his fun, the big baby," Shelly said.

My fun is just beginning, Lasker thought.

CHAPTER 32

"You two sound like an old married couple," Dr. Lasker said.

"Heaven forbid," Shelly replied.

"Oh, I don't think it would be so bad," Allen said, "Except of course we'd have to use your name, since I can't for the life of me-- Hey, that's funny -- for the life of me!"

"You're a riot," Shelly remarked, feeling so exhausted she was almost glad the professor was putting her up for the night in this building.

"Well, anyway, we'd have to use your name since I can't remember mine." Allen sighed. "Do you really think this quack can help me? He looks like he can't help himself off the chair."

"I don't know, but if he can help me get rid of you that would be well worth all this."

"I can't believe you can still feel this way after I saved you…"

"Three times. You're right. I'm just pooped," Shelly said. "Dr. Lasker, could you please show me where I'm going to sleep tonight?"

Dr. Lasker walked to a locked cabinet behind his desk and extracted a ring of keys. "Please follow me. Your room is at the other end of this hall. I think you'll be very comfortable."

Shelly no longer cared where she was going to be. She just wanted to flop down on a clean bed and crash. It had been a really long day. She felt as if she was going to stumble as she followed a slight distance behind the professor, who was guiding her with a flashlight since the hall lights were shut off automatically at 9:30 each night to conserve power and cut costs. Nobody was supposed to be here this late at night .

"Are all these doors your offices," Shelly asked.

"Some," Lasker replied. "Funding cuts have caused many to be vacant at this time. Bean-counters are a curse to science!"

"You scientists would spend every dime you could get your hands on if it weren't for so-called bean-counters," Allen shot back.

Shelly was surprised by his vehemence. This kind of response didn't sound like her ghost at all. "I'm too tired to argue this with you tonight," she replied.

"I suppose you support the bean-counters," Dr. Lasker said, clearly not happy with her response.

"No, I was talking to Allen," Shelly said.

Dr. Lasker stopped in front of a door marked B66. "This will be your room." He slipped his master key in the lock, opened the door and found the light switch on the wall.

Shelly was pleasantly surprised. She had expected a room resembling a prison cell, but this room was carpeted in a soft tan with clean, beige-colored walls broken up by regularly placed abstract paintings. A red fabric love-seat took up one of the walls, with a flat screen television -- she guessed forty inches -- directly opposite.

"Is this satisfactory?" Dr. Lasker asked.

"It's very nice," Shelly said, and promptly yawned. "Where's the bed?"

"In the bedroom, of course," Dr. Lasker replied. "Right through that door."

"Door?" Shelly pushed open the door and found herself facing a real bed, not just a dorm cot with its thin mattress, but a queen-sized bed with what looked like a thick mattress, covered by a neatly tucked-in tan blanket and tan sheets. Two pillows were leaning against a white headboard. The sight of the bed almost made Shelly cry. "Is this for real?" she asked.

"You know why the bed is so big, don't you?" Allen hissed.

Shelly wished she could hit him in the mouth and shut him up once and for all. "I'm so tired I wouldn't care who crawled into this wonderful bed with me." She thought about that and added quickly, "Except you."

Dr. Lasker's mouth dropped wide open. Was she inviting him? He couldn't deny he had some thoughts of something more with this girl…that was natural given her pretty face and attractive vulnerability…but was she really inviting him?

"Well then, I'll stay right here and keep you safe," Allen said.

"Oh no, you don't! Dr. Lasker, before I settle into this heavenly room, can we please take my friend to his 'locked cell'?"

Dr. Lasker extracted another key. "How do I know he's following me?" he asked as he started for the door, turning to look for footprints in the carpet, but seeing nothing, not even the tiniest of indentations.

"Because if he doesn't, I'm not going to help him," Shelly said. "Have I made that clear?"

"Loud and clear," Allen replied and muttered, "Ungrateful brat."

"I heard that," Shelly said.

Dr. Lasker shrugged his shoulders. Either this was the most important discovery he had ever made, or he was finally going crazy. Either way, he wondered just how this was going to play out. For years this department, Parapsychology, had been derided and cut back mercilessly by the university trustees, the hated 'bean-counters' -- but if this girl was genuine, and more importantly, if her ghost was for real, Dr. Lasker saw a bright path ahead. He had to keep reminding himself to take it slow and enter with extreme caution. But what if she wanted more? He sighed. Divorced five years earlier, he rationalized, he was too busy for women. He had found some of his assistants attractive, but never made a move on them. He just wasn't into it then, and wasn't that into it now. But if sex would seal the deal? *I guess I can think of worse ways to sacrifice myself,* he thought as he tried to imagine what she looked like under the lab coat. *Her legs are quite nice,* he mused. *And it has been a long time.*

"I don't want to be far from you," Allen said. "Just look at him. I can see what he wants in his face. He's positively drooling."

"He wants a room nearby," Shelly said, ignoring Allen when she saw that the Professor was scanning the rooms all the way down the hall.

Lasker nodded and slipped his key in the door opposite Shelly's. "I think Allen will find this room to his liking." He pushed on the light switch. "Can he…er…can he manipulate objects? Can he shut off the lights? Does he need lights?" *I can't believe I'm asking such stupid questions, but I realize how little I really know about ghosts -- or whatever this Allen really is. I just hope he's as harmless as she believes.* "I really don't know what he needs," Dr. Lasker said apologetically.

Shelly felt the ridiculousness of the situation and couldn't keep from laughing. "Why are you asking me? I have no idea what a ghost needs either."

"I don't need anything," Allen said. "It's actually kind of sad. I don't seem to need anything at all. It's like I don't exist… or maybe never did? I don't know!"

The sad tone of Allen's voice stopped her laughter. As much as she wished he'd never come into her life she found herself sympathizing. *Maybe it's because he saved my life? Three times, as he always says.* "Do you like the room?" Shelly asked, seeing that the room was almost exactly the same as hers. "You have a nice couch and a great flat screen T.V."

"I can't turn it on. I can't change the channels. Who's going to shut it off if I ever fall asleep? Which I never do."

Shelly sighed. He really had a rotten after-life. "Well, if I don't go to sleep now, I'm going to be like a wild bear in the morning," she said softly. "Good night, Allen. I'll see you in the morning, and we'll start working on helping you. I promise."

"Good night, Shelly." Allen suddenly added, "Shelly?"

"Yes?"

"I'm glad I saved you."

The way he said that totally unnerved her. She found herself staring into the corner of the room where she thought he was standing and watching her.

"Is he okay with this?" Dr. Lasker asked before she could reply.

Shelly closed Allen's door. "If you were a ghost and thought you had been murdered, would you be okay?"

Dr. Lasker sighed. "He really believes he was murdered?" He felt a wave of sadness, a sensation he did not generally give in to.

Shelly yawned and reached for her door. "Thank you for helping me. I really hope you can help him, too."

As he watched her door close, Dr. Lasker wondered if he could help Allen. He also wondered, if he did help him or the girl, if that would end his one chance to save his department and his reputation. *If the girl is freed from her ghost, if he is a ghost, then what good will she be to me? She is perhaps the best Ectoplasmic Researcher I've ever found, even better than...* He didn't want to mention the name. It still caused him too much pain, and perhaps even a little guilt, whenever he thought of what had happened to Dodd.

Lasker's flashlight danced on a door near his laboratory. A square of cardboard, a name card, taped to the wall next to the door was spotlighted. Dr. Lasker reached for the board and tore it off the wall. He used his fingernail to scrape off the tape residue from the wall.

When he returned to his office, he tossed the paper in his waste bin. *What if she accidentally checks that?* He fished into the bottom drawer of his desk and found a match. The card burnt brilliantly, and was soon reduced to ashes. The ashes were scooped up into a small plastic bag which he popped into his coat pocket. As he locked his office, Dr. Lasker frowned and thought, *So much for Dodd.*

CHAPTER 33

Shelly could hardly walk. "I'm pooped," she moaned, "But I also stink in these clothes." She wished she had a change of clothes with her. She stared at the white lab coat Dr. Lasker had given her. It looked clean enough. She reluctantly decided it would have to do. *No way am I sleeping in these things and then wearing them tomorrow again.* She let out a yawn.

Shelly had a sudden impulse and walked over to the door, assuring herself it was locked from the inside. "It really is a nice room," she mused as she undid her shirt buttons and slid her shirt onto the couch. "I hate wearing dirty clothes," she grumbled again as she slipped out of her skirt and tried to smooth the wrinkles.

A noise startled her. "Are you here?" she asked, now standing in only her white bra and panties. "I warned you what I would do." She held the lab coat over her front.

There wasn't any reply, but Shelly rushed on the lab coat. It covered most of her body, down to just above her knees. Satisfied she was now protected from any Peeping Tom, even a ghost, she pulled off her panties and slipped her bra through the sleeves of the white coat. "There's nothing to see, you letch," she said. "You may as well go back to your room now. I warned you!"

There still wasn't any reply. Shelly sighed. *Let him do what he wants. He's a damn ghost, and there's no way I can control him.* She straightened out her blouse on the couch, and walked into the bedroom.

Exhausted, she wished she could just fall on the bed and collapse, but her body was telling her she had one more duty to fulfill. She found the light switch and, still not sure Allen wasn't cheating, she locked the bathroom door.

The room smelled clean, not like the sickly smell of the dorm bathroom. She pulled aside the white tub-curtain and smiled. "It's spotless." What a difference from the shower stalls she had to share with the girls in the dorm. *This is like a hotel*, she thought, as she could picture herself stretched out in this gorgeous tub, water playing on her body... *No, not just water. Oh my god, a bubble bath and body lotions!* "This isn't what I expected," she said, as the contrast between the super-clean tiled walls and floors of this private...*oh boy, a private bathroom*...and the slimy-feeling, grungy tiles of the gang-style dorm bathroom imprinted itself on her exhausted brain. "How can I refuse this?" she wondered, as the toilet flushed the first time and did not require jiggling to make the flow of water stop. *No volcanic eruptions here.*

Even the medicine cabinet mirror was a real mirror, and not just a slab of metal screwed into the wall so it wouldn't be stolen or used for a suicide weapon. "Have you ever tried to apply makeup with one of those distorted crappy mirrors?" she had asked her mother when they joked about dorm life on the phone -- but now seeing her face in the mirror, a real mirror, for the first time in weeks, made her realize how much she missed even that little convenience.

She pulled open a drawer in the granite-topped vanity, and thought about not having to drag her hair dryer and bathroom necessities in that stupid little plastic carry-all with its fake chrome handle -- chrome paper that was already peeling -- to the bathroom every morning and night. To be able to keep all of her little goodies inside an honest to goodness bathroom vanity was a luxury in the dormitory of shared everything, dirty everything, slime everywhere. "This is going to be hard to give up," she thought. But it all came with one catch, one major problem -- Dr. Lasker, that arrogant, inconsiderate mad scientist...and, oh yes, her ghost. *Without Allen, the bathroom vanishes.* Shelly knew the score even if Allen thought she was naïve, even if Dr. Lasker thought she was just another stupid college brat, even if Dodd....

She stared at the real mirror, and saw for the first time how really tired and grungy she looked. What did Dodd think of her? Where the hell was that strange and mysterious mad scientist whose one-syllable name seemed to knock her for a loop? *Why the hell can't I stop thinking about him...even if he may have tried to kill me...or was it Lasker? Maybe he's the one who set this whole thing up. Maybe Dodd and Lasker are in it together.* She felt the headache starting again. *I need sleep.*

Shelly hurried over to a louvered closet in the bathroom. She pulled it open and stared in disbelief at neatly folded towels, all sizes and all uniformly tan in color -- no fade spots, no spots that the campus laundry could not seem to remove and which she had no desire to identify. "That's it," she said aloud. "That settles it. If he still wants me, I'm moving in."

Unable to stand any more excitement, Shelly shut off the bathroom light and walked barefoot the short distance to her bed. Flopping down on the thick mattress was one of the greatest delights in her life, after nearly a month on the thin university cots through which she could feel the bedsprings.

The hum of the air conditioner was incredibly smooth, no metallic bumping and grinding like the sounds emanating from the window conditioners in the dorm. She had been uneasy about the lack of windows, but the room without windows and heavily insulated kept it free from extraneous sounds. Soon the sound of Shelly's rhythmic breathing was a sign that she was finally asleep.

Shelly's sleep was undisturbed by dreams. Even her headaches had subsided. The bed was like floating on air, and she hadn't even crawled under the coverlet. The only thing hiding her body was the thin white lab coat -- which was slightly open, just open enough that if someone was in the room they would get a teasing glimpse of Shelly's firm legs, almost completely exposed up to her hips. One shoulder was almost bare, and a breast was barely hidden under the flimsy lapel of the coat. The thin coat revealed more than it concealed.

She really is pretty, Dodd thought as he stared at Shelly sleeping so angelically in only the oversized white coat. His eyes ran from her toenails up her ankles, one curled slightly under the other. He was tempted to run his hand gently up her thigh. He could almost feel her smooth flesh under his fingers.

He moved forward and leaned down. He could hear the rhythmic breathing, feel her breath. It came and went like a tiny warming breeze. Her head was against a pillow, her hair splayed across the beige fabric. Her eyes were closed so he wouldn't have to see them looking at him, making him feel guilty. Another pillow was nearby. Dodd felt that pillow calling him. A few seconds of pressing that pillow over the girl's mouth and nose, and she wouldn't be a problem anymore. So why couldn't he do it?

Dodd let his eyes wander below her chin. He saw her flesh from the vee of her breasts to her slender throat. He stared at this part of her for a long time, feeling a longing inside him that he had never felt before. He'd never had time before to let his sexual needs interfere. He had come to believe that part of him had been killed off by the horrors of his work, the price of being an Ecto. It was as if the sexual side of him had been overcome by the work to develop his sensitivity, the sensitivity that might have destroyed his sanity. At least that was how he understood his inability to function. He couldn't even make a decision anymore, or by now the girl would have been dead -- or he would have made love to her. As she lay alone on that big bed, her flesh peeking temptingly through the lab coat, the pillow waiting for his head, Dodd heard the voices arguing inside him and could not decide what he should do. *Murder or sex?*

Dodd's hand inched forward and he carefully lowered the flap of Shelly's coat so it covered up her legs. He waited until he was sure she wasn't going to move, and stood up. Looking down again, he felt the confusion inside him. The pillow was so damn close -- but she looked so innocent, sweet. She was nothing like what he had expected. Maybe she wasn't such a threat after all. At any rate, suffocating her with a pillow -- feeling her buckling under his pressing hands -- was a hell of a lot different from letting a bus or poison gas do her in. *No, I don't think I could stand that,* Dodd thought, discarding the pillow idea, at least for tonight.

He backed away from her, his wild-looking eyes searching for any sign that she was awake, that she had seen him. *She really looks like a child, asleep,* he considered, taking one last look at someone he had thought of as his enemy, someone he had wanted to destroy. Now he wondered what she would say if she woke up and felt him lying with her, pressing against her. He found himself seriously thinking of slipping off his jeans and shirt and sliding into the bed next to her. Could he find happiness that way? Would it make all the pain and horror go away? If only it would!

As he stared at her, Dodd couldn't help thinking, *it really is a shame to hurt someone like her.* He bent lower again and whispered, "Shelly, please leave and don't come back. I don't want to hurt you."

Shelly stirred in her sleep.

Dodd wondered if she had heard him. He hoped she would heed his warning. For his sake, and hers, he prayed she would finally take his warnings to get the hell out of his life.

CHAPTER 34

It had taken weeks for Shelly to get used to sleeping in a dorm room at Stonewall. Her roomie was a night-owl and loved to watch late-night television when she was home, when she was alone. It was much worse when Lisa brought someone back with her to the tiny room. That girl could make the walls rock when some guy was pumping her as if she was an oil-well. And it didn't seem to matter who the guy was. Shelly had tried talking to her, working out some kind of amicable arrangement, but some roomies just can't compromise -- so every few nights Shelly had to try to sleep with either the noise of the television, the sounds of people getting high on pot or whatever they could find, or the sounds of her roomie and whoever slapping bodies on the creaking springs of the dorm cot... and one time even the floor.

At first the loud springs of the cot had almost sounded funny to her, then irritating, and eventually Shelly had become resigned to it all, covering her ears with a pillow, but still hearing Lisa and whoever, going at it like rabbits in heat. She planned to ask for a new roommate at the end of the semester, but had not figured out how to break that to Lisa -- who assumed Shelly was okay with her, even if Shelly wasn't a party girl. Had Shelly known the reason for Lisa's fear of sleeping alone, she might have been more sympathetic. Lisa never told anyone about the ghosts in her house, but might have confided in Shelly if she had known about Allen.

The silence in this wonderful room was truly amazing. Shelly hadn't slept like this in forever, and had just about made up her mind that it would take dynamite to make her give it up. No more Lisa -- and her creaking bed and creepy bed-mates -- if she could stay in this room. Even working with an arrogant character like Lasker might be worth it for a few nights of real sleep and a bathroom all her own. Oh, yeah!

It didn't even raise an eyelash when Shelly woke up and found that her lab coat was completely buttoned and she was covered by the soft tan blanket. She assumed she had woken up and done that herself. And besides, the room was locked and no crazy roomie! "I haven't slept like this in ages," she murmured, trying to see the time on a clock resting on the white night-table. "Holy crap! It's after ten! I'm late!"

This is not a good way to start, she thought, especially since she decided she wanted to take up Lasker's offer. She still wasn't sure about this Professor and his strange Parapsychology department, and the Ectos -- whatever they were called -- and Lasker still reminded her of Dr. Frankenstein with his weird equipment and sinister laugh. But then again, what should a professor of parapsychology be like? "He works with ghosts, for goodness sake," she reminded herself. "And I've got a damn ghost." She had almost forgotten that detail.

She walked into the bathroom, and a motion-sensing fixture bathed the room in a delicate tan light. She looked at the shower as if she'd never seen one before. It was gorgeous, but most importantly, it was clean -- not one sign of someone else using it. "I've got to," she said happily, and reached for the faucet embedded in the tiled wall. She leaned down to feel the water. "Oh my God, it's perfect." Before it had a chance to become either too hot or freezing cold, she was about to step in, about to drop her lab coat to the floor, when she remembered Allen. "Are you here?" she asked. *It would be just like him,* she thought and then decided that even if he was, she didn't care anymore. She dropped the lab coat and stepped into the shower.

The water was amazing, the spray perfectly adjusted -- not hard-hitting needle-like, but almost gentle, landing softly on her skin and drifting slowly down the curves of her body. "This is heaven," Shelly said. She unwrapped a bar of soap wrapped in silvery foil. Against her body the soap felt smooth and aromatic, smelling of lavender. The bubbles were luxurious, and she could have stayed in the shower all morning -- except she realized that she had things that had to be done. She had made a promise to Allen. Reluctantly, she shut off the water and placed her feet on the bath rug, for once not afraid of what creepy crawlies might be hiding in the worn fibers of the dorm mats. She eyed the lab coat from last night with distaste, and suddenly saw a lush white robe hanging on a hook in the tall closet next to the bathroom door. "Lasker thought of everything," she mused as she slipped into the soft cotton robe, cinching it around her middle. "Now, I've really got to please him," she considered.

She rushed to the sitting room and stared with distaste at her clothes draped on the couch, worn the day before. "I have no choice." She slipped the panties on under her robe. "Allen, good morning. Are you here? Tell the truth. I won't be angry, I promise." *I know you've seen it before, you letch,* she thought, as she searched the room.

Not hearing a reply, Shelly slipped the top of the open robe off, down to her waist. Running had given her a trim and firm body, but there was no time for exercising today. She thought of not putting on the dirty bra under her translucent white shirt. "That would give that Professor a heart attack," she laughed, and reluctantly put it back on. Her blouse looked okay, but she wished she had a fresh one. *Fresh clothing always makes me feel better,* she thought as she gazed at the mirror.

Another thought occurred. "I'm starving! I wonder if there's a kitchen in this building." She headed for the door, and saw a key with a rabbit-foot on a lamp table next to the loveseat. She groaned at the sight of the rabbit's foot, a mix of light brown and white -- hopefully fake -- fur with a wire frame. "Someone around here is superstitious," she muttered, "But not me." She picked up the key and pulled open the door.

The hall was deserted. Relieved that the key fit the lock, she locked her room -- as she now considered it -- shoved the key and rabbit's foot in her jacket pocket , and walked toward Allen's door.

Leaning against the door, she tried to hear any sign Allen might be inside. She remembered another time, years earlier, she was eleven, when she had stayed outside a bedroom door and heard sounds that changed her life. Her mother was holding her hand, and her face showed that she was in pain. "Do you hear that," she asked Shelly.

Shelly had been too frightened to reply, but she had heard the sounds of a woman calling out repeatedly in what she mistook for pain. And then she heard a man's voice. It was a deep voice, and though she couldn't make out the words, she thought it was strange how much it sounded like her father.

Her mother yanked her backwards and aimed her eyes hard into Shelly's face. "Never trust a man. They're all sons-of-bitches," she hissed, and then dragged Shelly down the stairs. In a few days, her father moved out.

Shelly suddenly realized she had been following her mother's angry advice ever since that night. She backed away from Allen's door. She wondered if she could sneak by and get a few minutes to talk to the professor alone before Allen could hear and cause more trouble.

"What were you listening to?" a voice behind her made Shelly jump.

CHAPTER 35

"Are you trying to give me a heart attack?" Shelly shouted, realizing it was Allen playing his tricks again.

"What were you doing listening in at my door? Want to hear if I snore?"

Why *had* she listened at his door? "No way! I just wanted to see if you were awake yet... But you said you don't sleep?"

"I don't. I never knew how nice it was to sleep until I couldn't do it anymore."

"So what *did* you do all night?" Shelly asked, suspicious of the answer, still not willing to trust him. Had he been in her room after all? She wondered if ghosts really could get turned on by a naked body. She heard her mother warning her, "Never trust a man". *But what if he saved your life?*

"I listened," Allen said. "Have you ever sat around and just listened?"

"Sure, I have."

"Uhuh." Allen had a feeling that an A-type personality like Shelly never would take the time to just sit and listen to the sounds around her. "This building has a lot of strange sounds in it. I have no idea where they come from, but--"

"Good morning, Shelly," Dr. Lasker was gushing this morning, as he paced up the corridor. "I trust you slept well?" He had almost forgotten how cute this little blonde was, but her crystal blue eyes reminded him quickly. He had driven from his home early to confirm that yesterday's events had happened...that she hadn't escaped with her ghost. All night long, he had visions of how someone like her could add to his research -- if she was a true Ecto.

"Yes, thank you. It was wonderful. I love the bed. It's heaven after those army cots in the dorm!"

"You sell yourself cheap," Allen said. "One good sleep and you're ready to move in?"

"Maybe," Shelly said. "It is tempting. I'll admit that."

"I'll bet he's tempted too," Allen muttered. "The son-of-a-bitch is licking his lips."

"The only one licking his lips is you," Shelly said, and wondered why she sometimes felt about Allen the way she felt about her father. What was the vibe she kept picking up that made her so sarcastic when he was around?

"You were talking to our friend? He is here?" Dr. Lasker stared where Shelly's eyes were guiding him. "Good morning, Allen. I hope you slept well too."

"He doesn't sleep," Shelly said.

"No, I suppose not," Dr. Lasker nodded. "I have never heard of any ghosts sleeping. In all my years of experience..."

"Blah, blah, blah," Allen groaned. "Shelly, can't we get to work? I really want to find out what happened to me, and get the hell out of here before Loco over there does something horrible to you."

Shelly glared at him. "Doctor, is there someplace near where I can get something to eat?" She realized she hadn't eaten since the morning before.

"Sure. Feed your face and let me suffer," Allen complained.

"Let me guess. Ghosts don't eat?" Shelly sighed.

"In all my experience, I've never known a ghost to eat," Dr. Lasker pronounced. "Although, I suppose, if a ghost did choose to devour some poor innocent child or some defenseless small animal--"

"I do not devour small, medium, or large children or animals!" Allen roared. "He knows nothing about us ghosts, absolutely nothing! He's a fake and a fraud and I think we'd be better off without him."

"He is not a fake!" Shelly shouted at Allen.

"He said I'm a fake?" Dr. Lasker asked.

Shelly looked embarrassed. "He doesn't know what he's talking about. He's been completely wrong about everything so far."

"I have not," Allen protested.

"You have."

"Have not."

"Have. And I don't want to discuss this now. I want to eat." Shelly pulled the doctor's sleeve. "Unless you want me to go back to the student cafeteria in the SU, you'd better have some coffee right here."

Dr. Lasker smiled. "We have coffee and breakfast all ready for you. And while you are enjoying it, I will discuss with you your work in your new major. I have already made the necessary phone calls, and congratulations my dear, you are now officially a candidate for a Masters in psychology, majoring in parapsychology."

Allen groaned. "It's too late. You've been drafted into Loco Lasker's army."

"Loco Lasker? I like that." Shelly laughed despite being annoyed with Allen.

"What did you say?" Dr. Lasker asked, his temper about to explode at this new indignity.

Shelly shrugged her shoulders. "He called you Loco Lasker. Sorry. He's incorrigible."

"I don't even know what that means," Allen hissed. "But I do know loco, and this character is definitely that."

Dr. Lasker bristled at his new nickname, but refused to lose his temper, not when so much was at stake. He was beginning to believe that this ghost was for real, and if that meant he had to put up with a little ridicule, that would be fine. He smiled at Shelly, hoping to win her trust, perhaps even her affection, for he had made up his mind that winning this girl's 'loyalty' was an immediate goal. *No matter what it takes,* he mused, trying to excite himself by her shapely body and lovely face. *Let them laugh at me,* he thought, giving her a warm smile -- but in the end, just like with that idiot Dodd, the last laugh would be his. Loco Lasker, indeed!

CHAPTER 36

"This pastry is delicious. Want one?" Shelly held a cream-filled cake in the air. "Oh, I forgot you can't eat anything."

"That isn't nice, Shelly." Allen wondered why she was being mean. "And stop sneering at me with cream all over your lips!"

"Well, I don't like you making fun of Dr. Lasker while he's talking to me. I'll bet he thinks I'm making up these things you say. I'm sure he didn't like my laughing at Loco Lasker one bit."

"Okay. Fair enough. I'll only make fun of him when he's not around. Which is like never!" Allen was finding it increasingly difficult to not react to Shelly's flirtatiousness, or what he thought of as her flirting with every man around her. What the hell is wrong with me, he asked himself, totally thrown by these confusing emotions. Who knew a ghost could feel such weird emotions?

Shelly was frustrated too, but mostly by how difficult and sarcastic Allen sometimes sounded. "Don't you want him to help you? If anyone can do it, it's him. Why don't you like him?" Shelly gobbled up the Danish. "He's the most experienced in this field that we're going to find here. Last night when I told him how you thought you were murdered, I could tell he felt something. He looked sad, Allen, like he really cared."

"That guy only cares about himself and his work. He's an egomaniac who wants to build up his department and his own reputation. He'll use anyone he can to achieve his goals -- human or ghost."

"So what's wrong with that? He's ambitious and wants to build his department. Those aren't bad things. If we help him, he'll help us. Allen, we need his help. Something, or someone, has tried to kill me three times already."

"And I saved you three times."

"I know, and I'm grateful. But what if you're not there?" Shelly sighed, aware she had vocalized something she'd been worried about for a while. "Unless we find out who's after me, and why, there may come a time when you're not around, and--"

"That's never going to happen! I'll always be here to protect you. I don't know why, but I know that we are linked, destined to be together until…"

"Until I become a ghost too?" Shelly asked. *"Never trust a man"…or a ghost,* echoed in her brain. "Is that what you really want, Allen?"

"That's not what I was going to say," Allen replied, sounding upset. "I would never hurt you." But he couldn't help wondering if her becoming a ghost would solve everything. *Maybe that's why she was there two days ago. Is that our fate?* "I could never wish this for you," he said softly.

Shelly wanted to believe him, but she had also wanted to believe her father, and Jeff. "I believe you, Allen," she said, but knew she still had her doubts.

Allen felt what she was feeling and wished he could tell her what was in his heart: I would never want her to go through something like this…not even if she could be with me forever. "Shelly, you have to believe me. I'm only interested in protecting you."

Shelly smiled. "But you know someone is after me, and I know it could happen sooner than later, unless we figure out what this is all about." Shelly was trying to be calm, but the thought that someone wanted her dead was terribly frightening. She wanted to eliminate Allen as a suspect, but trust did not come easy for her. "I'm living on borrowed time now," she said. "There have already been three attempts. Who knows what's next?"

Allen was silent.

"Allen, are you here?"

"Shelly, I didn't think about all this before. I figured I would always be able to protect you."

"I believe you want to protect me, but if you find out who you are and where you belong, it wouldn't be fair to hold you here just to keep me safe. Please, Allen, please try and behave yourself, only for a little while, and let's give this doctor a chance. I've changed my major and I'm moving out of my dorm."

"You're what? You can't do that! It isn't safe here! I heard all kinds of sounds here. There's something weird going on. You can't stay here!"

"You'll be here with me. I'll be fine, and soon we'll have our answers, and then we'll both be free." Shelly wiped her lips with a cloth napkin, something unheard of in the student cafeteria, where they used brown paper towels that felt like sandpaper. "We'll both be free. Isn't that worth it?"

"We'll both be free?" Allen sighed. *How free can I possibly be without you?* he thought. "Okay. I give up. You are one strong female, and maybe you're right. I'll give this Loco Lasker a chance, but only for just so long, and only if he treats you right."

"Thank you," Shelly said. "And I promise to do whatever I can to help you find out who you are."

"Because you want to get rid of me," Allen said.

"No. Because I want my life back," Shelly replied.

"Don't you think I want that too?" Allen said. "I'd give anything I ever owned to have my life back."

Shelly heard the pleading in his voice, and immediately felt sorry for him. She wished she could grant him his wish, even if it meant giving up something she loved herself. "Allen, I wish I could give you that back. I really do."

"I believe you."

"I think you must have been a fine man," Shelly said softly. "I think you have a very kind and caring heart…when you're not busting my chops."

"I wish to hell I knew," Allen muttered and left the room.

"I bet you had a wife and children who loved you," Shelly continued, not knowing Allen had gone.

When Allen didn't reply, Shelly sipped silently at her coffee and finally called to him. "Allen? Allen?" He either wasn't answering or he had left. In either case, Shelly felt a strange emptiness in sitting alone at the table sipping her coffee. *Isn't this what I wanted?* she asked herself.

CHAPTER 37

Dr. Lasker was watching Shelly on a secret monitor in the lab, secured in the sub-basement. *Even when nobody's around, the girl is obviously having a conversation,* he thought. *Look how much she talks... Wait! Her lips have stopped.*

Had the ghost left? Was this the right time to approach her without that interfering invisible creature? He had sensed that the ghost, for lack of a better word, was suspicious of him, was helping her resist him. Now was the time to spring the trap. She had already taken the bait, staying overnight in that wonderful room. *How could anyone who ever lived in a filthy dorm ever turn down a room like that?* he mused, congratulating himself again for having insisted on giving his 'Ectos' such luxurious accommodations. *Little enough compensation for what they eventually have to go through,* he thought. *Well worth the price.*

He watched Shelly a little longer. He had to be sure. *No lips moving at all. Definitely the strangest thing I've ever seen...well, maybe not. But in someone so normal-looking? Very strange.* He thought of Swan, a former female Ecto, whose dark skin sometimes seemed to have a green tinge, whose eyes were black, but had reddish flecks in them. Where Shelly was small and petite, Swan, the descendant of Navaho shaman, was large-boned and intimidating. He had thought her invincible -- until the day she had fled from a house and he found her sitting in the dirt, tears flowing down her face. If she, with all her strength and ancestral bravery, could not survive the pressures of this unique kind of research, how would this delicate, fair-skinned, petite girl hope to survive? It almost made him want to release her, but not enough. "If it gets bad," he promised himself, knowing he might not have the willpower to save her.

Then another thought occurred to him. Dr. Lasker rushed to the door and made certain to lock it behind him. With Dodd on the loose, every room had to be secured. There was no telling what he might do.

Running, he reached the elevator and dashed inside. *I should have taken the stairs,* he thought, realizing how vulnerable elevators are to attack. He didn't breathe as the elevator rose two floors and finally reached the first basement. Only he and a few others knew about the hidden floor sandwiched between the basement and the sub-basement. It was accessible only from this elevator and with his special key. He had no time to check the floor now, so he pressed the B button and prayed he'd catch her before the ghost arrived and he blew his chance to be alone with her.

Shelly was rising from her chair as he came in.

"More coffee? I think I'll have one." He moved quickly to the samovar and poured a cup of the aromatic brew. "They make wonderful coffee here. Dinner will be lovely too."

"Dinner? I didn't see any cooking staff. I didn't think you ate here.

"With the cutbacks, we have only staff for lunch -- and dinner on the top floor of the building. We have a wonderful view of the woods from there, and of course the north side of this campus. Perhaps you'll join me for dinner tonight?"

Shelly shook her head. "I appreciate everything you're doing for me, but I'm not sure yet what I want to do."

He leaned forward looking concerned. "I thought you had pretty much made up your mind." He gave her a coaxing smile. "Didn't you like your new room? We can fix it up if there's anything else you require?"

"Well, yes. The room is lovely as is. Thank you." She thought he looked almost handsome when he smiled, and wondered what the beard hid.

A serious expression replaced the smile. "You did ask me to change your major for you? I took care of that already. Do you wish to switch it back to education now? While I think you'd make a fine reading teacher, I believe what I am about to offer you is far more interesting, challenging and rewarding."

"I'm still not sure. It's a big decision."

Dr. Lasker nodded. At least she hadn't turned him down. "Being an Ectoplasmic Researcher is not for everyone. Only a chosen few have the ability. I would like to offer you a job…not exactly a job, but more like an internship -- an internship with pay of course."

"That would help," Shelly said, knowing it was difficult for new graduate education students to find jobs on campus.

"Good. But as you know, we've had some cutbacks -- and I've had to let go most of my assistants -- but I believe you have the abilities I - this department requires to re-establish itself as the premier parapsychology program in this state, perhaps in the nation."

Shelly sighed, her ego a little deflated. "You mean, I have a ghost, and you want him for your department. Is that right?" Allen was right after all. Lasker was only interested in one thing, exploiting Allen and her for his precious department.

Lasker realized she had figured it out. He gave her a friendly smile. "Shelly, I won't lie to you. You may or may not have a ghost. I honestly don't know what you have yet, but I strongly feel we can help each other in a mutually beneficial way. I can use my considerable expertise, experience and staff to help you assist your 'friend' and thus free yourself again, while you can help me help the many people who have asked for our help with their unique problems."

Shelly noticed he had used 'help' in his last paragraph five times. "I don't understand. What kind of help do all these people want of you?"

Dr. Lasker pulled out his tablet. "Do you see all of these faces? I record them for my research. These are a mere sampling of the people who have come to us begging for help, much as you are doing--"

"I'm not begging," Shelly interrupted. "Do I want your help? Yes. Am I begging? No. If you won't help us, I'll just find someone else who will." Shelly felt indignant that he could think she was 'begging' for his help. *Arrogant idiot*, she thought. *How could I have thought he was anything but?*

"Calm down please, Shelly. I am not a diplomat, and I'm sometimes rather clumsy with words, but I assure you these people are in desperate need. First, there are few programs like ours anywhere else in this country. Second, and most important, I am going to help you, but to do so I must ask in return for your help." *Here goes,* he thought, trying to look casual and trustworthy when he knew he wasn't telling her everything. He cleared his throat. "On the off-chance that your 'friend' is truly a ghost, you may be the only one who can help all these people who are truly begging for my assistance. Look at their faces -- men, women, and even babies -- and tell me you won't take a little time and energy to help them. Please, just look?"

Shelly stared at the faces in an endless slideshow on the tablet. There were men with strained expressions, women with lifeless, dark-circled, pitiful eyes, children who appeared gaunt and emaciated and worst of all, babies whose eyes showed no luster, no sign of joy. "What happened to them?" she asked, unable to look at the faces, wondering if all this was some kind of cruel set-up to trick her into staying.

Dr. Lasker glanced at his screen. He saw the face of a young man with long brown curly hair and a tight-lipped smile. *Damn!* He shut off the program before Shelly could see Dodd's face. "Shelly, just like you, they all said they were haunted – and most still are."

Shelly was surprised. *I'm not the only one,* she thought, the faces stuck in her mind. "And they come to you for help?"

"Yes. Every year we get dozens who claim they desperately need our help."

"And you can't help them?" Shelly was beginning to understand what the doctor wanted. She just wasn't sure how she felt about it. She had a feeling she knew how Allen would feel. "I'm no guinea pig!" She could almost hear the anger in his voice. *But he said he would give it a chance...he did say that. Did he mean it? Can you trust a ghost? Can I trust Lasker?*

Dr. Lasker shrugged his shoulders. "Some of my assistants have been very good, and we've had some limited successes. We've been able to document some evidence of 'unusual' phenomena -- rare snippets of the supernatural world, that barely scratch the surface of what I suspect is the reality. Unfortunately, most of these cases remain unresolved." *And the more unresolved cases, the less funding we receive,* he added to himself. *Bloody bean-counters! Hence the shrunken department we now are fighting to resurrect.* "You have to understand that part of our funding is based on this kind of essential and desperately needed research."

"Your funding depends on solving cases of the supernatural?" Shelly asked.

Lasker was surprised at how quickly her mind worked. She was not the foolish young blonde girl he had assumed her to be. "To a very large extent, yes. That is why we are down to a skeletal staff. Most of our better assistants have sought greener pastures, better pay, at private universities and institutions elsewhere. I don't blame them, but I believe that, with your help, we can achieve much improved success -- and rebuild this department into something you and I will be proud of."

"This sounds like a bit more than I bargained for," Shelly said. "I was only looking to rid myself of a ghost, not sign on for a lifetime career as a ghost-catcher."

"We call ourselves ectoplasmic researchers." Lasker tried to look humble. "I fully understand, and assure you that you need not make a commitment at this time. All I ask is that you consider giving me one semester to prove the worth of our project and studies. I've already changed your major. I know it's a big change, but if you imagine the possibilities, I'm certain you will want to try this. And you will be paid, which should help your finances considerably"

"I don't know," Shelly said, thinking very hard about his offer. She suspected he wasn't telling her everything.

"I have a case right now," Dr. Lasker said, quickly pulling a folder out of his lab coat. He flipped open the folder. "This is a photograph of a beautiful antique house. It was built in the early 1800s and has belonged to many families ever since -- all with tragic histories. Why? Can a house be evil? All I ask is that you look at the photograph of this house, and tell me what you feel."

Shelly sighed. "You tried that ESP junk with me yesterday, and you saw that without Allen I just don't have it."

"I'm not asking for your ESP, I'm asking you to just give me your first thoughts on seeing this house. Once you do that, you are free to go back into teaching if you wish. I just hope you will want to stay with me and give this 'ghost-catching', as you call it, a chance. No obligation. I promise." He pushed the photograph in front of her. "Just one look is all I ask."

Shelly gazed down at the photo and felt a chill immediately race down her spine. She wiped beads of sweat off her forehead. "I feel cold," she muttered.

"My reaction exactly," Dr. Lasker said. Now look back on the faces of the current family, and say you will not help them."

Oh God, I wish I could say that. Shelly moaned, knowing she had fallen into his trap.

CHAPTER 38

"Allen," Shelly was calling him through his door. "Please talk to me."

"Why? You only want to get rid of me. I already said I'll do whatever it takes to help you do that, so let's get started. Did you ever think I might want to be free of you too?"

"It has nothing to do with that. Dr. Lasker has a job for us."

"I knew it! I told you he was a sneaky rat! I can't believe the balls on this guy!"

"Wait a minute! Will you just stop and listen for a change?" Shelly couldn't believe a ghost could carry on like this. She opened the door and walked in. "He's not a rat! He wants to help people who--"

"He wants to help himself, you mean. I told you and I told you. This guy only wants us for what we can do for him. He's a snake in sheep's clothing. He's a terminal rat."

Shelly was losing her temper. "Shut up and look at this picture." She threw the picture down on his table.

"What is it? What has that con artist conned you into now?" Suddenly Allen became quiet. "What is this place?" he asked. "I felt a chill race through my body. I didn't know ghosts could feel chills. Hell, I don't even have a body!"

"I felt it too," Shelly said. "It has the same effect on everyone."

"Even Loco?" Allen's eyes were drawn to the top of the large house in the photograph. It was like being drawn by a magnet. "The funny thing is, Shelly, I think I've seen this house before."

"You remember something?" At least he had stopped carrying on.

"I don't know, but there's something about this house that's drawing me to it. Is that how you feel about it too?"

"Yes, but I've never seen it before. You think you have?"

Allen studied the house closer. "The porch looks new…like it's been expanded. The gingerbread shingles on the side… I've seen this house before. I know I have." He tried to lift the photo with his fingers, but no matter how he tried, he couldn't do it.

"I'm going with Dr. Lasker to this house today," Shelly said.

"Oh no, you're not!" Allen shouted. "It's too dangerous! Something wants you there, and that's not good. You've already had three close calls, and--"

"Come with me. Help me help these poor people who live in this house." Shelly held the picture up so he could see it again. "That's all Dr. Lasker wants us to do. He wants us to help these people get rid of their pain and suffering."

"I told you! You are *so* damn naïve! Well, I'm not falling for his tricks. I'm not going! If he wants my help, first he has to help me."

"You're so damn stubborn! I'm going, with you or without you," Shelly stormed. "I know what it's like to be haunted, and I'm going to do whatever I can to help them."

"It's too dangerous for you! Please, let's think about this. Why do we have to do this right now?" Allen still felt that awful chill as he stared at the house in the photograph.

"This family is going through hell, and someone will be hurt or killed if we don't do something now," Shelly said.

"Oh, you're so stubborn! You remind me of… someone, but I have no idea who."

"You see? Maybe the more you try and help me, the more you'll remember. Isn't that worth a try?"

"I hate seeing that Loco Lasker get his own way. I don't trust him. There's something he's not telling us."

"With you to take care of me, I know I'll be fine."

"Flattery won't get you anywhere with me," Allen said, but he realized that wasn't true. He actually was surprised and flattered that she finally seemed to realize he had been protecting her. That was an improvement. "Okay. I don't like it, but this house gives me the willies, so I'm going to go with you this time -- but I'm not letting your mad scientist take advantage of me."

"Thank you, Allen," she said. "I knew you wouldn't let me down."

"You did, did you?" He kind of liked that at last she seemed to be showing trust in him...at least a little. "Just don't take me for granted."

Shelly picked up the picture again -- and suddenly an electric-like charge shot through her brain. She dropped the photograph and was afraid to pick it up again. It was as if she had dropped a lit match. There were tears of pain in her eyes.

Allen could not help but notice. "If just the photo of this house can do that to you, Shelly, then imagine what the real house must be like," he said, searching his memory to try and remember where he had seen this house before.

"I know you're right," Shelly said, "But Allen, I really want to help if we can."

"We?" Allen asked.

"We," Shelly replied and gave him a warm smile.

CHAPTER 39

When Shelly tried to find Dr. Lasker and notify him that Allen and she were willing to visit the house in the photograph, she was surprised to find his office locked. The doctor didn't appear to be anywhere in the building. Instead he had left a note on her door and a set of car keys. The note said she was to use the car to collect her things from the dorm and bring them back with her, ASAP. It also said he would see her at dinner on the top floor of the psychology B building, at four-thirty sharp.

Shelly noticed that the fob attached to the car keys was, once again, a rabbit's foot. "Someone must be very superstitious," she said as she went to find Allen, whom she supposed would be back in his room. When he didn't reply to her repeated calling, she decided to leave him a note taped to his door. It read, "Have gone back to dorm to get clothing."

Once she had taken care of that loose end, Shelly walked over to the stairwell and pulled at the knob. It wouldn't open. "Why would they lock this?" she wondered. She studied the key fob and tried a key marked with a red dot, nail polish perhaps. Sure enough the key fit, and she pulled open the heavy door.

The stairwell was very dark. She searched for a light switch, but was unable to find one. Shelly had to feel her way up the stairs, her hand gripping the banister. Usually she could run stairs, but not in the dark, not in an unfamiliar stairwell, not when she couldn't see where she was heading.

She climbed four sets of stairs and was surprised to find there wasn't a door on the landing. "I guess I have to keep going," she thought, wondering why the building was built so strangely. After the sixth set of stairs she saw the sign that said 1st Floor, and pushed open the door. "That's the darndest thing," she mused. "It took six staircases to go from the basement to the first floor. I must have miscounted." Or maybe one of the basements had an unusually high ceiling, like a gym. No big deal, though.

In the lobby she saw a different guard seated at the information desk. He was reading a comic book, which he quickly hid when the stairway door opened. He looked puzzled seeing her.

"Hi," she called. "I'm new."

"Hi," he gave her a quick smile. "I'm old."

Shelly laughed. "No, you're not."

"Thanks," he said, "Sometimes on this job I feel like I'm getting old." He leaned forward. "There isn't much to do here. Hardly anybody comes into this building." He shrugged his shoulders. "I'm Andy Weil."

"Hi, Andy. I'm Shelly, and brand new."

"You came from that stairway?" Andy was studying her face with its clean, intelligent lines, no heavy makeup (he hated that goth stuff) and sharp blue eyes. "Are you in psych?" He laughed. "I guess you must be, or what would you be doing in the psych building?"

"I'm with Dr. Lasker," Shelly said. "I'm thinking of becoming an assistant."

Andy looked around. Satisfied that nobody was nearby, he leaned forward. "I'm glad he got rid of his old one. He never even talked to me. He gave me the creeps."

"And I don't give you the creeps?" Shelly asked, knowing she was teasing him.

"That's it! You're flirting again," Allen hissed. "I can't leave you alone for one second."

"Oh no, not you again!" Shelly whirled toward where she had heard Allen's voice.

Andy looked confused. "Excuse me. What did you say? Have we met before?"

Shelly turned back to the guard, who was staring at her as if she was crazy. She saw he had a nice face, tanned skin, no beard or mustache, neatly arched brows and soft brown eyes. He looked muscular, but not muscle-bound. "No. I'd remember if we'd met before."

Andy smiled. "Yeah. So would I."

"I can't believe you!" Allen roared. "Why don't you just save the chit-chat and jump on his bones already?"

"I don't do that!" Shelly barked -- and saw the confused look in Andy's eyes. "I'm sorry. I didn't mean you."

The look on Andy's face told her he was protecting himself from the crazy new assistant who was replacing another crazy assistant. "It was nice talking to you Andy."

His look softened. "Me too," he said softly, as if afraid she would dissolve into madness again if he was too loud. "Good luck. I hope you get the job."

"That's not all he hopes," Allen hissed. "You really do need my protection. You just don't understand men." Allen wondered why he should even care that she flirted with every guy around, but as weird as it was, he did. No amount of logic seemed to take away the anger he felt when she appeared to be angling for a date. *Can a ghost be jealous?* he wondered. *What the hell can I hope for in a relationship with a mortal? I don't understand it at all.* "

Shelly gave Allen a dirty look and forced herself not to reply to him, knowing that would only serve to confuse anybody who was listening. "Thank you. It's a tough decision, but I'm thinking about it more now." She flashed Andy a brilliant smile. She knew it would aggravate Allen, but she didn't care.

"Well, I'll say one thing for you. You have a much nicer smile than the last guy."

"I'm getting sick," Allen said. "I'll wait for you in the car."

"What car?" Shelly said. "I forgot to ask the professor what car to take."

Andy looked into his desktop computer. "Professor Lasker has several cars listed in his department. May I see the key?"

Shelly handed him the key.

"Is that a rabbit's foot? I haven't seen one of those in years. Are you superstitious? They're supposed to bring good luck."

"Except for the rabbit," Shelly said, and laughed at her own joke.

"Oh, brother," Allen sighed. "We're losing time here."

"I guess you're right. I never thought about it before, but for centuries rabbits have had to sacrifice themselves so others could have protection from bad luck. Weird, huh?" Andy gave her a smile and went back to searching the key chart.

"I'm leaving," Allen threatened again.

Shelly sighed. "I never thought of it that way before." She also realized that she had never thought that, to protect some strangers from god-knows-what-kinds of monsters, Dr. Loco was willing to sacrifice Allen and herself. "I'm a rabbit," Shelly said softly.

Andy didn't hear her. "This key is from a Ford van. I see on our monitors it's parked behind the building." He returned the key.

"I was hoping for something more exciting," Shelly murmured.

Andy smiled. "I have a '66 Mustang. Original bucket seats."

Shelly smiled and then quickly looked serious, just in case Allen was still around. *Invisible chaperones are the pits*, she thought, wondering how much longer she was going to be saddled with her ghostly companion.

CHAPTER 40

"It's about time you stopped flirting and got out here," Allen said. "The van is in the back of the building, alright -- all the way in the back."

"I haven't jogged today," Shelly said, and began to run at a leisurely pace around the adjoining parking fields that separated the two psychology towers. "Look how many cars are in that lot," Shelly said, noting that there were only a few empty parking spaces by building A.

"I've got a feeling you're hitching up with a falling star," Allen said, easily keeping up with Shelly. "You know, I do remember one thing about my former life."

"You do?" Shelly stopped running. "Really?"

"I remember I enjoyed running."

Shelly started off again. "That's not much help," she muttered, thinking that with his personality he would have had to do a lot of running -- away from people wanting to kill him. But she suddenly recalled that Allen had been murdered, so this wasn't funny, not at all. As much as she wanted to be rid of him, she had to admit she was feeling sorry for him -- sorry for how he had died, sorry for his being so alone. *How can I have feelings for a ghost?* she wondered, but knew she did. "A lot of people like running," she said.

"You don't understand. The first time I saw you, you were running. I think, by saving you, I was able to remember that one thing about my past."

Shelly stopped jogging again. "What about the second time, when you saved me from the bus? Did that make you remember anything?"

"I think it did. I remembered I wasn't a bus driver."

Shelly groaned. "Really? Did you really think that, of all the things you might have been, you were a bus driver? Not that there's anything wrong with that, but somehow I don't see you driving a bus for a living."

"You don't see me at all," Allen said with some bitterness.

Shelly sighed. She was beginning to realize that this whole mess was tough on Allen too. "So we can rule out you being a bus driver?"

"Yes. I think so. But the funny thing is, I remembered hearing the sound of a bus...or maybe a truck...sometime shortly before I died. That bus almost hitting you brought that back I guess."

"Those aren't great clues," Shelly said.

"I know, but it's the best I have so far."

Shelly bent down and took several deep breaths. "What about the third time, when you saved me from being poisoned by gas?"

"I only had to leave a note. That wasn't as hard as materializing, like I did before. Maybe that's why I didn't remember anything."

"Maybe you did, but don't know it yet. It could be something so obvious you just overlooked it."

"Well, we can't overlook the van! Wow!" Allen wondered if Shelly was really going to try and drive this thing.

"That's the van? Are you sure? What a piece of junk!" Shelly stared at a large Ford van whose hood and sides looked like someone had poured acid on top. The paint looked as if it had bubbled up and started to peel. "This can't be right." Shelly tried the key in the door, and unfortunately it worked. "Figures he'd give me something like this. I'll bet he's got a Cadillac or something flashy for himself."

"I keep telling you--"

"Shut up, Allen!" Shelly yanked open the door -- and almost fell over backwards. "What's that smell?"

"What smell? Ghosts don't smell things. We also can't taste things, touch things or..."

"What is that awful smell?" Shelly repeated, recoiling from the distinctive odor. "Wait a minute. I've got to open the windows."

"What windows? This is a van, Shelly. There are only the driver and passenger windows."

Shelly pulled open the rear doors. "I'm not getting in this thing until some of the stink is gone. You sure you can't smell anything?"

"No," Allen replied, trying to inhale some of the odor.

"That doesn't make sense."

"What doesn't?"

"If you can't smell anything, how did you know the air in that lab was poison gas?"

"I never thought of that."

"But you did know?"

"Yes, I did. How do you explain that?" Allen asked.

Shelly took another whiff of the inside of the van. "You can't smell this awful rotten egg odor, but you did recognize the poison. Maybe that was the one thing you were able to remember."

"I recognized a poison gas? It was some form of chlorine, wasn't it?"

"I think that's what the professor said. Chlorine? Maybe you were a pool attendant."

"A pool attendant?"

Shelly burst out laughing at the image of Allen as a hunky pool boy in a tight red bathing suit. *With a voice like his? Much too old to be a pool boy.* "I'm kidding. But you did something where you learned to recognize the smell of chlorine gas." *But not sulfur.* She sniffed again and withdrew her head. "I think that every time you save me you remember another piece of the puzzle."

"So you're saying it's almost like a gift I get, every time I do something good for you? Is that what you think?"

"I don't know, but you did remember the smell of the gas because you were concentrating on protecting me. Maybe you were right all along. Maybe we are meant to be together, at least until you find out who you are."

"Don't you mean who I was?" Allen said, as he watched Shelly swing the van's rear doors shut, wishing he could help her. He couldn't help feeling she was in terrible danger, and there was very little he could do about it.

"No, I mean who you are. Allen, you may be a ghost, but you haven't changed. You're still the kind man you were when you were alive." She realized that she meant it. He really was a kind person, even if he was a pain-in-the-ass ghost. She pondered that as she got in the van, cinched on her seat-belt and started the engine.

Allen was silent. He wondered if ghosts could cry. He felt as if he could, but there were no tears in his eyes. "Thank you, Shelly. I hope you're right. I hope I was…I mean, am, the kind of man you think I was…am. Damn, this is confusing."

"Well, let me concentrate on my driving," Shelly said. "I've never driven a hunk of junk like this."

"Now you tell me," Allen said. "I should have known better than to get into a car being driven by you."

"Uhuh," Shelly said, "You're not being very kind." She gave him a warm glance.

"Look out!" Allen screamed.

Shelly peered out the window and saw a man standing in the middle of the road, just fifty feet in front of the van. She stepped hard on the brakes, which squealed in pain as they tried to grip the nearly bald tires. The van swung to the other side of the road, and Shelly struggled to bring it back. She turned the steering wheel as fast as she could and held her foot on the brakes. The rear doors exploded open and the van flipped over on its side, and then flipped over again and again.

CHAPTER 41

The first inkling Shelly had that she was still alive was she could feel pain where her seat belt had dug into her. She could taste blood in her mouth where her teeth had bit into her tongue, and she could feel her head throbbing as a thin stream of blood dripped onto her blouse. "What happened?" she asked, unable to move.

There wasn't any reply.

"Allen?" She searched the van with her eyes. "Are you okay?"

With no answer, Shelly tried to push the release on her seat belt. Her fingers couldn't press the release hard enough. "Damn, they hurt!" She looked. Her fingers seemed twisted. "Damn, they're broken," she groaned, settling back in the seat, waiting for someone to come and release her.

Someone would come soon. She would be alright if she didn't move. She let her eyes close. She couldn't stop them.

It was silent in the van, easy to fall asleep.

And then she smelled a familiar odor. She sometimes smelled it when she accidentally poured too much gasoline into her car tank. Her eyes opened. "Gas?"

She pressed the seat belt release again. Harder and harder, she pressed the red release button until her fingers ached, but it would not release.

The gasoline smell was stronger.

She peered out the window and in the mirror saw a puddle forming near the van. She had seen enough movies to know what was about to happen.

Allen? Where is he? He'll save me. "Allen," she called. "Allen?"

Why didn't he answer?

The image of her sitting in this van as flames roared up around her sent chills of fear down her back. Ever since she was a child she had always been afraid of fire. Scenes of burning bodies, often her own, terrified her in recurring dreams.

Shelly pushed at the release button again and again. "Why isn't anyone coming?" And then she remembered that the psych buildings were isolated from the rest of the campus, and this back road, a short cut, was hardly ever used.

Shelly screamed. The pain in her chest was worse when she screamed, but she continued desperately calling for help. "Damn it Allen, where the hell are you?"

Suddenly she saw someone walking toward the van. "Help me," she cried. "Please help me!"

The man reached up to the driver's-side window. "You're still alive," he said, and frowned. "I can't believe you survived again. You're like a damn cat."

Shelly felt as if she were losing consciousness, but was still able to see the leering smile as Dodd looked at the gasoline puddle forming under the van. "I tried to warn you," he said. "I did everything I could to warn you to stay away."

Shelly's eyes were closing, but she was fighting it, too aware of the smell of gasoline. She looked to where Dodd had been standing. There was nobody there. Was he real or was he imagined? She found it hard to believe any human being, really human, could leave another human being -- even if they hated them for some unknown reason -- to be burnt alive. He had to be another hallucination, another ghostly character, just as unreal as the imaginary friend she called Allen. Where was her imaginary ghost friend when she needed him? *There is no Allen. There is no Dodd. There is no Shelly in a car about to burst into flame.*

Her fingers kept pressing the release button even as she drifted into the sleep that would ease her trip into death. "Allen," she called, "I'm sorry."

Allen was focusing as hard as he could on materializing to save Shelly yet again. He had seen the man in the middle of the road, but it had been too late to prevent the accident. Now, blaming himself, he was unable to focus his energy on what he needed to do to save her. There had been something horrifying about the man in the middle of the road. He had stood there as if he didn't care if he were killed by the van. Allen had seen what looked like a smile on the man's face. He had barely enough time to scream a warning because the face had seemed familiar, a face he had seen before, but couldn't remember where…

And then he knew. It was the long hair and the desperate blue eyes… Dodd.

CHAPTER 42

Why had Dodd been standing in the middle of the road like that? Why wasn't he helping? Allen tried to push the safety belt release button, but his fingers had no solidity to them. It was like pushing with fingers made of water. "I can't save you this time," he moaned to the unconscious Shelly. "I'm trying. I'm really trying."

Allen's nose twitched. "I smell something," he said. His mind told him it was gasoline. An image flashed into his brain, sending an electric shock through his being. He saw a car suddenly burst into flame. He could not have told what kind of car it was -- its color, or if anyone was seated in the front and back seat of the car -- but the image was real enough to shock him away from all his distracting thoughts, just enough that he was able to concentrate on his right hand. *If only I can make that one small part of me real,* he growled, focusing all his strength on making his hand visible, palpable.

He saw it first as a grayish mist, and then slowly taking physical shape. It was forming so slowly…too slowly. The gas puddle was reflecting small dancing flames. Allen forced the nearly formed hand to reach for the release button. He strained every shred of whatever power he had left to push the release button again. "It still won't move," he moaned.

Desperately, Allen searched for something or someone that could help Shelly. He saw the man with the smirking face a short distance from the driver's door as the sparks from the sputtering engine finally set the gasoline alight. The man appeared fascinated by the tiny flame that seemed to be dancing taller, wilder, bright orange, on the plume of fluid leaking from the car. "Save her, damn you, Dodd!" Allen screamed, and then he saw the flames rise higher and move with more violence toward the front of the van. "Why the hell aren't you saving her?" he screamed at the statue-like figure. "I'll let you have her," Allen promised, in one last effort to make the man move. Nothing happened.

"She's out of time," Allen murmured. Never once tempted to let her die, even if she would be his ghostly companion for eternity, he spotted her fingers still automatically pressing down on the stalled button. She didn't have enough strength.

Dodd felt strange. He had heard someone calling his name, but who? There was nobody here except Shelly, and she couldn't have seen him. She was almost gone. The threat was over.

"Please, Dodd, she's a good person. Don't let her die! It's not too late for you." Allen was focused on making Dodd hear him. "All she wants is to be free of me. Help her! Dodd, you love her."

Dodd stared at the van. He saw Shelly, flames melting her flesh. He heard a voice crying that he loved her. "I can't do this!" he shouted and ran toward the driver's door.

Dodd pulled hard at the handle and the door swung open. The seat next to Shelly was already in flame. He could feel the intense heat as he reached over Shelly's skirt for the seat belt release. Shelly's hand seemed frozen on the red button. He pushed her fingers away and slammed his thumb on the button. It was stuck. He tried again, pressing down as hard as he could, his eyes on Shelly's face -- and the buckle finally released.

Smoke was filling his lungs and he coughed hard. It was difficult to see with the smoke and the flames licking at the back of the seat. Dodd reached under Shelly, and with all his strength he pulled her body off the seat -- and fell backwards with her clasped in his arms.

He clutched her as he pulled himself away from the truck. He could hardly see, and he was coughing from the smoke, but he had succeeded in getting her out of the van.

Then he heard a rumble and he had a vivid vision of the van exploding. He saw Shelly lying on the grass, blood covering her body, a large piece of metal sticking up from her chest and her eyes gazing at him in mute accusation. He tried to move, but he was exhausted from pulling her away from the van. "Too close. Too close," he murmured, as the flames roared just overhead. He closed his eyes.

"Help her, Dodd!" Allen shouted again.

Dodd heard the voice calling and opened his eyes. He didn't want to see what he knew was about to happen…what he had made happen. "I can't," he whispered, "It's done."

"Damn you, help her!" Allen screamed, unable to materialize enough to roll Shelly down the grass-covered slope, away from the car.

An explosion sent metal flying toward them. Allen threw himself over her, but a slab of metal from the roof struck her on her back. He realized he couldn't materialize again, not so soon after trying to release her from the van.

"Oh god," Dodd moaned, as something tore into his leg. Tears were streaming down his face, and his eyes were still blurry. "What have I done?" he asked, searching for Shelly.

Dodd saw blood oozing through her shirt. "I can't let her die", he said, rising weakly to his knees and then falling flat on the ground again.

"Get up, you useless piece of shit!" Allen shouted. "This is your fault!"

Dodd rose again. "Who the hell are you?" he asked, unable to see anyone near.

"Help her, damn you!" Allen said. "She needs you."

Dodd turned toward Shelly. "Shelly, you've got to move!" he shouted, shaking her, wishing he could have protected her from the pieces of glass and metal that were falling on her clothes and hair. "Come on, Shelly, get up!"

Shelly's eyes were barely open. "Who are you?" she said, unable to see anything but the smoke and flames from the van hanging halfway over the slope.

"Dodd, remember? You've got to move now!"

Shelly forced herself up on one knee and then fell back down.

Allen shouted, "Damn it, Shelly! Are you going to let someone kill you like this?"

Shelly's eyes opened and she began to cry. "I'm hurt. It hurts so much."

"I know," Dodd said. "Honey, I know. But you have to move! If you don't you'll die, and I can't let that happen."

Shelly saw the fire and smelled the smoke reaching toward her. "I don't want to die."

"I know." Dodd heard another explosion. "Roll down the hill. Just let yourself roll down the hill."

"I can't," Shelly said. "It hurts."

Allen focused on Shelly's face. It was covered with blood and black grease stains. Her hair was wild and blackened. He felt scared for her, and sad that Dodd could want to do this to her. He felt his anger rising -- and suddenly he was on the ground, his feet pressed hard against her, pushing her, but still unable to move her. "Help me roll her down the slope," he urged Dodd, who was staring at Shelly's face. "I won't tell her it was you if you help me now."

Dodd wondered who was urging him to help her. Was it his conscience? Had one of his voices finally overcome the others? It didn't matter. There was no time. He forced himself to crawl to her side, the pain from his leg excruciating. Knowing it was going to hurt horribly, he braced his legs against her. The sharp metal shaft was still in his right leg. He tried to reach it. His hand clutched the thin shaft, and he pulled hard. The sharp metal cut into his palm and he had to release it. He saw blood dripping now from his hands. He had caused this pain. He had caused Shelly to feel this pain. He wished he had something to protect his hands, but there wasn't any time left. He locked his hands on the sharp metal shaft and pulled. He let out an agonized scream as he finally dislodged the piece from his leg. He felt faint, blood gushing from his hands, but he braced his legs against Shelly's side. He heard someone shout, "Now," and with what little strength he had left he pushed his feet hard against Shelly. "Harder!" someone screamed, and with his eyes squeezed shut and pain shooting through his body, he pushed as hard as he could -- and finally Shelly began rolling down the slope.

"We did it," Dodd heard someone gasp. He looked around, but nobody was near.

There was a loud explosion again, as what was left of the van seemed to jump into the sky. A large slab of metal came rushing toward Dodd, and he threw himself down the hill. The car door slammed into his back, and he let out another cry of pain.

Allen had rolled down the cliff, holding onto Shelly. He was exhausted, unable to do one more thing to help her. He suddenly understood that each time he tried to save her, he was not only remembering something of his former life, but was also losing some of his strength. He gazed up at the flaming van and saw that it was teetering over the edge of the cliff.

Shelly was unconscious. He couldn't even materialize enough to shake her. Where was Dodd? This was his fault!

The noise of the van tumbling down the hill was like the roaring of a train, but it didn't wake Shelly.

Allen crawled toward her and covered her body with his own, but knew that, unable to materialize, he could not protect her. Suddenly he saw Dodd pulling himself up the hill. He watched silently as Dodd reached Shelly and covered her with his body.

CHAPTER 43

"Where am I?"

It seemed so trite, a cliché of a question, but what else could she ask? Shelly reached up and felt bandages on her face. She swore to fight the tears as she wondered if her face was still there. After that gasoline explosion, and all that fire and smoke, she had good reason to worry.

"You're at University hospital," a voice nearby replied. "You've been in an accident." He decided not to add, "And lucky to be alive."

Shelly moved her head slightly so she could see who was speaking. It was a bearded man with round wire-framed glasses and clear gray eyes. "You're Dr. Lasker," Shelly said, recognizing the doctor who was staring at her. Why did he look so worried?

Lasker moved so she could see without changing her position. "Are you okay? Is there anything I can do for you?"

Shelly felt the tears again. "Mom? Does she know?" She searched the room. If her mother found out about all this she would be up here like a shot, trying to drag Shelly out of school. "I told you to commute," she would say. And then she'd add, "You can't trust any man." Shelly sighed. "Tell me you didn't call her."

"I was waiting for you. The doctors say you'll be fine in a day or two. You have only mild abrasions, incredibly enough."

"Don't tell her," Shelly said. "She'll want to take me home."

"Maybe that would be best for a while," Dr. Lasker said, surprising himself. "You've had some very close calls." He found it hard to believe he was saying this, knowing what it might cost him, but he had been shaken when he saw what was left of his van. "Maybe you should take a semester off? I'll hold open your position until you come back." *If there's any department left after I report this van accident,* he thought. *Why did I let this accident-waiting-to-happen drive our van?*

"I'm not leaving. Not on your life," Shelly growled. "I've had it with whoever's trying to get rid of me. This makes me more determined than ever."

"Determination is close to stubbornness. Please consider taking a short break. I want you... That didn't come out right. I need your help, very much so, but not at the risk of your life." *Or of my department.*

"And I need you, to help me get rid of that ghost and get back to normal as fast as possible." She sank back into the pillow. Suddenly she felt the tears again. "My face? What will it be like?" She braced herself for bad news. She tried to tell herself she could be strong, but a face is something you get used to seeing in the mirror every day. A face is what makes each person special. *My face is me,* she thought.

"There's nothing wrong with your face, I am told – nothing worse than a sunburn The bandages are there to protect you until Dr. Medford, a friend and an excellent surgeon, gives you the all clear."

"No plastic surgery?" She felt the tears flow, unable to stop them.

"Yes, you're still the same ugly, stubborn, little girl as always," he said, letting himself smile for the first time. "Now, if you're strong enough, I would like you to tell me how you came to destroy my truck."

I knew his niceness wouldn't last, Shelly thought, as the idea that she was going to be alright began to sink in. And then she had another thought, a question which only she could answer: Where was Allen? Could a ghost be destroyed in a car accident? Had he been killed in the explosion? Wasn't he dead already? What do you call it when you 'terminate' a ghost?

"So? I am waiting, Shelly. Why did you crash my truck? I would never have lent it to you if I'd known you were unable to drive it." Dr. Lasker sighed. "I mean, I'm very grateful you are going to be okay, but I wondered if something happened before you crashed and drove it over the side of the road. Can you remember?"

"I'm a good driver... but something did happen." She tried to remember, which made her head hurt. She remembered Allen had screamed. When she turned her head she had seen..."

"What's wrong? What do you see? Is your ghost here? Hello, Allen....I wish I could see him." Dr. Lasker was out of his seat, searching the room in the hope he might finally see this mysterious creature known as Allen.

Shelly wished she could see him too... and hear him. "No, I don't think he's here. I haven't heard him since the accident. Maybe he's gone? Maybe he's had enough of all these crazy things, and gone back to where he came from." Shelly wasn't sure she was happy with that, even though she had wanted it from the first day she'd encountered this ghost. *I'm just in shock from the wreck,* she told herself, but she knew there was more to her feeling of loss than the accident could explain.

Dr. Lasker sighed. If the ghost had really left, the girl would be useless even if she was stubborn enough to stay. Even though he liked Shelly, definitely felt some sympathy for her current condition, the truth was that without her ghostly friend she was a luxury the department, he, could not afford. "Shelly, when was the last time you heard Allen?"

Shelly closed her eyes. The sound of Allen's screaming brought back too many frightening images. She saw the fire and smoke...could almost smell it, and she heard the explosion. Allen had screamed just before the crash. He was warning her about something, but what was it? Suddenly she remembered. "He was screaming at me that something was in the road."

"Something? Like a dog or cat?" Dr. Lasker asked, thinking how foolish and wasteful it was to lose a van over a stray animal.

Shelly opened her eyes. "No... It was a man...I saw him. He wasn't moving. I couldn't see his face, but he looked tall...and I think he had long, dark hair...."

Dr. Lasker's body tensed. He was grateful she could not see the look on his face. *Damn that Dodd!* he cursed silently. "Are you sure it was a man and not some animal?" he asked, trying to sound more relaxed than he felt. *What the hell is he up to now? It had to be him.*

"Yes. It was definitely a man." She closed her eyes and the face reappeared. The lips were tight. She stared at the lips and the intense blue eyes and gasped, "I think it was Dodd!" *But why?* she wondered. Why would he want her dead? Her mind was conjuring up his face again, but this time his lips were soft...she had wanted to kiss him...but his eyes had never softened...always steely and hard to read. *I would have made love to you,* she heard her brain saying, unable to understand why suddenly she felt afraid of him. She opened her eyes and saw Lasker studying her. *What does he know?*

Dr. Lasker frowned. "I've told you before, dear Shelly, I've never heard of anyone with such a name. It must be your imagination...perhaps some residual shock? Now get some rest, and I'll come back later today. Would you like me to bring you anything?"

He looks so caring, so concerned, Shelly mused for a second -- and then remembered who she was dealing with. She closed her eyes and thought, *Yes, bring me the damn truth.*

CHAPTER 44

It was hard for Shelly to stop thinking about all that had happened to her in the last few days. Even in the hospital she kept expecting to hear Allen -- or worse yet, see the unpredictable, perhaps evil, creature who had called himself Dodd. Allen she had finally come to accept as being a ghost, but what was Dodd*? Is he a ghost too? Can you fall in love with a ghost?,* she asked herself, remembering how she had wanted to feel his body in her bed, see his hair bouncing over his shoulders as he gazed down at her while they made love.

Shelly had first thought Dodd was kind of strange-looking -- dark, thin and mysterious -- and soon found herself responding to him, feeling her body wanting him, despite her efforts to be cautious. She thought he looked unique, like a mischievous boy, but in a wild-looking sort of way. He was mysterious, and she loved that even while she sensed he was dangerous -- and then he had tried to kill her... Had he? It had to be him...first poison gas...and then standing in the middle of a deserted street and making himself a target for Dr. Loco's van. Yes, she now was convinced it had been Dodd who was standing in the middle of the road, deliberately trying to force the van to brake hard and hurl her down the steep slope to a fiery explosion. And she was now positive it was Dodd whom she had seen standing and watching as the gasoline had leaked into a deadly puddle, just before she was finally freed from the safety belts. How could he watch so impassively, so coldly, as she was about to die? *I thought he liked me! It makes no sense. Why does he hate me?*

None of it made sense, but what did these days? Did believing in a ghost make sense? How about believing a ghost could be good, caring...loving? She thought of Allen and wondered where he was...and where is Dodd?

Dodd made no sense at all. Maybe Dodd wasn't real. Maybe he was a ghost too, a malevolent ghost with an advanced degree in materialization! Very confusing. Very scary. All these disturbing thoughts kept racing around in her brain as she recuperated in the hospital.

* * * * *

The bandages had all been removed, and Shelly was relieved that at least about her face Dr. Loco hadn't lied. As she examined herself in the mirror, she realized how close she had come to not only losing that irreplaceable part of her, but her life. And it had all started with Allen. Was it somehow his fault? Was he the real reason why someone was trying to kill her…why Dodd was trying to kill her?

Shelly found that all these thoughts whirring around in her head were driving her crazy. When Dr. Lasker returned in the afternoon, she had made up her mind about a lot of things and was ready for him.

"You look better," Lasker said. "I told you your face would be as lovely as ever. A few more days and you can go home and get some much-needed rest. I'll take care of everything." He gave her a reassuring smile. "We'll call it a recuperative--"

Shelly didn't smile back. "I'm not going home. I've made up my mind. I'm going to do whatever it takes to be on your team, and help myself get back to normal. I'm going to hold you to your promise to help Allen, and in return I'll work with you on your cases. I'll become an Ecto for you."

"No, no, no! I simply can't allow you to take such risks," Dr. Lasker said, a worried look on his face. "I was wrong to even ask you. I can find another assistant. I have many names on a waiting list…people who are not being threatened with murder at every turn."

"But none with their own ghost to help you." Shelly gave him a knowing smile.

Dr. Lasker felt anxious. She was definitely not as dumb as he'd once assumed. *Beauty and brains and a ghost is not a good combination,* he thought. "That may have been true—" he began.

Shelly cut him off. "You don't have to hide it. I know exactly what you want from me. I'm willing to give it to you, but you are going to do what you can to help Allen. That's the deal. Take it, or all those poor people you showed me will keep on suffering, and you'll miss out on the greatest research project of your career." She could almost taste his drool as he hungered for what having a ghost -- and her -- on his team would mean to his department, and to him.

Dr. Lasker got out of his chair and walked to the window. From the twelfth floor where the private rooms were, he could not make out faces on the sidewalk below. All the tiny creatures moving about in their 'ordinary' lives, far below, were barely distinguishable from each other to the doctor -- who wished he could see who was standing next to his car and gazing up at this room. *It could be Dodd, but how can I be sure? Damn that lunatic!* he thought, but hid his anger from Shelly. He wanted the girl on his team so badly, but realized it would be signing her death warrant. "Shelly, I'm afraid you are not safe here."

"Tell me something I don't know."

The doctor turned away from the window. He gazed into her eyes and felt strangely protective, not a usual characteristic. *It's just that she's so young,* he rationalized, but he knew it was more than that. He rested his hand on her bed, hoping she would place her hand on top of his. It didn't happen, but he hadn't expected it to. Not really. He gazed into her eyes and for once told her the truth. "I now believe there is someone who may want to do you harm."

"So now you believe me?"

"I never disbelieved you. But now with this latest incident… Yes, I believe you, and have come to the conclusion that you working with me, as much as I would desire it… " *Desire? Did I really use that word?* "At any rate, your further involvement in this department would place you in intolerable danger." He couldn't understand why he was doing this. Why was he feeling compelled to protect her? "I'm truly sorry."

Shelly sat up, her eyes stormy. "I don't care. As I see it, if I leave, Allen will go with me -- and that is what has put me in this danger. At least with you and him covering my back, I have a fighting chance of finding out exactly what the heck is going on here and why I'm suddenly a target. I'm safer working with you than I am on my own." She didn't tell him that she suspected he knew more about what was happening to her than he was letting on. "Doctor Lasker, with all due respect, nothing you or Allen say is going to change my mind. I'm here until I'm free of both of them."

Dr. Lasker was about to protest when Shelly surprised him by flipping off the covers and revealing that she was fully dressed. "I'm ready. No more delays and no more surprises. Well, maybe one. I need to stop at my dorm and pick up a few things. I've decided I need a good bath and a good night's sleep, so at least for tonight I'm moving in with you." She slid out of the bed and sat on the edge.

"Get up slowly or you may feel dizzy," Dr. Lasker warned, wondering if she realized exactly what she had said. Little beads of sweat were lining his forehead at the idea that she might have meant exactly what she said, that she was moving in with him -- just for the night. *Old idiot,* he scolded himself, *You know that's not what she meant.* But it was exciting anyway.

"Let's blow this joint," Shelly said in her best gangster imitation. "We have work to do."

Dr. Lasker followed her out of the room, hoping she didn't see the hopeful smile on his face.

"And by the way, Doc, when we get some time, you are going to tell me all about Dodd. No more bullshit!"

That took care of the smile.

CHAPTER 45

There hadn't been any sign of Allen in the three days Shelly had been in the hospital. At first she wondered if somehow the accident had destroyed him. She almost hoped it had, but that hope was fleeting and was replaced by the reluctant admission that she missed him and was worried about him. "Worried about a ghost?" she laughed to herself. "Who'd have thunk it?"

There was something so human about this ghost, though. He had surprised her in so many ways, from his gentle voice, his playful teasing, sometimes going too far, to his sudden bursts of what she was beginning to believe might be jealousy. Now that was a real surprise. *Can ghosts be jealous? How can that be?* The longer Allen was absent, the more she realized that -- even though he was a pest -- he had also made her feel protected. Sure, he was annoying, doing things like showing up when she was chatting-up guys, but maybe he wanted to keep her from making a painful mistake. She thought of Jeff. *How could I have been so wrong about him? He didn't call even once. What does that say about my judgment of men?*

Was Allen different? She was beginning to wonder if maybe Allen had somehow also been the one who had saved her from the burning van. How else could she have finally gotten loose from that seat-belt? How else could she have escaped before the explosion? It had to be Allen. But where was he? Had something happened to make him vanish forever?

The ride back in Dr. Lasker's eight-year-old Cadillac seemed unending. Even the smooth-riding car could not completely cushion her from the pain that shot through her body, the residue of the horrendous accident. It could also not erase the fear, the agonizing fear of another accident, a fifth attempt on her life by an unseen enemy -- whom she now believed had to be Dodd. But why?

Every time she thought of Dodd, she found it impossible to believe that someone who had seemed so 'interested' in her could really have been plotting to kill her. And yet the evidence seemed to be pointing at the wild-looking Dodd as the perpetrator of at least some of these plots against her. He'd been at her side during the bus and gas incidents...he, or someone who looked like him, had forced the van off the road, and incredibly had refused to help her when she was trapped inside. She remembered his face, a strange cold expression on his lips as he stood by watching the flames reach the gasoline. How could this be the same man she had wanted to make love to?

The doctor deliberately avoided the back roads, the short-cut, the scene of the accident. Was it out of consideration for her, trying not to offer reminders of her ordeal, or was it something else, something less altruistic? *He gave me the directions to use the shortcut! He also gave me his oldest and ugliest vehicle... Isn't there anyone I can trust?*

"Allen," Shelly muttered.

"Did you say something?" Lasker peered in the mirror at her.

"I was thinking aloud."

Dr. Lasker avoided talking about anything that might remind her of what she had been through. The more he thought about it, the more he realized he was glad Shelly was too stubborn to have listened to him about taking a hiatus. This little blonde girl was a treasure, if only he could exploit her to best advantage. *In attacking her, that idiot Dodd might have actually done me a service -- for now she's so damn mad that nothing will stop her. Dodd has more or less sealed his fate.*

"Tell me about the house," Shelly said, as she tried to maneuver the seat belt so it didn't land on the exact spot where the van's belt had cut into her flesh.

"We have time for that," Dr. Lasker replied, giving her a fast glance in the mirror again and then returning his gaze to the road. He was not taking any chances that Dodd might try to replicate the accident. *The fool might try to commit suicide by having me drive into him,* the doctor thought, as he slowed down just in case. Why couldn't Dodd have accepted it and simply disappeared like the others had? Lasker sighed. *I knew he wasn't normal when I first laid eyes on him, but then again, nobody who does this is exactly normal. She certainly isn't. Dodd was a terrible mistake. Is this one?* He gazed at her again as if the sight of her face, so attentive on the road, would reassure him. When she caught him looking, he gave her a warm smile.

Shelly was impatient, eager to get started unraveling all the mysteries that were making her life hell lately. "What happened at the house that created this frightening feeling you get just from looking at the photo?"

"Are you sure you feel up to discussing this now? We have time later." Lasker was surprised, but pleased by her apparent eagerness to get to work. Time was running out for the department. Now that Dodd was no longer active, it had been a long dry spell.

"The sooner, the better. You want to know if Allen is real, and I want to know that too. This could show us, once and for all."

Dr. Lasker realized she had changed. The young innocent girl was now humorless, a scientist, a detective, who wanted nothing more than answers. He almost regretted the loss of that child-like quality, her vulnerability, but realized there was little place for that light-hearted personality in a true Ecto. Her new determination might help her survive, might help her succeed where others had failed…where Dodd had failed.

Lasker chose his words carefully, knowing she was analyzing everything he said, hoping he was giving her just enough, but not enough to frighten her off. "There's much we don't know. The house has a violent history. It's become well known for its effect on all the families that have lived there. They all say it's haunted by 'evil spirits'."

"And you believe that?"

"There are striking similarities in the various descriptions of the manifestations they've witnessed...and experienced."

He wants this so badly, she thought, *so why not give it to him? Let him have this single success, and maybe he'll realize just how valuable his new assistant and her ghostly friend really are.* "From what you said when you showed me the family pictures, I don't think we can afford to wait. I'm ready now."

Dr. Lasker nodded. "Very well. As soon as we get back, I'll phone the family and see if they will allow us to spend the night in the house."

"Spend the night?" Shelly had been counting on spending her first night out of the hospital, with its constant noise -- of paging this doctor or that nurse, and the scraping of gurneys on the tiled floor -- in a clean room, a wonderfully cloud-like mattress, and a bathtub you could die for. *Die for? Did I really think that?*

"Of course we must spend the night there. Don't you realize most ghostly manifestations have taken place at night?" He had forgotten how little she knew.

Shelly sighed. *Just my luck to get a ghost who comes out not just at night but every dang day.* "Allen doesn't. He's around both day and night. Is that unusual?" *Maybe Allen isn't a ghost,* she thought, *But then, what else could he be?*

If only she knew just how unusual her Allen is, Dr. Lasker thought. "I believe there are significant differences between ghosts that haunt a specific sphere, a house for example, than a so-called 'unattached' ghost, a 'homeless' ghost, such as Allen appears to be."

"You think he's homeless? Could he have been homeless in real life?" Shelly had never thought of this possibility, but it made sense if he was homeless now. She thought of the mugger. Had he been homeless too? Did Allen know him? Was he somehow responsible after all?

"I suppose it's possible that Allen is a homeless spirit. From my extensive research and years of experience working with supernatural phenomena, I believe the routines of a ghost are generally established by the routines they followed in life. So the answer to your question is that, if Allen is homeless now, not attached to a particular place or building, I would guess he might have been in a similar situation in life."

"Poor Allen," Shelly said. *Poor me. I'm stuck with a homeless ghost. What else don't I know about him?*

There are far worse fates than being a homeless ghost, Dr. Lasker thought, as he steered the car into the nearly deserted parking lot outside Psych Building B. The family in the beautiful white house with its gingerbread shingles and perfectly landscaped lawn were an example of that. As the door of the car slammed shut, Dr. Lasker thought he heard a familiar noise. He listened again as the sound repeated every few seconds. He was almost sure that he heard an axe. But here on campus? It had to be his imagination, a memory…a terrible memory.

"Are you okay," Shelly asked, seeing the professor frozen, as if in a trance.

His words came slowly. "I think you're right. The people in case study 143 need our help immediately."

Shelly felt a chill race through her body. "I only hope we can help."

So do I, the doctor thought, as he made a mental list of what they would need. *If Dodd was still here, he would have packed the van for me. If Dodd was still here… I'd still need her.* Dodd had failed at their earlier attempt.

"It'll be okay, Professor," Shelly said. "Allen will help that poor family. You'll see."

The professor sighed. He knew he was sacrificing Shelly, much as he had sacrificed everyone else who had been part of the team -- yes, even Dodd. He was tempted again to release her, to protect her, but knew she would not accept -- and the greater good called for the sacrifice....

Besides Shelly isn't Dodd, Lasker told himself. *She isn't personally 'sensitive', a true Ecto, but is somehow linked just to one particular entity. That may save her. Dodd's 'sensitivity' was extraordinary, while he was sane,* Lasker thought bitterly, but quickly shoved all thoughts of his 'disturbed' assistant aside, just in case she could read his mind...or maybe the ghost could. "It will be fine," he told her, knowing he was lying, but praying it might be the truth. At any rate, he could not warn her -- and she could not know about his former assistant yet, not until she swallowed the hook. He knew once this 'hook' was swallowed, only the rare few could break free. And he was pretty certain that, as bright as Shelly was, she was not one of those rare few. *She will be mine,* he thought, with a mixture of pleasure and some regret, as he watched her shapely body limp toward the building that concealed so many secrets and so much promise.

CHAPTER 46

I could kill for a hot bath, Shelly thought after calling Allen through his door and not getting a response. Where could he be? Had the explosion finally destroyed him? Could a ghost be destroyed by an earthly event? *I never wanted that!* She let out a deep sigh. *Maybe I did?*

Shelly unlocked her door and saw that her clothes, retrieved from her former dorm, were neatly hung in the closet. *I'll have to thank someone for that,* she thought, and suddenly realized she hadn't met anyone else from the department yet. "All in good time," she could hear the professor say in his deep voice.

Thoughts about Allen kept hitting her at the strangest times. About to step into the shower, she suddenly wondered if he was watching her. *Just my luck to get a letch of a ghost.* "Allen, are you here?" She deliberately stripped off her blouse. "Come on, Allen. I know you're enjoying this if you're here?"

Knowing him the way she thought she did, Shelly knew he'd have some comment to make, or perhaps deliver a great wolf–whistle, at the sight of her topless. *I guess he's not here,* she thought.

A bath was so tempting, but she had no time for that now. First things first. She quickly stripped off the rest of her clothes and stepped into the enclosure. The shower water was cold, but quickly turned warm and then hot, perfectly modulated. The water felt lovely as the warm pellets messaged her aching body, and the soap smelled refreshing, lavender. She let her finger touch the welt along her stomach. *No showing that off to anyone for a while,* she thought, and then remembered how lucky she was to be alive -- most likely thanks to that troublesome ghost. She shut off the water and stepped out of the tub, a towel wrapped around her...

Then she gasped and whirled, around surveying the room. Someone had written a message in the fog of the mirror. It read,
U R Fre LU A
She read it again. Was it a warning? Was it a threat?

She sat down on the toilet seat. "U R Fre LU A?" She understood almost immediately what the message said -- "You are free. Love you Always"...no, "Love You...Allen".

Why did he have to write that? Shelly sighed. It must have taken a lot of his strength to materialize enough to do that. She could almost feel his struggle trying to make the crooked letters.

She got up and stared at the writing again. "It was him! He was the one who left that message in the shower, warning me about Dr. Loco. I knew it."

Shelly grabbed a washcloth and erased the message. She got to the LU and hesitated. "A ghost can't feel love," she said, and before she changed her mind rushed the cloth over the letters, wiping them out over and over. "Damn you, Allen! I wanted a bath and a nap, and now I've got to go and find you."

She dressed quickly in a fresh jogging suit and slipped on her running shoes. The hall seemed deserted The whole building seemed deserted. *This is the strangest university department I've ever heard of,* she thought as she headed for the stairway.

She trotted up the stairs and again looked for a door to the first floor after charging up four flights. There wasn't any exit on the landing. She wondered how that could be, as she headed for the final two flights. *I'll have to ask about that later.* "Loco," she imitated Desi Arnaz, "You got a lotta explainin' to do."

"Hi Andy," she said, smiling at the guard.

He nodded at her.

"How are you doing," she asked, casting him an even warmer smile.

He looked around as if wondering if she was throwing that warm smile at someone else. "I'm fine. Are you okay? I heard about your accident. You look fine."

She nodded. "I have to go find someone, but maybe we can talk sometime?"

A frown appeared on Andy's face. "My day off is Thursday." He looked furtively at his monitors and whispered, "Can't talk now."

"See you later," Shelly said, wondering why the secrecy. Was everyone in this building crazy?

Andy gave her a little wave and buzzed her out the door.

She wondered why he was so nervous. Was he afraid he was being watched? Why would anyone want to watch a guard? She looked back, but Andy was already reading his comic book.
"I don't know," Shelly muttered, uncertain if a comic-book reading guard was much of an improvement over a mysterious, perhaps murderous Dodd, a pompous and chauvinistic Lasker, or even a hard-to-figure-out ghost. "I have absolutely the worst luck with men," Shelly said, "Even dead ones."

Shelly hesitated outside the door. It was already getting dark. *Do I really want to do this now?* The parking lot was empty. "Where the hell are you, Allen?" she asked aloud.

She looked at the road leading away from the building. *On campus, I'm safe,* she thought. She bent down and did a few stretching exercises, and then began jogging down the same road on which she had driven the van.

There weren't any cars. It amazed her how empty the B lot was. Even the A lot had about a dozen cars splattered around its massive expanse.

Her sneakers were making a soft slapping noise on the asphalt. A man's shoes would make a heavier sound. Shelly knew that if someone was waiting for her, the sound of her shoes was a dead giveaway. She had a flashback of the mugger who had started this whole mess. She could almost see him running after a yellow-suited jogger, lunging forward and falling through a ghostly cloud. "Allen," she panted, "What the hell do you want from me?"

She tried to pace herself, but the recent accident and her lack of training were making this run difficult. She sensed that she was vulnerable, that danger could be anywhere. She had planned it that way, knowing that if he was near, if Allen still cared, he would know she was in danger and he would respond. The link between them had been forged, and until he was freed, Shelly knew they had to stay together. She believed it now.

"I'm waiting," Shelly shouted, advancing farther from the safety of the building.

Shelly had plenty of time to think as she was recuperating in the hospital. She decided she was tired of waiting for the next attack, fed up with searching every corner and alley, suspecting every car. She made up her mind that this time she would be ready for Dodd, or anyone else who took the bait.

CHAPTER 47

"Hi Shelly."

Even though she expected him, his voice startled her. She hadn't expected him to be so close. It was too soon. He must have been following her from the building. "You're not a ghost," she said, finding herself facing Dodd. He still looked handsome, but there was something sinister about the expression on his face. Why was he smiling at her like that, just as he had smiled at her by the van?

Dodd let out a small burst of laughter. "You thought I was a ghost?" He peered at her, his eyes mesmerizing. "Is that what Lasker told you?"

Shelly felt disarmed, suddenly unsure of what she was doing. "He knows about you?" Shelly had suspected something, but why would Dr. Loco hide this from her?

Dodd burst into laughter again. This time it was loud and insane, frightening to her. "He lied to you, didn't he? That wily old bastard."

Shelly wanted to back away, but Dodd was watching her every move. "Is your name really Dodd?" Shelly felt the sharp edge of the steak knife in her jacket pocket.

There was a look of amusement on his face. "Did you think I'd lie to you? Yes, my name is Dodd, Thomas Graham Dodd." He was studying her with narrow eyes. "Do you have any other questions for me?"

She detected a wild look in his eyes. "Yes. Why are you trying to kill me?" she asked, her hand now tight around the knife handle. "It is you trying to kill me, isn't it?"

Dodd stared at her and then smiled, his hands clenched at his sides.

When he smiled, Shelly thought he looked sexy again, his face unblemished, his chin and cheeks clean-shaven and his hair black, wisps straying wildly, provocatively. *He definitely has an interesting face...* It almost made her want to tell him she liked him and might have had a nice relationship with him...except that he wanted to kill her. Why?

"Why do you want to hurt me? Did I do something to you?" she asked, seeing he wasn't talking, just staring at her, as if studying her before he decided to attack. She had seen this frightening face on zombies in the movies, but Dodd was no zombie -- he was alive, and could strike at her with sudden and frightening speed. "I like...liked you."

He seemed to refocus, his eyes sizing her up, intense.

Shelly tightened her hand on the knife. "I liked you. I thought you were cute and..."

"I know exactly what you want. I know why you're here." Voices inside his head were screaming it at him.

"I don't want anything. What are you talking about?"

"Sure you do. That's why you wanted to see him."

"Who? I didn't want to see anyone but you." Was he jealous? *Is that what this was all about?*

"You know very well what I mean." His eyes and his voice were cold, cruel and menacing. "You pretend to like me, but you don't fool me. I know exactly what you wanted. You never should have come here. He didn't need you. He had me."

Shelly was confused. Who was Dodd talking about? And then it hit her. "Do you mean Dr. Lasker? I wanted Dr. Lasker to help me with a..." Shelly almost said "ghost", but stopped herself. Dodd couldn't know.

"Liar."

He had said that so softly, without emotion, that it frightened Shelly even more than if he'd screamed it at her. "Dodd, I'm not lying. I absolutely do not have the hots for Professor Lasker. I need his help. Trust me, that's all I wanted from him."

"No, dear, lying Shelly. You wanted my job."

"Your job? What are you talking about?"

"Don't pretend you don't know."

"I don't know anything! I'm telling you the truth. I wanted help with a problem I have."

"You have a problem? Okay, tell me, what is it? What, Shelly, is your damn problem?"

He sounded maniacal, vicious and threatening. *What's wrong with him?* Shelly hesitated. "I can't. I promised..."

"That's what I thought! I knew you were a lying bitch the minute I saw you...I knew I had to stop you."

"I don't know what you're talking about! Dr. Lasker is helping me and –"

"Damn you, stop lying! He gave you my job. *I* was his assistant! You had no right to take my job from me! It was my life! My whole damn life... I have nothing else! Nothing."

Shelly was about to speak when Dodd hurled himself at her, his hands reaching for her throat. The attack was so sudden and so swift that the knife fell out of her jacket pocket and was quickly lost in the high grass.

He grabbed her. "I didn't want to hurt you. I tried scaring you off, but you wouldn't stop. You had to worm your way into his heart with your devilish ways."

Shelly felt his hands tighten around her throat, and tried to pull them off. "I didn't! I didn't know about you!"

"At least stop lying!" he screamed, his tears landing on her face as his hands were clamping down tighter and tighter on her windpipe. "I could have loved you if you weren't a lying bitch! Even with that guard-- I saw you flirting with him!"

She couldn't speak. She kicked her feet at his legs, and he squeezed harder. She tried to knee him in the crotch, but he pulled away, never releasing his fingers from her neck. *How could I have been so stupid?* she thought, as she reached for his face -- that beautiful face -- and felt her nails scratch down from his eye to somewhere on his cheek. He released one hand to pull her hand off his flesh, and slapped the side of her face so hard she let out a sharp cry.

"Stop fighting!" he screeched, the madness taking complete hold of him, tears flowing freely as he prayed she'd finally die so he could show her how gently he would help her to the ground, how tenderly he would hold her as he waited for the police to come and place a bullet between his eyes. "Please stop fighting. It won't hurt as much. I never wanted to hurt you. If only you had taken my warnings!" He squeezed harder, tears falling, repeating over and over again, "I love you. I love you. I love you."

Shelly couldn't speak. She was trying to hold his hands, to pull them away, knowing her strength was giving out. Her brain still could not compute how someone who could say he loved her could also be snuffing out her life. "Dodd," she begged, but no words came out. His hands were too tight.

"Not again! Can't you stay out of trouble for five minutes?"

Shelly heard Allen's familiar voice as her hands stopped fighting against Dodd and her body grew limp. *Is this what you were waiting for?* She screamed silently as she accepted that she was about to become a victim of murder, just like Allen. And maybe that was what the ghost she called Allen had wanted all along. Maybe that was why he had been sent for her. …It didn't matter. It was time to let go.

CHAPTER 48

"Every time I turn my back, you go walking right into more trouble," Allen said. "Let go of her, you asshole."

Dodd dropped Shelly's body and was searching wildly for the source of the voice he had just heard. "This is impossible!" he screeched. "Nobody's here! Nobody!"

"Now, that's interesting," Allen said. He had been trying to materialize, but Dodd's reaction to his voice had disrupted his concentration.

Dodd stiffened and backed away from Shelly, whom he had killed, his eyes still searching wildly for someone who had just called him an asshole. Had he finally gone completely insane? As the doctor's assistant for eight years, he had experienced terrifying things, phenomena that had sapped his sanity, and he'd suffered severe mental trauma like a soldier who had been in battle too long. Eventually, all the nightmares he had suffered, all the pain he had accepted from others in his effort to help them, had worn away at his mental stability. He was now the one haunted, tormented mercilessly by the memories of the many horror stories he had lived, the pain of too many victims, internalized, and now driving him mad, so that all he had left was the delusion that he could still do his job, still work with the professor as the departmental link to the spiritual world he had always been, and would always be. Shelly could not take that away from him. Nobody could.

Allen bent over Shelly. "Dodd, you idiot! What have you done? She loved you."

Dodd's eyes raced wildly toward Shelly's body, where the voice had come from. But there was no one there. "Who are you? What do you want from me?" As much as he had searched for it all his life, he had never heard a ghost talk directly to him before; his abilities were limited only to sensing their presence, the cold chill that raced through his body. No matter how much he had sought them out, pleaded with them to trust him, to speak to him -- to make him their link to the department, the world -- the ghosts had never connected with him until now. "So why is this whore more worthy than me?" he screamed to Allen. "*I'm* the one you should have chosen! I gave up everything for my gift...my curse."

Allen was gazing at the fallen Shelly. "How could you hurt her? Don't you know she would have done anything to help you? She...liked you. She loved you." Allen wondered why it hurt him so much to say that.

"No!" Dodd screamed, thinking this was his conscience he was confronting. "She didn't love me. She stole my life." He was crying now, his tears uncontrollable. "He threw me away like garbage! It's all I have left. She was taking it from me. I stopped her. Now he'll need me again."

"You idiot, Shelly didn't do it! She didn't even know you worked for Dr. Loco. He never told her anything about you. He lied, and told her he had never heard of you."

"No. You're lying." Dodd looked confused. "He...He was like a father to me. He'd never hurt me like that. You're both liars."

Allen almost felt sorry for Dodd. "Dodd, he used you like he wants to use Shelly...and me," Allen said. "You let him. You let him drain you dry. That's all Lasker wants from any of us. He drains us dry and then throws the corpses away when he's done. He did that to you."

An animal growl rose from Dodd's throat. "No. That's not true. It was her!" Dodd had Shelly's knife in his hand. "I'm going to kill you!" he shrieked, and lunged toward where he thought Allen was standing. Over and over he slashed in the air with the knife, crying hysterically when all he felt was air.

"You can't hurt me," Allen said to the pathetic, insane, former assistant still flailing the knife at him. *Maybe you can,* Allen thought, as he stared at Shelly's lifeless body.

Dodd, finally exhausted, panting hard, turned his eyes to the inert body of the girl.

"Did you think you could kill a ghost?" Allen asked.

Dodd eyes and his soul were riveted on the girl's body. Was her chest moving? Did her fingers look as if they were moving, ever so slightly? "Why doesn't she die," he murmured.

Allen saw the look on Dodd's face and the meat knife in his hand. "Don't even think it," he warned.

Dodd walked slowly toward Shelly.

"No, Dodd! Dodd, no more. It isn't her fault." Allen saw the knife pointed at the center of Shelly's chest. In a second, it would be too late.

CHAPTER 49

Shelly opened her eyes when she heard a terrible scream.

In the instant Allen rushed Dodd and threw him to the ground, she caught a glimpse of the man who had become the ghost she called Allen. She couldn't have known it was him, having been unconscious as he struggled to materialize. His back could have been any man's naked back, strong, lean, but marked with several unusual scars. She let her eyes roam to his hair, almost translucent but clearly brown and wavy. An instant later, the man -- the physical being -- had vanished and Allen, the ghost again, lay exhausted on top of Dodd, the exertion of materializing to save Shelly sapping his strength.

I saw you, Shelly thought, and closed her eyes. She felt as if she had died. Maybe for a few seconds she had.

The sound of a siren caused her to open her eyes again.

"Are you okay?" she heard Allen's voice. "This is getting to be a habit…a really bad one."

"Are you…" she asked. "It was you who saved me again, wasn't it?"

"I had no choice."

"You did," Shelly said, trying to breathe normally. *You could have let me die and become a ghost with you,* she thought.

"I keep telling you our destinies are intertwined, linked. I had to come when I heard you calling me."

"I did call you. There was nobody else." *And you had to save me again, although you didn't do it right away. I thought for a second that you were going to let me die. I would have been murdered…just like you. We'd have been together then,* Shelly thought.

"I would never want you to be like me," Allen said, as if reading her mind.

Something in his voice made her believe that.

The ambulance pulled up and two men came charging out of the vehicle. "Are you okay, Miss?" one man asked, setting down a yellow defibrillator box next to her. "Are you in pain?"

"He tried to kill me," Shelly said, pointing to her throat.

"Who did?" the other man asked, moving a gurney toward them.

Shelly gazed at where Dodd had been lying on the ground. "He's gone," she gasped, aiming a puzzled look at where she thought Allen was standing.

"I couldn't kill him," Allen said as if apologizing. "I learned something else about me. I can't kill anyone, even if I want to…and I did want to. I wanted to kill him for what he did to you."

"You're not the killer type," Shelly said as the medic was taking her blood pressure.

The medic gave her a funny look. "Did you hit your head?" he asked. "Your vitals are fine. Other than a few scrapes and a sore throat, you seem okay."

"I am," Shelly said, slowly rising to her feet. She brushed dirt off her jogging pants. "…Thanks to you."

The medic smiled. "You would have been fine without us, but it always pays to be safe."

"That's what I've been trying to tell you," Allen said. "What on Earth were you doing out here on your own? You knew someone was gunning for you, so what were you thinking?"

"I was looking for you," Shelly said. "You weren't there, and I needed you." She didn't want to tell him she had missed him.

The medic with the gurney had returned to the ambulance, but the other medic had a look of concern on his face. "Are you okay, Miss?" he repeated. "What do you mean, you were looking for us? We're always here if you need us. Just call 911, or the campus police."

Shelly understood the young EMT's confusion, and remembered she had to talk to Allen when others weren't around. "I'm sorry. I guess I'm still in a bit of shock."

"That's understandable," the medic said. "Did you see who attacked you? Can you give a description? The cops should be here any second, and they'll be happy to help."

"No police," Allen said. "There's no way you can explain all this. They'll think you're crazy."

"I'm fine. I didn't get a look at his face. He came up behind me." Shelly suddenly had Dodd's face in front of her again, that handsome flawless face marred by an insane smile and wild terrifying eyes. "I'd like to leave now. I'm okay."

"Are you sure? The police will want to talk to you."

Shelly got to her feet, bent down and touched her toes. "Do I look like I need any more help? I'm fine. Thank you." Before he could protest again, Shelly was walking back to the Psych B building.

"Are you still with me," she asked Allen.

"Yes. For as long as it takes."

Out of sight of the medic who had been following her until she had turned off the main road, Shelly stopped walking. She was panting hard and felt a little dizzy.

"Seriously, are you okay," Allen asked.

"It just hit me that it was Dodd who attacked me, who was trying to kill me all along." Shelly was bent over trying to calm her breathing. She almost said, "I thought I could like him," but decided that wasn't a good thing to say to Allen, or any man, even a ghost, whom she had just kind of made up with. "And where were you? Why did you disappear after the crash? I thought you were gone for good."

Did you celebrate? Allen almost asked, but decided this was't a very good time for that. Besides, he knew she wasn't the type who would celebrate his disappearance. She might feel relief at being free of her ghost, but she would always wonder what had happened to him, if he was alright. That was the kind of person she was. He understood that now. He knew how he had felt when he thought she had been killed. And yes, he was ready to admit that at least this ghost could feel things mortal humans could feel, perhaps even love. "I'm sorry I left you without an explanation. I shouldn't have done that." He sounded genuine.

"Then why did you? I…I hate to admit it, but I was worried about you."

"We'd better get back. I don't want that maniac to get a second shot at you." Allen had been searching for Dodd around every tree along the park-like roadway. "I think he's really lost it. I wish I knew why."

He really sounds concerned, Shelly thought as she started walking quickly, aware that the doctor would be looking for her, suspecting that Dodd might be too. "We can talk while we walk," Shelly said. "You can do two things at one time, can't you?"

Allen realized she was teasing him, but he didn't laugh. He was watching her to be sure she was okay for the long walk back. He also knew he had been weakened by materializing for his fight with Dodd, and if she were attacked again he might not be able to come to her rescue.

"Why did you leave? I really want to know."

Allen sighed. "To tell you the truth, I couldn't stand to see you being hurt. You were almost killed three…four times…I'm losing count." He gave an uneasy laugh, knowing that he wasn't telling her the whole truth.

"All the more reason for you to stay," Shelly said.

"Not if I'm the reason you're in such danger."

Shelly stopped walking. "So you think the reason I'm being targeted is because of you?"

"It started after you met me."

"What about the mugger in the park? Was that your fault too?" Shelly started walking again, feeling a chill in the air as darkness approached.

"Do you believe there's a reason for everything that happens in life?" Allen asked.

"I guess I do now," Shelly said.

"I believe that now too. I think you and I were meant to meet, and that mugger was just part of the plan."

"Well, if that's what you believe, then you know we can't escape our destiny -- and right now you're needed right here, by me." Shelly found it hard to believe she was asking a ghost to stay and help her.

"That's why I came back when you were in trouble. Hey, you're always in trouble! Taking care of you is, like, a full time job." He had to lighten things up or he might spill how he really felt about her. "You need a damn bodyguard."

"You're hired...at least until I can be rid of you," Shelly said, and quickly added, "I'm teasing you. Don't get your sheet in a knot."

"Hey, that's pretty funny for a girl who can't afford to make any more enemies."

"Dodd. You had him and let him go?"

"I couldn't hold him once I dematerialized again. I wish they had an instruction manual for this ghosting business! I'd love to know how to control this tricky power. I can only stay solid for a few seconds, at most."

"While you had him, did he tell you why he wants to kill me?"

"Not really. Did you find out?"

"He was too busy trying to strangle me to tell me," Shelly said, wondering if Allen was keeping something back, just as she was.

"I have a feeling he won't try again after what I did to him," Allen said, remembering how Dodd had reacted when, for the first time in his life, he had made direct contact with a real ghost. *You should have seen the look on his face, Shelly, when he heard me yelling at him.* Allen thought of telling her what Dodd had said, but then he would have to tell her the rest. She would have to know that Dodd, maniac that he now apparently was, had once been Dr. Lasker's very sane assistant -- worn down by years of the kind of work she was about to undertake, work whose horrors had traumatized him to the point of insanity, work which Shelly was determined to do in order to help rid her of her ghost -- in order to help him find his murderer. How could he tell her that? He needed time to think, time to sort out his conflicting feelings about what Shelly was about to do. He knew his fate rested in her decision.

Shelly was quiet the rest of the walk back. She wondered what Allen was thinking about, since he was unusually quiet too. She wondered how he would react if she told him the truth about Dodd -- not that she knew he was still a terrible danger to her, but something far more significant, something that would ruin any hope she had of helping Allen. Shelly now understood that the agonizing work Dodd had done as Dr. Loco's assistant had taken a devastating toll on him. She didn't know if it was because he was already predisposed to madness, or if it was the accumulated burden placed on his brain from dealing with so many horrendous and perplexing cases. She only knew that, if she told Allen what she now believed had caused Dodd's sickness, the ghost would never let her sacrifice herself to help him. How could she let him suffer like that endlessly, without any hope of learning the truth about his life, his family, his murder?

So they walked back silently, neither wanting the other to know the terrible risks they were willing to take to help each other -- a ghost who was willing to remain unresolved and homeless rather than have Shelly lose her mind and risk her life, and a beautiful, young girl willing to sacrifice herself to inevitable horrors, that might result in madness, to help a ghost 'friend' find out about himself and finally have the peace she thought he deserved.

When the door opened to Psych B, Shelly and Allen were resolved to do whatever it would take to help the other survive.

CHAPTER 50

"Why didn't you tell Dr. Loco what happened to you today?" Allen asked, sitting on Shelly's bed. She had invited him into her room so they could talk without being overheard.

"I don't know if I can trust him." Shelly was searching the closet for a few things to pack in an overnight bag. Tonight was the night Dr. Loco had said they would visit the house he called Case 242. There was a good chance they would need to spend the night, he had explained. She wanted to be ready. No more delays. No more excuses.

"I've never trusted him," Allen said, wishing he could see through doors the way some television ghosts and superheroes could do, as Shelly walked past him into the bathroom to change her clothes. *I shouldn't be thinking like this,* he scolded himself, surprised as he always was when he thought ghosts should not have what seemed an obvious attraction for a living being. He tried to distract himself, but found himself staring at her open drawer, a pair of black lacy underpants hanging over the edge. He walked toward the drawer and reached for the silky black panties, but was unable to feel them. "Being a ghost rots," he said aloud.

"Being haunted isn't much better," Shelly replied, wondering suddenly if he could see through the bathroom door. The sight of his bare back as he'd struggled with Dodd...at least she thought it had been his; who else could it have been? His muscular physique had surprised her. His voice, usually soft and kind of mellow, had made her expect a much thinner man, a less well-developed man. *This is so damn frustrating,* she thought as she tucked her blouse into the last pair of fresh jeans she had in the closet. And then she realized it must be far worse for him. "I just thought of something. What did you remember about your previous life the last time you saved me?"

"You mean from that maniac, Dodd?"

"Yes. Was that time four or five?" She pulled her jeans on and wondered how long it would be before they were covered in grass, dirt, or -- worst of all -- blood. The way things were going, it seemed inevitable.

"Who's counting?" he said. "Actually, when Dodd was standing over you with a knife, I did get a flashback... but I can't remember exactly what it was." He didn't want to tell her he had seen his hand holding a knife over a naked female body. If that vision had frightened him, he could imagine how she would react. She'd probably never talk to him again. He wished he could have seen the knife clearer. He was afraid to see the body again -- it was young, and there was blonde hair spread across what looked like a table or bed. He remembered that, but nothing else.

"You can't remember what it was?" Shelly asked, stepping out of the bathroom, fully dressed. "The other times you seemed to learn things about yourself that might help us solve your mystery."

"Yeah, but they weren't that important. So I liked running? Millions of people like that. Not much of a clue. So I wasn't a bus driver? Big surprise."

"But what about the fire? You said you saw a car burst into flame. That's not exactly unimportant."

Allen sighed. "It's a piece of the puzzle, but only a small piece. A car fire like that happens somewhere, every day. I don't see how it can help me find out who I was if I have no idea where the fire was, or who was in the vehicle."

Shelly heard the frustration in his voice. "I promise, after we finish this first case I'll get Dr. Lasker to sit down with us and help you." She heard Allen sigh. "I know this must be very upsetting for you. I feel it too."

"You really do?" It was strange how each time Shelly faced danger, she seemed to become more attuned to his feelings. Each close call with death seemed to be changing him and her, making the link between them even stronger.

"Yes. I don't understand it, but I really do feel at least a little of what you're feeling." She straightened up. "Let's go, we've got a job to do."

"Shelly, that house we're going to... It gives me the willies. Are you sure you want to do this? It's not too late to back out. Don't do this just for me. I can be fine the way I am."

The picture of the house flashed back, and she felt that icy chill race down her spine again. "Stop trying to talk me out of it. I've made up my mind."

"And once you've made up your mind, nothing can change it."

"You know me pretty well by now," Shelly said, and stepped out of the room.

Allen watched her lock the door behind her. *Totally useless,* he mused. Did she really believe that crazy doctor would give her a lock that would keep him out? He and that crazy Dodd could probably enter her room any time they wanted. He hurried to catch up before she got herself into more mischief.

"Good afternoon, Shelly. How are you Allen?" Dr. Lasker was wheeling an unusual-looking black metallic suitcase behind him. It made a thin squealing noise as he walked toward them. "Are you ready for an adventure?"

Allen shivered, suddenly very afraid for Shelly, who was following Dr. Loco like an obedient puppy. He thought of Dodd, the shell of a human being abandoned after Dr. Loco had no more use for him, and wondered if she realized just what kind of a hell the 'good doctor' was leading her to.

CHAPTER 51

Shelly was a little disappointed that they weren't taking the Cadillac, but she saw that the unmarked white Chevy van was filled with lots of equipment. Cameras, tripods, several dozen flashlights, she easily identified, but some of the other objects were unfamiliar. "Is all this necessary?" she asked, after Dr. Lasker introduced her to a young Asian-looking man seated behind the steering wheel. "This is Chan Lee Pong. He's our driver and cameraman tonight."

Shelly smiled and said, "Nice to meet you, Mr. Pong." She noticed he was slight in figure, had jet black hair which was tied in a ponytail, and wore green sunglasses. His jaw-line was high and etched, skin stretched taut. She couldn't imagine him ever cracking a smile or laughing.

Chan said, "Buckle up. We're late to leave."

What's with him? Shelly thought, noticing that he had hardly looked at her. *Is everyone in this department crazy?*

"You can call him Chan," Dr. Lasker said. "He's a bit terse, but correct -- we are late. I want to get there before dark."

"We should have left earlier then," Chan said as he backed the large van out of its garage in the rear of Psych Building B. The door came down behind them, and Shelly noticed that it was covered with a concrete brick façade, making it almost invisible against the rest of the building. "That's a nice camouflage job," she said to Dr. Lasker, who was sitting next to Chan, riding shotgun.

"You mean the garage door? As I've explained to you, much of our work here is highly confidential. There are others who would do anything to obtain our secrets and equipment. When I designed this building--"

"You designed it?"

"Why, yes. I didn't tell you that?" He looked puzzled. "I'm getting old. Please forgive me. This line of work can take a lot out of you." *Now why did I say that?*

Damn right, Allen thought, wondering if the Good Doctor was ever going to tell Shelly the whole truth about the mysterious Mr. Dodd. *I'll tell her after this job is done,* he promised. *I won't let her risk herself just to help me.*

"So you really designed the whole building? I'm impressed." Shelly said.

"Ask him about the missing floor," Allen hissed. He had tried to pass through the walls, as he'd done easily everywhere else, but the floor was sealed in some kind of material that blocked all access. *Was it lead, like what blocks Superman's x-ray vision?* he wondered.

"What missing floor?" Shelly asked, forgetting Dr. Lasker was listening to every word she said to Allen.

Dr. Lasker felt his body tense up. "You mean why there isn't a 13th floor in the building? Most buildings don't have a 13th floor, for the same reason that all the keys here are on rabbit's feet. I have to admit I feel foolish, but I'm slightly superstitious." *In my business, you're a fool not to be,* he thought.

"He knows that's not the floor you mean. Everyone knows most buildings don't have a 13th floor, but I'm talking about the floor concealed between the basement and the lobby floor," Allen said. "I've never heard of a hidden floor like that before."

"Neither have I." She recalled how puzzled she had been when it took two extra flights of stairs to go from the basement to the lobby. In all the craziness, she had almost forgotten about that. "Dr. Lasker, I wasn't going to ask about the 13th floor. I know a lot of buildings are like that. I was more curious about why there are six flights of stairs from the basement to the first floor, when normally there would only be four."

Dr. Lasker turned abruptly to Chan. "You missed the turn. Make the next left, and we'll be on the Expressway. Pay attention, please. We're late as is."

"I did *not* miss a turn," Chan replied, sounding irritated. "You're the worst backseat driver. Everyone says--" He looked into the rearview mirror. "I mean... You must forgive my English. I sometimes make mistakes, like mixing who says something. You understand?" He saw the girl nod her head. It was okay. She hadn't noticed his slip -- or if she did, she wasn't going to ask about it. "You must let me be the driver, Dear Doctor, or take the steering wheel yourself."

"Don't be so sensitive," Doctor Lasker said, hoping he had distracted Shelly from her question.

Chan gazed back at the girl. "Isn't that what you want of all of us?" he asked the doctor. "Isn't our 'sensitivity' what you work us so hard to develop?"

Dr. Lasker tried to hide his displeasure. "I should have mentioned that Chan here, in fact all our grad student interns, are what we call 'sensitives'. They call themselves Ectos -- which, as you know by now, is short for Ectoplasmic Researchers."

"Does that mean they can hear ghosts?" Allen asked, remembering how Dodd had been able to hear him. "Please ask him!"

Shelly nodded. "Doctor, does that mean they can hear ghosts? Chan, can you?"

Dr. Lasker looked back at her. *She really is a pretty girl,* he thought, as her eyes looked so earnestly into his face. "I have never been able to document this ability successfully," he said, knowing he wasn't telling her the whole truth. "I would have to define 'sensitive' as perhaps being able to viscerally 'sense' the presence of some occult energy within a confined area."

"More double-talk," Allen said. "He's definitely hiding something." *So am I. I wonder what she would say if I told her what I saw when I held that knife.* He remembered the sight of a young, naked girl with blonde hair, lying on some kind of bed or table, with him—he was sure it was him—standing over her with a sharp knife in his hand. *How can I tell her that?* he thought, grateful she was not a true Ecto, nor someone with mind-reading ability. How could he tell her that what really frightened him was that he thought the girl under the knife was Shelly?

CHAPTER 52

Chan eyed Lasker, but said nothing. He had seen Asian mediums seem to carry on conversations with the departed. He remembered a particular incident, when he was a child on a rice farm not far from the Emperor's City. The city -- fabled, over-powering in its size -- was the home of generations of Chinese emperors. The houses for servants and laborers, not protected by the massive walls, were often plagued by the ghosts of fallen warriors, or the spirits of young women raped and butchered after being used by the royalty and the massive legions of men that served them. He had heard his mother just before she fell on a large sword wedged against the floor, screaming at someone invisible that she would never submit to his desires no matter who he might be. And though he had not heard the ghost's words, the laughter as his mother's blood spread across the sleep-mat, had echoed with him every night in the fifteen years since she had died.

Dr. Lasker theorized that Chan's sensitivity was the result of his exposure to a demonic ghost at such an early point in his life. But what to Lasker was a gift, to Chan was a curse, for every nightmare was the same -- a young boy, watching his mother deliberately forcing her body to lower itself -- inch by fraction of an inch -- onto her husband's sword, blood dripping onto the bed mat. While Dodd had been more sensitive, Chan seemed better able to cope with his gift/curse...at least for now, Lasker thought, wondering how long a true sensitive could last against all the terrible pressures they were exposed to in their search for something none of them could ever reach, the complete resolution of the frightening situations that had given them their gift in the first place. *Their destruction is inevitable,* Lasker reasoned, *So why not employ them to help others for as long as their power can be harnessed?* Ectos, true Ectos, were doomed to die early in life, either because their past caught up to them with tragic results, or through mental meltdown from the accumulative effects of their supernatural contact, the burden of carrying so much grief and horror. Lasker knew, and accepted that in turn each of his 'assistants', including the beautiful Shelly, would be burnt out by the experience dictated by their 'gift'.

Dodd, the most sensitive of all his twenty years of assistants, had crashed badly, much as Lasker had expected. He had tried to prolong the young man's employment, but the erratic behaviors had grown worse, endangering other Ectos and the department.

Almost a year earlier, Dodd had warned Chan that a new girl would soon be arriving -- a girl who, though disarmingly beautiful, was nothing but a selfish schemer who wanted to take their place. He had heard voices telling him that this young woman would beguile him with her sensual behavior and then betray him before Lasker, who would discard him in her favor, abandon him in this world and in the other world that called him with increasing regularity. "She will destroy my life," he told Chan, and then she will destroy yours."

"How can you be so certain?" Chan asked, wondering why Dodd seemed to be acting so strangely the last few months. He had seen alarming changes in his associate—he couldn't call Dodd or any of the others a friend, except perhaps Swan, because Lasker had turned them into rivals, competitors, to sharpen their senses, to turn them into the Ectos he needed for his department—changes he knew were attributable to his special talents.

"Believe me, I know," Dodd replied. "I've seen her. I know what she wants and what she's willing to do to get it."

"That has nothing to do with me," Chan said.

"So I guess you want to be sent back," Dodd said, a cruel sneer on his face.

That got Chan's attention. "How do you know that will happen because of this girl?"

Dodd's smile sent shivers through Chan's body. "I've had dreams, many dreams. Trust me, my dreams are never wrong."

Dodd's dreams seemed more real than the reality through which he walked like a dazed by-stander. In those dreams he saw her only as a blonde-haired, faceless nymph, offering herself to him as he stood still, refusing to embrace her. He saw her stretching up to touch his face with her tiny hands and reaching up to give him what at first was a tentative light kiss, but soon becomes harder and more passionate. He saw her looking curiously at him, with her pale blue eyes that seemed to probe his soul, asking why he wasn't moving, why he wasn't feeling what she was pretending to feel so hotly in her body. And then he saw her undoing his shirt buttons, one button at a time, teasing him with her fingernails, one long nail pointed at his jugular so that if he moved sharply the torment would be over. That nail was so tempting.

But he doesn't move, so she continues, running her fingers over his chest. He shudders and still fights the temptation of pulling her toward him, tearing off her thin blouse and crushing her breasts against him. But the voices, the visions, have told him she is malicious, out to destroy him, so he still doesn't move, won't let himself feel anything for her but hate. Even when she drops her hand to his jeans and he feels himself rising to meet her touch, he sees this only as evidence of her evil nature, her desire to control and destroy his will. So finally, when she lowers herself before him, her eyes gazing up at him to see if she has successfully cast her spell, conquered his resistance, he sees his hands drop on her lovely shoulders and he must decide whether to bring her up and press his body against her, feel her breasts against his hard-beating heart, pull off her jeans and those lacy black panties, press himself inside her and take her as she is, standing against the wall of her dorm room, making love to her at long last, give in to her... or move his hands slowly, ever so reluctantly from those sweet shoulders to her slender neck, pull away her hair, move his hands across her flesh and gradually, so she barely notices, begin to clamp down hard on her lying throat.

They were dreams that foretold her arrival, a nightmare that did not let him sleep. He could not tell Lasker, fearing his 'boss' would become frightened of his paranoia and fire him.

In his absorption he didn't realize that Lasker had become concerned about his behaviors months earlier, and knew it was only a few months at best before he would have to take action. He tried to warn Dodd, but knew warnings were in vain once the disease attacked. He had seen it before, but never with the intensity with which it attacked Dodd.

Lasker still needed him, but Dodd was already picking up signs that the Chairman was losing patience and confidence in him, and if he found a suitable replacement, Dodd would be cast aside like so much garbage. That's what possessed him, and what he wanted to have possess Chan, so he told the young Chinese student over and over again that the new 'whore' was incredibly 'sensitive', far more than anyone else he had seen -- except, of course, himself. He worked incessantly to recruit Chan in the effort to stop her from stealing their jobs, their lives, by harping on the one thing that Chan cared more about than anything in his life. Dodd hammered into him that he could not afford to lose his job because he would be sent back to China -- where he would be imprisoned for the murder of his mother.

The possibility of no longer being needed by Dr. Lasker and being returned to China was frightening to Chan, and he was prepared to assist Dodd, but now, having finally met the 'new assistant', he found it hard to believe she was the threat Dodd had depicted. Not as sensitive as Dodd, relegated to little more than serving as the cameraman for Lasker -- who had almost given up on his ever attaining the skills of a true Ecto -- Chan had so far been spared the debilitating weight of dealing with the misery of the haunted and the haunters, a misery that was eating away at Dodd's brain. So he told Dodd he would not do anything to hurt Shelly, and was shocked when Dr. Lasker had filled him in on her so-called 'accidents.' He might have suspected Dodd, who he thought had become increasingly unpredictable, egotistical, narcissistic, but he didn't consider him irrational or murderous. He'd never believed Dodd would take things so far -- perhaps frighten her off, but kill her? Chan knew he himself could never hurt and certainly not kill anyone, not after witnessing his mother's excruciating death. He had seen his mother's blood gushing from her savage self-inflicted wound. In his nightmares he could still see her body writhing slowly, inch by agonizing inch, toward death on the sword. He could never subject anyone, let alone a beautiful young girl, to such agony. Could Dodd? Chan didn't think so.

Chan caught Shelly smiling at him and returned her smile with one of his own. *It would be a shame,* Chan thought, as he studied her innocent-looking face in the mirror, *If she ended up like Dodd.*

Lasker had noted Chan's concerned expression as he'd been eyeing Shelly in the mirror. Not an Ecto himself, Lasker could not know what the young Chinese assistant was thinking, but coincidentally he was thinking about Dodd himself -- Dodd and Shelly, two gifted assistants, doomed by their gifts. He felt sorry for Shelly, and yes, even for Dodd. He had accepted his responsibility for what happened to the most sensitive of his Ectos, but hoped Dodd, and now Shelly, would be stronger than others who had worked with him in the past.

In Dodd, he had placed as much confidence as he could ever have done. In some ways, Dodd was the son he had lost years ago in a drowning 'accident', which he knew was not an accident, both being driven mad by a gift he both envied and cursed.

Lasker had been unprepared for the death of his fourteen-year-old son, and had hoped Dodd would be different. Now he almost wished his favorite Ecto would do what his son had done, and just drown himself before he hurt or killed someone. Death, the chairman reasoned, was quick and had ended David's torment, the nightmarish visions which Lasker could never bring himself to explain to his son, the secret from his youth that had somehow been laid at the feet of his innocent child. Hearing his son scream in terror and not being able to help him, even though he knew the cause, knowing it was his fault, was a torture he did not want to relive with Dodd. David's death devastated Lasker, destroyed his marriage, but eventually he concluded was merciful, compared to what Dodd was experiencing, this slow and apparently irreversible insanity. This was far worse than death, incredibly painful to witness, and, based on recent incidents, impossible to stop.

Lasker described Dodd's condition, in his secret case notes, as the "gradual and complete dissolution of a once caring and loving soul into a paranoid and murderous maniac." After the van incident, he added, "Prognosis hopeless."

CHAPTER 53

Shelly, weak from her stay in the hospital, was dozing as the van raced along the Long Island Expressway at the breath-taking rush hour speed of ten miles per hour. The traffic was horrendous.

"Isn't there some other route," Dr. Lasker asked.

Chan, who was sweating from being stuck in all this traffic, gave him a dirty look. "Whoever heard of trying to traverse the LIE during rush hour? I told you we should have left earlier."

And we all know what a psychic you are, Dr. Lasker thought bitterly. "I figured since we're headed toward the city, and traffic would logically be going the other way, we'd avoid it," Dr. Lasker replied.

Chan grunted. "Next time, listen to someone with experience."

Lasker shot Chan an annoyed look, irritated he had been compelled to answer a subordinate's question in front of the new girl. But of course, Chan was not just any subordinate. He had been deliberately recruited from China, after Lasker had been informed of his case by a well-respected Chinese professor of parapsychology he'd met at a conference. Dr. Wu had extolled Chan's powers as a sensitive, until Lasker had jumped eagerly at the chance to obtain him for the struggling department. Despite all the claims of Chan's abilities, Dr. Lasker had been disappointed. Dodd was far more sensitive than Chan, but increasingly unstable, so he felt compelled to keep Chan, believing eventually the young Chan would prove himself. Wasn't that how it had been with Dodd? Maybe taking Chan out of China was like taking a fish out of water, limiting his abilities until he became accustomed to his new environment. At any rate, with Dodd showing signs of depression and paranoia, he had no choice but to keep Chan and hope Dodd would hold up until a suitable replacement could be found.

Damn Dodd. Lasker shook his head. *What a waste!* Dodd was a weakling to have let himself be destroyed by their work. Lasker believed the 'weakness' resided in Dodd himself, much as it had been the weakness of his son that had led him to walk into the Great South Bay. *I know I am partly responsible,* he rationalized, *But it is their weakness that must bear the brunt of the blame.* That was what he assured himself. That was what he explained to the other three assistants after one of Dodd's explosive tantrums -- but only Chan had remained, paralyzed by the threat of Dr. Lasker removing his sponsorship and having him deported to China. He knew Chan would never want to risk going back. The Chinese courts were inflexible with children who murder their mothers. It gave Lasker a sense of power, knowing he could control Chan with the threat of one phone call telling the authorities where the boy could be found.

"This traffic is a bitch," Chan said. "I hate this. You'd think we'd learned our lesson from last time--" Chan glanced at Lasker's face and knew he had said too much.

Lasker stared at Chan's profile as if saying, "Remember who you're speaking to. I hold the key to your life and death."

Chan knew he had gone too far, perhaps trying subconsciously to impress the new girl. "It will be fine, Dr. Lasker, sir. We'll be there very soon, as you planned." He felt the professor divert his gaze to the front windshield. Dodd had been right about one thing; neither boy could afford to have their job snatched away from them by this female, Dodd, because he had nothing else in his life, and he because he had others who wanted to take his freedom away.

"Open the windows or the damn A.C. will stall," Dr. Lasker said to Chan, cranking his window down with an old-fashioned handle.

Chan quickly complied, lowering his window, though he hated the smell of the exhaust fumes from the long rows of cars ahead.

Shelly stirred, the smell from the car exhausts reminding her, even in her sleep, of the smell of gasoline that had oozed from the department's other van. In her sleep she saw a man who looked like a devil, tall, with long hair and a vicious snarl on his face, standing like a wall in front of her careening vehicle. She let out a scream when she saw again the white van hurtle over the embankment and begin a slow motion series of rolls ending in a massive explosion.

Allen sensed Shelly's discomfort even before she screamed. It was so odd feeling these erratic human sensations he seemed to be sharing with her. He hadn't told Shelly about this growing empathy because he was afraid she would realize that these human-like sensations were, he now believed, weakening him. He had a theory that this process might end with his eventual total loss of what made him a ghost, and his gradual disappearance into oblivion. It would not be heaven, and it would not be hell, but some existence/non-existence that would be far worse than any human had ever imagined. He only hoped he would be allowed to stay with her until he could be reasonably certain she'd be safe. He had selflessly given up on his own mission, of finding out who killed him, to protect this girl whose life was now entwined with his. That was a significant change. Allen still wanted to know about his former life and how he had died, but now there was something else more important to him, and nobody was more surprised or confused than he was. He found himself feeling concerned as he watched Shelly sleeping fitfully next to him in the van.

"I fell asleep," Shelly said letting out a yawn and looking confused.

"It's this traffic," Chan muttered. "I hate this road. We need a GPS. If we had that, we'd be able to find an alternative."

"Stop complaining," Dr. Lasker growled. "We're almost there."

Shelly felt anticipation and nervousness building inside her. She leaned toward the window. *How many idiots are on this road?* she thought, as all she could see were endless rows of cars.

"If I was stuck in traffic like this every morning and night, I'd probably kill someone," Allen said.

"So you don't think you commuted to work every day?" Shelly asked, forgetting that others could hear.

Chan looked back. "My English is not very good yet. Did you ask if I commute to work on this road every day?"

"No, she was talking to..." Dr. Lasker caught himself before he gave away his most treasured secret. Nobody must know yet about Allen.

"Yes. She was talking to?" Chan looked curiously at his boss. He had known for several days that Lasker was hiding something. He was sensitive enough to feel this, but not enough to know what Lasker was concealing.

Shelly saw that Dr. Lasker was looking nervous, and rushed in to rescue him. "I was asking if you have to travel on the LIE to get to the college every day, or if you live on campus."

Chan nodded. "I live in Building B, so no, I do not travel this godforsaken mess every day at all. Where do you live?"

"I live in Building B too."

Lasker jumped in to explain. "Chan lives in the sub-basement. We used to have several of our graduate students live there, but we've had some serious cut-backs lately, as you know."

"I used to enjoy it when others lived here too," Chan said. "I do not know many people in America, so I made friends with…"

"Don't miss the exit!" Dr. Lasker cut in again, wishing Chan would just shut up before he gave everything away.

"It's five miles away," Chan replied and then muttered, "Backseat driver."

"I just want you to concentrate. It's enough that we lost our other van this week." He had said that deliberately, hoping to get Shelly's help at diverting the conversation. "You'll have to use this for now."

"I'm very sorry about that. Was that your van?" Shelly asked Chan.

"It is okay. I understand you had a serious accident. The most important thing is that you are okay." He glanced at her through the mirror. *She really is cute.* Dodd had said that, but it wasn't enough to save her from his 'accidents'. *Dodd's a maniac,* Chan thought, as he seemed unable to stop from glancing in the mirror every few miles to see her face.

Shelly noticed Chan had sharp black eyes and jet-black hair. His face was vee-shaped but not wiry, and his smile was increasingly more open. He hadn't smiled at all at first, but seemed to be getting more comfortable with her. "Thank you, Chan. I'm okay," she reassured him.

"She's fine. Now pay attention. We get off here." Lasker wasn't taking chances on Chan spilling the beans. He didn't want either of them to mention Dodd's name. He had made up his mind he would tell her about his deranged former assistant, but not yet. He wanted just a little more time, so she would swallow the entire hook. He knew the kind of work they were doing was oddly intoxicating, an addictive high that, once Shelly tasted it, would become part of her blood just as it had become part of Dodd's blood, Chan's blood, mind and soul. *Just give me a little more time,* he thought as Chan guided the van down the exit ramp, toward a small seaport town on Long Island – a town whose biggest tourist attraction was an unfriendly-looking house which the natives believed was cursed.

Dr. Lasker thought so too.

CHAPTER 54

"Do you remember where it is?" Lasker asked Chan, who had come to a traffic light on Main Street in the heart of the neatly laid-out town.

"How could I forget such a place?" A shiver ran down Chan's spine. "None of us could."

"I don't like this," Allen said. "I'm frightened for you. He hasn't told you everything. I can feel it in my bones…and I don't have any."

Shelly ignored him, her eyes taking in the touristy storefronts. "This looks like a nice place to shop," she said, thinking about the clothing she had waiting to be washed back at the dorm. *When am I going to have time to do that?* she thought. "Maybe we can stop on our way back?" she asked.

Chan looked at her incredulously. What had Lasker told her? Didn't she understand where they were going? He looked at the professor, and detected a warning look on his face.

"The Chinese kid is looking at you like a lovesick puppy," Allen said. "Yet another conquest," he grumbled, again surprised he could feel such human emotions as jealousy.

It was all Shelly could do to not snap back an answer to him, but she was learning to not reply to his remarks with others present, no matter how snide some of them were.

"The next left," Dr. Lasker directed.

"I know," Chan replied, making the turn a bit too sharply, as if trying to punish Lasker.

Shelly saw large, well-kept houses positioned far back from the road. The houses were different from the homes she had known in Queens, much larger and with far more space between them. She would have killed for a porch like this one when she was little. "What a great place to play house," she said. She saw a little girl serving tea to several dolls on an expansive white porch.

"Don't let the expensive covers fool you," Allen said. "Some of these 'book covers' are hiding awful secrets. I'm getting a strange vibe already."

"The expression is, 'Never judge a book by its cover'," she replied.

Dr. Lasker looked back in surprise. "Do you feel something?" he asked. *Wouldn't it be wonderful if she did feel something this early?* he thought. "Try to concentrate my dear," he urged, still not fully believing in her ghost story, but knowing something was responsible for her uncanny test scores. If the scores were any indication, Shelly would be an even more attuned Ecto than Dodd had been.

So that's it, Chan thought. Dodd was right, the sneaky doctor was bringing in someone even more sensitive than Dodd or him. Even though Chan had more to lose, perhaps even being sent back to China, he had not fallen prey to Dodd's insanity -- but he knew he had to find some other way to fight, or lose his job and immigrant protection. "I feel a tingling sensation," Chan said, deliberately trying to place himself back into the psychic loop.

Shelly sighed. "Nothing specific so far. Right?"

Allen was deep in thought. If he told her what he was already picking up, the doctor would realize just how special having a ghost on his team, and therefore Shelly, really was. Shelly would be stuck here forever. Eventually she could end up like Dodd. But Chan hadn't been damaged that way. ...Or had he? Did Chan really feel something emanating from these houses, or was he just saying it to protect his job and his stay in America? Would he be the next former assistant to be let go if Shelly put on too good a show? "No. I don't sense anything so far. Not yet," Allen said. He hated lying to her, but felt caution was the best strategy until he could figure out what really was best for her.

"I feel the house is near," Chan said. "I feel prickly, skin tight, breathing harder…headache…."

"You know where the damn house is," Lasker sniped, shaking his head. "What do you feel, Allen?" Lasker asked, deliberately passing over Shelly -- who was staring at a large white house rising over a grassy front lawn that was showing signs of neglect, weeds taking over and ruts where the ground had dried in the hot summer sun. Grass and weeds were appearing in cracks in the concrete driveway that led to the house.

"That's the house in the picture," Allen said, feeling strangely alarmed. "Shelly, you can't go in there."

"Stop the car," Shelly said. "That's the house."

Chan stopped the car. "I thought her name is Shelly. Who is Allen?" he asked Dr. Lasker as he held the van door for him.

"I'll explain later," Lasker replied, realizing he had made an unfortunate slip.

"Yes, you will," Chan said, his mouth so close to Lasker's face the professor could smell garlic on his breath, "Or I'll have some explaining for your new little friend here." Lasker's shocked face told Chan he had finally found some leverage over the professor.

Dr. Lasker shook himself away from Chan, whom he now considered nothing more than a disloyal blackmailer. He forced a thin smile. "We are about to enter the world of American occultism. I'm certain you have seen such houses featured on television, several movies, and of course in some rather over-rated books. But the truth of such possessions is far more terrifying and disturbing than all the fictions and legends. My dear Shelly, this visitation is step one in our revitalized mission to help these poor souls, both the haunted and the haunters. It is for their sake that we must do what we can to--"

"Oh, brother," Allen groaned as he reluctantly followed Shelly up the gravel driveway that he feared would bring them to the threshold of hell.

CHAPTER 55

Shelly was confused. The photo of the house had sent chills through her body, but the real house -- white and welcoming with its expansive porch and comfy looking pairs of rockers, four in all -- seemed to have no such effect on her. "Do you feel anything," she asked Allen.

"Oh yeah," Allen replied. "Tell me you don't?"

"I feel the spirits are angry inside," Chan said, again trying to get the jump on the new girl. "They're warning her to stay out." Had Dodd been right all along about her? Was she just an ambitious bitch trying to take over?

"Are they?" Shelly asked Allen.

"I don't know what wacko telephone he's on, but I don't hear anyone talking, warning or moaning. I just feel this strange heaviness, like the air has become really thick and heavy. Do you feel that?"

"No," Shelly said softly.

"No what?" Chan asked. "Are you refusing to obey the spirits of this house?"

Shelly sighed and then charged up the three wide wooden steps that led to the front porch. "I'm here," she shouted in a challenging voice. "Come and get me, evil spirits!"

Chan scrambled up the stairs and stood next to her, hissing in a low voice, "What are you trying to do? If I lose this job, I'll be sent back to China. Is that what you want?"

Shelly sighed. "No. Of course not. Listen, I'm not after your job or anybody else's."

"Then why are you here? Why would anyone put themselves through this kind of thing if not for the job?"

Shelly saw Dr. Lasker puffing up the driveway and pulling himself up the stairs. "I can't talk now, but please trust me. I'm only doing this to help a friend."

Allen realized she meant him. He felt like telling her not to bother, but sensed from sharing her emotions that it was too late.

Chan pulled away from Shelly as he saw Lasker's curious eyes. He didn't know whether to believe her or not. She had been honest in admitting she hadn't felt any of the sensations he had falsely reported. She could easily have stolen the spotlight from him. Maybe Dodd was wrong. *It is possible,* he thought, *knowing how sick he is.* He gazed at Shelly, aware again of how nice she looked, not at all dark and sinister as he had expected of someone with her special gift and ambition…as described by Dodd. His gut told him to trust her, but he would keep a wary eye on her anyway.

"What is going on?" Dr. Lasker asked, sensing some sort of tension between the two Ectos, a tension he could not afford.

At that instant the front door of the house opened, and a small girl with dark brown hair and brown eyes was holding the ornate handle. "Momma, someone's here."

"I've told you not to open the door for anyone," a female voice reached Shelly's ears.

In an instant Shelly found herself face to face with a woman who could have passed for her older sister, almost the same color hair and the same light blue eyes, but there was one major difference; the woman's eyes were ringed by dark ashy circles, and red veins spidered across their surfaces. "Who are you?" she asked, looking pensively back into the house. "Please, go away! He'll hear you."

The woman gave off a strange breath odor as she spoke. Shelly recognized it as garlic, fresh garlic. Her thoughts immediately summoned up the vampire movies she had loved as a child, the dark circled eyes, pale skin, and the garlic hung all around to keep away the evil spirits and vampires. "Vampires are make-believe, aren't they?" she asked Allen.

Chan wondered who she was talking to.

"I always thought ghosts were fiction too," Allen replied. "Now, I'm not sure of anything. Are you?"

CHAPTER 56

Dr. Lasker held out his card. "I spoke to you this afternoon. I am Professor Lasker, and these are my associates. We were here almost a year ago and—"

Shelly gasped. A very tall man had appeared behind the woman. His eyes were bloodshot and circled in the same smoky-ash rings as his wife, and like her, he wasn't smiling. Shelly noticed something else; his hands, which were hanging down at his sides, were horribly bruised -- skin black and blue, with angry red splotches in the inside of his palms. He was staring at them, his face covered by a long beard and unkempt brown hair.

"I remember you now," the woman said, a worried look on her face. "It's okay, John. They're here to help us."

The man glared at Dr. Lasker, and Shelly heard him say, "We don't need no help. Tell them to leave, and close the door."

His sheer size and icy tone spooked Shelly. The only thing worse was the stony look in his eyes.

"He doesn't want our help," Allen broke the silence. "Let's get out of here. He looks like the Frankenstein monster…that Karloff character. I used to like that movie. Now, I don't know why."

"We can't leave," Shelly said, refusing to break eye-contact with the man. "One more puzzle piece?"

"Me, liking Frankenstein? I hardly think so," Allen muttered. "Unless you think I was some kind of mad scientist, like Dr. Loco here."

Shelly didn't reply. She was keeping a close eye on the woman's giant husband, his eyes never wavering.

"I've work to do," the man said slowly and lumbered back into the living room.

The woman watched as her husband moved back into the dark, looking more like a giant bear than a human being.

Through the still swinging kitchen door Shelly saw him cross the kitchen and pull open the side door. She lost sight of him when the kitchen door swung shut.

Suddenly the woman was animated, her arms waving and her words gushing out as if they had been corked in a bottle, but were now free. "Thank God you came at last," the woman whispered urgently. "Of course, I know who you are. He was furious that I let you come here. He keeps saying there's nothing to worry about." She looked furtively toward the kitchen door. "After last time, I didn't think anyone would ever come back. Lord knows, I kept calling." She glanced at the kitchen door again and whispered, "It's worse this time. Much worse. He's going to kill us."

Just then the little girl came bouncing into the room. The mother got quiet.

"Is everything okay, Momma?" the little girl asked.

"Yes, sweetheart. Go ahead and play in the kitchen."

"What's your name?" the little girl asked Shelly. "I'm Caroline Elizabeth Ross. I'm four years old. How old are you?"

"Nice to meet you. I'm Shelly. I'm twenty one."

"Can you play with me?"

Shelly looked at Dr. Lasker, who was frowning. "I'm sorry, Sweetie. Maybe after I get my work done."

The girl eyed Shelly curiously, and suddenly bounced back into the kitchen.

Once he had seen the girl leave, Dr. Lasker whispered, "Mrs. Ross, I did not want to give up on your case, but until now…" He glanced at Shelly. "I didn't think we could help…not after last time. I did tell you that someday we'd be back--"

Chan frowned, contemplating Shelly and wondering what her secret was. She didn't seem to be sensitive, not even as much as he was, and certainly less than Dodd... or even Swan.

Ah, Swan -- full name White Swan. Chan missed her a lot, but had understood when she wanted to return to her tribe. He had thought she was African American, Black, when he first met her. Her skin was dark and glossy, so he'd thought she was joking when she claimed she was one-hundred-percent Native American. The granddaughter of a Navajo shaman, called a 'medicine man' by the white man, Swan had suffered visions ever since she was a little girl. The most horrifying vision, the one that -- like Chan's nightmare -- repeated every night, was the one where her grandfather was hanging between two tall stakes while two white eagles were pulling off his flesh with their talons. Swan had taken it to be representative of what the white people had done to her ancestors, slowly but irrevocably stripping them of their weapons, land, and ultimately their heritage. She had always said she would someday go back to help her people, but this house had persuaded her to do it early.

Chan and Swan had worked well together even after she had proven to be more sensitive than he was, but not nearly as sensitive as Dodd. In those days, Dodd seemed to be someone who had it all figured out, and Chan had resigned himself to his two associates being together. He really didn't mind their fooling around...not at first, but then things began to change. Dodd seemed to become darker and more distant, even cruel. Chan could still hear them going at it like rabbits some nights, but the following mornings, instead of Swan looking happy, she seemed sad and began to isolate herself. One time, Chan noticed a bruise on her cheek. Another time, he thought he saw a welt on her shoulder. She never talked about Dodd, but Chan suspected Dodd was changing.

It was shortly after the incident in this house that Swan decided to leave the university. "It is time to go back and help my people, so many of them haunted by spirits. They no longer have the closeness to the Earth to see the ancestors and the sacred ones. I must return to help them." Chan suspected that the night in this cursed house had been the straw that broke her resolve -- the night Dodd had gone after her with an axe.

It had seemed to be a routine case, if any of their cases could be called routine. The three of them were working while Dr. Lasker tried to distract the family when, without warning, Dodd had sprung at Swan with an axe, an axe whose blade was coated with blood. Swan had said earlier that there was a demon taking possession of a soul in the house… After Dodd attacked, Chan had assumed the demon had possessed him, hitting at their most vulnerable member whose instability was already showing.

"What the hell are you doing?" Chan had yelled as he grabbed onto the axe, just before Dodd could swing it at Swan, who had barely ducked the first attempted blow.

Dodd held onto the axe with surprising strength as Chan and Swan tried to wrest it from his grip. His eyes were staring upward and his mouth was spewing thin droplets of white foam.

The calls for help had brought Dr. Lasker, who barked, "Dodd! Stop now!"

That seemed to enrage Dodd even more, his hands refusing to release the axe.

"He's going to try again!" Chan yelled.

And then, as suddenly as the attack had started, Dodd seemed to go slack, his hands dropping from the axe handle and his eyes refocusing on Swan. He wiped the foam from his lips with his sleeve. He shook his head and tears fell from his eyes.

"Wait in the car, Thomas," Lasker said firmly. "Go rest."

Dodd had nodded his head and slowly walked toward the car. Suddenly he broke into a run, and was gone before Chan could catch him.

As far as Lasker was concerned, it was the end of the road for his unpredictable assistant who seemed unable to cope with the horrors he had faced for five years. The misery of ghosts, the haunted and the haunters, had been gradually wearing him out until he could no longer function. Nightmares and paranoid delusions made him far too dangerous to continue this kind of work, but Lasker would have kept him on. There was no one who could replace him.

Chan had witnessed this irrevocable deterioration, and remembered too well the axe incident. He had always believed a demon had taken possession of Thomas in his weakened state, that Dodd had not had the strength to fight against it anymore. As he had studied Mr. Ross, he sensed a hollowness and hostility that made Chan wonder if the demon was claiming another soul. He felt afraid, not only for himself but, surprisingly, for Shelly too. If Shelly was truly as sensitive as Dodd had been, she would make a wonderful target for a malevolent spirit. And she didn't have Dodd's experience and expertise to fend off such a demonic foe.

CHAPTER 57

"May we sit someplace?" Dr. Lasker asked the woman, who gave a quick glance at her daughter in the kitchen.

"I'm sorry. I'm forgetting my manners." She gestured toward the couch.

Shelly noticed a large faded square on the wall above the couch, where a painting or mirror might have hung.

The woman sat down on a rocking chair, an old raw-wood type, from the period when the house was built in the late 1700's. She began to rock with a slow but steady rhythm.

Dr. Lasker sat down on the couch across from her. A puff of dust rose as he almost fell into the cushion. He signaled Chan to fetch a camera.

Shelly saw the dust cloud, and remained standing. She wondered why the frame of the couch looked fairly sturdy -- wood, again unpainted -- but the cushions were falling apart and didn't seem to fit right in the frame. Not being an expert, she didn't notice that most of the rest of the furniture in the room was made of unvarnished wood, held together by wooden dowels and hand-cut joints. It was an odd mix, as if collected from garage sales at many different houses.

Shelly suddenly noticed the professor was glaring at her, signaling her to stop gawking and sit down with him on the couch. "Go ahead," she said. "I'll stand here. I'm stiff from the long drive."

Dr. Lasker smiled at the woman. "Tell me, Mrs. Ross, how are things worse? Do you mean worse than last year?"

The woman shivered. Her thin arms looked bruised. "He won't sell the damn place. I keep begging him and begging him, but he won't sell. It's been a year of horror." She looked anxiously around again. "There are all kinds of noises and cold spells, but that's not the worst."

Chan was back with a camera. He was rushing to mount it on a tripod.

"It's not a very good seller's market right now," Lasker said. "Perhaps that's why he won't sell."

The woman looked down at her feet. "Don't you see what's going on? Are you blind?" She was becoming agitated, and said suddenly, "Calm down! I've got to calm down. You're here to help us. To help us… you're here."

"Yes," Dr. Lasker said, signaling Chan to start filming.

The woman arched her neck toward the kitchen, and then leaned forward into a whisper. "Do you remember what this house looked like when you were here last? Look around you. What do you see?"

Shelly looked around again. She didn't see anything unusual -- other than the fact that, for a big house, the furniture seemed more like that of poor people, old and shabby. Strangely, a large wall unit on the far wall looked modern and expensive.

The woman moved toward Lasker, her eyes almost touching his. "Damn it! Look at the furniture. It's all old! Hand-made! Don't you remember? We had just bought all new furniture after moving in here, after Caroline was born. I've got pictures somewhere…if he didn't throw them out? He throws them all out, but I hid a few. There was a glass wall unit over there -- on that wall, just like that one there. We had a sixty-inch flat-screen television, hanging between the twin columns of the wall unit. You remember now?"

"I do vaguely remember. What happened to them," the professor asked, looking into the lens of the camcorder.

Mrs. Ross leaned closer again, her eyes peering into the kitchen. "He chopped them up. He just came in one night with cold eyes, like a shark, and he just swung an axe until bits of furniture were all over the floor."

"She's lucky that's all he chopped up," Allen said. "Did you see that monster?"

"Stop joking around," Shelly hissed.

"I'm not joking," the woman said, giving Shelly a disapproving look. "The truth is, I do feel lucky that's all he chopped up...so far."

Dr. Lasker shot Shelly a dirty look. "My associate didn't mean you were joking," he said, giving Shelly another warning glance.

The woman looked confused, but continued, "I ran and locked Caroline and me in my bedroom. That's when I found out he'd cut the phone wires. I left my cell phone on the kitchen table, so we were stuck in the bedroom. I was praying for someone to save us. Caroline seemed to be in shock of some kind, her eyes weren't seeing me."

"That's awful," Dr. Lasker said to the camera. "How did you escape?"

Mrs. Ross brushed her hand on her dress. "He just stopped. I have no idea why. He never explained, nor mentioned it after that. And as you can see, John replaced some of the furniture he destroyed, but it's all old-looking. He built it himself. He says he likes it all old looking."

"He built all this junk?" Allen said. "He must be crazy."

Shelly bit her tongue so she wouldn't answer him. "It's amazing that he was able to do all this," she said to Mrs. Ross, hoping to make up for her previous comment. She'd have to talk to Allen about keeping quiet when clients were talking. That would definitely help.

The woman's eyes were cold as they aimed at Shelly. "What's really amazing," she said softly as if revealing a secret, "Is that John could never hammer a nail straight. He was an accountant by trade, and had never sawed a board in his life. Suddenly he's making one piece of furniture after another."

"Well, that's really quite an accomplishment," Shelly said.

Dr. Lasker sighed. "Miss Adams, you are missing the point."

Chan caught himself laughing. If Shelly kept this up, he had nothing to worry about. She'd be out on her pretty little butt in no time.

"You really are missing the point," Allen chided.

"Not you, too," Shelly said and then clapped a hand over her mouth.

"Good idea," Dr. Lasker said, shaking his head in disgust.

Shelly walked into the next room, feeling her temper simmering. "Are you here?" She hissed.

"I figured you wanted to talk to me," Allen replied.

"Exactly what point am I supposedly missing?" She felt explosive toward both of these macho idiots.

"Look at her outfit," Allen said.

Shelly shrugged her shoulders. "I don't understand why suddenly you're the fashion police." And suddenly she realized what Allen was saying. The woman was dressed in an ankle-length tan dress, a white apron tied at her middle and heavy-looking black leather high boots on her feet. "She looks like someone from another century," Shelly said, amazed she had missed this.

"Didn't you notice the little girl?" Allen was beginning to realize that Shelly had a minor weakness which, in this new 'business', could prove to be a major problem. "You're not very observant, are you?" he asked.

"I see things pretty well," Shelly argued, but suddenly she did remember the little girl had been wearing a similar tan patternless dress and odd-looking black leather high boots. "She had her hair hidden by a bonnet, too," Shelly said. "I thought she was playing dress-up."

"A likely excuse for a lack of observation," Allen replied. "Now do you understand what's going on here?"

Shelly shrugged. "I'm guessing the old man, the father, is, for some unknown reason, forcing them to dress like people did more than a hundred years ago. Is that right?"

"Bingo," Allen replied.

"And the furniture too," Shelly added, realizing she really hadn't been very observant. She wouldn't admit it to either of them, but she now knew she really had missed the point.

"Bingo again," Allen said.

"But why? Why would he do this?"

"What really scares me is why did he show so much rage when he chopped up the furniture?"

CHAPTER 58

Shelly groaned. "I really goofed, didn't I?"

"We're both new at this," Allen said. "I think we both have a lot to learn."

"Thanks, Allen," Shelly said.

"You're welcome."

Shelly nodded and, feeling humbled, returned to the living room.

Dr. Lasker gave her a curious glance. "I was discussing with Mrs. Ross some of the changes she sees around here."

Shelly had learned to keep quiet. She noticed that there were no photographs of the family anywhere in the room. She would have liked to have seen how they were dressed before what she assumed was a forced transformation to an earlier time.

"Mr. Ross refuses to allow us to remain in the house overnight. This is of course a big disappointment, but we will do the best we can until we must leave." He rose from the couch. "I must beg your pardon, Mrs. Ross, but I wish to discuss something with my assistant here. I shall return shortly." He grabbed Shelly's elbow and nearly dragged her into the next room.

"I'm terrified for her and the little girl," he whispered. "They didn't look anything like this when we were here last year. I don't like the anger I observe in Mr. Ross. I don't like the idea that he destroyed the furniture they had just purchased shortly after they moved in."

"You didn't tell me you'd been here before," Shelly said in an accusatory tone.

"That's not important now. We must focus on helping this family, and that's all."

"What can I do to help?" Shelly asked.

"Mrs. Ross has described several… shall we call them 'incidents', perhaps some imagined? I don't know, but I do know that the way these people are dressed, and the way Mr. Ross chopped up his new furniture, is sufficient to make me worry about their safety."

"I'm worried too," Shelly said. "That father looks--"

Dr. Lasker interrupted. "I want to protect Mrs. Ross and her daughter. I need you and Allen to see if this is an occult manifestation. That is essential. After that, we shall see."

"Do you mean a ghost?" Shelly asked.

"It is possible."

"How do we do that," Shelly asked.

Allen added, "I've never seen another ghost, but that woman is terrified, and I am too. You're right, Shelly, we've got to help her and her little girl. That big guy with the axe worries me."

"Allen wants to help," Shelly said, "But doesn't know how."

Dr. Lasker scratched his head. "I don't know, either. We've had no real success with a hostile spirit, but that is where you and Allen offer us a unique new advantage. They say it takes a thief to catch one. Perhaps…"

"It takes a ghost to catch another ghost," Allen finished the sentence.

"I won't lie to you, Shelly, this could be extremely dangerous," Dr. Lasker said, "But I'm certain that if something isn't done soon this young wife, her little girl and even her husband will join the others who have died here in the past."

"Others have died here?" Allen let out a low whistle. "Shelly, what have we let ourselves into?"

"We've got to help them," Shelly said. "Dr. Lasker, if you keep Mrs. Ross busy, Allen and I will try to discover what's happening here. Any suggestions on where we should start?"

"If I were an evil ghost, I would probably lurk in the basement or attic. But of course, there are no limitations on where such malevolent spirits may appear."

"Of course not," Allen grumbled. "Ask him if he's ever heard of an evil ghost destroying a good one. I'd like to know what I'm up against."

Shelly shot him a silencing look. "The basement it is." Shelly leaned closer to the professor and whispered, "What about Chan?"

"I'll keep him with me to stay filming, and just in case the father becomes a problem. She says that at night he goes down to the shed in the back yard, and chops up wood with his axe. It seems to be the only thing that stops the terrible headaches he claims are raging in his head."

"I saw his eyes," Allen said. "They scared me."

"Allen says the father's eyes scare him," Shelly repeated.

"I've seen those eyes before," Dr. Lasker said. "They're the eyes of someone about to commit a gruesome crime. I'd be scared too." Dodd's eyes had looked like that when he had gone after them with the axe. It was in this very same house, a year ago tonight. Why didn't he tell Shelly? *Because I don't want to lose her.*

Shelly felt a chill race through her body again.

Dr. Lasker took her hand. "I must go back to Mrs. Ross." He hesitated and then added, "Please be careful. Use the phone I gave you if you need me...or if the father finds you. Do not take any chances!" He started back, but turned and gave her a weak smile. "I'm grateful you are on my team, so please, Allen, watch over her for me. This could be very dangerous."

You're telling me? Allen thought, as he saw Shelly reaching into a bag and grabbing a large flashlight. He found himself admiring her as she bent forward into the bag. *This is not helpful,* he scolded himself. *Ghosts don't feel this way about humans, even cute ones like her,* he said, but it was no use. All this danger she was in had somehow sharpened his protective instincts, and as much as he wanted to fight what he was feeling, he realized it was hopeless. No matter what might happen to him, he had to protect her from whatever evil was waiting.

CHAPTER 59

"I've got the flashlight," Shelly said. "Let's find the basement and see what's ticking around here."

"That Loco has a lot of nerve," Allen sputtered. "First he puts you in danger, and then he acts like I need him to tell me to protect you. The man has balls bigger than— I have a good mind to just quit!" *It was worth a try,* Allen thought, hoping Shelly would take the bait.

"Come on, Allen! Don't get your undies in a knot over Loco. We've got work to do. Let's go."

"Now you're giving me orders too. This business of being your ghost isn't easy, and judging from this case, not fun."

Shelly walked back into the hallway. She noticed that the walls showed empty squares where pictures had once been. She gazed through the swinging door that led to the kitchen. "What do you think?"

"I hate this house, is what I think," Allen said, having already passed through the door.

"I wish I could do that," Shelly said as she swung the door open, and found herself in a kitchen that seemed to be unable to decide what century it was in. The table in the center and the four chairs were all made of rough-surfaced wood, held together by dowels, not one nail anywhere, while the refrigerator was modern, a stainless steel-side-by-side with an ice-maker in the door. The stove was far too small for the space it was in. Shelly saw the outline on the wall that was a giveaway. Before this ancient-looking woodburner stove had been put in this spot, there had been a far larger, modern stove with a gas hook-up still in the wall. "He's probably in the middle of redoing this kitchen back to the 1700's," Shelly said. "Weird!"

"The basement door is there, near the side entranceway," Allen said.

Shelly was about to pull open the door to the basement, when she heard a loud crack and the sound of someone cursing outside. She stared through the back window, and in the growing dark saw what looked like a lantern, an orange flame burning dully inside. Lit by the flame was the silhouette of a gigantic man, a large axe swinging high over his head. The violence of the axe slamming down on what looked like a flat-screen television made Shelly let out a frightened yelp.

"Shh, he'll hear you," Allen hissed. "Get away from the door."

"That's Mr. Ross out there, Allen. He just axed what looks like a new television." She peered out the window again. "Oh my God, the little girl is with him!"

"It is okay, Shelly. They're talking, and he's eating it up like candy."

"Are you sure? Can you hear them?"

"I guess I can." Allen was surprised he had been able to hear them through the door, and wondered if once again his fear for a human being -- this time not even Shelly, but a little girl talking to her axe-swinging father -- had somehow made it possible for him to hear through the kitchen door. *Is fear the secret?* he wondered. "Anyway, she's sitting a safe distance away and chattering like a happy little magpie. I can't hear what she's saying, but she should be okay."

"Allen, I don't want anything happening to her while we're on a wild ghost chase in the basement."

"Look yourself. If anything, she seems to be bossing him around. Kids! ...I wonder if I had any."

"Let's go," Shelly said, starting down the basement stairs. She tried the light switch, but no lights came on. "Maybe he didn't pay his last electric bill."

"That would explain chopping up the T.V., "Allen said.

"Listen to that guy chop," Shelly said. "Do you really think that sweet little girl is safe?"

"For now, but let's see if we can find a way to stop this thing."

Shelly flipped the switch on her flashlight. "Can ghosts see in the dark?"

"I guess we can. Let me go down ahead of you."

Shelly waited on the stairs, her flashlight aimed down at the basement floor.

Suddenly there was a loud crash behind her, and the door slammed shut so hard that Shelly lost hold of the flashlight and it fell to the floor. "Allen, I dropped the light."

There wasn't any reply.

"Allen? Where the heck are you?" Shelly reached back for the door handle. "Of course it won't work," she muttered. "Allen, I'm locked in. Come on. This isn't funny."

"Come down," Allen said. "Use the railing, and come down."

Shelly placed her hand on the wood railing and moved down the stairs one step at a time. "Allen, where are you?"

"I'm here. Follow my voice."

Shelly felt along the wall. It was rough–textured, like stone. She was groping along the wall when a hand slammed down on top of her hand and held it. Shelly felt her hand turn to ice, and in the dark felt a sticky fluid oozing from under her palm. "What are you doing, Allen?" she screamed as she smelled blood seeping from her wound. "Allen!"

CHAPTER 60

"What the hell is wrong with you? You've cut my hand!" Shelly was trying to yank her hand free, but the pressure on her hand grew stronger -- and suddenly Shelly knew this could not be Allen. He would never hurt her, and he was unable to materialize unless he was focused on saving her.

"You're not Allen!" she shouted, but the hand was pressing harder. "You're trying to hurt me! Why?"

She couldn't see anyone, maybe because it was too dark, or maybe because whatever it was pressing down on her hand wasn't real.

It is worth a shot. "You're not real, you're not real," she chanted again and again -- and suddenly the weight on her hand was gone.

Shelly raised her hand off the rough wall, holding it up to her eyes. In the dark it was impossible to see the wound or the blood. "Allen," she called, "Please, where are you?"

There was a flash of light as a plume of flame spat out across the room from an old oil furnace.

In the brief flash of light, Shelly saw what looked like a man's body shackled to the basement wall. Even with the head hanging down over the top of his torso, Shelly sensed it was Allen. She stifled a scream as she scanned the darkness for another glimpse. The man was naked, muscular, his face hidden…was he unconscious? What had happened to him? "Allen," she called and saw the man's head move. *He's in trouble.*

The flames shooting violently from the burner were blocking her path. Fire had always terrified her. The flames were like a wall. Gazing around the basement, now lit up by the burner flare-ups, she saw what looked like a Native American blanket draped on one arm of a wooden chair.

She hurried toward the blanket, and saw it was covered with strange hieroglyphic-like symbols. *Probably Navajo,* she thought, wrapping it around her shoulders and over her hair. *Whatever you are, I hope you can protect me,* she said to the spirits of the blanket.

The flames seemed to be lashing out at her like fiery whips. She hesitated, wishing she had another option, but Allen needed her. He had saved her when she needed help, and now it was her turn. *My turn, to save a ghost?* That even sounded strange to her, but it didn't matter. She now understood that the link between Allen and her was strong, but was it strong enough to make her walk into the flames?

She gazed with fear at the fire shooting out from the furnace like fiery hands. "One. Two. Three!" She charged through the flames with the blanket held tightly around her. The heat and the brightness of the fire made it seem forever until she broke through. Her breathing was rapid and she felt as if she was in the furnace, but she was through. The blanket was alive with flame, so she threw it off her shoulders and stomped the flames with her shoes until they went out.

The flames were no longer shooting at her from the furnace. Shelly was plunged into darkness again.

She felt along the wall, groping her way toward where she thought she had seen Allen. She moved cautiously, afraid the phantom hand would once again slam her against the jagged surface of the rough stone wall and draw more blood. Step by cautious step, she crept forward. Finally her hand landed on what felt like naked flesh, his arm. "Allen," she whispered, "I'm here. Tell me you're okay?"

"It's your fault," Allen said, his voice hoarse. "You were warned to stay away."

"I only wanted to help," Shelly said. "You know that."

"We don't need your damned help," a thunderous voice, not at all Allen's, seemed to rise all around her -- and Shelly felt a hand clamp around her wrist.

Allen's voice begged, "You must release me. The key is by the furnace."

Shelly felt the hand free her, and she dropped to her knees to search for the key. She found a small metal box, and inside was a key. She grasped it and hurried back to Allen. "I have it," she said.

"Use it quickly. Set me free. Hurry, before they get here."

Shelly reached forward and fit the key into the leg shackles. One twist and they opened. Next she reached for the thick collar around Allen's neck. This lock was more stubborn, but she finally felt it give way. She was exhausted but reached up to his wrists, standing on tip-toe, her body inches from his naked torso. *I'm feeling his chest, his naked chest,* she found herself thinking as the first lock turned. Finally the second lock gave way, and she dropped away from him, wondering what he was going to do next.

"I'm free," he said, his voice soft and enticing. "I've waited such a long time for you," he whispered.

Shelly felt herself melting. He had waited for her, but how did he mean that? She suddenly realized she had been waiting for him too. And now she could see him. How was that possible? She didn't care. She could see his body, and it was strong and handsome. She felt strange, as if a fire was starting inside her. *Have I wanted this all along*? she asked herself, as she couldn't help staring at his naked torso, his muscles clear and powerful, more powerful than she had expected.

He reached for her with his hand, and pulled her toward him. It was happening. It was impossible, but yet it was happening. At long last, she was seeing and feeling this person who had grown so close to her. He was raising her lips to his and she could see him. He wanted her, and she wanted him. She knew that now. *I want him.* His fingers were strong. His grip held her and pulled her forward and up. She felt his chest pressing against her breasts. She felt her body responding, even though he was rougher than she wanted, holding her hard against him as if years of want were exploding inside him.

Shelly reached up toward his lips and suddenly saw his eyes. "You're not Allen!" she gasped, as she focused on eyes that were red and cruel. Shelly screamed as the hand relentlessly pulled her closer to his lips. Shelly screamed louder as two blindingly red lights, his eyes, seemed to burn into her. "What are you? You're not Allen! Let go of me!"

The hand was holding her against his body. Another hand on the back of her head was pulling her mouth toward his mouth, which was now open and waiting. A strange odor was coming from his mouth. It made her stomach turn.

"All I want is a kiss," Shelly heard Allen's voice taunting. "Isn't that what you've wanted all along?" The hand pressed harder and Shelly's lips were about to touch the monster's blood-red lips -- its tongue, snake-like, long and pronged, was forcing its way through her teeth. "I know you want me. I've felt your heat for days," Allen's voice taunted her. "You love me. Don't resist. I've smelled your heat."

It sounded like Allen, but she knew instinctively it was some monster imitating him. He'd never talk like this. He'd never be so rough. "No!" she screamed. She kicked and kicked, but her sneakers met only steel-like bone, almost breaking her toes in her effort to break away.

"Why are you fighting me?" the man asked with Allen's voice. "I know you want me. I've wanted you, too." Bony fingers ripped open her blouse. Shelly tried to break the grip of the hand that was holding her arm behind her back, but it was far too strong. She felt a long nail pull at her bra. "How lovely you are," the voice hissed roughly yanking the bra over her breasts. "I'll so enjoy taking you. You're delicious."

Shelly struggled, but the monster now had his hand on her breast, squeezing hard. Pain shot through Shelly's body, and she let out another scream as the monster laughed at her agonized kicking and clawing in a vain effort to break free. This was surely not Allen! He could never be this cruel and brutal. Her arm, pinned behind her back, felt as if it was breaking, but still she tried to fight free.

Shelly shuddered as she felt long nails moving slowly from her breast, down her stomach, the nails drawing thin trickles of blood as they trailed through her flesh toward her jeans. "Isn't this fun?" the monster asked, licking the blood off his fingers. "It's like unwrapping a Christmas present."

Inches from the fangs, the sulfur smell overpowering her, Shelly felt the beast pulling at her jeans. "You want me," Allen's voice repeated, as he pulled her jeans down to her knees. "Your legs are wondrous," he hissed, his hand moving up and down her leg. She felt a nail slice a thin path in her thigh, and he released her from his lips just long enough to taste the blood from his finger.

"No!" she screamed, but his tongue darted into her mouth and began inching its way down her throat. She felt faint, being held up by this monster now viciously spreading her legs apart with sharp talons. "Allen, help me!" she screamed, feeling a sharp fingernail pushing under the hem of her panties. He moved her hand lower on his body, and she felt his immense organ ready to take her. "Allen, please help!" she cried, as she felt his organ pressing between her legs, unable to stop him.

Suddenly Shelly felt the forward motion stop, and something pulled her backwards and flung her across the room -- where she landed hard on the concrete floor. Tears stinging her eyes, she fought to get to her feet, but fell backwards, unable to stand. She screamed in terror as she saw the thing's grotesque face. It was almost upon her again. Suddenly the creature turned. "What the hell do you want?" it roared, no longer disguising its voice.

Shelly wondered who it was shouting at. She peered through teary eyes, and was horrified to see that there were now two spectral figures in the smoke pouring from the burner.

"Oh no, not two of them," Shelly groaned, as she fell back on the concrete, unable to move, staring at the creatures outlined in the smoke.

"Did I hurt you, Shelly?" Allen said, as he turned from the fiery monster a few feet in front of him. "I had to get you away from it."

"Allen?" Shelly's eyes cleared, and she realized that one of the creatures, body outlined in the smoke, had to be the real Allen.

CHAPTER 61

Shelly couldn't believe she had finally caught her second glimpse of Allen. But she didn't want it this way, not with him about to go into battle to protect her from some creature that looked like it had come from hell. The other figure was huge and covered with scales. The hands, which Shelly realized she had felt running down her body, were made up of four sinewy fingers, each with long nails that could cut through flesh as if it was butter. She still felt the thin gashes where the monster's nails had ripped her to taste her blood. She pulled her jeans up over her legs and tugged the sides of her blouse together.

The figures were a few feet apart. Allen, if it really was him, was thinner, but taller than the less human hulking creature which he was facing. Shelly wondered if he was a match for the terrifying monster who seemed to be measuring his opponent before attacking.

"Let her leave with me," Allen said, his eyes never leaving the monster's glaring red eyes, "And we'll let you escape. They'll destroy you otherwise."

"You can't stop me! She and they are mine!" the monster roared, and hurled himself toward Allen.

Shelly was terrified Allen wouldn't be strong enough to fight such a powerful entity. They were wrestling now, one a nightmarish hulking mass of fleshy red muscle, eyes glowing like red flame, and the other, taller, more slender, with skin color almost transparent, like smoky crystal. The latter, the human-like fighter, she now was certain had to be Allen. She wished she could help him. She tried to scramble away, but her legs seemed unable to move. She was forced to watch in fear as she saw that Allen was struggling to hold onto his much larger opponent, a creature with huge red horns on his head and a double row of spikes on his back. "I can't hold him much longer," Allen shouted. "Go! Save yourself!"

I can't! Shelly, unable to move, was also unable to stop watching. It was the fascination of witnessing a fatal car accident, horrified by the damaged cars, the bloodied bodies, but unable to take eyes away from the gory scene. Shelly had to see Allen, stay with him, even if she knew he was badly out-powered by his opponent, even if she knew she would be the next target of the monster's lust and rage.

The two combatants were now punching each other, flames shooting out from the larger creature's body. The monster let out a ferocious roar, and Allen was being bent backwards, his hands struggling to keep the claws of the monster from shredding his smoky flesh, reaching his throat. "Run, Shelly!" Allen gasped. "I can't hold him."

So this is Allen, Shelly thought, still mesmerized by her first real sighting of her ghost. She wished she could see his face, but first things first. Somehow she had to do something to help him. She didn't want to lose him now, not like this, not when he had endangered himself to rescue her yet again. *Can a ghost be destroyed?* Shelly didn't know, but she didn't want to take that chance. "Hey, ugly!" she impulsively screamed at the monster. "Pick on someone your own size."

The monster was distracted for an instant, and then threw Allen across the room. He took two steps toward Shelly, who let out a terrified scream, backing away against the wall.

"You are still mine!" the monster roared, reaching for her with his talons.

Allen charged at him again. This time he knew that if he didn't win, Shelly would be the monster's next victim. The fearful image of that monster savaging her, raping her, ignited a surge of incredible energy and Allen gripped the monster's throat, refusing to let go no matter how hard the creature tried to free himself. "Go!" He gasped again. "Get Loco!"

The creature bucked under him wildly, but Allen refused to let go of the scaly throat, twisting its head, his legs locked against the spiny torso. Again and again the creature tried to pull Allen's hands free, slicing with his claws, but Allen's eyes were locked shut, his brain filled with the vision of a naked Shelly, bloody and torn, being ravaged by this hideous beast, a vision that Allen would never let become real.

Suddenly there was a blood-chilling scream. Flames, then dropped to embers, leaving the basement almost dark.

"Allen!" Shelly cried, thinking he had been sliced in shreds by the demon's claws. She knew the creature would come for her, and pulled her body as far away as she could, awaiting its stinking breath and clawing hands. She held the top of her jeans and swore she would fight him so hard that he would have to kill her before he could do what he wanted with her body. She was ready to die, ready if she could join Allen. Braced against the wall, she saw a smoky figure bent over on the dirt floor. It didn't look like the monster. It looked like a naked man, his face almost touching the floor. "Allen?" she asked, afraid and excited at the hope it was him.

"What happened to him?" Allen gasped. "Are you okay, Shelly? Are you okay?"

"Are you okay?" Shelly was staring into the smoke, where a vague outline of Allen was still visible, but fading quickly. She crawled toward him, her hands pulling her body, legs unable to move. It hurt, but she wanted to get to him fast so she could see his face. "You're fading. Are you okay?"

"I think so. I don't know. I'm a ghost, remember?" He gave a little laugh, but felt very weak, drained again of energy in his effort to remain materialized to save Shelly.

Shelly, relieved he seemed unhurt, inched toward him, not believing she was finally able to see at least an outline of this man, ghost, who had become such an important part of her life in just a few days. "Allen, show me your face before the smoke is gone," Shelly asked. "Allen, please before the smoke is…gone."

He turned toward her. "Did he hurt you? I had to stop him."

She reached up, searching through the fading gray mist.

It was too late. The smoke had drifted away, and Allen was invisible again.

"Damn," Shelly moaned. "I wanted to see your face."

He coughed. "That's what you think about when I've almost been demolished by a creature from hell?" Allen asked, as he searched the basement in case the creature was still there, hiding, waiting to attack again. "Females," he teased. "All you want is our bodies."

"I saw you for a second." Shelly smiled sadly. "You've got a nice butt." She laughed, pain shooting up her legs and chest.

"Great," Allen said. "Every ghost wants to hear that. Can we please concentrate on business here? We've got to find that horrible thing. I know I didn't kill it."

Shelly sighed. "You're right. I was just curious."

"Curiosity killed the cat -- and the ghost-catcher," Allen said. "Now, do you want to know what I just learned from our fiery friend?"

Shelly nodded. "I hope it's something we can use to save this family."

"Our ghost, if that's what it is, killed his parents and his little sister one hundred years ago. And guess what he used?"

"An axe?"

"Right. As I was holding him, it was like his horrors were pouring into my brain."

"Wait a minute! You said he killed his sister? How little was the sister?"

"About the age of our little girl," Allen said.

"Shit! How do we stop him?"

"Do you think he would tell me that? There's something else you should know. This guy killed his family one hundred years ago tonight. The professor knew that. That's why the sly sonofabitch brought us here exactly tonight."

"One hundred years ago? That's why the old furniture and clothing," Shelly gasped. "He's recreating the scene of the crime!"

"Hey, you're getting good at this. Shelly, he's been taking over the father's soul because, as a ghost, just like me, he is limited in how long he can stay materialized. He needs a human body to swing the axe. I'm sure that's it."

"We've got to tell Dr. Lasker," Shelly said, standing for support against the wall, already groping her way in the dark toward the stairs.

"I wish I could help you with the steps," Allen said. "I used up all my energy… I need to recharge, I guess."

Shelly grimaced as she pulled herself up the wooden stairs, holding the wood banister tightly as each step seemed to torment her pained body. She no longer cared that her blouse was open and her bra was swinging loose. Her only thought was to reach the top of the staircase and open that damned door so she could get help for the little girl and family upstairs.

Allen was watching her struggle up the stairs in growing admiration for her courage, knowing she must be in terrible pain still. He felt almost as if he was feeling her pain shoot through his invisible body. *Could the link be that strong?* he wondered.

"Allen, the door is locked. I can't get out." Shelly began to bang on the door furiously. "Damn! Nobody is answering. It may already be too late!"

CHAPTER 62

Shelly was still pounding at the door. "Allen, you're going to have to do this. The basement is locked and nobody is coming." She sank to the floor.

"Shelly, even if I can get through the door, I can't tell that crazy doctor. He can't hear me."

Shelly realized Allen was right. The doctor had not shown one sign that he was a sensitive too. *But what about Chan?* He had to be somewhat capable. Why else would Loco keep him on? "No, but maybe Chan can hear you," Shelly said, her body wracked by pain, still smelling the horrible sulphur odors permeating her hair and torn clothing.

"The Chinese kid? He's not going to help you. He thinks you're after his job. He'd like you to fall flat on your cute little ass." Allen was immediately sorry he'd said that. It had slipped through before he could stop it.

Shelly decided to ignore his remark, but pulled her blouse over her breasts. "I don't think he's like that. I think he'll want to help the family. You've got to try. That little girl is in danger!"

"Okay, so you want me to go upstairs and get that Chinese kid to let you out? Is that the plan?"

"There isn't enough time for that. That demon knows we're onto him. We may have forced his hand." She shivered at the remembered sight of the creature. "Is that what all ghosts come to look like?" she asked Allen, wondering if he was doomed to become a demonic creature someday too.

"I hope not! That's why I've got to find out who I am. I don't ever want to be like that thing, my soul so lost I could hurt a child."

Shelly gasped, "The child! That's it! Allen, he's going to go after her first. Get up there and tell Chan to get that little girl away from here. And keep her away from her father!"

"Shelly, are you sure you want me to leave you down here in the dark?"

"That monster isn't here anymore. I know he's going after that girl. Go! Go now! I'll be fine. If you fail to stop that thing, then no matter where I am in this damn place, it won't matter."

"I'll be back for you as soon as we rescue the girl and her parents," Allen said.

There was a slight whooshing sound as Allen forced his body to pass through the door. Shelly regretted sending him away, feeling alone and exhausted. "Please, Chan. Please hear him!"

Upstairs, in the living room, Chan was getting bored. The camera was on a tripod and recording the conversation between Dr. Lasker and Mrs. Ross while he stood behind it. *They don't need me here,* he thought, feeling resentful that Shelly seemed to be getting the choice assignment. This was not what he had counted on when the doctor had recruited him, with promises of adventure and the kind of new knowledge that would help him someday resolve his own personal haunting. It was these lures, and the release from a mental institution to which he had been sentenced for the murder of his mother, that had convinced Chan to accept the mad doctor's offer of a one year trial internship in the department. "With the proper training, my dear Chan, you will become as fine an Ectoplasmic Researcher as any in the world," Dr. Lasker had promised. It hadn't happened. He guessed it was because he just wasn't Ecto material, but he had to keep trying.

Chan's real dream was that with more experience, he would one day be able to talk to his mother and find out what had driven her to push that sword into her stomach. Only then, he believed, his nightmares would end and he would once again be free.

This is not getting me anywhere, he thought, as the conversation droned on. *And where is that new girl?* Chan wondered. *Having all the fun?* Maybe not, but Dr. Lasker was making it very clear that there was a new star in the parapsychology department, and it wasn't him. It was a slender, dumb-blonde model-type, who should be on a runway instead of running after ghosts. *And yet,* Chan mused, *she seems nice*...not at all the way Dodd had described her, while trying to enlist his help in frightening her off. *I wish I could tell what is in her soul,* Chan thought, not used to having such conflicting emotions in his very logical mind. *Am I judging her by her looks?* he asked himself, well aware that her body and face were arousing something inside him that he had never experienced before -- since most of his life had been spent in institutions for the insane in China.

"I'm going to the john," Chan said, not caring if he interrupted, but embarrassed when he realized his statement was recorded by the whirring camcorder.

"Go," the professor said, waving him on impatiently. "Be sure the camera is on. You'll edit it later." He shot Chan a dirty look.

He really doesn't care if I come or go, Chan thought, wondering if it was time to follow Swan's lead and set up shop somewhere else, but knowing in his case it was very risky. *I wonder if I can get sponsorship at another university... Maybe Indiana? They have a good parapsych program. Damn! I can't go back yet!* The thought of being sent back to China and facing charges for killing his mother terrified him. He had already spent years in a youth prison for the insane for the crime. Without witnesses, and evidence, Chan's story of the ghostly rapist had fallen on the judge's deaf ears. His sentence had been tempered by his being considered a child at the time. He knew if he returned as an adult now, he would be institutionalized with other criminally insane men, murderers, rapists, serial killers… He'd never let that happen. "I'll die first," he had sworn to Dodd, when he had first been warned of how dangerous the new girl would be.

Chan stepped into the bathroom, half expecting a ghost to come jumping out at him and yelling for him to shut the damn bathroom door! *This is a strange business,* he thought, as he remembered how Dodd and he had run out of this very same house a year ago. The crazy professor had reamed Chan good for the broken camcorder, and had not believed him when he said something had knocked it over and then chopped it to pieces. "I should have left when Swan left," Chan said, as he settled own on the toilet seat, relieved to see that the roll of toilet paper had not been eliminated in Ross's attempt to recreate the 1800s in this crazy house. He wondered what they used in the 1890s for toilet paper. "What do I care?" he laughed, as for the first time all night he felt a little relaxed. "I do my best thinking here," he mused, as he tried to use an exercise he had learned in the Chinese prison to erase all his thoughts and tension, make his mind go blank.

The locked bathroom gave him a feeling of security in a house that he knew had suffered terrible pain. A year earlier he had felt almost nothing, but watched as Dodd and Swan had reacted to unseen forces in the house. He had learned from them, and now he did feel something strange, but could not define it. He thought it felt like the heavy air before a storm. Not being a true sensitive like Dodd, Swan, or apparently this new girl, he realized he was only capable of picking up the slightest hints of the sensations they felt. "This place gives me the willies," he said. "Let the new girl deal with the ghosts this house hides. Let her be the next Dodd." He shivered. *The last thing I want is to end up like that poor sonofabitch.* "Let the girl have her fun," he said. "It won't last long."

He smiled at the image of pretty little Shelly being chased from this house by its ghostly inhabitants. He could see her running, her perky breasts bouncing as she fled through the door. *Now, that would be something to film,* he thought, suddenly feeling better. *The image of breasts, even imagined, always makes me feel better.* Chan sighed. He knew he was fooling himself. He had realized in the car, gazing at the girl's trusting eyes, that he could never hurt her. If Dodd wanted to scare her off, he couldn't stop him, but he wouldn't help him either.

"Five more minutes," he told himself, savoring the silence of the john.

...but that silence was about to be broken in ways Chan had never expected.

CHAPTER 63

Allen had searched for Chan all over the house, and finally realized he had to be in the bathroom by the kitchen. He hesitated outside the bathroom door for what seemed like hours, and then -- knowing time was running out for the girl and her mother, Shelly too -- he decided to do something he hated. He passed through the bathroom wall. *At least I know one thing a ghost can do,* he thought as he saw Chan with his pants around his ankles. *Just what I always wanted to see. Now how do I talk to this idiot without scaring the crap out of him?* He laughed at his unintended pun.

"Please don't be scared," he said in as gentle a voice as he could muster, considering the urgency of the situation.

Chan did not react. He was lost in thought, in the room lit only by his flashlight aimed down at the floor.

He doesn't hear me, Allen thought. "What did Shelly call you? Chan! That's right. Chan," he said louder. "Can you hear me? Hey, Chan! Mr. Chan!"

Chan thought he felt a breeze. He reached up and checked the window behind him. It was closed and locked. "I hate these old houses," he mumbled, reseating himself.

"Chan! Chan! Chan!" Allen was now shouting. "What's wrong with you? You're an Ecto, aren't you? You're supposed to be able to hear ghosts!"

Chan looked up. He felt strange. His arm was covered with goose bumps. He searched the room with the flashlight's beam. *There is nothing here,* he assured himself.

Alan felt hopeful. "Chan, Shelly needs you! You can be the hero."

Chan felt his ears tingling. He searched the room again, feeling suddenly anxious. He yanked up his pants and cinched his belt. "It is nothing. My imagination is running amok."

"Please, Chan!" Allen shouted at the boy who was now looking hungrily at the doorknob. "You've got to hear me!"

Chan was feeling increasingly uneasy. "What is going on?" he muttered.

He can't hear me, Allen thought. He closed his eyes and concentrated as hard as he could, repeating the phrase, "Shelly needs me. Shelly needs me."

A thin layer of dust coated the bathroom mirror. Allen tried to press his finger into the dust, but the finger was like air and couldn't move even the lightest of matter, dust.

The boy reached for the doorknob.

Allen felt fear and panic surging like an electric current and suddenly his finger hardened. He moved it to shape letters on the mirror, in the dust.

Chan stared as the letters formed in slow motion in front of his amazed eyes. His hand turned the doorknob, but he'd forgotten he had locked the door. Terrified he was trapped, he couldn't take his eyes off the mirror. And then he read the message scrawled in shaky letters in the dust:

Hep grl

At first Chan didn't understand, and stared at the words a long time. Then he heard the sound of something loud outside. It was a crashing sound. He had heard it before, but now it was coming faster, more regular. *What is that sound?* "Who wrote that? Is someone here?"

Allen wished he could answer him, wished Chan could hear him. "Help the girl!" he shouted. "Help the girl!"

Chan thought he heard someone's voice, and whirled around the room searching for anyone who could be in here with him. "That's crazy," Chan said and burst into laughter at how ridiculous he was.

"Damn it!" Allen shouted. "Girl! Girl!"

Chan froze. There was that sound again…like a crashing sound…broken glass? Another crash…silence?

"He's got the axe!" Allen shouted. "Damn you," he screamed. "It's an AXE!"

"Who said that?' Chan whirled around again, now certain he had heard someone shout out a word that sounded like…axe! Suddenly Chan remembered the mother talking about her husband charging into the house and smashing all the furniture they had recently bought -- with an axe. "Oh my God! AXE!"

Chan gazed at the mirror:

Hep Grl

"Help girl! What girl?"

Allen wished he could get Chan to understand.

"My God! The girl…the axe…the father!" Chan suddenly gasped, "I've got to warn her." He took one last look at the note in the mirror, unlocked the bathroom door and ran from the room.

Allen was exhausted from just materializing one finger after his battle with the monster, but he followed Chan knowing there was little he could do to help him.

"The living room!" Chan shouted as he ran to find Dr. Lasker.

The room was empty. "Where the hell are they? Where the hell is that Shelly?" Chan heard the sound of the axe outside. "I've got to be careful," he reminded himself, his knees shaking from fear. "Where the hell is everyone?" He had the sinking feeling he might be too late already.

He pushed open the swinging door and peered into the kitchen. *Nobody.*

The crashing sound was louder.

Chan moved past the swinging doors, holding them so they would not make telltale noises.

No lights?

He aimed his flashlight around the room.

The sound was coming from just outside that door.

The window provided a good view of the yard, but the darkness of night made it hard to see. And then Chan saw what looked like a giant figure raising an axe high over his head and then smashing it down hard, on some unseen object resting on what looked like a large sacrificial stone.

CHAPTER 64

Chan stared in terrified awe as the axe crashed down and sent splinters of wood flying in all directions. *What the hell is he chopping?* He couldn't see the little girl. "Where is she?"

The kitchen door to the yard wasn't locked. He pushed it open very quietly, and -- trying to remain hidden -- sneaked as quietly as he could toward the site where the man was poised again with the axe.

On a large stone altar, behind the man, Chan saw black boots struggling against a thick rope wrapped around their ankles. "Oh my God!" he screamed.

"Kill him!" a shrill voice commanded as Chan stared in horror at the scene before him. "I said, kill him!" the daughter screamed as the father turned slowly toward Chan.

"Holy crap!" Allen shouted. "It's the girl! It's not the father who is possessed. It's that little girl!"

"You and your friends just had to butt into my business!" the girl said with a menacing tone, into Chan's terrified face. "Now you'll all pay! Kill him now!" she screamed in a shrill voice.

The father raised the axe again, and this time it was aimed at Chan.

Chan raised his hand over his face. "Please, don't let him kill me!" he cried to the girl. "I'll go and never come back. Nobody will know."

"Now!" the girl screamed, her face contorted with rage. "Kill him now!"

The man swung the axe. Chan, relying on his reflexes, ducked beneath the weapon by falling to the ground. "Stop it!" he screamed, but the axe was being raised again. "What the hell?" He looked at the man's eyes and saw they were devoid of feeling, a blank expression on the giant's gaunt face.

Chan saw the axe begin to smash down again, and -- hoping he had timed it right -- suddenly rolled over.

The axe clanged noisily on a patio block a few inches away.

"You missed him, you idiot!" the girl screeched. "Again! Do it again! And this time you'd better not miss. I want that boy's head, now!"

The father raised the axe obediently over his head.

Chan's eyes were on the massive blade. There was blood on its edge.

"Kill the sonofabitch!" the girl commanded, her eyes red flames, red-tinged foam salivating from her black lips.

"No! Please!" Chan begged, knowing the odds were against his dodging the blade.

"Kill him! Kill him!"

Chan waited for the giant to lower the axe, but nothing was happening.

"You made a big mistake, demon," Allen hissed. He had jumped in front of the girl, blocking her view, so she couldn't control her father -- who was frozen like a menacing statue.

"You again! Why are you butting into my business?" the demon asked from the girl's lips.

"You give ghosts a bad name!" Allen shouted. "What kind of ghost uses a little girl to commit murders?"

"That's part of the fun," the girl said. "Nobody suspects these sweet angelic children. It's always the fathers or mothers who get blamed. It's great fun. You should try it some time. Now let me get on with it, or you'll pay the price."

"What were you in your former life?" Allen asked, still blocking the girl's view of her father. "What kind of tormented person could you have been?"

The girl laughed, but it was a cruel, vicious sound, full of fury. "You don't know? I thought you knew it all! I killed my own parents and my little sister. I chopped them up with this very axe." The girl appeared to be trembling. "And now I'm going to have this man who looks like my damn father chop up his pig wife -- and then I'll let this sweet child help the father feel such grief at what he's done that he'll hate himself. He'll kill himself, and his soul will be lost forever. Now get the hell away from me!" The girl moved toward Allen, her eyes glowing with rage.

"Is that what you did?" Allen asked. "Is that why you're cursed?"

The girl stopped moving. "You mean blessed, don't you?"

Allen sighed. "No, you're cursed. You couldn't stand what you did, so you killed yourself after you killed your father, mother and baby sister. That's why *you* are cursed forever, isn't it? You hated what you did, and you killed yourself!"

The girl's eyes glared at Allen and her lips tightened with hate. "I hated them. I hated them all. I was glad they died!"

"Then why did you cover your sister in that Native American blanket after you killed her? Why is the blanket covered with your tears?"

The girl looked shaken. "You're lying. That's not what happened!" the demon's voice shouted. "I hated them. I killed them all. They deserved to die. I felt no guilt. None!"

"Then why did you kill yourself?" Allen repeated again and again. "You killed yourself. Why?" He kept moving to block the girl's view of her father.

"I didn't, I didn't..." the demon said, but his voice sounded weaker, more doubtful as Allen kept up the barrage.

Suddenly Allen shouted at the girl, "Caroline, fight him! Fight him off!" Allen kept urging the girl's soul to rise and fight the demon, sensing he had robbed the terrible creature of some of its strength while it was most vulnerable, locked in the young girl's body. "You can do it!" he shouted to the girl's spirit. "I'll help you." He focused on the girl as hard as he could, every ounce of his will pushing his soul into the girl's body. "Fight him with me!" he shouted. "Together we can defeat him!"

Chan was now kneeling on the ground. He saw the axe still suspended in the air. "Oh my God!" He shrank back, but the man wasn't moving. He appeared to be frozen like a statue. *What happened? Why is he like that?*

And then Chan remembered. It wasn't the man screaming like an enraged lunatic. It had been the girl. *It is the girl who is commanding the father!*

CHAPTER 65

Chan found it impossible to believe that a girl four years old could be orchestrating all the horrors of this house. "But I heard her," he muttered. "She must be insane!" He had to get help. He turned his head slowly away from under the axe and saw the girl. She was glaring into space and looked as if she was yelling at someone, but there was nobody else there. "What the hell is going on?" Chan cried.

Suddenly he sensed something strange was happening to the girl. She was trembling, her fists clenched tight and her face twisted into an expression of terrible pain. It was as if something was tearing her up inside. "Help us!" he heard a man's voice seeming to emerge from the child. "Help us!"

Chan stared in terror at the axe still suspended in the air. "I can't! I can't move! He'll kill me!"

"Mom," the voice moaned. "Free the mother!"

"I can't," Chan said again. The axe...if he moved would the axe come crashing down?

"Chan, free the mother!" Allen said, feeling that the girl was losing her battle against the demon, even with his help. He had been weakened by his battle in the basement and was struggling to contain the demon in the girl's body where it was most vulnerable. "Chan, you must help us!"

"The axe," Chan whimpered. "He'll chop me in half!"

"Help us," the man's voice said -- and suddenly a child's voice echoed weakly, "Help me..."

"Oh, God! It's the girl! I hear her," Chan whimpered, his eyes riveted on the axe. *I have no choice. If I don't stop him we're all dead anyway.* He backed away slowly from the axe, his eyes never leaving the bloody blade. Nothing happened.

Relieved that the man still hadn't moved, still was frozen, Chan took the long way around the yard and finally reached Mrs. Ross. She was alive. "You've got to wake up," he hissed, untying the ropes that were tied around her wrists. "Your daughter needs you," he said, as he freed her ankles. "She can't do it without you." He helped her up, letting her head rest on his shoulder.

"Who are you?" Mrs. Ross moaned -- and then saw her daughter standing in front of what looked like an altar made of concrete patio blocks, writhing in pain. "What's happening? My baby!" the mother asked, her eyes searching Chan's face.

"You have to help her," Chan said.

The girl let out a furious scream in the demon's voice. "You'll all die! Die, all of you!"

"I don't understand," the mother gasped, staring in horror. "I thought it was John! I never suspected it was Carol! My sweet baby--" She looked as if she was going to faint, but said, "What can we do? I can't let him hurt my girl!"

Chan shouted, "It's not her! It's a demon, and she's fighting him off. I don't know how she's doing it, but you've got to help her!" He held her up and moved her behind her husband, who still wasn't moving.

"What can I do?" Mrs. Ross asked, horrified by the transformation of her daughter into some kind of wild-eyed fury. "I'll do anything. Please!"

"I don't know," Chan said, afraid the daughter was lost already.

"Hug her daughter," Allen said, his voice even weaker than before. "Hold her... don't let go."

Chan wondered who the male voice was that seemed to be trying to help them. It didn't matter for now. He sensed that the girl had only minutes left, if she had any chance at all. He turned to Mrs. Ross and said, "You've got to hold her! Hold her now!" He wondered if she could summon the courage to do that.

The mother inside her was moving her closer, but the fear of the demon was holding her back. "I can't," she moaned. "I'm afraid."

Chan had been standing to one side, terrified of moving toward the monster, but now he gripped her shoulders and steered her forward. "You don't think I'm afraid?" Chan held her tightly. "Now hold her, and I'll hold you. Just close your eyes and pray, as you squeeze her with all the love you have for her."

The mother's arms cautiously wrapped around her daughter, and Chan locked his arms around them both. He felt the agony of the souls struggling inside the girl's body, and wondered how someone so young and so frail could survive the horrible battering she was being forced to suffer by this heartless demon, ghost, or whatever evil thing this was.

"I'll kill you all!" the demon screamed in a terrible distortion of the girl's voice. "You, Chinese boy, your mother died like a slit pig, her honey-tasting blood dripping all over you as you tried to save her, but I can bring her back to you. You can learn the truth from her own tender lips. Isn't that what you want? Isn't that peace what you've always wanted?"

Chan felt tears burning in his eyes. "No!" he screamed. "You can't have her!"

"Your mother is waiting for you, Chan," the demon taunted. "Your mother, who was the only woman who loved you. She gave up her life for you. They didn't want her. You've known all along, they wanted you."

Chan held on. He had told no other person the truth, but this demon seemed to know it all. It wasn't his mother the ghost had come for, it was Chan -- the last male descendant of the soldier that had killed him in battle. His mother had killed herself to keep the ghost from taking him. She couldn't have known that the young boy would never get over his guilt for what she had done to save him. She couldn't have known that he would be punished as a criminal for telling the truth.

"Let your mother free you," the demon urged. "No more guilt, no more pain…you can go home again, a free man."

Chan was tempted, but he couldn't let this child be sacrificed for him. He had already enough guilt burdening his life from the sacrifice of his mother, so many years ago. "You're afraid!" he shouted at the monster. "We'll beat you!"

"I don't need you, Chinese bastard!" the demon snapped, "Not when I have another who'll be all too glad to accept my gifts!"

Chan wondered who he meant as the demon seemed to be addressing someone else, someone Chan couldn't see, but whose voice seemed to be coming from the girl as well.

"And you, you poor, lost soul of a ghost," the girl said in a syrupy voice, "I have a gift for you. I know what you want. I can tell you how you were murdered."

Who is he talking to? Chan asked, struggling to hold on.

Allen tried not to listen, but he heard the demon continue, "You are of the spirit world. You're like me. You should care nothing about this girl, or the others, so leave them to me and I'll give you what you want. Peace! I can set you free, so you may have your rest at last"

Allen knew these were the things he wanted most, but couldn't let this girl die and become a lost soul -- and he couldn't abandon Shelly, who he knew would be the demon's next target. "Tell me first," Allen said, his voice quivering with the struggle of remaining inside the girl's body with this monster's depraved soul, fighting for control.

The demon's voice was harsh. "Do you think I'm a fool? I have been here long before the boy killed his parents. I've been here before the Indians were betrayed by the Europeans. And I'll be here long after your little friends, these mere mortals which you and I should regard as fodder, are all dead. They will all be dust, and I will still be here no matter what you do. But you, you shall remain unfulfilled and desperately alone, a wandering soul for all eternity -- unless you accept my generous help. I am the truth you seek! Can you turn away from your one hope for answers, for your well-deserved rest?"

"You may survive, but not in this innocent girl's body," Allen said, forcing himself to focus all his energy, whatever was left, on merging the girl, mother, Chan and himself into one unified force against this monstrous creature who he had trapped in her body.

"Keep holding her," Allen wheezed. "Don't let go."

Chan was exhausted. He had no idea who was speaking to him from the girl's body, but sensed the being was trying to help the girl. The mother had almost passed out from her exertion, but Chan was holding her up. *We can't hold on much longer,* he thought, wondering what the demon would do if he won. He caught sight of the father, the axe still held over his head, and had an idea. "Whoever you are inside helping us, the father -- can you help me call the father to help us?"

Allen was afraid his strength was almost gone. The demon seemed weaker, not screaming any more, but they were weaker too. "Mr. Ross! he called, "John, your daughter loves you. She loves you so much. Help her! You must help her!"

Chan echoed the ghost's words. "Your daughter loves you! She loves you so much..."

Together Allen and Chan repeated the words as if they were a magical chant.

Suddenly Chan heard the sound of the axe striking something on the ground. "Say it again! Again!" Chan shouted. "He's chopping again!"

CHAPTER 66

Allen's strength was nearly gone, but he refused to stop fighting. He felt that the four-year-old girl was unable to resist much longer. None of them could, without help. "Caroline, call your father! Tell him you love him!"

The demon laughed. "That won't work! I control him! I made him destroy everything I hated. Now he'll destroy you."

Chan saw the large man gazing down at the axe as if he was going to pick it up again. "Now, Caroline! Call him now!"

Allen echoed Chan's call.

"Daddy," a weak voice barely audible rose from the girl's lips. "Daddy... I love you."

"No!" The demon screamed. "Pick up the axe and kill them all! *I'm* your daughter and I want you to kill them all!"

Chan felt panic surge inside his body as the giant man hefted the axe again. "Oh God, no!" He was tempted to let go of the others and run...just as Dodd, Swan, and he had run from this house of horrors a year earlier... But this time it was different. There was someone invisible helping. "Call him! Call him again," he rasped, feeling that he was about to collapse from exhaustion.

Allen shouted, "Caroline, now! Call daddy!"

"Daddy, I...love...you," the girl wailed. "I love you so much."

Chan saw that the man's face was still unchanged, as if he was locked in a trance.

"Kill them now," the demon's voice hissed. "They're hurting me."

"Daddy? Daddy!" Caroline called.

Chan was praying for any sign that his daughter had reached what was left of the father's soul. Suddenly he saw the man's tortured expression turn to one of confusion. "It's working," he said trying to hold onto the others.

"Daddy, I love you!" Caroline called, her voice weaker.

"Look at your daughter's body," the monster taunted, raising the skirt until a white undergarment was revealed. "They are plotting to take her, to defile your sweet, innocent, child. The axe! Chop off their heads, and save your daughter from their filthy lust."

"He's lying," Allen shouted. "Chan, you must tell him."

Chan strained to see who the man was that was talking to him, but saw only the girl. He suddenly realized that a miracle might have been happening, he might have been at long last talking to a ghost. He wished he had time to question whoever this unknown entity was, but saw the father was staring at them with confusion. "The monster is lying," he shouted, "Listen to your daughter. She loves you!"

"Daddy, please hug me," Caroline managed to say, but the monster was overpowering her and his voice screamed out, "I am your master! You will obey me. Kill them. Kill them!"

Chan stared at the axe. "Would your daughter talk like that? You taught her to love, not to hate."

The man lowered the axe and stared at it as if he didn't know why he was holding it. "Where am I?" he murmured, and then he saw his wife and Chan holding their arms around his daughter, who was barely visible in the huddle. "What's happening?" he asked, his eyes clearing.

"Hold her," Chan gasped. "For her sake, hug her -- now."

The man was on top of them instantly, his arms wrapped around Chan, and his wife and child. "What's happening to her?" he begged. "I didn't hurt her, did I? Please tell me I didn't--"

"Tell her you love her. Keep telling her that," Allen said.

Chan could barely speak. "You love her. Tell her – and mean it. Keep telling her."

"I love you. I love you. I love you," the father repeated, tears falling from his eyes.

"Damn you all!" the demon screamed, and the girl cried pitifully in a terrifying convulsion.

"Hold her!" Allen shouted, struggling to remain with her.

"Hold her!" Chan repeated, squeezing harder.

Suddenly there was a bone-chilling scream, and the demon seemed to burst from Caroline's tiny body, push his way up past their heads and escape out into the night air.

"Don't let go!" Allen said. "Don't let go!"

"Don't let go!" Chan repeated, surprised that he was weeping, searching for the source of the mysterious voice.

The man looked at his daughter who was barely able to stand and said, "I'm never going to let go again."

How long they stayed in the embrace nobody knew, but they refused to break away, believing that as long as they were one, the demon could not invade again.

"I'm hot," the girl moaned in a weak voice. "Why are you hugging me so hard?"

"Carol baby, is that you?" the father asked.

"Daddy, are you hurt?"

"No, sweetheart, I'm fine. Mr. Chan, it's okay. You can let her go now,"

Chan sagged to the ground. He was covered in sweat, and his clothes had an acrid smell. His eyes searched the girl's face. She seemed pale, but okay, her body being hugged by her father and mother, who was now crying with joy.

"You saved us," the father said to Chan. "I don't know how to thank you."

Chan nodded modestly. *It wasn't me,* he thought, *But who was it then?* Who was the male voice that had called him to help? He stared at the girl, wondering if the spirit that had saved her was somehow still locked inside her. Had the spirit, ghost, or whatever it had been, sacrificed itself for the girl and her family?

"I'll never be able to thank you," the father said again.

The mother's eyes, wet with tears, were enough to show Chan how grateful she was. *This is what it's about,* Chan thought, for the first time in his life feeling some sense of having done something right. "I must find the others," Chan said to the Ross family. "I pray they were not hurt by…" What should he tell them it was? Time for that later. "I must go," he said, giving Caroline a smile.

"Do you want my help?" the father said, still clutching his wife and daughter.

"Please enjoy your family, Sir." Chan envied him. He walked back to the living room. What had happened to the Professor? Had he run off, the way they had a year ago? He couldn't blame the man if he did.

Chan suddenly heard a banging sound. It was a dull sound, hard to hear. He tried to follow the sound, but it was erratic. "Where the heck are you?" he shouted, hoping it wasn't another evil ghost.

CHAPTER 67

Chan scanned the foyer with his flashlight. "Are you here? Professor, is that you? Shelly?"

Three small thumps were the only answer.

Chan's flashlight picked out a wooden door, its paint scraped off as if by a knife. "Are you inside this closet?" Chan called.

Two thumps.

Chan pulled the door knob. "It's locked." He searched for a key, but couldn't find it. "I'll be back," he shouted.

"I need your help, Sir," Chan said running up to Mr. Ross.

"Whatever you need, son," the man said, and kissed his wife and daughter.

"We're coming with you," the mother said.

"Do you have a key to the front hall closet?" Chan asked.

"That door doesn't have a lock. Let me take a crack at it." The man turned the knob and pushed at the door. "Something's stuck behind the door." He leaned forward and shoved harder. "Move away from the door!" Mr. Ross shouted.

"I can't," someone whimpered.

"Is that you, Professor?" Chan asked, his ear pressed against the door.

"I'll have to take her down," Mr. Ross said, and gripped the door with both huge hands, tearing it right off the hinges.

"Oh, my God," Chan exclaimed.

"Don't look," Dr. Lasker moaned.

Chan blinked in disbelief. Dr. Lasker was stuffed into what looked like a large wire dog crate, completely naked. "What the hell happened to you?" he asked. "Where are your clothes?"

The mother pulled her daughter back into the living room.

"Dr. Lasker, where are your clothes?" Chan asked, as Mr. Ross pulled open the dog crate.

"Get something to cover me up, you dolt!" Lasker shouted. "I've never been so humiliated! Someone is going to pay for this!"

"I'll get something," Mrs. Ross said, and hurried to her bedroom.

"Sir, what happened?" Chan asked, trying not to laugh at the image of his boss locked naked into a dog crate.

"I have no idea! I was searching for Shelly when suddenly something slammed down on my head. The next thing I know, I'm in this damn cage in this lamentable position. Now get me the hell out of this cursed house! And find my damn pants!"

Chan couldn't stop himself from laughing at the remembered sight of his boss trussed up like a featherless turkey in the cage.

"Try these on," Mrs. Ross said, handing him one of her husband's shirts and a pair of his jeans.

"Thank you," Dr. Lasker said, grabbing the clothes. "And you'd better stop laughing, you idiot, if you want your job," Dr. Lasker was grumbling furiously as he shoved his legs into the pants -- which were so large he looked as if he was drowning in them. "Chan, you idiot, find my clothes now, or you're fired! And stop laughing!"

Mr. Ross grabbed him by the shirt collar. "Don't you yell at that boy! He saved my family. He figured out how to get rid of the demon that was in my daughter and controlling me. You should thank your lucky stars to have him working for you. If he hadn't stopped that monster, I expect you'd have ended up on its plate, along with the rest of us."

Dr. Lasker was shaking with fear. Even not under the demon's spell, this man was gigantic and frightening. "I'm sorry. Chan, I apologize," he stammered, but shot Chan a dirty look even as he stuffed himself into the oversized shirt.

Mr. Ross released the professor who, though sputtering mad and looking like a furious child in the oversized clothing, realized he'd better control his temper. "Is this true, Chan? Did you save them?"

Chan nodded, expecting another explosion. "But I had help."

"Shelly helped you?" Dr. Lasker suddenly was aware the girl was not in the room. "Where is she?"

"No. Not her," Chan said, wondering if maybe he'd imagined the male voice coming from the girl. *How can I explain what I don't understand?* Had he finally heard a real ghost?

"There's nobody else here," the doctor was about to blast, but saw Mr. Ross staring at him.

Chan nodded in agreement. "I know, but there was a man's voice. He was inside the girl. It was like he was battling for her soul with some monster also inside her. He told me what to do."

Dr. Lasker looked anxiously around him. "You say you heard a man's voice inside the girl? Perhaps you are an Ecto at last? We shall hope." Lasker wasn't ready to celebrate yet. It could have been Shelly's Allen, or it could have been another ghost in the house. At any rate, he didn't want Chan to know about Allen, not yet, not until he figured out exactly what he wanted to do with the girl and her ghost. "You probably imagined it. People who are frightened imagine all kinds of things. Where is Shelly?"

Chan didn't feel like arguing now. Shelly was his first concern. "I don't know. She might still be in the basement." He turned to Mr. Ross. "Where is the basement door, sir?"

"I'll show you," the man said.

Dr. Lasker was grumbling as he tied on a pair of Mr. Ross's huge shoes. "I've never been so embarrassed," he roared now that Mr. Ross was out of the room. "Bloody ghosts! Who needs them?"

CHAPTER 68

"Shelly? Shelly, are you down here?" Chan shouted through the door. "It's locked. What is it with this place? Every door is locked."

Mr. Ross gripped the door handle and pulled. The heavy steel door wouldn't budge. "I'll be back," he said.

Chan waited and suddenly his eyes grew wide. Mr. Ross was back, and he was carrying that awful axe. "Not again," he moaned.

"Stand back boy," the man ordered.

Chan had no desire to be anywhere near that all-too-familiar weapon. He moved as far away as he could.

Shelly suddenly heard a loud crash on the door. *Oh my God, it's him!* she thought, searching the dark. She crawled to a corner of the wall, cowering in case the demon had returned.

The axe struck again.

Shelly wondered where Allen was. Had the demon destroyed him? She had witnessed him fighting with the monster and believed he was no match for the gruesome creature. "Allen, where are you?"

The axe struck again and the door burst open.

Shelly screamed at the sight of the giant Mr. Ross, the axe in his hand, as he towered over her.

"It's okay, Shelly," Chan said, scurrying past Mr. Ross. "You're safe now." He bent over her and Shelly, relieved to see that the father had lowered the axe, reached up and pulled Chan toward her. Her grateful tears fell on his face and shoulder.

"Thank you," she whimpered, and kissed him on the cheek. "I was so terrified, trapped down here. Thank you." Her head rested on his shoulder, her legs still rubbery as Chan held her in his arms.

Chan found himself not wanting to let her go. As he held her he wondered how he could have wanted to hurt her. Dodd had warned him she was after their jobs and he'd be sent back to China, so he had been silent as Dodd had launched his attacks on the girl. He understood Dodd's anger and fear, had shared them, but that wasn't enough to try and kill her. He felt guilty that he hadn't tried to stop Dodd, even as he found himself feeling tenderness for Shelly, his supposed rival, that he hadn't expected. "Come on, Shelly, it's okay now. I promise you, it'll all be okay from now on."

Allen had been completely spent by his efforts to fight the demon and save the girl, and had only just been able to come downstairs to check on Shelly. He was relieved to see she was okay, but surprised to see her snuggling into the Chinese boy's shoulder. He winced at the almost inaudible sound of her lips kissing Chan's cheek.

"Is she going to be alright?" Mr. Ross asked. "Do you need help carrying her up the stairs?"

"I can walk," Shelly said, and, leaning on Chan, managed to stand. "Thank you Chan," she said. "Thank you for rescuing me." She wondered where Allen was. Was he okay? She felt that he was, but still didn't trust her ability to share his emotions.

"He's a hero, this Chinese kid," the father said. "He saved my whole family, singlehanded."

"I didn't," Chan said, wishing he understood what had really happened.

"He's being modest," Mr. Ross said. "Without him, we'd all been cooked."

"I'm not a hero," Chan said wanting to tell Shelly about the voice that had driven him to help, but she was smiling so warmly at him that the words failed to emerge from his mouth.

"I won't forget your bravery," Mr. Ross said.

"Neither will I," Shelly murmured holding Chan's arm.

That's right boy, you take all the credit, Allen thought, wondering if Shelly was ever going to call for him. Didn't she want to know where he was? Didn't she care if he'd survived?

Shelly stumbled.

"Please Shelly," Chan said, "Let me help you up the stairs."

Shelly felt weak. "Okay, but give me a minute."

Chan thought she was still dizzy or faint, so he held her around her waist as he waited.

Shelly was searching the basement. She wanted to call Allen, to see if he was okay, but couldn't risk it surrounded by all these people. "I'm ready now," she said and, with Chan's help, she pulled herself up the stairs and back into the light.

Allen watched her silently from a corner of the basement. He saw her head drop down on Chan's shoulder, her arm nestled in his arm. He felt weak, and wondered if he was going to recover this time. It didn't matter. Shelly was safe. She had Chan to help her now. He had never thought of Chan as someone she could be interested in. Dodd, that insane mysterious character, he had been the one Allen had thought was the real threat. He had picked up Shelly's interest in the wild-eyed Dodd, had even gotten glimpses of her desire for him… And there had been no such romantic images of Chan. *But there you have it,* he mused, *Women are totally unpredictable.* And Shelly, he had long ago concluded, was very much a woman with needs he could never hope to satisfy. So why did he feel so jealous? Was that what he was feeling as he heard her kiss that young man's cheek? He didn't mind when the basement door was closed and he was left alone in the dark. It was as if he belonged here.

CHAPTER 69

"Let's get the hell out of here," Dr. Lasker grumbled, barely able to walk in Mr. Ross's overflowing clothes and shoes. He had to hold his pants up with one hand or they would have fallen, revealing that he wasn't wearing any underwear. "I will not wear anybody else's underwear!" he had roared at Chan. "And you," he aimed his fiery eyes at Shelly, "What kind of Ecto are you that you can't find my clothing?"

Shelly couldn't help laughing at his discomfort, swimming around in those oversized clothes. She tried to stifle it, seeing he was giving her a dirty look.

Mr. and Mrs. Ross would not let go of their daughter as they thanked Chan for all he had done for them. Chan kept trying to shift the credit to the unseen ghost and Shelly, who he felt was somehow responsible for their success. He had other things on his mind as well. He was absorbed with trying to understand if he had finally heard a ghost. That possibility gave him his first positive hope that someday he might be able to speak to his mother, and learn the whole truth of what had happened to her when he was a child. Why the ghost came for him was still a mystery he had to unravel. Maybe Shelly would help him. He now understood why Dodd had been so worried about her. Chan worried now that Dodd could still be out there, waiting to do her harm.

All the way back to the university, Dr. Lasker grumbled, "Whoever heard of a ghost who steals a man's clothing?" and other complaints about the way the night had gone, but then he became quiet when the realization that, despite his personal humiliation, something amazing had happened in the house. Somehow, in a way which he did not understand, Chan might have finally heard a ghost, and therefore might someday be able to replace Dodd. He kept speaking of hearing a man's voice coming from the girl. Could it have been Shelly's alleged ghost, Allen, or some other benevolent spirit that had miraculously appeared to help them? And what of Shelly? She had been locked in the basement and had been silent once liberated, conspicuously letting Chan take the spotlight, but something told him she was hiding something. *Nobody lets another take credit for something they do. It is just not human nature,* he thought, his own deviousness coloring his view of others. *There is more to this than she is letting on.*

Lasker turned to grill Shelly about what she had experienced, but saw that the girl's eyes were closed. As he studied her features in sleep, he found himself feeling something for her that he would never admit to anyone. What it was precisely, he couldn't answer. *Tenderness, maybe? Enough to protect her from Dodd's fate?* He'd have to give that some thought.

Allen was sitting in the seat next to Shelly. He was still weak, and sensed her exhaustion. He couldn't deny he felt protective of her as she slept. But he was also conflicted about his feelings for her. He had thought about remaining in the house with the Ross family, but he knew they were now safe and no longer needed him. He was tempted to return to the park and leave Shelly to lead her life without him, but Dodd was still loose and a threat in more ways than one. He had disturbing visions of Shelly, naked, before the enigmatic Dodd, reaching up to give him a kiss, with his long fingers clutched around her slender throat. How could he leave her when her life was still in danger, when her sensations were so intertwined with his? And he still had hopes, slim at best, that the wily Dr. Loco might live up to his agreement and somehow help him find out about his past. He had to know who had killed him, and why.

So Allen had many reasons to stay, but as he saw and felt Shelly sleeping next to him he wondered if it was worth it. Was it worth risking Shelly's sanity? Could she end up like Dodd? Could his staying with her risk her life?

As she slept, Allen felt a warmth surge through him. He called his ability to share her feelings their 'link', but he didn't understand what he was feeling, perplexed that a ghost could still have such feelings for a mortal human being. There were times when he thought he loved her, wished to hold her in his arms and kiss her, but there were other times when he felt angry and jealous -- and then hated himself for not being able to rationalize those feelings, tell himself that he had no right to love her, want her, because he was not solid, not able to touch her, to hold her. When he contemplated Shelly falling in love with Dodd, or Chan, or even that security guard, he couldn't help feeling upset, wanting to get as far away from her as he could.

But in the end, Allen knew he couldn't leave her until he felt she would be permanently safe. There was an undefinable link between them he couldn't deny, a sense of wanting to protect her. His anger at being forgotten, as he stood waiting for her in the basement, had mellowed into an acceptance that a ghost to a human is just a ghost, a bodiless being, no feelings, no hopes, no dreams. A ghost is only a rare phenomenon to humans like Shelly and Lasker, that when one miraculously appears must be exploited fully. *It's not your fault, Shelly,* he told himself. *It is what it is. And for now, it will do.*

In her sleep, Shelly saw a young man, well dressed in a dark suit, tie, and leather shoes. His back was toward her, but she could see he had soft light-brown hair and stood very straight, almost like a soldier. He was powerful looking, muscles well-toned, but not muscle-bound, and his voice was gentle yet masculine.

"Allen," she called.

The man slowly turned toward her. His hands were clean and smooth as he reached toward her.

"Allen," she said again as her eyes, pleased by the appearance of his six foot body, moved up toward his face.

But there was no face. There was only a ceramic-like white mask where a face should have been.

She stared in silence, with no screams, no fear. "I'd give anything to see your face," she said, reaching with her hands and lips to touch him. She couldn't believe how soft his lips felt, how gently he held her and kissed her. "Please show me your face," she whispered, as he held her in his arms, drawing her breath away.

The dream figure vaporized, and she awoke.

"Are you here?" she whispered.

"Yes. Are you okay?" Allen asked.

"Yes. Are *you* okay?" she replied, realizing she cared.

"Yes."

"I was frightened for you," she said, no longer questioning why.

Chan smiled back at her in the rear view mirror. "And I for you," he replied, wondering if that meant what he thought it did.

Shelly returned Chan's smile. What else could she do? How could she explain she was talking to a ghost, her very special invisible friend?

Dr. Lasker wasn't listening to their conversation. He had little patience for such mush. He was busily thinking of how next he could use this promising new team of his. This first surprising success might be enough to change the bean-counters' minds. He could see a new van with sparkling new equipment. That would be first on his agenda. *Yes, all we need is a few more successes.*

His mind raced through his files. He'd search them as soon as he got back, and come up with just the right kind of case, one that would make a good book…perhaps a great movie? *I'll need a ghost writer,* he laughed, but was serious about the book idea. Which of the many reported hauntings and unexplained phenomenon languishing in his file cabinet would be the most promising, the most lucrative? Which supernatural manifestation would do the most to promote his parapsychology department?

He was itching to get started…or was that itching from that idiot Ross's clothing? *What kind of a ghost takes a man's clothes?* He roared inside, but even that anger did not take away his growing sense of excitement, exhilaration. *Chan and Shelly! Shelly with her alleged ghost, and Chan, who is finally showing the talent I suspected in him. They'll be a good starting lineup for our next jobs. Who knows? Even that insane Dodd might still come in handy. Nothing is impossible.*

THE END

Look for ECTOS 2

About the author:

Mark is a multi-award winning teacher and author. Born in Germany to Holocaust survivors, he loved teaching in Central Islip, New York, and SUNY Old Westbury. He was named Teacher of the Year by the New York State Reading Assoc., 1989, among other honors.

Mark's books include The Rockhound Science Mysteries, Learning Magazine's Teachers' Choice Award, 2001 and The Midnight Diet Club, First Prize, Florida Writers Association 2011, YA published fiction. Awards for his adult short stories include being a winner in the Writers' Digest Short Story Competition (2012); 2nd place in the Creative Writer's Notebook Story contest (2013) and a winner in the 2014 Tales2Inspire anthology contest. See www.markhnewhouse.com.

Mark is the founder/leader of the Children's Author Team, contributor and Editor-in-Chief for The Story Shop and Holiday Helpings (Court Jester Publications}, profits donated to charity

Mark's BA and MA are from Queens College, New York. He was co-producer/host of AUTHOR'S BEAT internet radio, and is now co-producer/ co-host of Boomers Plus Radio. Mark prides himself on being willing to do almost anything to help children stop bullying and provides free materials at www.bullystoppersclub.com. You can hear Mark at www.boomersplusradio.com

Other Solstice title you may enjoy…

Waking up Dead
By Margo Bond Collins

When Callie Taylor died, she expected to go to heaven—or maybe hell. Instead, when she was murdered in Dallas by some jerk with a knife and a bad-mommy complex, she went to Alabama. Now she's seen another murder, and she can't just let it go; she must find a way to make sure the police figure out who really killed Molly McClatchy before an innocent man goes to prison, all the while trying to determine how and why she woke up dead in Alabama.

The Ghost Catcher
By: KC Sprayberry

A gift to know when people are in trouble of the ghostly type puts Hailey Hatmaker in the middle of a major problem – one that winds up getting her into more hot water than she can handle. In true Hailey Hatmaker fashion, she dives into what turns out to be a battle with Limbo, her number one nemesis.
Can Hailey rescue two friends before it's too late? Or is she forever condemned to losing to Limbo?

For more Solstice books, please visit our online store: http://solsticepublishing.com/bookstore/

Made in the USA
Charleston, SC
20 July 2014